AS THE
FOG CLEARS

Jacquie Roberson

FriesenPress

Suite 300 - 990 Fort St
Victoria, BC, Canada, V8V 3K2
www.friesenpress.com

Copyright © 2015 by Jacquie Roberson
First Edition — 2015

Cover image by Kathy Root-Marys.

This book has been written for entertainment purposes only. Although it is based on some facts
pertaining to the War of 1812, it is not meant to read like a history book. It is not the intention
of this author to slander, debase or cause embarrassment to any historical event or person.

ISBN
978-1-4602-6343-3 (Hardcover)
978-1-4602-6344-0 (Paperback)
978-1-4602-6345-7 (eBook)

1. *Fiction, Historical*

Distributed to the trade by The Ingram Book Company

Newark: Niagara-on-the-Lake
Shipman's Corners: St. Catherines

This book is dedicated to my brother Ron; who loved to read, to my mother; who taught us the joy of reading in the first place, and to my family; Dan, Melanie, and Danny, who encouraged me to write, supporting me through the whole process.

Acknowledgements

———

Thank you to my editors: Margaret Jeskie, Robin Clegg, and Jeana Lowes.

Your input and suggestions were greatly appreciated. I could not have done it without you!

Thank you to the staff at the Laura Secord Homestead, who patiently answered my many questions.

Thank You God, for giving me the incentive to write.

The Redcoats and the Blue

The British redcoats clashed with blue
As guns roared oe'r the land,
The fifes and drummers too were heard
As each side took its stand.

With musket fire and cannon blasts
The smoke mixed with the fear,
As people waited anxiously
for the fog of war to clear.

Jacquie Roberson

Prologue

———————

It was a beautiful spring morning; the sun beamed down its warmth on the earth below. Birds chirped intermittently from their hidden perches in the treetops overhead. An elderly woman stood in the peaceful surroundings, her eyes locked for a moment on the little house across the road. It seemed to be waiting there for her like an old friend she hadn't seen for many years. Her oldest son, Thomas, stood quietly at her side, curiously surveying the house for the first time as he gently encircled his mother's arm. He seemed as anxious as she to further explore the deserted property, and so, led her across the dusty road for a closer inspection.

The house had changed some over the years, and yet there was still a lingering familiarity about it. Standing lost and empty now, it looked so forlorn with broken windows and a weather-beaten frame. In her mind's eye, she could still see the pleasant white frame house that had once welcomed many weary travellers within its walls. Two chimneys, standing proud and erect at either end of the building were now crumbling to dust. The beautifully kept gardens and hedges that had once surrounded the front yard were now replaced by tall field grasses concealing the foundation, and voracious weeds devouring everything in their path. The summer kitchen was gone; along with the profitable dry goods store that James was so proud of. In fact, there were no other visible out buildings left; just a few scattered piles of wood blackened by fire and hidden amongst the weeds. She sighed wistfully as tears of both sadness and joy filled her eyes and her mind flooded with treasured memories, overshadowed by this sagging, unkempt structure that remained. Sensing his mother's conflicted emotions, Thomas broke in.

"So, this is the famous Secord farm that I have heard so much about." Turning to face her then, he caught a glint in her watery eyes. "What are you thinking of, Mother? You seem a million miles away."

"Oh, Thomas, when I look at this dear old place something your grandfather once told me comes to mind. He said: 'Remember, Katie Brianna, things can seem to change, but still, they remain the same.'" She smiled at her son then. "You know, dear, I never really understood what he meant until this moment. This visit is indeed bittersweet for me. I am disappointed at the destruction I see and yet happy to be back here at last." Her mind and gaze wandered from one thing to the next. "Life was hard then, Thomas, even before the war. When the work was finally done, though, we did occasionally have time to enjoy ourselves. I thank God for all the blessings that he gave us."

"It's really a shame, Mother, that this place has been allowed to fall into such disarray. It should be cleaned up and rebuilt to look the way it used to when Laura Secord lived here, especially with her being a war heroine. This homestead could be her monument and her legacy. Her story should be told."

"Yes indeed, Laura is definitely a war heroine," she replied, gently patting his arm. "It really is inexcusable that it has taken this long for her to be recognized. Just imagine, Thomas," she added excitedly, "the Prince of Wales himself is finally going to give our dear Laura the credit she so rightly deserves for that long, treacherous walk so many years ago. Just think! This small, inconspicuous place is where it all began." Energized now, she began walking once more, pulling her son with her. "Even though other families lived here after James and Laura moved on, it is my belief that the house has stood empty for quite some time. You are right, my dear," the lady confessed. "It would be nice to see this homestead restored."

As they strolled around the property the lady gave her son a running commentary of what used to be here and what was done there, pointing to each site as they went. She showed him where the summer kitchen had once stood; the place where she and Mary, Laura's daughter, had spent many an afternoon peeling potatoes and baking bread for the evening meal. She also shared with Thomas how one day Mary had come running out the door of that very kitchen, laughing and screaming at her 'Not to dare do it' as she chased her threateningly with a pot of cold water. "I do not recall the reason for the chase now," she reflected. "I do suspect that it was all done in fun though." She then told Thomas of Laura's stern reprimand that followed, just in time to save Mary from a good dousing; all of which seemed to amuse her son. When they came to the side of the house near the front yard, she began reminiscing out loud.

"The store must have stood here ..." and on the occasion Laura could spare her, she would help Mr. Secord sell his goods. "I thoroughly enjoyed watching James banter with his customers, always ready to make a deal," she declared. Realizing that she was painting a pretty picture of those early days, she remembered that life was not as easy and serene as she let on. She immediately fell back into a melancholy state.

Thomas knew the truth, however, and heard her silence as clearly as her words.

"I am so relieved that Laura is not here to see this; she was so proud of her beautiful home," the elderly lady said. "You know, Thomas, I do not think that she has ever been back here since moving to Chippawa, and frankly, I cannot believe that it has taken me over forty years to return here myself."

"Mother, if I don't soon see that lovely smile back on your face, I'm going to think that you are not enjoying yourself. I will have no other option but to take you home," Thomas cajoled, trying to cheer her waning spirits. He turned her to face him then and pulled gently on a loose strand of her greying hair.

Smiling weakly, she gave her son's arm a loving squeeze. "You remind me so much of your father, dear. He was forever teasing me and tugging on my hair too."

"It's nice that memories of Father can still make you smile. He is part of your history here too, isn't he?" Thomas then reflected on a private memory of his own. "I miss him too, Mother. We all do, but need I remind you that we are celebrating a happy occasion. Remember?"

She smiled then, quite thankful to be sharing this trip with her son; and told him so. Of all her children, Thomas was the one who enjoyed her stories the most, listening intently when she would weave embellished tales before sending him off to sleep as a little boy. He gave her an inquiring look and, at her affirmative nod, proceeded to lead her up to the front door of the house, both anxious now to have a look inside.

Curious, she stood beside her son in the doorway, their eyes adjusting to the dim surroundings as they tried to take it all in. She recognized the old wooden hutch that leaned perilously against the far wall at the opposite end of the entryway, where Laura once kept her special pieces of china and silver cutlery. The wood surface, now covered with scratches and gouges, had two doors at the top hanging limply on their hinges. The bottom cupboard lay open, showing a mass of dusty spider webs inside. What a shame, she thought sadly, it had been a beautiful piece of furniture at one time.

They entered the kitchen and once again the woman felt herself melting into visions of her past. She recalled the large wooden table that had once stood in the middle of the room where the evening meal was enjoyed, and the small pantry where the many herbs, spices and preserves were once stored all those years ago. Her heart ached now at the sight of the table lying in a broken heap on the floor, and the only things occupying the pantry these days were dust, cobwebs and mice. Her visit through the remainder of the house was just as bittersweet. She would enter a room remembering how it had once looked, only to have her happy nostalgia dashed by this new reality.

The run-down property had once been a social centre before the war, occasionally sharing hosting of picnics and dances with the local inns and Fort George. She reminded Thomas of that and of her memorable meeting with General Isaac Brock and his fiancée, Sophia Shaw. She secretly wondered what their thoughts would have entailed had they been there today. The woman knew that she had regaled Thomas with most of these stories in the past, but he let her ramble on uninterrupted, chuckling and cooing at appropriate intervals. While holding her arm he carefully escorted her through the rest of the house, skirting the clutter and debris littering the floor. There were sections of the dilapidated walls where mouldy paper coverings sagged limply, and a damp, musty, pungency permeated their nostrils, mouse droppings everywhere they looked. Lost in her private thoughts, she allowed herself to fall back over fifty years, to the time when she had first come to this memorable homestead.

"Thomas," she said, laughing now. "I will never forget my first day working here. What a day that was! I thought for sure I would be sent on my way before I even had a chance to start. You see, we always had Hannah to help in our house. My chores at home mostly involved farm work. I had no idea what I was doing in a kitchen. Thank goodness Laura and Mary were there to teach me."

The two then slowly climbed the stairs to explore the floor above.

Later, Thomas led them out of the house, his mother quietly reflecting on the amount of time gone by. So many years had brought so many changes. The Americans had invaded Canada in 1812 causing a war of such devastation that many families never recovered from the loss and destruction. Some even declared it a senseless war in which no one really wanted to fight. It made heroes of some; Major-General Sir Isaac Brock for one (now there was a man!) and Laura Secord for another, while also making cowards of others. It had reached its ugly arm out to the communities of the Niagara frontier and beyond, snatching away men, young and old. When it finally ended, lives were rebuilt with the tools and materials left at hand; with some residents not just trying to repair their homes, but their sanity as well. Eventually, with the continuous influx of settlers arriving from across the Atlantic, the population of the country had grown.

The birth of the railroad promised to change transportation forever, and, with the invention of the telegraph, methods of communication would become faster and easier. Steamships were transporting passengers across the water, and were proving very prosperous for Canada's import and export businesses. During their journey here today, she could not help but notice how built-up the entire Queenston area appeared now, and, when they had stopped earlier for some refreshment, an innkeeper had informed them that more families were arriving almost daily.

The once dense and hostile woods had thinned and most of the wild creatures, along with many of the Indians, had gone. Laura Secord's trek through that very same bush all those years ago was filled with fear and danger. She had travelled over rough terrain and through mosquito infested swamps, just to reach Fitzgibbon in time to warn him of the secret American attack. Much of that same bush had been cut down now to accommodate the area's vast growth. It was tame and much more settled. How right her father had been: '*Remember, Katie Brianna, things can seem to change, but still, they remain the same.*'

"Yes, Thomas dear, during that horrible war I was a lonely young woman. I could not find my family and I was so grateful to both James and Laura for taking me in. I felt so lost and frightened!" Her son had become her rock since the death of his father, allowing her to lean on him often for comfort, as she did now. As he smiled down at her, she remembered the young, frightened woman she had once been, desperately afraid of an advancing war. "One night in particular will forever be etched in my mind, Son," she reflected, as he held her in a reassuring hug. "I was so terrified then, and had no idea of how soon my life would drastically and chaotically change ..."

Chapter One

The early evening light was fading; the sun descending into the distant horizon with darkness in its wake. A young woman, walking along the deserted country road, stopped for a moment to let her eyes adjust to the change, praying for the moon to come out from behind the ever darkening clouds. The unsteady air threatened to let loose a storm that would surely bring heavy rains and strong forceful winds. Presently though, all was still and quiet, all except the loud throbbing of her heart. She was frightened ... very frightened indeed, and she hurried her step hoping to arrive home that much sooner. The only sounds were the constant chirping of crickets and the continual croaking of frogs in a nearby pond.

Kate Sullivan was sixteen years old; too old to be a child but not quite old enough to be considered a fully-grown woman. She had a pretty face that held a promise of beauty in the near future and her fair complexion was unblemished and rosy, except for the few freckles that dotted her small, slender nose. Her dark green eyes had heavily lashed lids and slightly arched brows. Young men in the area were beginning to look at her with great interest, but their amorous attentions only proved an embarrassment to her. She wasn't used to being admired. She really had no idea that she should be feeling some vanity now that womanhood was fast approaching. When home on the farm, she worked alongside her older brother Kevin and their hired hand, Carl. She dressed just like them in her brother's old hand-me-downs; her workload the same as theirs, as she would have it no other way. Kate donned a cotton dress and a pretty hat whenever she went to church or to the Secord's, but she always felt more comfortable in her work clothes.

She undid the single braid in her hair with a doleful sigh, unleashing the long, auburn tresses that now framed her face in a crowning glory. She clutched her light shawl tightly around her shoulders as the warm evening wind suddenly picked up, whipping her hair wildly about her face and wrapping her dress tightly around her legs. Kate wasn't normally afraid to walk down this road alone, but tonight she had left the Secord's house later than usual and the one mile trek in the dark made her all too aware of her vulnerability, and her anxiety increased. Was that a noise coming from the bush that skirted the roadside? Was something menacing lurking there ready to pounce? Kate shook her head, scolding herself for being such a coward as she tried to keep her overactive imagination in check. If only she had not overheard that conversation at the Secord's dinner table tonight. Why did she not let James escort her home?

James and Laura Secord had been close friends and a neighbour of the Sullivan's for as long as Kate could remember. James had built a small clothing and dry goods store on the homestead and he often required Kate's help with cleaning, stocking shelves, and selling, when she wasn't busy helping Laura in the house. The Secord's had a large family but welcomed her as one of their own. Mary, the eldest of the five children, was closest to Kate's age and her best friend. They often worked together in the late afternoon, helping not only to prepare the evening meal, but to serve it and do the washing-up afterwards. Kate always felt safe and happy in the Secord home.

Tonight was different! James Secord had a uniformed dinner guest this evening, a captain named Percy, and, while serving them, she had overheard some of their conversation. The British officer had said such terrible, daunting things to James that even now, as she trudged quietly along in the dark, she recalled the entire incident and was left feeling disturbed and frightened; the captain's terrible words still ringing in her ears:

'President Madison will declare war on us James, to be sure. I have it on good authority that Thomas Jefferson was heard boasting quite loudly that all they need do is march up here and take over.'

Kate persevered with her harrowing journey home, her thoughts still centred on Mr. Secord and his illustrious guest. The captain had spoken earnestly of the mounting tensions that existed between the Americans and the British. Kate had also overheard his sharp declaration that:

'We now suffer from a vast shortage of soldiers, as Britain is still too busy fighting Napoleon to offer us any assistance in providing additional troops. I am positive that we will be outnumbered by approximately ten to one.'

Kate then recalled how drawn she had been to the conversation and how she had continued to eavesdrop even though their words struck fear into her heart. She remembered that they also mentioned the grim suffering and misery that many would face if war did come, implying mainly hopelessness for the British defenders. The British seemed to be placing all their hope and trust in a new leader; a Major-General named Brock. Captain Percy had described their commander as a no-nonsense officer who genuinely cared for the welfare of his men. The captain's confidence, however, did little to quell Kate's anxious fears. Her pulse now quickened and her head pounded at the implications. She gave her head another desperate shake. Despite the warmth of the evening, an icy shiver ran through her body as she continued her lonely walk home. She just could not forget what she had overheard.

"Dear Lord, it cannot be true," she exclaimed aloud. "Surely those men are not certain that war is coming, or are they?" They had talked so calmly when they first began, she thought, and they seemed so relaxed while they drank their wine and smoked their cigars. Maybe it was just the debate that had caused the discussion to grow louder and more intense. Is that not what usually happened whenever the men sat down together? No! It had to be a mistake. It just had to be! "Father will know," she reasoned aloud. Kate hoped that upon hearing the news, her father would just smile and express an ardent wish that she not worry herself over nothing, and tell her that all this talk of war was just nonsense. "He is always saying that I should not believe everything I hear," she said. Even though Kate's anxiety eased slightly her pace still quickened. When the modest farmhouse finally came into view, she ran towards it. Racing through the back door into the kitchen, she nearly toppled Hannah who had come to greet her.

"Good heavens, Child! You are terribly late tonight; we were all worried," Hannah exclaimed, clutching Kate in a warm hug. Sensing the young lady's anxiety, the troubled housekeeper pulled away, eyeing Kate with concern. "Is there something the matter dear?"

It was then that Kate noticed the deep tension lines now straining Hannah's ordinarily relaxed brow, and she immediately felt guilty for all the distress she had caused. "I am sorry," she said, desperate to regain control of her frazzled emotions. Kate then treated Hannah to a hasty shrug and an impish smile in a meagre attempt to lesson her friend's worry.

Hannah knew that something was upsetting Kate and wanted desperately to help her, deciding instead to send the girl to her over anxious father and let him offer the comfort. "Your father was just talking to Kevin and Carl about searching for you. He is in the parlour, my dear, and is extremely worried I might add, so you had better go in there and ease his mind." Hannah gave Kate another quick hug before gently pushing her from the room.

Kate loved Hannah; she took the place of her own mother who'd died from pneumonia when Kate was just a little girl. She never mourned her mother; she had no real memory of her. She only vaguely remembered being held in the arms of a loving young woman who softly lulled her to sleep. Hannah, however, was a mother, a sister and a friend, all rolled into one. As Kate grew older, she became aware of the love between her father and Hannah, often wondering why they had never married. Even so, she still believed that they were a family. Hannah had been hired as the housekeeper and caretaker for the Sullivan children and their father, and she ran the home like it was her own. She was a kind, gentle, spiritual woman, one with a loving heart and ready to lend a hand whenever needed. Yes, Kate thought as she headed for the parlour, something is very wrong Hannah, but hopefully Father can make it right again. When she entered the room, she discovered her father smoking his pipe and anxiously pacing the floor, stopping on her arrival, relief instantly flooding his handsome face.

"What a night! I am sorry to be so late, Father, but the Secord's had a special dinner guest this evening and there was a lot of cleaning up to do." Kate approached her father, hugging him tightly while kissing his cheek, hoping to allay his fears along with any potential admonishments. "You see, Mr. Secord was entertaining a British officer from Fort George and so I politely declined his invitation of an escort home, not wishing to interrupt their visit you understand, and as it was not yet dark, I decided to walk. I hope I have not worried you overmuch Father!"

Thomas Sullivan smiled patiently at his beloved daughter, returning her hug before taking her hand and leading her to a chair. "Come, sit down Katie Brianna. You are shiverin' me darlin'. Is it that cold out then?" he inquired gently, knowing full well that the outside temperature had nothing to do with his daughter's distress. "Aye, me girl, I was very worried indeed, and do not mind sayin' that I am greatly relieved at your return. But now I see, upon closer scrutiny, that ya' are not cold at all, but that somethin' or someone has upset ya.'"

"Oh, Father, you will not believe it! The Americans want Upper Canada!" Kate blurted out in anguish, tears now filling her eyes. "The dinner guest at the Secord's this evening was a British captain in the 41st Regiment, and he said that the Americans want to just march up here and takeover our country. They would not dare; would they Father?" Kate pleaded. She jumped instantly from her chair and began to imitate her father's earlier performance by nervously pacing the room. "Walking home tonight, I kept telling myself that the men were mistaken and it just could not be true," she continued, involuntarily wringing her hands. "I am such a coward! I even imagined that there might be American soldiers hiding in the bushes just waiting to pounce on me. I was so afraid! I cringed at every noise! It sounds ridiculous I know, but I am frightened! The whole idea of a war petrifies me!" She inhaled deeply, forcing herself to calm, and after clearing her throat and wiping her eyes, she continued on. "I just could not wait to come home and have you reassure me. Please tell me how silly I am Father and that all is not as bad as it seems!"

"The first thing ya' need to be doin', me darlin', is ta' calm down," Mr. Sullivan stated, as he seated his daughter, still distraught, back into her chair.

"But Father, the men also spoke about other consequences of war, declaring all the atrocities that would happen if we fought the Americans: death, sickness, and shortages. Our whole way of life will change. The men painted such a bleak, ugly picture of the future it upset me so; I am desperately afraid and utterly ashamed of my cowardice."

Thomas Sullivan gazed with compassion at his only daughter. How lovely she is, he thought, and so like her dear mother; God rest her soul. He had brought his own young wife Brianna all the way from Ireland to this new land, and she too was afraid and as meek as a lamb. He'd learned too late that she was not strong enough to endure the hardships of this rough, sometimes unforgiving country and she'd died young, leaving him with two little children to raise. It worried him now to witness a similar fear and weakness in his young daughter. He wanted more for his Kate. She needs to be strong now more than ever, he reasoned, because the war with the States will surely come and she will have to cope or be destroyed. Her death was too horrible to consider. Looking at Kate sitting there so dejected, he could see worry marring her lovely features and could hear the terror in her voice. He knew that she waited expectantly for reassurances that he just could not give. Instead, he sighed heavily and decided to tell her the truth.

"I am sorry Katie Brianna, but tis' quite probable that war will come." Thomas watched helplessly as more tears welled up in his young daughter's eyes, spilling down over her cheeks and causing her to whimper softly. His mind slid quietly to the past, remembering Kate as a little girl and how easy it was to comfort her then, especially if she was hurt or frightened. This was not so simple as a bump on the knee he could kiss better, or a nightmare he could soothe away. With a heavy heart and a wavering sense of duty, he pressed on. "Tis' my opinion, me darlin' girl, that the conversation ya' unfortunately overheard earlier this evenin' is indeed, true, but I would also like to add that the Americans are really not the monsters ya' make them out to be. If ya' will recall, some of our friends and neighbours are from across the border," he said, thrusting his arm out in a southerly direction. "Laura Secord for one; she came from Massachusetts, and what of our own dear Hannah? She also came from somewhere over there too. Has she not taken excellent care of both you and your brother all these years? She couldn't of loved ya' more if she were your own sainted mother." Thomas looked at his frightened child now peering up at him with her mother's sad green eyes, and sighed. He knew there was nothing more he could say to lessen her fear, so he gently lifted her chin and continued.

"If war does come, me girl, t'will happen whether we want it or not, and our only recourse is to meet it with a strong, brave front. We just cannot hand over our country without a fight! Ya' do see that, do ya' not me girl? So many people have worked so hard through the years, meself included, and sweat and strained to build a life here. Both you and your brother have worked this farm too. Sometimes, me darlin', ya' have to fight for what ya' believe in; for what is yours!"

Kate sighed and looked away from her hands and up into her father's tender face, still eyeing him miserably. She understood what he was trying to convey but his explanation did not calm her fears. She was a sensible young woman and even though her father had dashed all her hopes and left her feeling like a naive little girl, she did not want to worry him further. I will not have him look upon me as a weak little child who is terrified of her own shadow, she decided. Kate wanted so much to be brave and make her father proud, but, no matter how hard she tried, she just could not shake the overwhelming feeling of foreboding that now clung to her; refusing to let go.

Mr. Sullivan noticed Kate's stifled yawn, her face now showing signs of fatigue along with the fear. She was in dire need of a good night's sleep, he surmised. "Believe me Daughter, there will be sacrifices on both sides of this war. Let us just leave the future to take care of itself for now, shall we? No one really knows for sure what's goin' to happen, but one thing I am certain of, and that is nothin's goin' to happen tonight."

He pulled Kate from the chair then, gently kissing her forehead before ruffling her hair. "Enough of this now; off to bed with ya'. Nothin' can be solved at this hour and I'm hopeful that all will be of little consequence in the mornin.'"

"I do hope you are right Father," Kate replied, trying to stifle another yawn. "Good night then." She kissed her father on the cheek before dragging herself slowly from the room, her disillusion showing in each step.

Thomas was left alone now with conflicting thoughts of his own. He was well aware of how miserably he failed to cushion the blow of war for his Kate, but she needed to know the truth. "Not so confident now are ya'?" he muttered quietly as he poured brandy into a glass and lit his pipe. "Sacrifices indeed!" The brave front he spoke of and had just put before Kate was as much a facade as hers had been. What he refrained from telling his sweet, innocent daughter was that he too was worried. His son could be killed in this godforsaken war. His thoughts were now in an uproar. Kevin is only twenty years old! His whole life is ahead of him! What of Carl? He's like a son to me. But Carl is in fact an American; where will his loyalties lie?

Thomas' earlier speech to Kate was momentarily forgotten as he found himself agonizing over his friends and neighbours, most who were settlers from the colonies across the border. What of the horror and devastation that usually accompanies war? he thought, recalling briefly the destruction and terror brought about by the American Revolution. More importantly, what if the Americans should win? So many questions that, at the moment, he had no answers for. He shook his head sadly and, lifting the glass to his lips, he drained the brandy in one swallow.

"Tis' a shame," he said aloud, holding the now empty glass towards heaven. "Ya' will forgive me Lord, will ya' not, if tonight I get drunk?" Thomas Sullivan proceeded to the sideboard where the whiskey was kept and, pouring himself a liberal amount, took the bottle and returned gloomily to his chair.

The moon brightened the night sky with a piercing light, casting a glow through the bedroom window and landing on Kate, lying restlessly in sleep in the middle of a tormenting dream. She was on a battlefield somewhere surrounded by a thick, eerie fog, shivering uncontrollably from being both frightened and cold. The dampness clung to her like a shroud and a feeling of claustrophobia wrapped around her like a heavy blanket. The ominous mist blotted out everything, leaving a film of black and grey on all it touched. Kate could see nothing, giving the startling illusion that she had suddenly lost her sight. Where was she? How did she come to be here? What was that noise coming to her from inside the fog? The blinding and bewildering shroud separated her body and mind from control and she found herself at the mercy of the elements and the unknown entities that seemed to be surrounding her. Kate tried moving her feet so she could find a way through the heavy mist but found them immobilized and restrained somehow, making it impossible for her to walk. She shuddered in her dream. How do I escape this madness? She attempted a feeble plea for help, only to discover that she was unable to utter a sound.

A deafening crescendo of screaming and wailing lamented all around her then. She covered her ears. In the next instant the voices faded into the distance and all was quiet: too quiet. Kate stretched out her arms in front to search the unknown blankness for something: anything ... Nothing! Crying out in dismay, she welcomed the return of her own voice. Waving her arms and hands madly about, she felt isolated, help-lessly trapped within the oppressive, empty air. The uneasy stillness that enveloped her now proved just as eerie as the fog.

Drawn suddenly to a whimpering noise coming from the seeming abyss below her, Kate dropped instantly to her knees, relieved to find that she was able to move once more. To her dismay she discovered an injured soldier collapsed at her feet, black blood oozing from a musket wound in his chest. Was it safe to help him? How could one tell in this world drained of colour whether he was British or American? Did it matter? Oh, dear God, his face is as featureless as the fog! Cowering alone in the dark, Kate screamed. The creature was devoid of a face: no eyes, nose or mouth. How could he whimper without a mouth? Kate stood up suddenly, wanting to escape the daunting scene below her, crying out again in alarm at her recurring immobility, one which almost caused her to topple backwards; trapped once more by the elusive fog. Kate glanced down and was shocked to discover that the dead soldier had disappeared.

The pathetic wailing returned. This time the shrieks seemed to echo and multiply, growing more intense and alarming each second: hideous screams and low guttural moans, lamenting lost souls, penetrating through the nothingness from the other side of the black wall. Kate tried to cover her ears, but her arms were still paralyzed. Just as before, the screaming crescendo ceased abruptly, leaving Kate feeling frightened and uncertain of what was yet to come. Fearful and wide-eyed, she strained to hear something: anything, discomfited now with the all-too-quiet stillness of her surroundings. She felt inevitably trapped by a smothering fog that was slowly closing in and threatening to swallow her whole. She shrieked at the unknown entity to go away and leave her alone.

Kate suddenly became aware of a low humming sound and her fear intensified. The noise grew increasingly louder and stronger, creeping threateningly towards her through the mist. She squeezed her eyes shut and, wrung cold, clammy hands together. She waited helplessly for impending doom. The anonymous creature was about to descend upon her and then she too would disappear just as the dead soldier had. Kate was cold, but perspired profusely, feeling streams of sweat running everywhere over her body. Her heart raced. She shivered uncontrollably. She then became aware of another sound; a steady drumming, droning on from within the surrounding blackness. Shaking her head, she watched in horror as a dark, unknown shape crawled slowly out of the fog, clawing the hard ground as it approached.

"I cannot fight this any longer!" she screamed in resignation, consumed by convulsions as the evil entity paralyzed its prey. The frightening apparition wavered threateningly before her. Kate moaned in defeat, her knees buckling as she fell into the tunnel of blackness that awaited her. Silence swallowed all into oblivion.

Kate Sullivan awoke the next morning perspiring and trembling in fear. She realized that every aspect of the nightmare possessed the power to terrify her, even in broad daylight. The dream frightened her as no other had before and it carried a feeling of impending doom that just could not be ignored. Opening her eyes she found herself safe at home in her own bed and relief soared through her body. Familiar sounds drifted up to her from the kitchen below: the clatter of dishes and the hymns that Hannah sang as she prepared the morning meal.

Kate yawned and stretched, squinting in the bright sunlight that streamed through the open window. She groaned in aggravation, immediately rolling over to protect her sleepy eyes from the imposing glare, berating herself for not closing the curtains the night before.

"I need more sleep," she whined, tired and miserable and thinking again of the dream. She punched her pillow a few times before wrapping it snugly around her head, shutting out the sun, the noise, and the horrible nightmare. Kate rationalized that the dream was most likely the result of her cowardly display of last evening. Surely this dreadful news had frightened others too, leaving them also concerned for their families and anxious for their futures. Kate pressed her lips together, giving her pillow another firm whack, determined to put this whole incident from her mind. She did not want to worry her father as he was most likely concerned not only for her welfare, but surely this news of war had unsettled him as well.

"I must hide my fear," she whispered, silently praying for the strength and courage to accomplish the task. I am such a coward, she thought dismally, after concluding her request to the Lord with the customary 'Amen'.

"Katie Brianna! Rise and shine, darlin', or I'll have Hannah throw your breakfast to the hogs."

Kate came out of her stupor instantly upon hearing her father's voice. She jumped out of bed and raced to the basin. She quickly splashed cold water on her face to wash away any traces of sleep and combed her hair with her fingers. After stepping into her slippers she promptly grabbed her dressing gown from the back of a nearby chair, throwing it on in haste and tying it securely, as she descended the stairs. She was so thankful that there was no standing on ceremony in this house. She often enjoyed drinking her tea and eating her breakfast before getting dressed for chores. The men were already seated at the kitchen table with their emptied plates pushed aside, engaged in a serious discussion about the threat of war. Their dubious conversation ended abruptly when she entered the room and all eyes fell on her.

"So nice of ya' to join us this mornin', me girl," her father teased, welcoming her soft kiss on his forehead. He studied his daughter for a moment, noticing the dark circles beneath her eyes and the slight puffiness of her lids. "And how did ya' sleep?" he inquired with concern.

"I slept well, Father. Please, do not fret on my account," she lied, trying to sound more confident than she felt. Kate realized that she must look a fright from her restless night of interrupted sleep, but she smiled at him anyway and continued with the charade. "I am terribly sorry for my childish behaviour of yesterday and I can assure you, Father, it will not happen again; I promise you that." There is no need to worry him more than I have already, she thought. But with her father inspecting her so closely, Kate was uncertain if she had succeeded in fooling him. She sat in the chair directly across from her brother Kevin and their hired hand and friend, Carl Phillips, treating each of them to a charming, though phony, reassuring smile. "Anyway, Father, you will be relieved to know that I woke this morning and decided that I refuse to let this war nonsense concern me any further, although I must confess that I do not like this President Madison very much."

"T'is' happy I am to be hearin' that Katie darlin'," Thomas replied with imminent relief, his features suddenly relaxed. "Ya' cannot ignore any future conversations concernin' this war, as I am quite certain that tongues will be waggin' throughout the county this very mornin.'"

He smiled at Kate then, and she was thankful for the second time since waking, convinced that her family now believed her; that she was no longer disturbed by the hostility to come. Her delight was cut short however, when her father, satisfied now, turned away to resume his discussion with the boys. They too seemed more at ease with the topic, certain that she had come to terms with the matter. Kate felt the slight pangs of hunger as she smelled Hannah's delicious biscuits wafting to her from the nearby fireplace. She welcomed the distraction, eating the flaky delights quietly, pushing away all thoughts of war and willing herself to remain calm.

"Sorry, Father," Kevin interjected. "I have to agree with Carl. If the British would just stop boarding American ships and stealing their sailors then maybe we could ward off any more trouble."

"No, lad, do ya' not see? There's too much political unrest between us and them blasted Americans that t'would take a lot more than that to end this thing. Ya' see, me boys, their dander's up now and they'll not be backin' down. Besides," Thomas added, as he picked up his pipe and paused for a moment to light it. "I know for a fact that some of them sailors were indeed British seamen who were desperately needed to fight that Napoleon fellow over there in France."

"Some Americans were taken by mistake, Thomas," Carl pointed out. "I know that for a fact because my cousin was one of those unfortunates."

"It maybe so, maybe so; I am not disputin' that the British are causing a stir and doin' us no favours, boyo," Thomas declared, pointing his pipe at Carl. "What I am tryin' ta' tell ya' both is that there's a whole hornets' nest stirred up here and even if we started kowtowing to the Americans now, t'would no good come of it. They're all riled up lads. They want this country come hell or high water, so there'll be no changin' their minds!"

"You men are not solving a thing," Kate scolded, dropping her half eaten biscuit onto the plate. "And you are spoiling my meal." She quickly gained control of her emotions, squashing the anxiety building inside and hiding her turmoil from the family. She noticed Hannah leaving the kitchen then and decided to follow her out. "Tomorrow is Sunday," she stated, eyeing each of them sternly. "When we all go to church I suggest that we pray for a peaceful solution to this whole mess. Now, if you men will excuse me, Mr. Secord requires my assistance in the store this morning." Kate rose from her chair then, scraping it across the floor, and the men followed suit, rising in unison while staring after her in wonder, as she beat a hasty retreat to her bedroom.

Thomas Sullivan broke the silent confusion with his few inspirational words. "Well, lads, I guess we'll be puttin' in a full day's work today and goin' ta' talk with the Lord himself tomorrow."

Chapter Two

———

The following week was a flurry of activity, gossip spread quickly throughout the Niagara frontier. There were mixed feelings regarding the known tensions between Canada and the States but, until war was actually declared, life would carry on as usual. Those who didn't concern themselves with the threat of an American attack were busy making plans to attend the ball that was to be held at the Coach House Inn, a few miles up the road in the town of Newark. Everyone in the county was invited and there were even rumours that a few of the soldiers from Fort George would be attending; Isaac Brock included. Some of the women argued that, although they would enjoy seeing the soldiers, the ball was deemed a happy occasion and talk of war should not be permitted. The majority of the men disagreed, of course. They compromised however, saying that any discussions pertaining to the dreaded invasion would take place in private, away from the ladies' hearing.

The young ladies in the county found it quite difficult to contain their excitement while they waited for the ball and were very preoccupied with deciding what to wear. Their eagerness mounted with each passing day as some in the more prosperous families were anxious for their gowns to be finished on time, while others were having older dresses fitted and altered by their mothers. Spirits seemed generally high among the local people and they anticipated a night of dancing and merry-making. Kate Sullivan, however, could not be counted as one of them. All the pomp and finery meant nothing and seemed in very bad taste to her, considering the threat of war nipping at their heels.

"Honestly, Mary, I really do not understand what all the fuss is about. It is just a silly little ball," Kate commented one morning as they finished dusting the last of the shelves. Today was Monday, the day when she helped James clean the store thoroughly and restock all the dry goods. Unfortunately, he was ill and in bed with a terrible cough. Laura was afraid of pneumonia setting in, so she made him promise to stay put. Mary was instructed to take his place and assist Kate, as news of the upcoming ball was proving extremely good for business.

"Oh, Kate, you cannot possibly mean that! Attending such a grand occasion will be a dream come true. I have been having such difficulty lately concentrating on my chores because this ball is all I think about."

"I certainly do mean it; every word," Kate replied indignantly, shaking her head in frustration at her friend's idle foolishness. "Mary, you are too young to entertain any thoughts of attending this dance, are you not?"

"I know that I have never been to a ball before but I am so looking forward to this one, Kate. The only other dances I have attended were the ones that Mother and Father hosted here. Even then, I merely sat on the sidelines watching everyone else enjoying themselves. You remember Kate? You were with me some of the time. Anyway, Mother has agreed to let me go," Mary exclaimed, crossing her arms in front of her chest. "She said that it was a special event and that there may not be another for quite some time if this silly war does come. So you see, I will be going, and I, for one, intend to have a good time."

Mary Secord was three years Kate's junior but, seeing them together, people often mistook her for the older of the two. Kate had often wondered why she was not more inclined to be like her friend, who seemed so ladylike in many respects and quite comfortable with her sex. Mary loved to preen in front of a mirror when she was alone, if time and her other siblings permitted. She carefully inspected her appearance, satisfying herself that she looked her best. She selected the proper clothing and ensured that no hair was out of place. Kate often became frustrated and impatient while waiting for Mary to prepare herself for any outing they chanced to go on together, wondering sometimes at their friendship and their differences.

Kate was the exact opposite to Mary. She gazed at her reflection only long enough to braid her hair, taking no pains whatsoever to ensure that every little strand was where it should be. She had no time for such vanity! When she awoke in the morning, she threw on her work clothes with no undue thought or care for her appearance, just as long as she was clean. Kate could never be accused of being vain.

Hannah would chuckle and smile in her own secret amusement while regarding Kate, knowing full well that one day things would change. It was only a matter of time; that and meeting the right gentleman, of course.

Kate's life was a busy one and, by far, not an easy one. She divided her responsibilities between the farm and housecleaning chores at home, which were plentiful, and her work at the Secord's a few afternoons each week, leaving very little time for her own pleasure. Life was hard for most people on the Niagara frontier; sometimes crops failed or livestock became sick and died, leaving families straining financially and at the mercy of the elements. The Sullivans were no different from their neighbours, which was the main reason that Kate began working for the Secords in the first place, as they were considered one of the more influential and prosperous families in the county.

"I am so excited, Kate," Mary said. "I am all prepared for the ball. Mother and I have just completed the changes to my gown. I do not intend to sit aside watching others having fun this time. I truly hope some of the soldiers ask me to dance," she added, smiling nervously.

"I have never been to a ball either, Mary, but thank goodness I am not acting as silly as you at this moment. Listen to yourself. You are only thirteen, a mere child in the eyes of the grown men who will most likely be attending this ball. I should not count on any dances if I were you, other than with your own father of course." Kate realized the moment she uttered the cruel words that she had hurt her friend and longed to take them back. It was not her intention to cause Mary pain; she just wanted to spare her young friend any disappointment the night of the ball.

Mary had turned abruptly away from Kate, desperate to stop the flow of tears that threatened to fall, proving Kate's point that she was a child after all.

"Oh, my dear, I am so sorry. I should be rendered speechless for that undeserved cruelness towards you," Kate repented. "I did not mean to hurt you; I hope you realize that. Truly, I only meant to warn you." She approached Mary then and encircled her in a gentle, soothing hug. "Honestly, dear, I cannot imagine what came over me to speak to you in such a fashion. I am so ashamed of myself. Will you not forgive me? I am sure you will enjoy many dances," she added, trying to appease the unfortunate situation.

Kate pulled away slightly. Looking at her friend, she smiled warmly as she wiped away the last remnants of Mary's tears. Mary smiled again. Soon both girls were laughing and all was forgotten as talk of the ball resumed. Kate would rather they discuss some other topic, but when her friend spoke once more of her desire for a dancing partner, she listened politely, offering that maybe her brother Kevin would oblige, or perhaps Carl? Mary suddenly appeared nervous and confused.

"You are mistaken, Kate. I was only speaking of dancing with some young soldier."

"You are not fooling me, Mary Secord, I am well aware of your infatuation with my brother," Kate replied in a teasing tone.

Mary shrugged her shoulders and smiled sheepishly as her thoughts turned to Kevin. He was handsome and seemed to always have a kind word for her whenever they chanced to meet. She had known him all of her life and still had no idea of how he felt about her, or if he even thought of her at all. I am not sure of my feelings for him either. Oh, I wish I were older, or that he would at least wait for me to grow up so I could find out. Kate is right, Mary berated herself, I am still a child. In her next breath Mary attempted to draw the unwelcome conversation away from her and Kevin.

"Please, tell me that you have your ball dress ready, Kate."

"I have not the slightest notion of what I will be wearing, nor do I care if I even attend," Kate replied dryly. "Oh, Hannah will probably alter one of my mother's old dresses. It is of little consequence to me," she added, after noticing the shocked expression on her friend's face. Neither of the girls had heard the store's front door open and were just as unaware that Molly Hogan stood in the doorway quietly observing them, until she spoke.

"Listen Kate, dear Mary is right. This ball promises fun and exhilaration for all. You just wait and see." Molly laughed gaily as she approached the girls, infecting only Mary with her good humour. "Just imagine, Kate, we can dance with those handsome men in uniform all evening and engage ourselves in silly conversation while drinking our punch." Following that happy outburst, Molly began twirling herself gracefully around the small storeroom, dancing with an imaginary partner and humming a popular tune. She was a pretty young woman with a friendly disposition, rather silly at times, but she was like a sister to the girls and Mary, for one, admired and appreciated her. "I could easily fall in love at this cotillion, Kate," Molly confessed, as she stopped dancing to peer closely at her friend. "Maybe at the end of the evening, when we are strolling quietly in the moonlight, I could share a goodnight kiss with my soldier. I just love a man in a bright red uniform," Molly whispered, as she clasped her hands together and smiled.

"Yes, that would be so lovely," Kate replied, rolling her eyes. "Then your handsome and unsuspecting soldier will leave you to fight in this ridiculous war and be killed, lying alone on a battlefield somewhere. How nice for you both! Honestly, Molly, I think you are acting just as foolish as Mary about this silly ball, and she is a lot younger than you."

Molly had always tried to allow that a person was entitled to his or her own opinion, but at present, she found Kate's attitude somewhat baffling. "I do not understand your reasoning Kate. Why are you being so negative about this particular event? Can you not just try to forget your troubles for one evening and set your mind to having fun? Please, do not let this war frighten you, my dear. This could be the last dance for quite some time." Molly Hogan noticed the forlorn look marring Kate's features and could only guess at her friend's thoughts. She gave Kate a comforting hug, trying to reassure her that she truly believed that the ball would produce nothing but good for everyone. "Let us dance and laugh while we are still able," Molly said.

"I do not know how to dance," Kate whispered in embarrassment.

"Well, goodness gracious my dear, I am quite convinced that there is no time like the present to learn." Molly took hold of Kate's hand. Armed with both a smile on her face and determination in her heart, she began humming a tune while proceeding with her instructions. Mary sat on a barrel beside the counter clapping her hands and giggling softy as she watched. Miss Hogan proved an excellent teacher, showing Kate the pivots and turns of each dance step, and even instructing Kate in the newly performed waltz that her father had taught her on his return from Europe.

When the lengthy lesson was completed, the young and graceful pupil had a fair knowledge of the *Waltz* as well as the old faithful *Minuet* and *Quadrille*. With Mary's assistance, Molly also taught Kate the ever popular *Country Dance*. To her amazement, Kate discovered that she really did enjoy dancing. Molly was proud of her protégé; and told her so, proceeding then to also give Mary a quick further instruction of the waltz.

"Oh, my goodness," Molly exclaimed breathlessly at the conclusion of both lessons. "I am late and I almost forgot what I came in here for." She quickly made her purchases, gave each of the young ladies a hug and, after both girls thanked her once again, went dancing merrily out the door. "See you two at the ba .... all," she sang.

Chapter Three

The Sullivans and the Secords arrived at the Coach House Inn at the same time, greeting each other cordially with handshakes and laughter. An elderly gentleman, Samuel Forbes, stood at the end of the walkway near the road, ready to offer his assistance to any of the ladies alighting from their carriages. He was meticulously dressed for the occasion in his old military uniform, and he performed his duty with reverence and patience, greeting each guest with a smile as they entered the inn. Kevin and Carl had the distinct responsibility of parking both family rigs behind the building, with Carl ushering the Secord carriage in behind the Sullivan's. In their absence, the rest of the party greeted other arriving guests with smiles and waves, as all the ladies waited to be escorted into the ball.

The Coach House Inn was delightful. Its exterior boasted a light yellow colour and its windows, twenty in all, were trimmed in royal blue shutters, giving it the appearance of an elaborate two story cottage. The front entrance was framed in brightly coloured red roses that encircled the door and there was a rose garden showcasing the flower's various colours under each of the two large front windows, and continuing down each side of the walkway. The walkway itself was a work of art consisting of multi coloured flat rocks carefully laid in a decorative pattern, running from the roadside up to the front door of the inn.

Kevin and Carl both joined the party at the same time, and Kate was pleased to see that her charming brother had offered his arm to

Mary. Kate was amazed at how much older her friend seemed when all dressed up, and she could not help but feel abundantly proud of her. She is handling herself beautifully, Kate thought, while I am as nervous as a kitten. I shall try my best to emulate Mary this evening, if only to please Father. Searching the crowd of guests for him, she smiled, noticing that he had given his arm to Hannah and was now escorting her inside. When Carl approached, Kate graciously accepted his cordial offer of accompaniment into the ball.

The inn was crowded with neighbours laughing and talking excitedly. Anticipation filled the air. Some had already started dancing, others formed small groups and were catching up on the latest news. The men discussed the current crop and livestock prices. After looking around mischievously, some quietly mentioned the devastating effect a war would have on their farms. The women were too wrapped up in their own excitement to pay the men any mind, sharing recipes, admiring some gowns while criticizing others, and lamenting various household problems.

The main floor of the inn was divided into three separate rooms. There were two large public rooms joined by an archway, one in front, which was now being used as the drawing room, and beyond that was the second room, which was now the ballroom. There was also a small kitchen located at the very back of the inn. On the second floor, there was an assortment of rooms where one could find lodgings for the night.

This evening, the drawing room was for socializing. Tables had been set for both the card playing guests and for those who only wished to sit and talk while enjoying refreshments. A long table covered with a fancy crocheted cloth was situated along the wall at the back of the room. It displayed a variety of meats, breads, puddings and other delectable desserts. Sitting beside it was the small beverage table, where one could help themselves to a glass of punch. The stronger beverages were available at the bar counter, situated under the stairway between the two rooms. The ballroom of course, was for dancing, where people were already turning and bowing in rhythm with the music. Some of the guests were sitting on chairs at the side of the room, entertaining each other as they observed the dancers, while others mingled outside under the illuminating lights of the lanterns.

Kate and Mary were both mesmerized by the wondrous sights before them, and since this was their first ball, they were both hard pressed to control their excitement. Even as she noticed the red uniformed soldiers that were present, Kate momentarily forgot her uneasiness and misery regarding the probable war. How wonderful everyone looks, she thought. It appeared as if the whole county were here tonight, seeking gaiety and merriment. Kate waved, greeting Molly Hogan who was helping herself to some punch. She also noticed Johnny Thornston leading Sylvia Crane to the dance floor. Kate and Mary were thrilled. While weaving their way through the crowded drawing room, they were passing a table of whist players when one of the elderly ladies called out to them.

"My goodness, Kate, how lovely you look!" said Mrs. Collins. "You seem to be a pretty young lady in that dress. I very nearly did not recognize you, my dear."

"Thank you very much," Kate answered, curtsying shyly and feeling her cheeks growing warm at the unaccustomed compliment.

"And Mary, you look lovely too, as always."

"Thank you, Mrs. Collins," Mary replied as they moved on.

Hannah had pressed Kate to take extra care in dressing this evening and she had obeyed, even asking for assistance, informing her beloved housekeeper that she wanted so much to appear as a gentle young lady should and not prove an embarrassment to her father. Earlier, when Kate looked into Hannah's full length mirror, she could not believe that the reflection staring back at her was her own. Gone were the oversized work clothes and dishevelled hair. Like Mary, Kate was dressed in a white cotton gown, but instead of the plain lace and ruche adornments, her dress was more detailed, with venice lace and satin ribbon that trimmed her sleeves, bodice and skirt. Her beautiful auburn hair was held in place by skillfully applied combs. Her mother's black cameo choker encircled her slender neck. On her feet Kate wore dainty white slippers, and both arms were covered with long, white gloves. Hannah had really outdone herself this time, Kate thought with satisfaction, attributing none of her appearance to her own natural beauty.

"Please God," she whispered. "Let my manners match my gown."

Both of the young ladies were in high spirits as they finally entered the ballroom, and Kate's relief was quite apparent finding that her first dance partner was to be Carl Phillips. She felt comfortable with him; it would be like dancing with her brother. He will not care if I miss a step or two, she thought, although I am sure he will tease me about it later. However, as they danced, Carl offered a humble apology for his own noticeable awkwardness, confessing that Mr. Sullivan had kept him too busy of late to attend many dances, but extending his compliments for her ease on the dance floor. She offered a smile of encouragement to Carl which seemed to relax him. At the conclusion of their dance, he escorted Kate back to the drawing room and her family, bowing to all the ladies before departing to seek out another dance partner. Kate then accompanied Hannah and Laura to a glass of punch, enjoying a brief nonsensical conversation before they were each escorted into the ballroom once again.

Kate's partners for the minuet and quadrille included both Kevin and her father in turn. Thomas exclaimed joyfully how proud he was of his Katie Brianna and how much she resembled her dear departed mother, while Kevin laughed and teased her, asking if she knew what had become of his little sister. Kate's next dance was with a young soldier, and after introducing himself as Private Matthew Dunsford, he proceeded to lavish her with compliments, and kept her laughing at his antics throughout the entire dance. He then invited her for a refreshment in the drawing room where they could talk in comfort. After noticing her slight hesitation, he assured her that this would be quite acceptable; since even though he was not an officer as yet, he most certainly was a gentleman.

The drawing room was a hub of activity, filled with other guests who were of the same mind as Kate and her soldier. Private Dunsford managed to find a vacant table, and as they sat together sipping their punch, he entertained her with his witty conversation. The private had a wonderful sense of humour and Kate found herself laughing merrily at all of his jokes. As they continued their casual talk, the subject suddenly turned to more serious matters. Kate listened intently as the young soldier spoke of the high regard that the entire regiment at Fort George had for their commander, Major-General Brock.

"He is such a kind and considerate gentleman Miss Sullivan, and people seem to respect him. The concern he shows for his men is admirable and we all genuinely feel honoured to be under his command. I wish you could visit the fort and meet the general for yourself. I am positive that you would find him quite affable. Perhaps a tour of our small fortress would interest you? I am sure that time can be set aside from our busy schedule to enlighten our friends and neighbours. Would a tour interest your father perchance? Especially with this ghastly threat of war on everyone's mind," he added. Kate felt uneasy at his mention of the word war. She knew he couldn't help it; he was a soldier after all.

"I would be very interested in meeting such a man, sir, but do you mind if we change the course of our conversation to a more agreeable subject? Let us not spoil this evening's festivities with such talk since it upsets me so." Up to now Kate had been successful in avoiding any conversation that even remotely pertained to the dreaded war and she was determined to keep it that way. She tried desperately to win the battle over her emotions, hoping to hide them from her bewildered escort. It was not the private's fault, she reasoned. He was quite unaware of her fear regarding the matter. She prided herself a moment later though, with how quickly she was able to collect herself and go on, displaying only a fraction of her concern to the young soldier.

"Please, forgive my inexcusable blunder, Miss Sullivan. I assure you my only intent was to alleviate any fears you may have at present regarding this terrible threat, and to show the magnificent post that is in place to protect the region if war does come."

The young private, noticing Kate's discomfort, quickly changed the subject to something more appealing, regaling her instead, with some amusing stories about his family back home in England. Soon they were both laughing again. Kate could feel a difference within herself, blushing with each compliment. This is not like me, she thought. It is as if this dress holds an enchantment over me; when I wear it, I become a lady.

She had been comfortable with all of her dance partners this evening, attributing some of her success to her recent dance lessons, and she now found herself at ease with Private Dunsford who, for the moment, seemed quite taken with her light, flirtatious mood.

Nick Brannigan had also been sitting in the drawing room quietly observing the young couple, feeling almost resentful of their apparent happiness. He was drawn instantly to the young lady's spirited beauty as she giggled coquettishly at some witty tale that the soldier was relating. Nick thought that the lady was young and, in her innocence, she was most likely unaware of how attractive and vibrant she appeared. He felt his own mouth widen into a smile as he listened to her gaiety. Damn, but her laughter is infectious, he thought. The young soldier certainly knew how to entertain the girl. How long had it been since he had expressed any abandoned amusement, or even made anyone else that happy? For some reason he could not fathom, Nick felt drawn to this young woman; a matter which he found rather confusing. He usually sought out older and more experienced women. This one lady was definitely not his type. He heard her chuckle again, and the melodic sound tickled his insides and warmed his heart. Nick realized then that it was her laughter and not her beauty that first caught his attention. That thought too was most perplexing.

Kate observed a handsome man sitting alone at a table just a short distance from where she and Private Dunsford were conversing, and she shivered slightly at his penetrating gaze. She returned a quick appraisal of her own, appreciating his tanned complexion, coal black hair, clean-shaven face and those dark, piercing blue eyes; which, for the moment, she found very unnerving. She also noticed how attractively dressed he was for the occasion: a white silk cravat and shirt, grey waistcoat, black velvet tailcoat, and cream coloured pantaloons tucked neatly into black hessian boots. The man smiled and Kate immediately turned back to Matthew Dunsford, deciding that he was closer to her age, so she should forget about the admiring glances of the handsome stranger. In their mutual distraction however, both Kate and the young private missed the approach of an older, slightly intoxicated British captain.

"Private Dunsford! You are to return to the fort," the captain stated, surprising the two young people.

"No, sir. I mean; yes, sir," the private responded, as he stood instantly to face his senior officer. He was slightly confused at the change of his orders and offered an explanation. "Sorry, sir, but, as I was instructed to return to the fort later with the other men in my company, I decided to enjoy myself for a time."

"You are to return now, private! Do not fear, Dunsford," the belligerent captain added, leaning in close to Kate and quickly grasping her hand. "I will take care of the young lady."

Private Dunsford shrugged apologetically to Kate, helplessly portraying his inability to refuse his captain, and, after making the proper introductions, bowed and left immediately.

Captain Walter Clarke brought Kate briskly to her feet and ignoring her agitated refusals, pulled her hastily into the ballroom. Kate's plight attracted the attention of the other patrons close by, though no one seemed willing to interfere with a captain of the British army.

Nick had been approaching Kate with the intention of introducing himself, only to watch in frustration as the lady was led away by a British officer, whose intoxication was quite apparent. He scowled deeply at their retreating backs, cursing the drunken man under his breath as he followed. The captain appeared to have left all of his manners and courtesies at the fort, Nick thought upon reaching the dancers. He was definitely not acting as an officer and a gentleman should. Nick's eyes never left Kate, or her lecherous partner, and he wondered how to assist without causing a disturbance. Since he was not a British soldier himself, the inebriated captain failed to intimidate him.

"Sir, please!" Kate exclaimed helplessly, trying to keep his busy hands from roaming where they did not belong. He was leering down at her as though he would devour her at any moment, his breath smelling stale from whiskey; his hands dripping with perspiration. She found this man to be obnoxious and utterly contemptuous, and for the first time this evening she felt extremely uncomfortable and completely powerless. Captain Walter Clarke had a strong, rough hold of her arm and an instant panic rose within Kate as she realized that he was now pulling her through the kitchen towards the back door. Once outside, she would be at his mercy. She quickly surveyed the room in open fear and frustration, but no one dancing seemed to notice her predicament; or perhaps they did not care.

Nick Brannigan noticed however, and he immediately weaved his way towards them.

"Excuse me, sir, but I believe the lady owes me a dance." He then took Kate gently by the arm as the drunken captain stood agape, unsure of how to reclaim his stolen prize. As Nick guided Kate to the dance floor, he spied the belligerent scoundrel staggering up to them, fists at the ready. Nick groaned in annoyance. Grabbing his assailant by the scruff of his coat and, twisting the captain's arm behind his back, he opened the door and heaved the blackguard out. One punch rendered the dumbfounded oaf unconscious. However, Nick's humour did not improve upon re-entering the ballroom. He saw his flustered dance partner being escorted away by Thomas Sullivan and a British officer. Shaking his head, he scowled and swore under his breath, deciding to wash his hands of the entire situation and have a drink.

Kate stood spellbound as she observed the handsome stranger discarding the wretched captain outside. She was just forming the thank you that she intended to offer him, when she heard her father's voice behind her and felt him pulling her from the room. Kate turned helplessly towards the stranger, noticing the scowl that darkened his features. She immediately disengaged herself from her father's grasp, pleading with him to let her go so she could properly thank the gentleman.

Thomas Sullivan glanced at the man in question, acknowledging his presence with a grateful smile and a quick nod of recognition. After watching his daughter, now bereft of any shyness, actively pursuing her champion, he whispered something to the officer at his side before they both turned back to the vicinity of the drawing room.

"Wait! Please," Kate called to her gallant rescuer. "I did not have the chance to thank you for your timely interruption." Nick turned to face her as she approached. "Sir, you must think me terribly rude," she exclaimed breathlessly.

"Not in the least, miss. No apology is necessary, I assure you," he replied, smiling once more. "I was glad to be of some assistance. However," he added, his smile now changing to a rakish grin. "I do think that you owe me a dance."

"Just the same, I do not know what would have happened had you not intervened. I did not want to cause a scene, you understand, so you can imagine how grateful I am to you, sir."

"My name is Nick ... Nick Brannigan." Nick bowed to Kate with the introduction, kissing her gloved hand. "I thought it only polite to introduce ourselves, before we dance."

"You may call me Kate," she replied, dipping into a curtsy.

Nick grinned mischievously, and winking, he pulled her a little closer. "Well, Miss Kate, I think I will lead you in the scandalous waltz. Have you any objections?"

"N-no, I suppose not," she replied nervously at the word scandalous.

A few of the older gentry shook their heads in disbelief as they watched the couple circling the room. Nick tried not to hold Kate too tightly or closely, so as to keep her reputation intact. He had already noticed the disapproving glares levelled at them from a few of the shocked guests, some even mumbling how sinful and vulgar the dance was and how Miss Sullivan should be utterly ashamed of herself. Nick saw that Kate had overheard their uncomplimentary remarks and noticed their dire expressions, though she said nothing. His admiration towards her deepened and he chuckled softly as he noticed more daring couples approaching the floor.

"It appears that we are not alone in our endeavor," he commented with amusement, drawing Kate's attention to the other dancers. "Relax, Katie, and let yourself enjoy the moment."

Kate had never felt this way before. Not even earlier with Matthew Dunsford, she thought. The amorous attentions of the neighbourhood boys suddenly came to mind. There quite simply was no comparison; they were boys, but Nick Brannigan was definitely a man. She was gradually becoming more comfortable with the waltz and she loved the feeling of being held in Nick's arms, albeit loosely, while they danced. She noticed Molly Hogan waltzing nearby with Private Dunsford, the latter winking slyly at them while Molly smiled brightly and waved. Kate was confused, wondering why the young private was not back at the fort by now as ordered, but she soon directed her attention back to her partner. Kate liked it when Nick called her Katie; it sounded so endearing. Although she had just met him, she was well aware of the rigid decorum that was expected. This particular situation was quite new to her though, so she was unsure of how to handle it properly.

Kate was giddy with excitement and feeling very contented, even though she now knew how much the waltz was frowned upon. She felt relieved that she had the presence of mind earlier this evening, to discard all of her unpleasant opinions regarding the ball, choosing instead to listen as Hannah offered stalwart instructions of how to dress appropriately and how to carry herself as a young lady. Kate was very grateful indeed to the dear woman for spending many a leisure moment altering the ball dress that had once been worn by her mother, and for fixing her hair just right. She was having a wonderful time and, although being held by this handsome man caused butterflies to flutter frantically about in her stomach, she truly felt beautiful for the first time in her life. Nick's penetrating gaze was very distracting, however, and Kate experienced some difficulty when trying to concentrate on the steps. If only this dance could last forever, she thought. But, much to her dismay the dance did end, and all too soon. Nick escorted her back to the drawing room to join the rest of her family.

"Well Nick, me boyo, I hope it was not your intention to make a spectacle of me young daughter," Thomas Sullivan stated with amusement, noticing Kate's confusion as he guided her to the awaiting chair beside Hannah.

"I do apologize, Thomas, for any embarrassment my actions may have caused," Nick replied. "I do feel, however, that a few eyebrows needed to be raised. Would you not agree, sir? It was all quite harmless, I assure you, and only in fun, you understand."

"No harm done, lad," Thomas laughed. "Indeed, it will give some of them ol' crows somethin' to go on about." Nick took a seat at the table then as introductions were made and a brief conversation ensued. A few minutes later, Thomas approached Nick, and slinging an arm over his shoulders, he motioned for him to stand. "While I have ya' here, me boyo, there is a wee matter I wish to discuss with ya'. Will ya' please excuse us ladies?" Both men bowed politely and Nick gave Kate a quick glance before being ushered away to another table for a private conversation.

Kate looked baffled, her eyes following Nick and her father. How long have they known each other? she wondered, and why had she not met Nick before? Kate sat quietly, glancing frequently in the direction of her father and Nick, feeling very bewildered. Another puzzling thought struck her. Why was her father not concerned that she had danced the notorious waltz?

"Oh, Mary," Kate remarked later in the evening, the two of them sitting on a bench outside. "I am so tired. I am sure that I could not dance another step, even if the king himself were to ask me."

"I am tired too but, my goodness, Kate, this has been the most wonderful night of my life," Mary replied dreamily. "Your brother is such a nice young gentleman; he has danced with me numerous times this evening. You do not think he was just being polite, do you? Oh, I wish I was older, and then maybe he would look at me differently. He thinks of me as a child, Kate, I know he does."

"You must be patient, Mary, and perhaps in a few years Kevin may well notice you in the way you desire. You are only thirteen, remember? When you are eighteen and he is twenty-five, the difference will not seem so great then."

"Five years is such a long time, Kate. What if he does not wait for me?"

"Then it just was not meant to be. There may be someone else intended for you, Mary."

"You should know how I hate waiting; it is not one of my strong suits."

Kate put her arm around her friend's shoulders to offer some comfort. "Hannah always says that we wait on God's time, Mary, not our own."

"What about you, Miss Kate?" Mary chided, quickly changing the subject. "Mr. Nick Brannigan is a very handsome older man, I should think."

"He is handsome, is he not? So distinguished looking too," Kate remarked tenderly. "Mary, tell me truly; did I shame myself this evening dancing the waltz? Molly should have warned me of how inappropriate some people consider it to be. I know Mrs. Collins and Mrs. Foster were appalled. I heard them both gasping loudly in shock. I am sure there were others who also felt as they did, and yet, my own father seemed unaffected by it."

"Honestly, Kate, I thought it was wonderful. You both danced beautifully together. Maybe your father will let you know his concerns in private, but I really do not think that he was upset. Anyway, who cares what those old ladies say. They were probably jealous," Mary giggled. "I was convinced that you and Private Dunsford had developed an understanding earlier this evening, Kate, but then I noticed him paying a lot of attention to Molly Hogan. They even waltzed together. Then, when I watched you and Mr. Brannigan, I noticed how happy you looked. I have never seen you like this. You seem different somehow."

"Mary, I was surprised to see Private Dunsford dancing with anyone. Was he not ordered back to Fort George by that ... captain, Captain Walter Clarke?"

"I heard Mr. Secord declaring that the captain had deceived the private and General Brock agreed," Mary stated. "The general also said that Captain Clarke was a cad; that he only ordered the private back to the fort so he could dance with you. Really, Kate, that man treated you abominably." Mary giggled once again, and leaning into her friend, she whispered a confession. "I also heard that General Brock was very displeased with Walter Clarke and that the captain left the ball extremely upset with everyone, but most especially with Mr. Nick Brannigan."

During the rest of the evening Kate danced very little; not for lack of offers, but due solely to her preoccupation with Nick Brannigan. She hadn't seen him since his earlier conversation with her father, and she searched for him everywhere; he had just simply disappeared. Kate would not consider that he might have already left. She liked Nick and hoped that after sharing one dance together, he might seek her out for another; but he did not. What a fool I have been, she thought. He probably forgot all about me when our dance ended. I suppose I am too young to attract the attentions of a man like him. Angry at herself for behaving so foolishly, Kate also speculated whether she should even care. It was just a silly little dance. Was it not just last week that she had declared as much to both Hannah and Mary?

This was all so new and puzzling. What had come over her? She recalled how occasionally, throughout the night, she had inspected her appearance, convincing herself that she did it for her benefit, not for Nick's. Had she now become vain as well? All for a man who did not appear the least bit interested in her. Kate was plagued by many new emotions. She felt as though she were drowning in a tidal wave of strange and uncertain feelings. She was eager to find Nick. Without him, there was no hope for rescue.

The festivities were quickly coming to an end and still there was no sign of Nick Brannigan. Kate was standing at the top of the stairway looking down into the ballroom below, anxious and frustrated, when she suddenly saw him. Her young face lit up as she quickly descended the stairs, trying to catch him before he vanished again. Kate had just about reached Nick when she stopped short. He was smiling warmly and leaning in close to a beautiful young woman who was speaking to him with her arm looped through his; and he was gazing down at her with absolute devotion. Kate was livid. Who was this woman?

She scolded herself mentally for wasting her time with the likes of him. I do not believe what I am seeing, she thought. How naive can I be? She felt angry and embarrassed. She was confused. Nick seemed so charming and attentive when we danced. He saved me from that lecherous Walter Clarke. How could he do this to me? And him being a friend of Father's too! She remembered then what Nick had said earlier regarding their waltz together: 'It was all just in fun.' Kate gasped when Nick's gaze suddenly turned in her direction but she darted around the nearest corner unseen. She felt tired, foolish, miserable and completely ashamed. This would prove to be a most memorable evening after all, she thought in despair; but not for the reasons she had hoped.

Kate left the ballroom and slowly made her way back to the drawing room where she found her family. Her father was standing with a British officer and his young lady. Their heads turned in her direction as they regarded her lazy approach. The officer had a kind, handsome face and was dressed in full military attire, from gold shoulder epaulettes to silver spurs on his boots. They greeted her warmly, and her father introduced the betrothed couple as Major-General Isaac Brock and his fiancée; Miss Sophia Shaw. He informed her then that the general was the same officer who had accompanied him when she was in the clutches of Captain Clarke. General Brock offered an apology to Kate on Clarke's behalf and Kate had thanked him for his efforts.

When the general then turned to resume his conversation with her father, Kate smiled politely at Miss Shaw, exchanging pleasantries and all the while longing to be home. Kate was relieved when the evening finally did come to an end, feeling tired and anxious for her own room where she could collect her thoughts and try to make sense of a most confusing night. How could one evening that had begun with such excitement and expectation end so dismally? Kate was experiencing strong feelings of regret and loss that she did not understand.

Both families gathered at the front of the inn once again. Kevin and Carl retrieved their prospective carriages and, after tiredly saying their farewells to one another, the Sullivans and the Secords left the ball in the same way that they had arrived: together.

Chapter Four

The excitement and gaiety of the ball seemed to wane as the week progressed and the little community of Queenston settled back into its regular routine. Kate and Mary secretly held onto their own memories of the occasion, good and bad, not even sharing them with each other. Molly Hogan finally had her handsome young soldier in her arranged understanding with Private Dunsford; Captain Walter Clarke received his comeuppance from his superiors at Fort George; and Kate had heard nothing from Mr. Nick Brannigan. She had her chores to do around the farm to occupy her time; feeding the few livestock they owned and mucking out their stalls. She even weeded both the vegetable and flower gardens and helped Hannah with the wash. She still went to the Secords most afternoons, giving her the chance to see Mary, but she did not turn down a ride home again, if it was offered. The war scare seemed to have been pushed to the background for the time being, around the women anyway, and life carried on as usual.

The morning dawned brightly but the ground was still wet and muddy from the heavy rain that had pounded the earth the night before. Kate had just finished feeding the pigs, grunting noisily now in their muddied enclosure, fighting each other to reach the trough. She'd always had a fascination for these peculiar animals, ever since she was a little girl, so she now climbed up and sat comfortably on the fence rail to observe them more closely. There was no semblance remaining of that beautifully dressed young lady at the ball the week before. Once again

Kate was dressed in her brother's old cast offs and her hair was tucked beneath the brim of an old straw hat. Since returning from the ball, she had wanted to dress more appropriately as a young lady should.

"I can hardly wear a dress and apron out here in all this filth," she reasoned aloud. "It is easy for other girls like Mary and Molly to look like ladies; they work mainly in the house." Maybe someday she could work strictly with Hannah, she thought, but for now her father needed her out here. Kate had no way of knowing that since the night of the ball, her father and Hannah had been quietly observing her, both watching with interest, for any changes in her outlook and appearance. Kate's mind wandered now as she studied the pigs. She became so preoccupied with her thoughts that she was unaware of the visitor riding leisurely up their drive.

Nick Brannigan dismounted from his horse and, after tying it securely to the fence post, his attention was drawn immediately to the noisy pigs in their pen. He noticed a young boy perched on top of the fence rail and decided to inquire from him the whereabouts of Mr. Thomas Sullivan. He quietly approached, stopping just a few feet behind the lad in question.

"Excuse me, boy, I am loo ..."

"A-a-a-ah!" The sudden sound behind her startled Kate and, jumping up, she lost her footing on the fence, plunging headlong into the filthy pig-pen, surrounded by squealing, frightened pigs and covered from head to toe in muck.

Nick reached the enclosure in an instant and, taking one look at her drenched body, began laughing. "I am sorry," he said regaining his composure. "I did not mean to startle you." He then climbed up and leaned over the fence, hiding his amusement as he held out his hand to offer his assistance. "Here, boy, give me your hand. The least I can do is to help you out of there."

Kate's anger had been ignited the moment she landed in the muck. The pigs were riled too, displaying their outrage by squealing and splattering mud around the pen, most of it landing on her. She recognized Nick's voice as soon as he spoke. Her recollection of the way he had so easily discarded her at the ball, along with her jealousy over his infatuation with the unknown woman there, now added insult to injury; increasing her anger. She felt embarrassed and betrayed. Nick actually believed that she was a boy? She retaliated the only way she knew how, her manner too, now devoid of any resemblance to the dignified lady who had attended that ball.

"How dare you stand there laughing at me! You, sir, are not the gentleman that I thought you were and I certainly do not require any assistance from you!" Kate finally managed to stand, knocking the proffered hand away and missing Nick's shocked expression, as she continued with her tongue lashing. "I should think that you would have had sufficient education to be able to tell the difference between a woman and a young boy!" After voicing her outrage, Kate then climbed indignantly over the fence and jumped to the ground.

All the commotion had attracted an audience from both the house and the barn. Her father and Hannah stood on the back porch laughing at the scene before them, neither one affected by Kate's foul temper. Kevin and Carl had been working in the barn and now they too found her predicament quite humorous. They stood in the doorway calling out teasing remarks which only proved to add fuel to Kate's already blazing fire.

"Are ya' alright then, Katie darlin'?" Thomas Sullivan inquired, not even attempting to hide his mirth.

"I will go in and fix a bath for you dear," Hannah added, as she disappeared inside the house, shaking her head and laughing.

Nick stood in a state of confusion, scratching his head and gazing at the young woman that only a moment ago he could have sworn was a boy. He was astonished by his mistake; but he thought in his defense, Kate did not even remotely resemble the beautiful lady that he had met and enjoyed dancing with.

"I am dreadfully sorry, Miss Sullivan. I had no idea that it was you straddled in all that muck; I thought you were a farm boy." Nick's intention was to appease Kate's anger but, instead, he only managed to insult her again. "Listen to me," he insisted softly, reaching for her once more.

"Leave me alone, sir, you have done quite enough!" Kate shook off his hand and, with as much dignity as she could muster, marched steadily and determinedly towards the house, large clumps of mud falling from her clothes and a messy trail behind her. Nick shook his head once more before walking the short distance to the barn to join Thomas, who now stood snickering beside Kevin and Carl.

"Never mind, lad, me daughter can be a bit willful at times, especially when ya' find yourself on her bad side. T'wasn't your fault, boyo, she'll soon see that. Come now; let's go in for a wee cuppa, eh lads?"

"I still find it hard to believe that was Kate," Nick muttered, following the men into the house.

Hannah was in the kitchen preparing Kate for her much needed bath. When the water was almost ready Kate undressed, covering herself in a blanket and throwing her filthy clothing into a nearby washtub to soak. She watched silently as Hannah filled the bath tub.

"Okay, dearie, the water is ready. I brought you some of my scented soap that you so enjoyed using on the night of the ball, remember?"

Kate tested the temperature of the water with her toe. "Please, do not remind me of that night," she pleaded, as she lowered herself into the tub.

"You know, dear, your falling into that pig-pen was just an accident." Hannah began lathering Kate's beautiful long hair as she talked. "It really was not poor Mr. Brannigan's fault; you do realize that do you not? I am quite sure that it was not his intention to startle you and, as for him mistaking you for a boy, it was an honest oversight dressed as you were."

"Oh, Hannah, I truly have never felt so foolish and ashamed in all my life. It was awful enough that he had to see me dressed in Kevin's old clothes, but to be covered in all this filth too! At the moment, I do not know whether to be angry or embarrassed. One thing is for certain; I never want to see him again." No wonder Nick chose that pretty lady at the ball over me, she thought miserably.

"Try and cheer up, Kate," Hannah said. "It really is not as terrible as you might think. I also know that two weeks ago this would not have bothered you in the least. I have to wonder, my dear, what has come over you. Now, just relax and let me rinse your hair and then I will scrub your back."

Kate smiled at the soothing voice, recalling how Hannah could always calm her when she was upset. She uttered one more sigh before giving in, allowing herself to be doused with the warm rinse water.

"So, let me see if I'm understandin' what ya' were sayin' when we last spoke, Nick me boy," Thomas Sullivan remarked as he puffed steadily on his cigar. "Did ya' mean to say that all a man need do is clear his land and grow grapes to make wine? Is it really as simple as that then? Has anyone tried it here?"

Nick nodded his head before answering. "They are special grapes, Thomas, and yes I have seen it done; quite successfully I might add, down in the warmer climes south of the border. I have also heard of a gentleman who has tried it in this area as well but, to be honest, sir, he apparently did experience some trouble developing the right grapes. I am positive, however, that it could become a lucrative business once the problems were sorted out."

"Father, how do you suppose this could work?" Kevin inquired doubtfully. "I can see you are interested enough to try it, but what about this threat of war? I do not wish to be rude, Mr. Brannigan, but are you not an American? If your country does invade ours, where would your loyalties lie? We cannot possibly enter into business with the enemy, Father."

"I'll be needin' to work this all out in me mind lads," Thomas stated, as he eyed each of them individually. "Ya' see, Nick, my son has brought up a valid point. It may not be the most opportune time for startin' a business, what with this damnable war threat in our midst; whether ya' turn out to be the enemy or not. I must confess though, and I mean no disrespect mind ya'," he added sheepishly, "but the question of your loyalty t'would surely be a concern."

This definitely was not the type of discussion that Nick had antici-pated when he arrived. He almost felt deceived. First Kate had attacked him, albeit he did insult her, and now this. He had what he surmised to be a sound business enterprise and he thought Thomas would make an excellent partner. Damn this threat of war. He was confused. Last week at the ball when Thomas first expressed an interest in joining him, there had been no talk of war and his loyalty had not come into question. Nick was disappointed, but he did agree that perhaps both Thomas and Kevin were right regarding the ill timing of the business venture, although he did feel the need to reassure them of his loyalty to this country.

"I can promise you gentlemen, all of you," he responded, looking at each man in turn. "If the Americans do attack Upper Canada, I fight with you. Kevin, I live here now and this is my country too. I am indeed one of you and can be trusted. We are all friends here. Are we not, gentlemen?"

"What about me?" Carl Phillips interjected loudly, fixing both Kevin and Thomas with an accusing stare. "I am also from the American colonies; are you worried about my loyalties too?"

"Come lads, let us not start squabblin' amongst ourselves. The war has not started yet, and hopefully it never will. However, if the worst thing imaginable does happen, and we find ourselves pitted against our neighbours to the south, then will be the time to question loyalties, not before. For now, Nick is right. We are friends." Looking directly at Nick, he continued. "I am very interested in your idea to be sure, lad, but maybe t'would be best to hold onto it for a wee bit longer, just until this war mess is cleared up. Agreed?" Nick slowly nodded his head and the matter was immediately dropped, their conversation changing to something more enjoyable. Kevin and Carl both reluctantly returned to work leaving Thomas Sullivan and Nick Brannigan alone to finish their beverages and cigars.

While the two men remained in the parlour, Kate was putting the finishing touches to her appearance. She had moved from the kitchen after her bath and was now dressed and sitting on her bed, while Hannah brushed the tangles from her freshly washed hair. Feeling much better, she reflected on her earlier behaviour towards Nick, deciding that she just possibly might have been too harsh with him. I suppose I did rather resemble a boy in those dirty clothes, she relented, and I guess I was quite unrecognizable covered in all that mud. After all, I barely know him. We shared one dance together and there was nothing implied.

"You are right, Hannah," Kate declared, "I should apologize to Mr. Brannigan. He is Father's friend and I really was terribly rude to him. I also agree with you that he did not intentionally startle me."

"That is just what I wanted to hear, my girl! I am very proud of you," Hannah replied.

A short time later Kate was making her way to the parlour in hopes of joining the men when she heard voices coming from the front of the house. She opened the door slightly, peering out just in time to see her father waving good-bye to Nick as he galloped down the lane and out of sight. Her heart sank. I am too late, she thought. Sighing heavily she sat down on the porch step and waited for her father to join her.

"Why the long face child? Surely you're not still bothered by that pig-pen debacle? Are ya'?" Thomas inquired, taking a seat on the top step beside Kate.

"No, Father, but I do feel ashamed now of my behaviour towards Mr. Brannigan. I had fully intended to offer my apologies before he left, but I see now that I spent too much time bathing and have missed my chance."

"Not to worry, me girl. I am quite certain that your prospects'll be brightnen' considerably in the very near future. Shall I tell ya' a wee secret then?"

Kate answered with an enthusiastic nod.

"Perhaps ya' just may have an opportunity to convey those apologies to Nick tomorrow when we visit Fort George, seein' as he'll more n' likely be there too." Thomas chuckled then at the look of surprise on his daughter's lovely face, marvelling at how quickly her features could change from despair to delight.

"Oh, thank you, Father, you are wonderful!" Kate exclaimed, treating him to one of her most exuberant hugs. Kate listened with interest as her father began explaining in great detail how the invitation had come about and what was planned during the visit, adding that there was nothing to thank him for. Her feelings regarding the possible war had not changed, but Fort George did hold a certain fascination for her now, especially since her brief meeting with General Brock not long ago. Kate learned that they weren't the only family attending the outing; a few of their neighbours had also been invited. The small tour was to take place in the afternoon, as that was the quiet time at the fort, and in the early evening they were all to meet in the Officer's Mess for some light refreshments. Kate took great pains to hold her excitement in check as she concentrated on what her father was saying.

"There was even some mention of music and possibly some dancin', if all were agreeable of course," Thomas added mirthfully. "Now Katie, me girl , ya' can start preparin' yourself for another excursion, mind ya', this one bein' a wee bit less formal than the last."

Kate was reminded of the ball and dancing the infamous waltz with Nick, and of the eyebrows that were raised. "Father. You did not seem too disturbed at my dancing the waltz. Were you?"

"Katie Brianna, I have seen that blasted dance done before and will again no doubt. Ya' must remember, me darlin', that this is not England; the waltz is more accepted here, by most anyway, so I gave little attention to the comments and stares. I have been well acquainted with Nick Brannigan since he was just a wee lad and I know him to be a gentleman. No harm was done, and I was not offended in the least."

Thomas leaned in closer to whisper in Kate's ear. "Now, ya' will recall too, Daughter, that I did not miss his rescue of ya' from the hands of that sot, Walter Clarke. That man has been a continual nuisance and an embarrassment to the British army as he has proven time and again. Well, General Brock himself was privy to that scoundrel's actions this time, if ya' remember, and he will most assuredly be answering for his offensive behaviour, mark my words. Brock is fair, but even he has his limits." Thomas Sullivan smiled warmly at his daughter. Patting her hand gently, he rose to leave, stating that he should get back to work before the boys came searching for him. After her father had gone, Kate was left alone to ponder her father and Nick's history together.

Kate wasn't needed at the Secord's that afternoon and, not wishing to dirty herself with chores so soon after her bath, she offered her assistance to Hannah in the house. Later, when she finally found a few minutes alone, she decided to check her mother's old trunk for another dress.

The following afternoon Kate could be found talking excitedly with Mary Secord just outside the massive gates of Fort George. She had recently arrived with the rest of her family, with the exception of Carl, who had remained home to take care of the farm. James and Laura Secord were there too, along with Laura's brother Charles Ingersoll and his wife, with the remainder of the tour group arriving shortly after. The guests all congregated noisily in anticipation, anxious to be inside, until the sentry on duty finally ushered them through the gates. Kate walked with Hannah and her father, at his request, and they obediently followed their military guide to the guardhouse, where all visitors were to report immediately upon their arrival.

Kate was not impressed with the small, dark structure. It carried an air of doom and gloom, and her opinion did not improve upon venturing inside. She noticed a large wooden shelf in the corner where the unlucky soldier on guard was allowed a few hours of sleep, while the unfortunate prisoners were confined in small, dark and extremely cramped cells. However uncomfortable the soldiers may have been with their sleeping arrangements, the prisoners lodgings were considerably worse. There really was no room in the tiny cubicles for anyone to lay down or even stand up comfortably. Kate glanced piteously towards Mary, quietly thanking God that at the moment all the cells were empty. Both girls felt stifled in the depressing, cramped quarters, opting instead for some fresh air and sunshine, so they immediately left their group to roam around outside.

Strolling slowly to the opposite end of the building, they stared in horror as they once again came upon another oppressive sight. Kate and Mary gazed in disbelief when they inadvertently found the whipping post that now stood boldly, and thankfully empty, in the centre of the horrible punishment triangle. Gruesome images of unknown soldiers and their cruel punishment formed in Kate's mind, leaving her feeling daunted by this terrible building's interior and exterior. Kate pulled Mary away to rejoin their group, now gathered in front of the Officer's Quarters across the way.

The remainder of the afternoon, however, proved to be a very interesting one. The visitors, twenty in all, were shown the many different features of the fort, and were introduced to some of the soldiers that inhabited the structure, with Kate frequently scanning the area for any sign of Nick. They'd met General Brock during their brief stop at the Officer's Quarter's, and later they chatted at length with a few of the soldier's families who resided with the men in the large blockhouses. The visitors were well pleased with their guide. He was friendly, courteous and extremely knowledgeable as he escorted the small group from the powder magazine to the gun shed, and from the wood yard to the flag bastion, where they enjoyed a beautiful view of the Niagara River.

Black iron cannons seemed to dominate the whole inner sides of the palisade surrounding Fort George, each one weighing several tons, and Kate noticed, much to her chagrin, that they all appeared ready and waiting for battle. She felt a slight shiver flow through her as her gaze fixed apprehensively on the site across the river, realizing just how close the American's Fort Niagara was to them. It loomed there so quietly on the other side of the water, reminding her of a wild animal hunched threateningly in the bushes, waiting to strike at its passing prey. Feeling uncomfortable yet again, Kate hurried away to rejoin her group.

The visitors had just passed the sentry box at the front gates and were crossing the green, back towards the Officer's Quarters at the conclusion of their tour, when they paused to watch the soldiers on the parade square. Some were practicing their battle drills. Others could be seen marching or just cleaning their weapons. All these were considered very important tasks in preparation of war.

"Enjoying yourself, Katie?" A familiar voice whispered softly in her ear and Kate, who had been intently watching the display in front of her, was startled once again by the same deep, rich voice from yesterday, but this time she welcomed it.

"Why, Mr. Brannigan," she cooed softly, turning to face him and offering her sweetest and most beguiling smile. "I am happy to see you again, sir. You see, I feel utterly ashamed of my behaviour towards you when we last met. I was so disappointed upon finding you gone before I could apologize. I feel just dreadful. Will you not please ease my distress, sir, I beg you, and tell me that I am forgiven?"

Nick could not believe his ears. Considering her mood of yesterday, he had anticipated that nothing short of begging for her forgiveness would do. Instead, here she was, begging him. He was quite happy with the encouraging turn of events, offering an apology of his own.

"Only if you will allow me to express my apologies for my callousness of yesterday, dear lady. I truly did not mean to insult you. Come, Kate, let us forget that whole incident and immerse ourselves joyfully in the remainder of the day," he added, humour now present in his voice. "I do insist on one thing however; you must call me Nick."

Their tour guide then informed the guests that it was time to join General Brock and his staff for a light meal. Everyone welcomed the chance for a rest and enjoy some refreshment, as they had a very full and tiring afternoon. Chattering excitedly, they followed the soldier to the Mess Hall.

"Thomas, I would like you to meet Captain Percy of his Majesty's 41ˢᵗ Regiment, who is also a friend of mine, I might add," James Secord declared with a broad smile. The two men, who now stood together by the unlit fireplace, jubilantly shook each other's hand. "The captain shared some supper with us a short while ago, and brought the unfortunate news that we would most likely be engaged in a war soon."

"Aye, sir. Then you are the culprit that upset me Kate," Thomas remarked with a smile. "I am afraid she had overheard your conversation that evenin', and it frightened her, to be sure. My main reason, sir, for havin' her accompany me this day, is ta' show Katie Brianna the fortitude of strength that ya' have in place here, should war in fact break out. To calm her fears, so to speak," he added.

"Please, accept my most humble apologies, Mr. Sullivan. I am terribly sorry for upsetting the young lady. I assure you that we were unaware that our conversation was being overheard," Captain Percy replied.

"I, too, offer my regrets for that unfortunate situation, Thomas," James Secord added. "I promise, sir, to be more careful in the future."

Thomas instantly raised his hands, waving them about in a gesture of good will and shook his head before replying, conveying to the gentlemen that they need not concern themselves. "Not to worry, lads, there's no harm done. If war does come, we will all have to face it; our women and children, too."

The afternoon had slowly melted into evening and the Officer's Mess was now a hub of joyous activity. Instead of the expected light refreshments, the visitors were served an elaborate meal of roast duck brought to them on silver platters and fine china. The women were now enjoying a cup of tea while the men sipped wine from the general's private stock. Brock proved a most excellent host, calling upon his own military band to entertain the small gathering with delightful music, and requesting that the tables all be moved aside for dancing; all but two, and those were to be reserved for the card players. Kate sat in a group that included Kevin, Private Dunsford and Molly Hogan, Mary and Laura, and Laura's brother Charles and his wife. They were all laughing and talking together when Nick, previously locked in a private conversation with General Brock, finally joined them.

The musicians started with the well known *Chain Cotillion* dance, but it wasn't until they began the more traditional *Gravel Walk* that most of the dancers found the floor. Kate watched with delight as Molly and Matthew gaily invited others to join them in the fun. Kate's heart skipped a beat as Nick, with his hand resting gently on the small of her back, directed her to the floor. In that moment, nothing else mattered. She was so very thankful to be here and was having the time of her life; her fall into the pig-pen forgotten now, as was Nick's mysterious lady at the ball.

As she danced with Nick she surveyed the room. It was filled with such merriment! Her attention was drawn to Kevin as he danced with a local beauty; and when she searched for Mary, Kate found her happily dipping and turning with a young soldier as they followed the others on the floor. With the next dance, the music tempo quickened slightly. Nick took Kate gently in hand, and following the others, led her to the two lines that were now forming, partnering the ladies and gentlemen for the minuet. Nick then bowed to her and she smiled as she curtseyed before him, both pointing their toes and crossing with the music. The music changed yet again and the group laughed gaily, dancing around each other, twirling in a circle as they performed the exhilarating *Country*

Dance. Kate was being swept happily away, enjoying herself once more with the rest of the dancers.

When the evening came to an end and everyone bid their farewells, respectfully thanking their host for a most informative and joyous day, the visitors left the fort just before the sentry closed and locked the heavy gates. Nick had excused himself after the last dance, and had not yet returned, leaving Kate to wonder where he disappeared to. He merely said that he had to leave and would see her later. Now, climbing into the carriage, she noticed him standing beside his horse talking to someone that she could not see clearly. When Nick moved aside and the moon gradually brightened overhead, Kate gasped aloud and her heart plummeted in shock. Nick was with the same unknown woman from the ball. Dear, Lord, she thought miserably. Surely this could not be happening again? Not after sharing such a wondrous night with him? Thomas Sullivan also noticed the couple and loudly beckoned to them, and Kate's vexation grew as she stood motionless by the carriage step, dismally watching the approach of Nick and his young lady.

"Thomas, you remember my sister Ellen?" he said, proudly displaying his coveted sibling. "Ellen, this is Thomas Sullivan and his family."

"Well, the saints preserve me! How good it is ta' be seein' ya' again me girl. It has been many a year ta' be sure. Do ya' remember me? How lovely ya' are," he declared, laughing boisterously and enclosing Ellen in an affectionate hug.

Ellen nodded quickly in reply.

"Now, love," he said, pulling away and indicating Kevin and Kate. "This tyke here is Kevin; him bein' me oldest, and me beautiful Kate here, is me youngest."

Ellen and Kate both dipped into curtsies during the introductions. Kevin responded with a courteous bow, placing a kiss in the air just above Ellen's gloved hand.

Kate could barely contain herself; feeling overwhelmed by so much excitement and relief. She is his sister! Oh, how happy she was with those words but, oh, how foolish she felt. Kate silently observed the siblings for a moment, wondering how she could have ever missed their resemblance. I imagine that I was much too busy glaring at Nick to really notice the similarities. How beautiful she is, Kate thought, feeling elated. Nick's sister is as beautiful as he is handsome. They both had raven black hair and piercing blue eyes, although Nick's were a slightly darker shade, and each possessed a tall, lean frame, although Ellen was petite where Nick's build was muscular. She resembled a grand lady while his very presence reminded her of a handsome rogue. It was quite evident that Nick adored his little sister and Kate could not have been happier. Before they left, Nick promised that he would bring Ellen to the Sullivan farm for a visit.

All the way home Kate felt like she was riding on air; her young heart soaring amongst the stars and dancing on the clouds. Fort George would always remain dear to her heart now, she vowed, as the earlier events of the evening floated dreamily along with her. Even though the afternoon was somewhat daunting at first: the dreadful guard house, the alarming punishment triangle, and the sight of so many guns, it was all forgotten now; lost in glorious memories of a delicious dinner, being with friends, and dancing with a most courteous and handsome partner. This night had definitely outshone the Newark ball in every way possible.

Kate's thoughts once more drifted quietly back to Nick and his seemingly growing affection for her, and she was happy. And Ellen! Would it not be lovely if she could become friends with Nick's sister? Kate gazed longingly up at the sky, and closing her eyes, she made a secret wish, whispering softly into the night.

"I wish that someday Nick would love me as much or maybe even more, than he does his sister.

Chapter Five

The month of June was welcomed in by the glowing warmth of the sun. When the spring rains finally stopped, the summer came in full force, with each day that passed seeming hotter than the last. The open carriage left Fort George, winding its way quietly through the small town of Newark, finally stopping at a newly constructed two storey home belonging to John Powell and his wife Isabella. General Brock stepped lightly from the conveyance and, turning, offered his assistance to Kate. They were greeted at once by a young woman whom Kate recognized instantly as Sophia Shaw, the lady who had captured the heart of the widely respected general. The two women regarded each other for a moment, and smiling politely, they displayed their mutual and immediate approval. They had met only briefly the previous month, but Kate saw a kindred spirit in Miss Shaw and Sophia Shaw saw a young, vibrant woman whom she could call a friend.

"Please, do come in you two. Isabella and I have tea waiting in the parlour," Sophia invited warmly, looping one arm through Brock's and the other through Kate's as they climbed the steps to the elaborate house. Earlier that morning Kate had met General Brock at his quarters in Fort George for a prearranged escort to the home of Isabella Powell; Sophia Shaw's sister, so she could begin a temporary position there. Sophia had arrived recently from York to live with her sister and brother-in-law in order to be closer to her intended.

Mrs. Powell was currently awaiting a visit from her other sister Charlotte, expected to arrive the following day. Kate was to be a temporary nanny to Mrs. Powell's nieces who were accompanying their mother on the trip, and entertain the two little girls during their short stay. The three sisters would then be free to spend time together, socializing with old friends and seeing the sites of Newark, or just simply sitting together over a cup of tea, reminiscing about days gone by.

Isabella Powell had made inquiries throughout the region with the hope of finding a responsible young woman who would suit the position. Isaac Brock had most generously offered Kate's name and Sophia agreed. To Isabella, Sophia relayed her having spoken briefly with Miss Sullivan at the previous ball, finding Kate to be a very affable and affectionate young lady. Miss Shaw further stated that she was indeed united with Brock in his confident referral of Miss Sullivan, and Kate was hired immediately. "After all," her father had remarked. "A reference from Brock cannot easily be ignored." General Brock was more than happy to take time from his duties at Fort George to provide an escort for Kate, at the gentle bidding of his fiancée, of course.

"The tea and cakes are delicious my dear, as always," the general declared a few moments later. "I shall look forward with anticipation to more of these delectable treats after our wedding day." As John Powell was not in attendance, Brock shared his witty anecdotes with the ladies, impressing them with his humour. When the tea pot was finally empty and only crumbs remained on the cake plate, the general set his cup and saucer on the table and rose from his chair. "Alas, dear ladies, duty calls and regretfully I must take my leave." Isaac Brock turned to face the three women and bowed politely. "I thank you again for the tea, and please Mrs. Powell, extend my regards to your husband. Convey to John how much he was missed." To Kate, he expressed his hope that she find enjoyment in her new post. He held out his arm to Sophia, who then escorted him to his awaiting carriage. What a lovely couple they make, Kate thought, as the door closed behind them.

The sun was streaming down over the same peaceful manor the following morning when Kate awoke in a strange bed. Hearing joyful screams and bubbling laughter coming from the adjoining room, it took her a moment to realize where she was. When memory finally dawned, she jumped from her bed and grabbing her robe, she immediately left the room to see to her two little charges who were now up and about. Mrs. Powell had told Kate the girls' names the night before, but she had been unable to meet them. They had arrived quite late and were sound asleep when the coachman carried them in. She did manage to meet their mother Charlotte though, but just briefly, due to the late hour and everyone's fatigue.

Kate followed the excited sounds of the children, and entering their room, she discovered the two girls, Betsy and Lillian, engaged in an extremely exuberant pillow fight. They stopped abruptly however, when they noticed her standing quietly in the doorway, and stared back at her in wonder, searching her smiling face. Sophia had heard the loud commotion above and rushed up the stairs to make the necessary introductions, but was pleasantly surprised at seeing Kate laughing and playing along with the children.

A short while later, Kate was seated in the dining room enjoying a delicious breakfast and chatting merrily with the family, as if she had known them all her life. John Powell welcomed her into his household and his wife Isabella expressed a wish that she would be happy during her stay, adding that she was to make herself right at home. She was to have fun with the girls, but also make them mind.

"Do keep them out of trouble," Charlotte pleaded.

Isabella informed Kate that she and her two sisters had a full afternoon planned, which included a brief stop at the military fort and visits to a few of their affluent neighbours. Kate was on her own to entertain the girls in any way she saw fit; within reason of course. Kate had then requested permission to take Betsy and Lillian on a little excursion of their own and Mrs. Powell generously offered to make the appropriate arrangements.

"I will help the girls dress for the outing," Kate stated. "Then we shall be off." She escorted the excited children from the room then, in the midst of lively chatter and exuberant laughter.

Kate and the two little girls walked out onto the front porch, their eyes squinting at the bright sunlight as they glanced expectantly about. When they spied the open carriage that awaited, they were delighted. Kate recognized the driver as Samuel Forbes, the elderly gentleman who had greeted her at the ball. Mr. Forbes now stood beside the carriage step, waiting patiently for them to climb in. Once they were seated comfortably, the girls giggled cheerfully, anticipating the day ahead. After turning left at the end of the drive, Mr. Forbes swivelled around in his seat to further inform them of Mrs. Powell's instructions. She had suggested that they go sight-seeing throughout Newark, maybe visiting the park and the quaint little shops that the town offered. Their venture would take them past Fort George, Mrs. Powell had said, but they were not to go inside. At the conclusion of their outing, they were to stop at the Coach House Inn for some refreshments before heading home.

The starting point for the afternoon was the village common, a small piece of land situated in the middle of town; a place where people sometimes gathered to share news. Visitors could pass the time of day there too, while scanning a notice board with the hope of finding information on local activities and amusements. As the carriage rattled along the streets of Newark, Kate noticed the pretty flowers and pointed them out to the girls as they passed. Some adorned window boxes while others displayed their beauty in colourful beds. She also showed them the numerous manicured hedges running evenly between some of the homes and the many groomed bushes standing so serenely on front lawns. Not to mention the whitewashed picket fences and their attached gates that, when opened, led you up to a front porch or into a decorative garden.

I am always amazed at the elegance of this town every time I visit," Kate remarked softly. "What a charming place."

Mr. Forbes pulled the carriage to a stop near the square and Kate alighted first, with Betsy and Lillian soon in tow. As she glanced around in search of the information board, her eyes fell upon a little theatre that was being set up a short distance away. A small audience had already gathered in front of the stage and there was a wooden sign on display. *A Punch and Judy Puppet Show* would be starting soon. The girls were delighted, laughing with unsuppressed glee, clapping their hands as they watched a jolly looking man playing his pipes for the people that had begun to loiter nearby. When the girls asked Kate what the man was doing, it was a passerby who answered. He explained to them that the man was called a *Bottler* and that by playing his music, he was enticing all of them over to watch the show. As they made their way to the puppet stage, Betsy and Lillian rushed ahead excitedly, leaving Kate to follow quickly behind.

The tiny wooden theatre was covered in a red-checked cloth, leaving only the small stage exposed to the public. The series of short scenes that consisted of Punch and Judy hitting each other, and their rivals, while poking fun at anything and everything, evoked shocked laughter from the crowd. The girls clapped happily and joined the others in the group, yelling out warnings to Punch when he was about to be clobbered by Judy. When the show ended, the children wanted to visit behind the little stage to meet the two famous puppets, but were disappointed, finding them gone.

The general store was to be their next stop. Once there, Betsy and Lillian both bought some rock candy and a few handkerchiefs while Kate purchased some tea. They then strolled leisurely along the main street, exploring some of the quaint little shops situated there, making a few minor purchases before continuing on. Next on the agenda was a stop at the park on the Niagara River where they rested for awhile, observing the many birds in flight above them. They watched with interest and delight as the stately winged creatures swooped purposely between the trees, screeching loudly and aggravating the busy squirrels who lived there. The girls laughed joyously when the bushy tailed animals chirred angrily back at the birds, who then glided gracefully away, spreading their wings over the water.

"I am hungry!" Betsy declared at last, looking expectantly at Kate.

"Let us eat then, shall we?" Kate stood up and folded the blanket they had been sitting on and directed the girls back to the carriage.

Nick Brannigan entered the Coach House Inn and after choosing a table in the back corner, he doffed his hat before taking his seat. A serving maid approached and he ordered an ale and some food. He had just pulled a wrinkled letter from his pocket, scowling deeply as he read over the galling words for a second time, when he was interrupted by an elderly gentleman, standing before him in an indecisive state.

"I do apologize for bothering you, sir," the stranger said. "I was told that you are the man I am seeking."

Nick turned to regard the gentleman. "Am I? And just who is it that you are looking for?" Nick inquired impatiently, throwing the hateful letter down onto the table.

"You are Mr. Nicholas Brannigan, are you not, sir? The innkeeper kindly pointed you out to me."

Nick nodded slowly. "Yes. I am Nick Brannigan ... I no longer answer to Nicholas. How can I be of assistance to you, Mr...?"

The stranger removed his hat and held it in both hands like a shield. "My name is Jeb-Jebadiah Jones, sir. I am a friend of your father's and have been recently sent here to speak with you."

Nick gestured towards the empty chair across the table from him. "Have a seat, Mr. Jones." The stranger complied and Nick continued, "Now, just what could my father possibly want from me?"

"Well ... ah ... young man," Mr. Jones began nervously noting Nick's impatient tone. "He was hoping that I could persuade you to return home with me to join forces with him; to fight on the side of your birth, if war is declared, sir." Mr. Jones had no way of knowing that Nick had just finished reading the distasteful letter from his father, and how raw his emotions were at present.

Nick's jaw clenched in annoyance and he was about to speak, but was interrupted by the serving maid, bringing his refreshments. "I assume you do not mind if I eat?" he inquired dryly.

"N-no, sir," was the quick, agitated reply.

Nick nodded and returned to the business at hand while he ate, not enjoying the meal half as much as he would have if this gentleman had not arrived. He quietly chided himself, realizing that this unfortunate man was only the messenger and it was his father that deserved his contempt.

"After all that has transpired between us Mr. Jones, surely my father could not possibly expect that I would even consider such a ludicrous suggestion?"

"Begging your pardon, sir, but I left your father in quite a distressful frame of mind. He wished me to convey to you that a son's place is at his father's side, and I quite agree."

The fork dropped from Nick's grasp, loudly hitting his plate, and he snatched the letter roughly from the table, waving it in front of the disconcerted gentleman. "He disowned me, did he happen to mention that? I have already heard from my father, sir, and you can tell him that the answer is still no!" Nick slammed his fist down on the table so hard that he knocked his tankard of ale over onto his unfinished plate. Swearing under his breath, he shot a icy glare at the innocent stranger.

Jebadiah Jones swallowed hard and peered nervously around the room. He noticed they had gained the attention of the other patrons, watching them with interest now, and he felt his cheeks growing warm. He cleared his throat and clutched his hat even tighter, crumpling it in both hands. He replied then, tripping over his words.

"Would you be so kind, sir, as to pen a small note to your father stating your adverse objection to his request? It is of no consequence to me you understand, but upon my return I would much rather that his anger be spent on you and not myself."

Nick offered a quick, curt apology to the stranger, reassuring him that he was not to blame, and left for a moment to acquire some writing materials from the innkeeper. After hastily scribbling the note, he handed it to the stranger and bid him good day. Mr. Jones departed immediately. Nick then gestured to the serving maid to remove his plate and bring him some whiskey. He seized the bottle in one hand, the glass in the other, and poured himself a drink before slumping into his chair. My Lord, he thought, with all that man has done to our family, he has some nerve expecting me to drop everything and return to fight by his side. Nick downed his whiskey in one gulp, shaking his head in disbelief as he poured himself another drink.

The mantel clock at the Coach House Inn chimed three times when Kate, accompanied by Betsy and Lillian, entered noisily, chattering amongst themselves as they found a table. The inn was not crowded, but a few people glanced their way momentarily, before turning back to their own conversations. Samuel Forbes remained in the carriage out front enjoying the little snack that his wife had packed, stating that he would just as soon eat outside if they didn't mind, as it was such a nice day. Kate, unaware of the promise that her driver had previously made to his wife regarding his abstinence from the devil's brew, cheerfully assured him that they would try not to be too long.

Mr. Fields, the innkeeper, was a short, skinny man with a very friendly disposition, who just happened to be well acquainted with Mr. John Powell. He therefore greeted the new arrivals with pleasure, stopping at nothing to ensure their comfort and satisfaction. Kate ordered tea and biscuits, politely thanking the young serving maid when she brought them to the table. Betsy and Lillian continued to chatter excitedly, giggling and squealing happily while expressing the high points of their day. Kate was beside herself trying to hush them, quietly suggesting that they enjoy their refreshments.

Nick Brannigan's foul mood had improved considerably the moment Kate entered the inn. His eyes followed her slender form appreciatively as she was shown to a table with two little girls. He found himself wondering who the children belonged to, and he watched with interest as they laughed together. He chuckled quietly to himself when he noticed Kate's ongoing struggle at keeping the two little girls quiet. How beautiful she looks, he thought, and he recalled once again how he loved the sound of her laughter. He decided to remain inconspicuous for the time being and not intrude on their little interlude; preferring to admire her at his leisure. He had put all thoughts and contempt for his father out of his mind for now; plenty of time to dwell on that later.

Kate sat sipping her tea and enjoying the peace and quiet as the girls had finally calmed; the tea and biscuits now demanding all of their attention. She had just taken another bite of her biscuit when the hair on the back of her neck began to prickle, leaving her with the unmistakable feeling that she was being watched. She gazed about the dimly lit room in search of the culprit when her eyes suddenly settled on Nick. He shot her a devilish grin and then nodded, noticing at once how her eyes widened in surprise, and deciding that since he had now been discovered, he should be a gentleman and greet them properly.

Kate returned a shy smile, hoping to hide her embarrassment at suddenly finding Nick ogling her like an infatuated suitor. I must look a fright, she thought dismally, quickly running a hand through her untidy hair. Well, thank goodness she could console herself with the fact that Nick had already seen her at her worst; at least today the mud soaked clothes were missing. Kate heard a chair scraping across the floor and turning again in Nick's direction, she watched hesitantly as he strolled towards them. Smiling to herself now, she knew that he was curious about Betsy and Lillian.

"I do hope you ladies are having a wonderful afternoon," he said, gazing intently at Kate.

Kate shifted nervously in her chair, turning her most charming smile up to Nick. "Mr. Brannigan, how wonderful to see you again. May I present Betsy and Lillian Evans to you, sir?" she inquired, indicating the girls with her outstretched hand. "Betsy, Lillian, this is Mr. Nick Brannigan. You see, Nick, I have just recently been employed by their mother," Kate explained. "I am going to take care of these children for a few days. And yes, we have indeed had a most pleasant day; I do thank you for asking."

Nick bowed politely to the little girls. "I am very pleased to meet you both," he said, casting a questioning glance at Kate. "May I be so bold as to inquire who their mother is?"

"Why of course, sir. Their mother's name is Charlotte Evans. She is, in fact, the sister of Miss Sophia Shaw; who is the fiancée of General Brock. I trust you are acquainted with that gentleman, are you not?"

"I am indeed, Miss Sullivan; he is a most admirable man."

The girls giggled continuously over the next few minutes as they were drawn into a silly conversation with Nick and Kate. Nick entertained them with harmless teasing, causing both girls to expel little squeals of delight at his antics. He was enjoying himself immensely now, and after suffering with his dark mood earlier, hearing their laughter was a salve to his wounds.

A short time later the innkeeper's wife approached their table carrying an empty tray. Mrs. Fields was a large, matronly woman who, like her husband, loved to please her clientele; but she also harboured a special motherly feeling for Nick. They had helped him when he first arrived in Upper Canada, providing him with a place to stay at a reasonable price, for as long as he should desire it. He returned the favour by doing odd jobs and keeping the place free of any troublemakers. Mrs. Fields exchanged pleasantries with the small group as she cleared away their empty dishes and Kate was full of compliments for her talents in the kitchen. She praised the delicious biscuits, claiming that they were even better than Hannah's. She also confessed that although she had a few culinary skills of her own, she still had a lot to learn.

The mantel clock chimed again and Kate realized that the afternoon was waning. They were expected home.

"I am afraid we have stayed too long," Kate declared, rising swiftly from her chair. "Come Betsy and Lillian, we must leave now. I do not wish to cause your mother any undue worry. We must not forget about poor Mr. Forbes who is waiting for us outside," she added, ushering the girls to their feet. "It was very kind of you to speak with us, Mr. Brannigan, and I do hope we shall see you again, soon." The two girls waved goodbye to Nick, exchanging giggles as they headed for the door.

Nick leaned in close to Kate, whispering softly in her ear. "You can count on it Katie." He flashed her his most dazzling smile then, tugging gently on a strand of her hair. After admiring her retreating form, Nick headed for the stairs, and he too quit the room.

Kate left the inn quite baffled not only by Nick's behaviour, but by her own as well. She was not actually afraid of him, but his stares and gestures today made her feel a little nervous, just to the point that she was not sure what to expect next. What a wonderful day this has been though, Kate thought, and the girls had such a glorious time. She smiled down at Betsy and Lillian, so exhausted, that they now snuggled together on the carriage seat beside her and slept soundly. Kate sat quietly, reflecting on the day's events and her feelings for Nick Brannigan, smiling to herself all the way back to the Powell's.

Sir Walter Clarke was seated at a table at the back of the inn, having relocated there following Nick Brannigan's untimely entrance. He had overheard the heated words exchanged earlier between Nick and the nervous stranger, and for some reason, just knowing that this man; this buffoon who pranced around like a king, was estranged from his own father, brought an unexpected comfort to Clarke.

Walter Clarke too, noticed Kate's noisy entrance and he seethed inwardly while observing Brannigan's light, easy banter with her. She welcomed Brannigan's company and loathed his! His mind reeled once more, recalling the horrible night of the ball and Miss Sullivan's blatant refusal to dance with him, and then Nick Brannigan's angry retaliation that followed.

"I just wanted to dance with her," he mumbled angrily to himself. He shot a vile glare at Nick then, as he observed the simpleton's display with the lady. That beautiful young woman treated him like dirt under her feet, he jeered, and by God, he would get even with both of them if it was the last thing he did. Sir Walter felt truly innocent of any untoward actions during the ball, believing that he was unjustly put upon by Nick Brannigan, also blaming Kate for not choosing him. He now cast a cynical smile in their direction, his presence still unnoticed.

"There will be another time, dear lady; I promise you that," he rasped, glaring heatedly at Kate. As soon as the cheerful group left the inn, Mr. Clarke dropped some coins loudly onto the table, swearing quietly under his breath. He then strode angrily out.

Chapter Six

The candle flame flickered in the warm summer breeze casting eerie shadows along the walls and ceiling, illuminating the two men sitting at the table in the middle of the dimly lit room. With a sudden gust the wind grew stronger, whipping the window curtains about frantically and scattering off the table all the loose papers that the younger man had been reading. Nick rose abruptly, cursing the wind and the older man who sat across from him. Striding angrily to the window, he slammed it down, then returned to gather the dishevelled papers from the floor and shooting a venomous glare at his unwelcome guest: the current cause of his foul mood. The man persisted in hounding Nick about his heritage.

"Nick, I do not understand this boy, you know as well as I where your loyalties lie. I do not care what you say, you are and always will be, an American!" The last few words were yelled out emphatically which only proved to raise Nick's temper to the boiling point and he retaliated in kind.

"I have no allegiance to your country Father, as I have told you before. I live in Upper Canada now. This is my home and that is that!" Nick forced himself to calm down. Gaining some control over his rampant emotions, he then continued in a much quieter tone. "I made that decision a long time ago and my mind is set, no matter how many Mr. Jones' you send to try and persuade me otherwise. That was low Father, even for you," he added accusingly. "I almost strangled that poor man in your stead. Did you even read the note that I sent back with him?"

"I read it. But for the life of me I could not understand what I was reading. I cannot fathom a son of mine being treasonous. I will not stand for such behaviour! You have had sufficient time to come to your senses my boy and my tolerance, as you can well imagine, is wearing thin."

Nick threw his arms up in disgust and exasperation, realizing once again that he could not reason with this man; that he never could. "I am at a loss, Father," he said, heaving a frustrated sigh. "The reasons I left have not changed; I wish to remain loyal to the king. There are also the other matters which apparently, and most conveniently I might add, have slipped your mind." Nick noticed the look of confusion displayed on his father's distorted face and uttered a short, heartless laugh. "Come, man, surely you could not have forgotten that you disowned me? So in that regard, I am puzzled why you would even want me to return with you. Please, do not misunderstand Father, your estrangement makes no difference to me."

Mr. Brannigan senior slammed his fist on the table, almost toppling the candle, and yelling out his anger, his face now purple with rage. "That was a long time ago! Do you not have it in your heart to forgive, boy?"

The extent of his father's anger startled Nick but he just shook his head.

"Well now, maybe I will just see what your sister has to say about the matter, shall I? the elder Mr. Brannigan inquired spitefully. Maybe I will just take her back home with me. What do you say to that, you ungrateful bastard?"

Nick slowly leaned over the table, his jaw tightening, his eyes flashing with hatred, and with a low snarl he ground out his reply through gritted teeth. "Listen to me and listen well old man. If you as much as look at Ellen, I will kill you. Do you understand me? I know what you did to my mother, and I am sure as hell not going to allow you to hurt my sister." He watched in disbelief as his father shook his head in denial. Nick continued with his vile tongue lashing. "You deny it? You killed my mother!" Nick shouted these last words at his father, but Mr. Brannigan senior just shook his head, and shrugging his shoulders in confusion, he eyed his son with a most bewildering stare, which only succeeded in increasing Nick's anger. "How can you sit there so innocently and deny what you know to be true?" Nick then slammed his own fist down on the table and continued with an icy confession, jabbing his finger towards his father. "You see, I have known for quite some time how Mother wanted us all to join the loyalists and come to Upper Canada. I also know how you turned her in, your own wife, to be murdered with the rest of the Empire Loyalists that had been captured that night."

"You are mistaken, boy. Who would tell you such a lie?"

Nick leaned in even closer, eyeing his father with contempt. "You did not notice me that night. I came downstairs when I heard the commotion and I saw the men at our door rough handling my mother. And you ... you were accusing her of treason, just before they dragged her away screaming and crying out for her children. I vowed then and there that I would never forgive you, I also swore an oath that I would leave as soon as I was old enough and take my little sister with me. But, for your information, Father dear," he snarled, "I also kept a very close eye on her, and you, while we remained in that house together. I was ready to come to Ellen's aid anytime I saw fit."

Nick backed away then, repulsed by the stench of his father's foul breath.

"You are just like your mother boy; a traitor! You have no claim on this country. Maybe you think that if you remain here, you will not have to fight at all. Are you a coward too!"

Nick's temper ignited at his father's accusations and he lost control. "You may have sired me old man," he bellowed, "but know this, I hate you from the very core of my being; you are not my father!!" He then toppled the table with one arm, sending the burning candle to the floor, which thankfully, extinguished itself on impact. After emitting an angry growl, he grabbed his father roughly by the collar with both hands. Hauling him crudely to the door, he swung the wooden portal wide open in a violent rage; dragging his struggling father mercilessly down the stairs, oblivious of any pain inflicted, through the crowded drawing room of the inn. After tossing him outside, he yelled out one last warning. "Get the hell out of here and never come back! Stay away from me and my sister! Ellen and I are through with you, do you understand?"

Mr. Brannigan senior lay stunned for a moment staring up at the madman that used to be his son, recoiling at his next hateful words.

"If you Americans do attack us and I happen upon you on a battle-field somewhere, do not for one moment think that I will not shoot you." Nick slammed the door hard, the thunderous sound reverberating throughout the building. Scowling, he turned to face not only the startled patrons in the inn, but the innkeeper and his wife as well; all staring back at him in wide-eyed astonishment. "Just clearing the place of a giant size rat," he declared, turning abruptly on his heels to escape the room.

The days passed quickly, and even though her three day stint at the Powell's had stretched into two weeks, it was almost time for Kate to return home. Sophia and her sister had planned a little soiree this evening in Charlotte's honour, adding that it would also be a nice send off for Kate. The house was now a flutter of activity as plans were being carried out and each person had their own responsibility in making it a success. Kate and the children were kept busy all morning helping Abigail, the Powell's maid, by making sure that the downstairs was clean, organized and spotless. Betsy and Lillian actually did more playing than working, but Kate didn't mind, as long as they were entertained and stayed out of mischief.

Isabella Powell took charge in the kitchen, collaborating with the cook to ensure that the menu was clear and that the dinner prepara-tions were now underway. Charlotte kindly accepted the task of setting the buffet table in the dining room, and with Sophia's assistance, they saw that it was covered with a large lacy cloth, adorned with special china, silverware, platters and crystal glasses. When all was finished to Isabella's satisfaction, they retired to their rooms to relax and ready themselves for the evening's festivities.

A few hours later, Kate came prancing down the stairs to a house full of guests, noticing familiar faces among the crowd as well as a few new ones. John Powell had informed her that she should enjoy herself on her last evening here, and she fully intended to do so. Mrs. Evans had politely requested that her two daughters be given something to eat and then later, perhaps she could read them a story and put them to bed.

Kate scanned the large drawing room looking for Nick. She had heard his name as one mentioned on the invitation list and wanted so much to dance with him again.

Mr. Powell was standing with a small group of soldiers obviously discussing war issues, and over in the far corner she noticed Sophia Shaw and General Brock together at the small pianoforte, listening attentively as Betsy and Lillian entertained them with their rendition of *Meet Me By Moonlight*. At the conclusion of their recital, both girls giggled nervously in the sudden silence, and then the whole room applauded in admiration at their performance. Kate smiled and clapped along with the others. She quickly made her way towards them, unaware of the piercing blue eyes that followed her.

Nick Brannigan watched with interest when Kate descended the stairway and proceeded to walk towards him. He stepped out from behind the group of men that he and John Powell had been conversing with, to greet her. He was disappointed in the next instant though, when she suddenly veered off in another direction, heading instead towards the two young Evans girls at the pianoforte. He followed with determination, fully intending to spend some time with her this evening. However, upon reaching the musical instrument, he groaned in frustration as he watched Kate disappear into the kitchen. She obviously had not seen him, he concluded, but when he followed her, he found his plans thwarted once again; a few ladies had approached him just as he reached the door.

"Mr. Brannigan, may I present my daughter Lucy to you?" the eldest of the entourage inquired, ushering a beautiful young lady forward.

"Nothing would please me more Mrs. Bascombe, I assure you," he replied dryly, bending to kiss the proffered gloved hand of Miss Lucy Bascombe. Although Lucy did posses a rare beauty, Nick's mind was otherwise engaged, but this lovely lady's mother would not be ignored.

"I am sure you must dance, Mr. Brannigan," Mrs. Bascombe stated presumptuously, quickly placing her daughter's hand into his as the band began to play. Nick held his mounting annoyance in check, trying to hide his frustration with the matriarch's forward rudeness, realizing that he would have to wait awhile yet before joining Kate. Since he was a gentleman, and not wishing to be discourteous to the lovely Miss Lucy, he had no recourse but to dance with her. Thus decided, he smiled and bowed to the lady. Tucking Lucy's arm through his, he led her resolutely to the dance floor.

During the past two weeks Kate had enjoyed being in the company of her delightful little charges. She found them both to be polite and happy girls, who never failed to keep her amused. Tonight, however, she sat with Betsy and Lillian at a small table in the kitchen, watching impatiently as they slowly finished their evening meal. Like Nick, she too was frustrated with the turn of events and, on hearing the music coming from the other room, she was anxious to join the dancing. Kate was leaving tomorrow and unsure of when she would be in Nick's company again; she was determined to seek him out. Now!

"Please girls, do hurry," she pleaded, rising impatiently from her chair. "I am sorry to rush this way, but I am eager to join the other guests. I want to dance!" At the word dance, Betsy and Lillian, who also wanted to have some more fun, emptied their plates in an instant and, after quickly wiping their mouths on napkins, followed Kate as she hastily left the room.

When Kate entered the drawing room, she noticed Nick dancing with a striking young woman and felt mildly annoyed, but the sight of Miss Shaw soothed her, and she decided to join her friend. She had been anxious to see Nick and was determined to speak with him at the conclusion of the dance. But, when Nick finally sought her out, she was busy dancing with General Brock. When their dance ended, Brock immediately pulled Nick away, declaring that he had a matter of utmost importance to discuss with him in private.

Sir Walter Clarke had also received an invitation to the Powell's soiree, along with the other officers from the fort, but he had to issue a solemn promise to General Brock to behave as an officer and gentleman should. A repeat performance of his actions at the previous ball would not be tolerated.

The illustrious Mr. Clarke was born in a small cottage on a grand estate just outside of London England. He was the son of a lord and his mother was a maidservant in his father's house. Lord Denton Clarke was a confirmed bachelor of means, and not welcoming the hindrance of a wife, especially one that was so far beneath him, refused to marry the maid when she found herself with child. Therefore, Walter Clarke not only came into this world as the sole heir of an English lord, but also as a bastard. Since Lord Denton was unaware of any other children that he might have fathered, he took a great interest in Walter. The young maid was permitted to remain on the estate to raise their son until he was old enough to live in the manor house with his father.

Sir Walter resided in the small, quaint cottage with his mother, but he did not love her. Sadly, as he grew, she realized that her son was incapable of sharing that particular emotion with people. However, he learned at an early age that he did love money and power. Young Walter had longed for the day that he could move into the elegant manor house with his father. He held no love for that parent either, but his shallow character allowed him the pretence, enabling him to gain money, power and prestige. He blamed his mother for his not being raised in a more refined manner, and continuously unleashed his temper on her. Horrified, she could only conclude that he must surely have been spawned by the devil himself. Walter Clarke had repeatedly screamed out ugly accusations at his mother, often confessing his wish that she were dead. His father would have to take him them.

Lord Denton doted on his son, paying him frequent visits and taking him riding or to tea at the manor. He filled the young boy's head with such glorious plans for their future together, causing Clarke to become even more restless and all the more anxious to join him. Walter continued to ridicule and scoff at his mother, showing her nothing but contempt, and on the day that his father finally came to collect him, he did not look back. Lord Denton didn't banish Sir Walter's mother when her son left; instead they both just ignored her presence. One fall day, however, after she'd been living alone for quite some time, they were informed by the under gardener that she'd died in her exiled cottage. She was buried by the servants, but neither Clarke nor his father attended the funeral.

Now, with General Brock's stern warning in mind, Sir Walter, who had arrived late, confidently approached the Powell's drawing room and paused briefly in the doorway, scanning the large crowd for a lovely dance partner. He thought himself quite the dashing figure and he displayed his arrogance with every leer that he bestowed on any unsuspecting ladies. Sir Walter Clarke was indeed the embodiment of a true scoundrel, and most of the guests wondered how he ever came to be knighted. He continued his appraisal of the room and his eyes eventually fell on Miss Sullivan and he smiled wickedly. There is the young woman I want, he thought, I shall dance with her. He devoured her then with his lecherous gaze, watching intently as she danced happily with a handsome soldier from his own regiment.

At the conclusion of their dance, the gallant soldier escorted Kate to the back of the drawing room where they were implored to join a small circle of men and women. As the group laughed and chatted together, the two little Powell girls played ring-around- the-rosy in the corner, out of the way. When the soldier excused himself to dance with another, Kate decided to join in the game with Betsy and Lillian, and with hands clasped together, they sang nursery rhymes while dancing around, laughing with each step.

With a lascivious grin, Sir Walter Clarke noticed that his fellow soldier had suddenly abandoned Kate. In his arrogance, he presumed that he could just whisk her away for a much longed for dalliance. He silently rehearsed an apology that he intended to offer her before they danced, the sincerity of the words sounding foreign on his tongue, and he worried that he would surely choke in the telling of them. He really was not sorry for the way he had acted at that blasted ball and he truly believed that it was her fault; Brannigan's too, but he was trying to make her soften towards him. Sir Walter convinced himself that once he was forgiven and she realized that he was not only a gentleman, but a captain in his majesty's army, he would soon be holding her in his arms and enjoying a waltz.

He was twenty years her senior and had been in the company of more beautiful and alluring women, usually of questionable character, but this little vixen had refused his advances and he would not accept that. He was a lord and a knight; she should be groveling at his feet and thanking him for his attentions. Her blatant refusal only proved to make him want her all the more, and by God, he would have her! Relentless now, Sir Walter weaved his way through the throng of guests towards Kate.

Squealing with excitement Betsy and Lillian whirled Kate around and around in a circle going faster and faster with each turn, until Kate finally called a halt, professing dizziness and fatigue. She scanned the room once again for any sign of Nick. It was almost time for her to take the girl's upstairs for their story before bed, and since she had no way of knowing how long it would take them to fall asleep, Kate feared that Nick would leave before she returned. Her anxiety to see Nick Brannigan again had been so intense that earlier, she actually thought of putting the girls to bed then and rushing through their story, but she had a sudden attack of guilt, knowing that they would be very disappointed.

It really is not their fault that I was unable to speak with Nick. It seems I find myself searching for that man whenever we attend the same functions. I hope this is not how it will always be. Oh, I can just hear Hannah now, Kate thought, shaking her head slightly. If she were here at this moment she would tell me not to chase the gentleman; a lady always lets the man approach first.

"Oh, for goodness sake," Kate muttered aloud to no one in particular. "A month ago I would not have been bothered by any of this. I was happy wearing Kevin's clothes and not attending balls. She gasped suddenly, noticing Sir Walter Clarke slithering through the crowd and heading straight for her. As she watched him she was reminded of the huge corn snake she saw one day, hunting prey in the barn, only now she was the unsuspecting little mouse. She immediately gathered the girls, guiding them quickly up the stairway to their room. Kate felt anger and frustration with Sir Walter once again. "Why did he have to come tonight? Why does he keep pestering me?"

"What is the matter Miss Kate?" Both Betsy and Lillian inquired in unison, staring in concern at their nanny.

Not wishing to distress the girls, Kate hid her aggravation, making light of the situation. "Well, my dears," she replied with a forced smile. "You need not worry about me, for I am fine. I suspect that I feel just as you do though, having to leave the party so soon, just when we were having such fun. However," she added a little sternly, "it is your bedtime, long past I would imagine, and I did promise to read you a story, did I not?" Both girls nodded. "I beg you, hurry then so we may begin." Betsy and Lillian complied immediately, helping each other undress and then squealing excitedly while splashing cold water on their faces as they washed. Kate only half listened to the girls. Her thoughts were once again on Nick, and she wondered if he was searching for her now. They had not been able to speak, let alone dance with each other all evening; someone always seemed to get in their way.

She felt her frustration rise again as the loathsome memory of Walter Clarke suddenly invaded her thoughts. Kate clenched her eyes tight in an attempt to dispel him from her mind, but his stubborn image remained fixed in her head.

"What a despicable man," she groaned quietly. "He has a complete lack of scruples and possesses no honour that I can see. He is the most unsavoury braggart that I have ever had the misfortune to meet. He is so in love with himself, that there is no room left in his heart for loving anyone else. I can well imagine that his so called knighthood was bought and paid for by ill-gotten gains." Kate tried once more to extinguish her anger for the girls' sake and remain calm. She willed her troubled thoughts to disappear so she could concentrate instead on her two little charges now lying obediently in their beds, waiting for the story to begin.

Nick's conversation with Brock had ended when the general left to escort Miss Shaw home, and he scoured the room for Kate. Unfortunately, he was waylaid once again by John Powell, drawing him into a political discussion with some soldiers from the fort. When he suddenly recognized Kate's distracting laughter emanating from the back of the room, he allowed his attention to wander towards the sound, and as his gaze searched through the many guests, he noticed her dancing joyfully in a corner with the two Evans girls. Nick was impatient to be with Kate. When he noticed her sudden hurried steps towards the staircase, he politely excused himself from the group to follow, but his departure was rudely interrupted by an ill-timed Walter Clarke.

Walter Clarke too had quickened his step when he noticed Kate escaping up the stairs with the children. He had no use for little girls; they were just a nuisance until they were old enough and beautiful enough to have a satisfying rendezvous with. His arrogance was such that he could not fathom Kate purposely avoiding him. In his rush to catch her, Clarke plowed through the conglomerate of people, paying little heed to what he was doing, or to who might be in his way. Ignoring the hard stares directed at him, and the even harder shoves in retaliation, he did not realize his error until it was too late. He forcefully collided into the back of Nick Brannigan, the impact severe enough that both men were knocked off balance. Nick was able to steady himself however, but Sir Walter was deposited, without dignity, upon the floor.

Isaac Brock's warning was forgotten in that instant as Clarke, pale and shaken, tried to stand. A young soldier, the very one who had been dancing with Kate earlier, had offered his assistance, but was shaken off with a curse, and Mr. Clarke gained his footing of his own accord. He swung around to face a startled Nick, and his dark eyes glared with hatred and disbelief. His temper flared and he uttered another curse, directing all of his anger and humiliation at his rival.

Nick tried to ignore the oaf's ungentlemanly behaviour, wondering at the incredible audacity of the man. How can he possibly blame me for this? John Powell and the other guests standing close by heard Clarke's curse and witnessed the icy glare levelled at Nick. They turned away from the ridiculous scene, shaking their heads and quietly professing Clarke to be all kinds of a fool. Nick was exasperated at finding that this imbecile had once again prevented his attempt to meet with Kate. He watched in mounting frustration as the lady in question disappeared up the stairs and out of sight, seemingly oblivious to all that had just transpired. His anger was just as strong as Clarke's and his hands clenched into fists, but he relented suddenly, not wishing to spoil the evening for the other guests or causing any embarrassment to his hosts. Nick turned away from Clarke and the calamity that had just taken place. Attempting to regain his composure, he offered an apology to John Powell for the disturbance.

Walter Clarke, the unrefined scoundrel that he was, extended no such courtesy. Instead, he continued with his angry insults to Nick, although somewhat quieter this time, but when he became aware of the laughter directed at him, he left the room in a huff. Some of the other guests poked fun at his clumsiness and bad temper, while their jabs and jeers followed him out the door, and he quietly cursed Nick, along with everyone else in the room. That insufferable buffoon has made a laughing stock of me for the last time, he thought, his blood boiling, I will not be treated this way. Someday I will make Brannigan pay!!

Nick shook his head and shot a contemptuous glare at Sir Walter's retreating back. Still finding himself in a foul mood, he knew his anger and frustration would not easily be appeased. To make the situation worse, he noticed Miss Lucy Bascombe and her overbearing mother, nuisances all evening, approaching him now with determination. He cursed quietly, and looking around for an escape, dashed unnoticed out the back door. Frustrated now with the lateness of the hour, Nick knew all too well that he would have to see Kate at another time.

A short while later Walter Clarke secretly crept back into the Powell's front hall, his temper much improved, and seeing no sign of either Miss Sullivan or Nick Brannigan, he approached the stairway. With one hand on the railing and a wide grin plastered on his face, he began to climb.

"... and they all lived happily ever after." Kate finished the last story and was relieved to see that both girls were sleeping soundly. She had read two stories to them but now, after pulling covers up to chins, and placing a light kiss on each forehead, she quietly tiptoed from the room. Kate was just about to descend the stairway when she darted back suddenly, moaning softly at her poor timing and bad luck.

Walter Clarke loomed at the bottom ready to come up, searching for her no doubt, she assumed dismally. She uttered a sigh of relief in the next instant however, finding that his ascent had been halted by two inebriated soldiers whose slurred speech begged him to join them in a drink. Kate did not wait for the outcome and wasted no time in making her way back down the hall and out of sight. Where could she go? She quickly decided that her only recourse was to seek refuge in her room where it was quiet and she could think more clearly about how to escape. She recalled the obvious determination on the drunken captain's face and was acutely aware that he would not be detained for long. She was trapped!

Kate was standing anxiously at her bedroom window, rocking nervously to and fro, trying desperately to figure out how to get away, when she heard the mantel clock chime melodically. "Good heavens! I have been standing here for over half an hour," she murmured, now anxiously pacing the room. A moment later she stopped abruptly, the worried frown disappearing from her face as an idea formed in her mind. The plan had come to her so quickly that Kate spared no time in thinking it through before acting on the impulse. She had no choice. At that precise moment she heard Walter Clarke's loud, slurred voice bidding farewell to his friends as he began to slowly climb the stairs. She had to get away now! Kate immediately swung the window open and after quickly removing her shoes and stockings, she stepped out onto a branch of an awaiting tree.

She gingerly tested each limb during her descent, praying to God that she would reach the ground in one piece. She had climbed many trees in her youth, but never in a calico dress, and this one was definitely hindering her progress. The thought came to her that she should just slip out of it, but for the second time that evening she imagined the irate scolding she would receive from Hannah, so she continued her diligent descent. After placing her foot down on another branch, Kate was breathing hard and concentrating on her escape, when she heard a loud crack! Startled, she let out a small scream and holding tightly to the limb above, she felt the rotten wood suddenly give way beneath her foot. Kate looked down in horror, but was instantly relieved at finding that she was only a few feet from the bottom. Chuckling at herself now, she let go of the branch and dropped safely to the ground.

"You certainly are a very unconventional young lady Miss Sullivan, and full of surprises, I might add." Nick Brannigan had come out from behind the tree that he had been leaning against, to face a much bewildered Kate.

He had startled Kate yet again and she gasped loudly. Turning in his direction, she noticed the shocked expression adorning his handsome face and was suddenly thankful that she had dismissed the idea of removing her dress.

Nick had known a moment of concern as he watched her risky descent. He was greatly relieved however, to discover her standing safely on the ground nearby. In an instant, he threw down the cigar he had been smoking and rapidly closed the distance between them, his features softening when he realized that she was unharmed. Nick shook his head in resignation then, laughing after he reached her, his eyes portraying a look of both admiration and humour.

"I do not suffer any disillusions my dear, for I expect that I shall never have a dull moment where you are concerned, Katie my love," he teased.

"I-I am sorry, sir, that you had to witness my silliness," Kate stammered nervously, wishing at this very moment that she were dead. She reminded herself then that no one she knew had ever died of embarrassment. Just the same, she was abundantly thankful for the growing darkness as it hid the blush that was now spreading to her neck. "I am a-afraid that I feel rather foolish, sir, I was not expecting an audience." Kate was close to tears and at a loss as to what to do or say next, so she turned away from Nick, avoiding the witticism she saw growing in his eyes. He was making fun of her again, she thought, mortified. *Why is it that I seem to always find myself in the most compromising and embarrassing situations whenever I am in Nick's company? It is like being in the pig-pen all over again.* She continued to blush profusely, chewing the corner of her lip and unconsciously wringing her hands together. She was feeling rather awkward and her heart was longing to stay here with Nick, but her pride was screaming at her to run away and hide.

Nick leaned in close to Kate. "May I inquire as to what you were running from dear lady? Something or someone terrible I should imagine, for you to go to such drastic lengths to escape. Was it the dreaded bogeyman perhaps?"

"Sir Walter was coming up the stairs after me and I was trapped. I did not know where to go, so the window was my only means of escape." Kate backed slowly away then, her eyes filling with tears of anguish and humiliation.

Nick's lighthearted humour faded abruptly and his hands clenched into fists at the mention of that degenerate's name. The man was a nuisance and some day, he promised himself, he would deal with him; but not tonight. Nick realized that he was upsetting Kate and had the distinct feeling that she was about to flee, so without any thought or hesitation, he pulled her into a crushing embrace as his mouth took hers in a sensual, searching and demanding kiss. He knew this kiss was a result of his frustration at not being able to be with her all evening, and his first thought was merely to keep her here with him, but all the irritation and annoyance that plagued him since first meeting her, poured liberally out when their lips met. He did not want to frighten her, so he softened the kiss slightly, allowing Kate to catch her breath.

Nick did not think about any repercussions that he could face, nor did he care. He only knew that he needed her, especially now. War was coming; he might not survive. He might never see her again. Nick satisfied himself that this simple reasoning was enough to condone this present impropriety of his. For some reason, this innocent young lady had come to mean a great deal to him, and he was not sure why. One moment he wanted to throttle her, especially when she did silly things like climbing trees, and the next moment he felt he needed to comfort and protect her, like this evening with Walter Clarke lurking in the shadows. She had etched her way into his heart. He was pleasantly surprised at the moment with the way she returned his ardent kiss. Nick vowed that he would do all he could to keep that skulking, poor excuse of a man from harming Kate, or he would die trying.

Kate had never been kissed like this before and she knew Nick was older and more experienced, so she allowed herself to enjoy it. Her lips were entrapped with his and her mind reeled from the flame of passion that seemed to burn through her. She felt her eyes close automatically, while her limbs became weak and her body began to tremble slightly. If this was how it felt to be a woman; she liked it. Kate also knew that she should be putting an immediate stop to this kiss, but the man took her very breath away. Her head swam with delight. When he finally drew back from her, Kate was sure she would swoon, finding that she had to lean against him for support. A momentary silence passed between them then and as Nick gazed down at her she waited for the heated blush to wash over her body, but it did not. Kate was amazed to find that she felt no embarrassment at returning Nick's kiss so fervently and with a passion that seemed to match his.

He smiled at her then as he gently reached to clutch her chin, pulling her face to his and placing a soft kiss on her lips.

"Well, Katie, you do realize that we have that scoundrel Clarke to thank for this? After all, he did chase you right into my arms, so to speak. Decorum would dictate that I had definitely acted shamefully just now and that I should not have kissed you, particularly in that manner. But I am not sorry, are you?" Kate could only smile, shaking her head as she stared up at him, unable to make a sound. "Tell me, Miss Sullivan," Nick inquired with amusement. "It is one thing to climb down a tree wearing a gown, but do you often accomplish the task in your bare feet?"

Kate gasped loudly in surprise as she followed his gaze to the hem of her dress.

"My goodness," she sputtered. "My shoes. I had forgotten that I removed them. I could not have climbed down safely otherwise." Kate's mood lifted and she chuckled softly, suddenly feeling giddy and playful. His kiss had brought such lightness to her heart that she wiggled her toes before twirling around and around in front of him, laughing merrily as she danced.

Nick chuckled softly at her antics. Reaching out, he pulled her into his embrace once more, releasing her only when they heard voices and saw other guests approaching. He smiled lazily, tugging on a loose strand of her hair and promising himself that one day she would be his, with no one getting in their way. Kate left him then, entering the house through the back door. Nick watched her leave; there was so much more that he had wanted to say to her.

"Another time, Katie," he promised, looking up to the darkening sky. He moved to the covered porch then, and as the thunder roared, he lit a cigar, puffing on it with satisfaction just as the rain started.

"I am returning home tomorrow, Nick," Kate whispered solemnly into the darkness.

A pair of black, menacing eyes burned through the stairway window that looked out over the yard. Sir Walter Clarke stood on the landing, his face distorted and livid with rage, pressed tightly against the pane. He was observing the man and woman below, locked in a passionate embrace. They teased him with their kisses and mocked him with their laughter. He was sure their merriment was at his expense. A man gone mad, he blamed Nick for stealing the lady from him. In his demented mind Kate belonged to him, and that Brannigan lout had no right to hold her like that; to kiss the lips that were meant for him.

"Now, more than ever Mr. Brannigan, you should fear me. You are a pompous ass. You have not won this day. I will best you and win the lady; I promise you that!" He spat out his malicious oath with spittle dripping grossly from his chin. Raising a fist to the blackened sky he proclaimed madly. "I am an officer and a knight. Sir Walter Clarke, the owner of fine lands and in possession of a huge fortune. You, Mr. Brannigan are a knave; the holder of nothing!" he sneered coldly. Had Nick or Kate looked up to the window at that moment they would have witnessed the ravings of a madman, the very devil himself. As if to seal the bargain, the wind blew in a sudden gust, causing the clouds to clash together, as thunder rocked the sky.

The following morning dawned with a vengeance. There were red splashes of colour spreading erratically between the heavy clouds, fore-telling the turbulence of a storm that was now brewing. The ground was still soaked from the pounding rain of the night before, and the wind blew stronger now, forcing clouds to race across the heavens. Kate was saying her final farewells to Sophia, Charlotte, Isabella and John, while Betsy and Lillian stood to one side sobbing loudly. Using their little aprons, they wiped away the tears that continuously spilled from their eyes.

When she finally approached the children, Kate hugged them both tightly, trying desperately to swallow the large lump that had gathered in her throat. She had had no idea that it would be this difficult to say goodbye to the two little girls.

"I love you, and will miss you both, always," Kate choked out through her own tears. "I will never forget you; I promise. Will you remember me too?" Betsy and Lillian both nodded their heads in answer; too upset to speak. Pulling away from them, Kate promised that if at all possible and the good Lord was willing, she would see them again. Climbing into the waiting carriage, she wiped her eyes once more. Holding her handkerchief out the window, she waved goodbye. The carriage then rambled down the drive, splashing through puddles thick with mud, before disappearing around the corner and out of sight.

Chapter Seven

Kate Sullivan stared listlessly out of the window, wondering how a day begun with so much happiness and excitement could have changed into this gloomy, restless and dismal evening. The beautiful sun that had been shining so brightly this afternoon had disappeared, and a steady rainfall had taken its place. She shook her head. Her slender fingers traced the tiny rivulets of water running down the outside of the window glass. She thought once again of that evening not so long ago when she had first been disturbed by the news of a possible war. She was only frightened then, she recalled, but now that war had actually been declared, she was terrified. There was no sense in anyone ignoring the fact now, because the war was here!

Major-General Brock had hosted a dinner party at Fort George earlier in the evening, generously sharing his table with some of the American officers from across the river at Fort Niagara. Once again he sought Kate's assistance and she graciously agreed to help the other ladies prepare the meal. They had just served the officers their dessert, and were sharing a meal of their own in the kitchen, when the women noticed the messenger's arrival. He entered the Officer's Mess abruptly, handing the note bearing the dreaded news to General Brock. There they were, Kate thought, bemused; the British and the Americans sitting together at the same table, laughing and sharing stories, unaware that one week previous, President Madison had declared war.

Kate had stood dumbstruck in the doorway, watching in disbelief as Isaac Brock implored all his American guests to please finish their meal in peace. To her further amazement, all of the officers then stood together, wine in hand, and toasted one another. Well wishes mixed with regret had been expressed on both sides, she recalled unhappily. The men had struck up a friendship of sorts during the evening, each sadly aware that their next meeting would very likely be on the battlefield. Kate had dragged herself gloomily back into the kitchen feeling tired, miserable, frightened and alone. She was greatly relieved when a soldier had finally arrived to escort her home.

That night Kate tossed and turned restlessly in her bed, sleep escaping her. When she was finally able to succumb to her tiredness, it was only to find that the horrible nightmare she experienced a month ago had returned. She was lost once again in the dreaded dark, colourless mist, feeling cold and unable to move, while a screaming and moaning continued its cacophony all around her. The dream was the same as before, leaving her shaken and terrified. When she awoke the next morning, she felt tired and cross. Kate slowly donned her robe, and solemnly made her way downstairs for a much needed cup of tea. She inhaled deeply upon entering the kitchen; the pleasant aroma of Hannah's hot biscuits and savoury coffee filled the air. She loved the smell of coffee, but could not abide its taste.

"You look frightful, my dear," Hannah remarked, watching Kate enter the room and sit glumly down at the table, looking pale and shaken. "Did you not sleep well?"

"No, Hannah, I did not; the fear of war plagued me for most of the night. I am just so afraid! What is going to happen to us; to our lives and our home? I prayed to God almost every night for over a month Hannah, asking Him to please keep this terrible war from coming. I guess he was not listening. Maybe President Madison prayed to God too, only he probably asked him to let there be a war." Kate sniffed quietly, wiping her eyes and trying very hard to gain control of her fears.

"The Lord always listens, my dear, but He may not always answer the way we like. Whatever you do Kate, keep on with your prayers; that is all any of us can do for now." Hannah placed the tea service on the table in front of Kate, her own heart aching now as she too thought sadly of the war and the repercussions they could all be facing.

"Where is Father?" Kate inquired limply.

"He has gone to the fort with your brother and Carl. Your father suggested that since James Secord is a sergeant in the 1st Lincoln Militia; he would prefer that the boys join under his tutelage. I think your poor father hopes that James will do his best to keep an eye on them." Hannah shook her head and plunked herself roughly down beside Kate, tears now spilling over her cheeks as well. "Oh, this seems like such a horrible nightmare. I just cannot believe that it is happening. You see, Kate; you are not alone in your fear. I would not be surprised if the whole Niagara peninsula is feeling devastated this morning. I was so sure that things would work out and war would never come." Hannah shook her head sadly. "I am sorry, my child. I should be offering comfort to you and easing your anxiety. Instead, I am only adding to your worry. Well," Hannah said with conviction. "I truly think the best we can do for now is to keep ourselves busy; life goes on, does it not?" She wiped her eyes on her apron before giving Kate's hand a gentle pat. "Yes. The more I think about it, the more the idea appeals to me. I prescribe a full day of cleaning; that should occupy both our minds." Hannah rose from her chair then, her mind already on the day's work ahead. "I will give you some breakfast my dear, and then we can begin."

Kate was taken aback with Hannah's surprising outburst. Somehow, just knowing that her usually stoic housekeeper was also afraid of the war, actually had a calming effect on Kate. She did not feel so childish and cowardly. Her beloved Hannah was frightened too. However, nothing could stop the feeling of an impending doom from overtaking her.

The next few weeks passed much as they had before, but with some noticeable changes. Any discussions pertaining to the war were no longer stifled. People still tried to carry on with their normal daily activities, but there was a definite air of uncertainty surrounding the region and the gossip spread from Fort George to Lake Erie. Some were heard to remark that Fort Niagara fired their cannons across the river at Fort George, to which our side responded in kind. Others claimed that a few American soldiers were seen skulking around the countryside after dark. Other such stories promptly circulated throughout the area and many people were uncertain of what to believe. Kevin and Carl spent most of their time at the fort now, training to become soldiers in the militia. The fort was bustling with activity as the men practiced their drills and prepared for battle. Kate was needed at home to help on the farm, so she had seen no one for quite some time. She did not even see Mary since her job at the Secord's had ended with the onset of war. She missed the camaraderie she had shared with Mary and Laura, as well as the many customers that she had chatted with in James' store.

The month of July rolled in, bringing with it an intense heat which seemed to antagonize an already anxious community. Gone were the social gatherings of the past, when neighbours periodically enjoyed picnics or country dances together. The illustrious Fort George was off limits too, unless you were otherwise invited. Most families were satisfied with just keeping to themselves, even on Sundays, with church services now being held in the privacy of their homes. There was also an air of expectancy that spread rapidly throughout the county. Tempers flared at the slightest provocation. The majority of the inhabitants thought that any day now the Americans would be marching into their lives bringing turmoil, devastation and death. Serious discussions would break out when men were grouped together, some claiming that war was necessary, while others stated emphatically that it was not only a waste of time but a waste of men as well. Kate did learn however, that a few of their closest neighbours had secretly pulled up stakes in the middle of the night; presumably leaving to join the American cause.

One evening, towards the middle of the month, James Secord had accompanied Kevin and Carl home from the fort, bringing Nick Brannigan with them. Kate had not seen Nick since the night of the Powell's soiree when he had kissed her with such passion. The men sat comfortably around the kitchen table discussing local current events, while Kate and Hannah kept the coffee and nut bread in abundant supply. Thomas Sullivan wiped his hands on a napkin and with one eyebrow raised, he questioned Sergeant Secord.

"Well, James, is it true then man? Has there been some riotin' down there in the States over this blasted war?"

"It is, Thomas. It seems their declaration of war has created a great sense of patriotism to sweep their nation, causing a huge backlash against any anti-war sympathizers that have made themselves known. They are not necessarily sympathetic to the British, you understand, but unfortunately they are still regarded as treasonous. I have also been informed that one of their prominent newspapers printed an article that stated very strongly: 'He *who is not for us, is against us.*' It appears that any people found sympathetic to the British, or against the war in any way, were assaulted. Some even died of their injuries."

Kevin regarded James Secord for a moment. "Are you certain, sergeant?" he asked, frowning now and looking at Carl for support. "We had heard that it was just the blacks that were killed."

"I am afraid that James is right, Kevin," Nick replied solemnly. "My sister Ellen has been writing to a friend in Baltimore and the lady wrote back telling her briefly of the deplorable situation down there. She assured Ellen that it was not just the black people; it was anyone, man or woman, who spoke out in favour of the British. It seems history is repeating itself gentlemen. If you will recall, this is exactly what happened with the Empire Loyalists years ago."

"What puzzles me lads, is this. Why did they stay?" Thomas inquired. "Would it not have made more sense to keep their traps shut and come to Upper Canada?"

"In this case, I think that they still wished to remain Americans, Thomas, but they just did not like the idea of war." Nick stated.

The room grew quiet for a moment while each man sipped his coffee and sampled the nut bread, letting their private thoughts wander where they may. Nick took this opportunity to sneak a glance at Kate, who at the moment had her back to him, making an apple pie for the next day. He was unaware of the dreaded sick feeling that had settled in her stomach as she listened to the men talking, and he was also oblivious of the effect that his presence in the room was having on her already unsteady nerves. All he knew at the moment was that he wanted to gather her in his arms and kiss her as he did that night at the Powell's.

Kate was very conscious of the fact that Nick was ogling her once again, and glancing briefly over her shoulder, she met his ardent gaze. Her heart pounded heavily as the intensity of his stare proved very unsettling, causing an instant blush to colour her cheeks. She turned away to resume her work, as an odd sense of elation settled within her. Kate was confused. With everything that had recently passed between them, why should she feel nervous now? It is because there is a room full of people, she surmised. Her cheeks flamed as she recalled the provocative way Nick had held her that night; kissing her so passionately. My goodness, she thought self consciously, and I kissed him back! Kate was indeed perplexed. There was no embarrassment then, so why was she blushing now?

She stole another look behind her. Nick's piercing stare consumed her, body and soul, holding her gaze so transfixed for the moment, that it was impossible to avert her eyes. He spoke not a word, but even in her naiveté she could see the desire in his eyes, and his bold glare made Kate feel as if she were on fire. The heat in her cheeks spread to her neck and her hands trembled as she stared back at him. She tore herself away suddenly, and the spell was broken.

Thomas Sullivan, however, did not miss the pulsating exchange between his daughter and his friend and lowering his head, he tried his best to hide the lopsided grin that now adorned his face. He knew that if anything were to happen to him, this man would take care of his Katie Brianna, of that he was certain, and a small part of him was at peace.

Kate had managed to avoid Nick for the remainder of the evening; he busy conversing with the men and she, seeking to be alone to discern her tattered emotions. I am so young, she surmised quietly; maybe that is why I feel this way. Nick appears so calm and unruffled; he is older and probably more immune to the affects of such strong feelings. A twinge of guilt invaded her thoughts as she went over all the things that had happened during the past month: the confusing, but exciting journey to womanhood, her fear of the war, her repulsion with Walter Clarke and her love for Nick Brannigan. Kate felt guilty for the happiness she experienced when Nick kissed her, and for the way he had gazed at her this evening. It reminded her of the afternoon when she and the Evans girls met him at the inn; she caught him staring at her the same way then too. He must be in love with me, she thought.

Oh dear, how could she possibly condone the joy and excitement in her heart, now that the war had come? Many lives would be at stake in the future, maybe even their own, and property could be destroyed. Her emotions were in complete turmoil and she was utterly confused. She experienced another stab of guilt after realizing that during all of this chaos, it was Nick's soothing arms that she desired to have around her now, not her father's. Kate decided that the only way to ease her shattered emotions was to avoid Nick for the time being.

The sun had fallen below the trees as the men mounted their horses to return once again to the fort in Newark. Kate and Hannah stood on the front porch with Thomas, watching in silence as the four men galloped down the drive, yelling goodbye and waving as they left. What will become of them? Kate wondered sadly. For that matter, what is in store for all us? Both Thomas and Hannah shared her desolate mood and hugged her close as they waved goodbye to the men. Kate held tightly to the childish hope that the war would not last too long and her family and friends would survive unscathed.

Most of the families in the Niagara frontier kept their men with them longer than was first anticipated. Kevin and Carl, however, were at the fort almost every day performing additional duties besides their training drills, unlike some of the other men who had trained no more than three times in the past month. Kate had voiced her concerns to Sophia Shaw one day when they met in Newark, informing her of the apprehension that the family now felt regarding Kevin and his contributions to the war effort at Fort George. Sophia confidently reassured Kate that she had heard from an extremely reliable source that the militia were only called out when needed, unless they volunteered to sign on for the duration of the war. Feeling very much relieved, Kate then turned her attention to Sophia, offering cordial wishes to her and her family and also making polite inquiries after Isaac Brock. Sophia's demeanour changed slightly then, as she confessed that the general had recently left for York and she was uncertain of his return.

A few nights later Kevin joined his family for their evening meal and Kate mentioned her meeting with Miss Shaw, telling her brother about their conversation. Unfortunately, Kevin informed them that he was indeed training to be a long-term soldier and that he had most definitely signed on for the duration of the war. After noticing his family's immediate disappointment, however, he attempted to appease their concern by offering a heartfelt explanation.

"There are just too many who have refused to fight! The British are drastically short of men," he exclaimed. "The militia needs me!"

In the end, the only good news from Sophia that day was that Charlotte Evans had written to her from York, happily proclaiming that the war had not affected their lives as yet.

Chapter Eight

———

In the ensuing days it became abundantly clear to the region that the war had indeed begun. The arrival of the American General William Hull at Sandwich, near Amherstburg, caused some anxiety in Upper Canada, especially after he read and then posted a threatening proclamation for all the inhabitants to see. Part of Hull's belligerent announcement stated that they (the Americans) had now invaded Canada, but no inhabitant need fear; they were free to join the American cause or stay right out of the war altogether. No harm would come to anyone who did not take up arms against them. He also went on to decree that if any man joined with the Indians to fight against the Americans; he would be killed. That intimidating announcement had sent some of the newly joined militia men scrambling back to their homes, some even packing up their families and disappearing to parts unknown.

General Isaac Brock found himself trapped in York during this time, encased in frustration and turmoil, wishing fervently that he could escape this remote country and display his military prowess across the ocean, fighting alongside Wellington in the war with Napoleon. Brock had been expecting a war in Upper Canada for the past few years and his exasperation with the civil authorities seemed to grow daily. They are a nuisance to me, he thought, an impediment to everything I try to do. He shook his head, his frustration mounting, as his thoughts turned to the militia in Canada. He found their courage, morale and skill all lacking, especially when compared to the great army he was used to.

They are the most inexperienced, disorderly and unruly group of rascals that I have ever come across, not to mention that the majority of them do not even realize the seriousness of this war. To make matters worse, Brock was all too aware of Hull's arrival in Upper Canada, knowing full well that his hands were tied.

The aggravation that the general felt towards his superior, General Prevost, knew no bounds. *That man is forever restraining me; chaining me to his side and preventing my freedom,* he thought. *He is constantly thwarting my efforts to deal with our American adversaries as I see fit.* Brock also felt his time was wasted in York and he was desperate to leave. He felt that his place was with his men now. *Plans had to be made! The enemy must be dealt with!* Isaac Brock was certain that he was the man to get it done. Instead, he was forced to remain at his post in York, nothing more than a glorified messenger, relaying any new orders from his superior to the commander at Fort York, also advising him of any new information regarding the Americans.

Sadly though for the Americans, General Hull was so intent on terrifying the people of Upper Canada with his declaration that he neglected his duty in protecting the forts on Lake Michigan. As a result, both Fort Michilimackinac and Fort Dearborn were instantly overtaken by the British and their Native allies; the capture of the former was accomplished without one shot being fired. The British surrounded the American fort and a portion of the regiment manoeuvred their six pounder cannon into place on a small rise overlooking the enemy. The remainder of the soldiers, along with some fur traders and a handful of Indians, marched up to the front of Michilimackinac and commenced banging loudly on the enormous gates while the Indians yelled out their horrendous battle cry. The American commander, Captain Hanks, knew that he had enough of a defence force within the fort to fight the British soldiers, but did not want to risk the lives of the families enclosed with him to an Indian bloodbath, so he surrendered.

Fort Dearborn's demise, however, was not without incident. The Americans referred to that surrender as a bloody Indian massacre that included not only the soldiers inhabiting the fort, but their families as well. The recent British ruckus at Michilimackinac, prompted

Commander William Hull to order Captain Heald to evacuate Fort Dearborn, surrendering it to the British. The Americans made a deal with the area natives promising to leave their supplies, guns and ammunition behind in exchange for safe passage to Fort Wayne. Captain Heald reneged on the deal however, fearing that the local Potawatomi would use the arms and ammunition against the Americans. Therefore, when the small wagon train of women, children, officers and soldiers, escorted by a band of Miami Natives, left Fort Dearborn after the surrender, they were attacked by a large band of angry warriors. The outcome of the ambush was disastrous. There were approximately twenty-eight killed, including the women and most of the children, re-enforcing to the Americans once again, of just how savage they considered the Indians to be.

Following the massacre, the British confessed that the Natives' deplorable actions during that surrender were probably prompted by not only the lack of bloodshed at Michilimackinac, but also by Heald's deception. No explanation was offered in regards to the slaying of the women and children. Even though they were not directly involved, the incident still proved an embarrassment, a proverbial thorn, sticking into the side of the British army.

When news of the slaughter reached the people of Queenston, Kate was appalled. This was the first known grotesque and terrifying incident of the war and the mere thought of it was unimaginable. She had convinced herself that it would not have happened if Fort Dearborn had been in the hands of a commander who possessed Isaac Brock's leadership capabilities. If General Brock had made a deal, he would have kept his word, of that she was sure! Kate had put the general on a pedestal from almost the first time she had met him, as did most of her neighbours, holding him in such high regard and feeling that he could do no wrong. They instilled all their hope in this one man, trusting him to finish this war quickly so life could return to normal. Kate relayed this sentiment to her father one morning and he had offered her a candid reply.

"Remember, he is just a man after all, make no mistake about it, albeit a seemingly great one to be sure. He's an aggressive commander,

I'll give ya' that, but I'm thinkin' that he still has his orders to follow too. He still has to answer to his superiors. I do agree with ya' darlin' that if left to his own devices, our friend Isaac Brock could no doubt win this godforsaken war for us."

The acclaimed General did display his military prowess to the fullest a while later however, with the surrender of the American Fort Detroit. In early August, he was suddenly summoned to Amherstburg for the purpose of directing operations on the Detroit front. Brock was elated by the news and anxious to be off. With determination and high hopes of spoiling any possible American attack, he dispatched a short, yet decisive message to Nick Brannigan. It read:

'Pray sir, gather as many volunteers from Queenston as you are able to muster in the shortest amount of time. Come directly to Port Dover; post haste, where you will be graciously greeted by myself and the York and Lincoln Militia. It is my utmost desire that boats will be at the ready upon your arrival and we can all journey to Amherstburg together.'

Nick quickly scanned the message and complied immediately, with Kevin Sullivan being one of the selected men.

When the large flotilla finally set off from Port Dover, Nick and Kevin were aboard the same boat that carried Brock. The men remained in good spirits even though they were plagued with unpredictable weather at times, pounded by heavy winds and rain one minute, and finding all was calm and dry the next. They grew exhausted from shortage of sleep and the constant rowing, but they never complained or lost their admiration and respect for General Brock. During their voyage, Brock's boat struck hard against a hidden rock and became trapped. Nick immediately instructed Kevin and the rest of the crew to grab oars and poles to try and free her. Unfortunately, the boat was stuck fast and the men suffered through many failed attempts. The crew were tired and sore, longing for rest. Nick, not wanting to give up, was conferring with Kevin as to what they should do next, when they heard a loud splash. The crew stood on deck, flabbergasted for a moment at witnessing their revered general leaping overboard into the murky water. Nick Brannigan and Kevin Sullivan, and some of the crew, dived in after their leader and with their assistance, along with the men on board, Brock was able to pry the boat free.

Later, when all were safely back in the vessel, Isaac Brock shared a glass of spirits from his personal liquor case with the men, conveying his appreciation for a task well done. Word spread rapidly from each boat, telling of the generosity of their stoic commander. The morale of the entire flotilla remained high for the remainder of the journey.

Shortly before midnight on August 13th 1812, General Brock, his aide Captain John Glegg, and Nick Brannigan, accompanied by Kevin Sullivan and the rest of the floating entourage, finally reached Amherstburg. The moment they disembarked, the men were immediately greeted on shore by Matthew Elliott, the British Indian agent, and Brock made the necessary introductions. Their conversation came to an abrupt halt however, as the Indians decided to welcome them by firing muskets into the night, whooping and dancing in euphoria.

"What a dreadful waste of ammunition," the general stated, casting a concerned glance at Mr. Elliott.

"The natives are simply expressing their excitement at your arrival with so many reinforcements, sir," explained the agent as he escorted the gentlemen to his private lodgings.

"Mr. Elliott, before the hour grows much later, do convey to our Native allies that I wish them to cease this unnecessary clamour, and advise them that tomorrow they will be informed of my plan for Detroit," Brock concluded.

The bluish-white moon sat serenely in the sky overseeing the sleepy earth, as a flickering candle flame cast dark silhouettes around the walls of the dimly lit room below. It was beyond midnight now and General Isaac Brock sat quietly in Mr. Elliott's study, inspecting stolen American dispatches and some area maps that littered the top of a large wooden desk. Earlier, he had sent Nick and Kevin on an errand with the Indian agent to speak with the Natives, appealing to them to desist their celebrating and obtain much needed rest. He was left in the room with Captain Glegg, now sleeping soundly in a nearby chair.

The study door opened suddenly, breaking the quiet stillness of the chamber, and General Brock found himself staring in awe at a most magnificent looking Indian. The man posed a striking figure with his dark eyes, dark skin, and jewelled aqua-line nose, standing proud and erect between Nick Brannigan and Matthew Elliott. He was dressed for the occasion in a tan deerskin jacket and pants, his feet encased in leather moccasins that were adorned with dyed porcupine quills, and there was also a very impressive medallion of King George III around his neck, dangling proudly at the end of a coloured wampum string. Captain Glegg woke instantly when the prominent Native entered the room, and no one uttered a sound. All eyes were momentarily fixed on the Shawnee Chief standing before them. Seconds past before Brock finally found his voice and clearing his throat, he rose to his feet, stepping forward to shake the visitor's hand.

"Do I have the pleasure of meeting the great Shawnee Chief Tecumseh?" Brock inquired with delight, as he ended the handshake. Tecumseh smiled warmly and nodded in reply, feeling a mutual admiration for the major-general. "Please, allow me to commend you, Chief Tecumseh, for the leadership and courage that you have exhibited in your recent engagements against the Americans. The British army welcomes you most heartily as our allies, and may I add that you are indeed the Wellington of the Indians!"

"My Indian brothers and I, make a treaty with you and your father, the king, promising to help you fight the blue-coated enemy, and you, the red-coats, promise to aid our confederacy. We fight together with honour to the finish," Tecumseh replied, boldly slapping his fist against his chest.

Brock nodded in agreement. "We have fought against the enemies of our father across the great water to the east, proving ourselves worthy of our king's trust . I come now to make war against his enemies here on this side of the great water, but desire for you and your warriors to teach us how to fight in your vast forests," the general replied. He then turned to Nick. "Would you please be so kind Mr. Brannigan, as to search out the remainder of my officers and inform them that I request their presence without delay."

When Nick returned with the men a short while later, it was to find their commander and the Shawnee Chief slumped over the desk,

Captain Glegg holding a candle over their heads, while Tecumseh, knife in hand, carefully scratched out a map of the area on a long strip of elm bark. What a striking pair they make, Nick thought, silently regarding both leaders with respect. Later, during the course of their late night meeting, Brock had informed all present of his plans for a swift attack on Fort Detroit.

"Gentlemen, it has been brought to my attention that General Hull has left our Canadian soil and retreated back over the river to his fort at Detroit. Alas, I feel it is quite evident now that the aging general is extremely weak in his command. Therefore, I wish to exploit the apparent weakness and attack as soon as possible." When the meeting finally concluded in the wee hours of the morning, Brock was adamant that they would indeed attack Fort Detroit, turning a deaf ear to the strong dissent of his officers. The men had their orders. The battle plan was discussed in detail. All that remained now was for the officers to brief their own men before retiring.

General Brock decided to request a surrender before the attack. When General William Hull refused the demand, he retaliated by directing an artillery barrage at the American fort, with the cannonade lasting on into the night. Together, Brock and Tecumseh had deployed an Indian scare tactic to frighten Hull, easy in light of the recent massacre at Fort Dearborn. Brock had simply penned a small note of warning to the general, informing him that his army was accompanied by a large band of Indians, who, at the moment, appeared overzealous at the prospect of doing battle with the Americans within that stockade. His letter also stated quite strongly that he would have no control over the Natives once the confrontation commenced.

Hull, who was deathly afraid of the Indians and feared for the lives of the inhabitants of the fort, including both his daughter and granddaughter, surrendered without a fight, mortifying his own officers and soldiers. Hull's men expressed their outrage at the surrender, declaring that they were not afraid to defend their post, believing their general had displayed an unforgivable cowardice in his yielding so quickly to the British.

At the conclusion, General Brock and the Shawnee Chief Tecumseh entered Fort Detroit together, signifying the American defeat; a great victory for Brock and Upper Canada, but leaving Hull to face his own countrymen in complete and utter disgrace.

Chapter Nine

Nick Brannigan arrived at Fort George, directly following the glorious capture of Detroit. He was accompanied by Kevin Sullivan and the rest of the volunteers. James Secord and the 1st Lincoln Militia, including Carl Phillips, were expected to arrive later in the day. The volunteers were to disperse, returning once more to their farms, while Nick and Kevin had orders to hold fast in Newark and await the return of Brock. Captain Walter Clarke however, was there at the fort ready to greet the men, welcoming them wholeheartedly and offering a friendly suggestion that they join him in a glass of spirits before heading home. For the most part the captain ignored Nick's presence, just briefly casting an insidious glare in his direction before inviting the rest of the men to follow him to his quarters. Standing alone, Nick swore angrily as he watched the retreating backs of the men. A sudden feeling of uneasiness swept over him. That scoundrel is up to something, he thought. I am sure of it. At the moment he was too exhausted to pay any more attention to the matter. After shooting one final glance at the unfathomable captain, he turned abruptly on his heels and marched determinedly towards the blockhouse and his awaiting bunk.

While General Brock had an exemplary victory on land at Detroit, Captain James Dacres of the British ship *HMS Guerriere* met with a devastating defeat on the water. The ship had been engaged in battle with the *USS Constitution* off the Grand Banks of Newfoundland, both sides showing no mercy as they bombarded each other with cannon balls. After two hours, the battered and defeated British vessel finally surrendered and Captain Dacres was listed among the many severely wounded men, being shot in the back while cheering his crew on during the battle. With the arrival of fall though, relief filled the countryside, and the war seemed stilled for the time being. The women welcomed the temporary peace with open arms, thanking God for the small reprieve and cherishing the company of their men once more, knowing that it would not be long before they were snatched away again.

One morning early in the month of October, Kate wandered into the kitchen after oversleeping to find her father sitting quietly at the table, a letter clutched tightly in his hands. He greeted her absentmindedly when she bestowed a light kiss on his forehead, his mind totally immersed in the words of the note. Hannah had begun to clear the dishes away, but not before Kate noticed the three dirty plates, suggesting that they had had a guest for breakfast. She directed a questioning glance at her father, seemingly lost in his own thoughts.

"I must have slept in Father," Kate exclaimed loudly, jolting him to attention. "Did you have company this morning?"

"Oh, aye, me darlin', Mr. Brannigan was here," he replied distractedly.

Kate sat down next to her father and waited for him to elaborate, but he did not. She hid her mounting frustration and, leaning in closer, continued with her curious prodding. "Oh? How is Nick doing? It has been quite some time since I have seen him. Do tell, has he joined the army too?"

Thomas Sullivan turned to face his daughter then, treating her with a long searching glance before answering. "Well, yes and no! Ya' see darlin', he is workin' with General Brock, somethin' ta' do with them Indians, but he has not really joined up so to speak. He was ... er... is volunteering, working with a group of regulars, whippin'm into shape." Thomas laughed distractedly before continuing. "Brock says them boys are just a rabble of young lads that do not seem ta' be takin' this war too seriously." Thomas turned all his attention back to the letter then, leaving Kate to finish her breakfast. He was determined never to disclose its contents to his lovely daughter. She's upset enough about this blasted war, he thought dismally. She need not know every sordid detail that goes on during it, especially these recent shenanigans with that bastard Clarke. I cannot abide that lout! He's a disgrace to the uniform and to his country. Nick Brannigan is one hundred times the man that imbecile is.

Thomas continued to read between the lines of the unpleasant letter, more convinced with each missing word that no good could come from worrying his Kate. But damn that man's worthless hide. Oh, aye, he seems to be gaining ground at every turn and after reading this disturbing note there was no way of knowing how much or how quickly that evil scoundrel would acquire even more power. Thomas was indeed perplexed. He was also extremely concerned for his Katie Brianna. That villainous Clarke was quite taken with his young daughter, of that he was sure. Thank the good Lord that there were men like Isaac Brock and Nick Brannigan to keep that man at bay, he thought gratefully, glancing quickly at Kate. He silently prayed for her safety. The world has surely gone mad, he concluded, sighing dismally.

Later that day Nick sat at a table with the celebrated general in his headquarters inside Fort George, engaged in a private conversation. "I am quite certain that you are well aware of my reasons for coming to this meeting earlier than the appointed time," Nick asserted, levelling a steady gaze at Brock.

"I would have to assume that your reasoning pertains to that damned note, does it not?"

"It does, sir. I wanted to speak with you alone before the others arrived, to inquire how this situation could have possibly come about. Why am I being so callously replaced? Especially by Clarke? You must be aware of what a blackguard he is, sir? I would be very interested in knowing who issued such a ridiculous order." Nick's frustration was escalating. He suddenly remembered though, that Brock, although charitable and sympathetic, had more important worries on his mind, and not wishing to add to his burdens, Nick quickly reined in his temper. "I am sorry, sir, but I do not understand how Clarke has managed to take command of my regulars," he stated quietly. "He is a loathsome, disreputable man and I do not trust him!"

General Brock took a sip of his wine, eyeing Nick with a speculative glance before rising from his chair to slowly pace the room. "I am afraid that in a small way I may in fact own some responsibility in this distasteful matter, Nick," Brock explained. "You see, I disobeyed direct orders from my superior, General George Prevost, regarding the surrender of Fort Detroit. His solution at the time seemed to be to do nothing, suspend hostilities as it were.

As you will recall, I knew we needed to act swiftly, so I took the initiative and gathered my men together to confront General Hull. Luckily for me, the outcome proved victorious and General Prevost decided to let my insubordination go unpunished, but his aggravation towards me was, and still is it seems, quite apparent." Brock stopped for a moment to consider the situation. "I shudder to think what the circumstances would have entailed had we not won the day." Shaking his head and finding his chair once again, Brock gazed steadily at Nick. "There are two pertinent facts to consider here. One, my superior had to congratulate me, most grudgingly I might add, which most certainly did not sit too well with him."

"And the other fact general?" Nick inquired stiffly, holding his annoyance in check.

"The other fact is simply this, Nick. General Sir George Prevost and Captain Sir Walter Clarke are old friends and have served together for quite some time in his majesty's army."

Nick groaned and clenching his jaw tightly, banged his fist angrily down on the table.

"You see, Nick," Brock continued, "Sir Walter, or should I say Captain Clarke, approached General Prevost with a most ardent request to replace you in your command, undoubtedly painting a very disagreeable picture of you as well. I would also assume that since Clarke possesses the rank of captain and you hold no such privilege, and my superior is at least acquainted with Clarke and knows you not, the captain's request was granted. I do, however, suspect that this action has more to do with my being punished by my superior, rather than him honouring a request from an old acquaintance. An unfortunate situation this." At Nick's apparent frustration, Brock continued on. "I have appealed to General Prevost's sense of duty and his military expertise without displaying any malice towards Clarke, hoping to sway him from his folly, but alas, Nick, he would have none of it. I am terribly sorry for my hand in this situation and heartily wish the outcome could have been otherwise."

Nick snarled and leaped angrily from his chair. He remembered that he was in the presence of a British general however, and instantly apologized for his unthinkable behaviour.

Brock immediately vacated his own seat and approached his friend, empathizing with him while trying to appease his mood. "I assure you, Nick, I did all that was possible, but General Prevost is damnably hard to reason with, especially when he is dealing with me. I agree that this is a very unfortunate situation, for I too do not trust Captain Clarke and think him the vilest of libertines. I did all I could to try and sway Sir George, but to no avail. You must remember, my friend," Brock added candidly, patting Nick affectionately on the shoulder. "Whatever happens from this moment on, I am on your side. I always stand by my men; and with my friends, even more so."

Nick sighed in defeat, slumping down into his chair.

Relieved that his friend seemed pacified for the moment, Isaac Brock too, returned to his chair. "Do you by chance still possess the little note that I sent?" he inquired curiously.

"No, general, I do not," Nick replied, calmer now. "I brought it to the attention of Thomas Sullivan this morning as a strictly precautionary measure. You see, sir, there is more to this than meets the eye. The lady you mentioned in the note is the gentleman's cherished daughter Kate, as you may well know, and Walter Clarke seems to be harbouring a reckless, infatuation for the maid. You recall the ball last month? And were you also informed of his unreasonable behaviour at the Powells? Need I say more, sir? He is becoming quite a nuisance to the young lady and I felt the need to notify her father, who is also a friend of mine, and yours too, it seems; to keep him abreast of the situation. I guess that I just feel uneasy with any circumstances regarding that devil."

"I have indeed had the pleasure of meeting Miss Sullivan and I quite agree with Captain Clarke's infatuation, however displaced it may be. I also agree that Miss Sullivan should most definitely be protected from him. That will undoubtedly be your concern Mr. Brannigan, will it not?"

Nick tightened his lips in conviction before replying with a slow, steady nod.

"Would you agree, sir, to remain after the forthcoming meeting is adjourned?" the general asked. "There is much that I wish to convey to you, in private."

Before Nick had a chance to reply however, their conversation was interrupted by the arrival of General Brock's officers; Captain Walter Clarke included. Nick Brannigan and Captain Clarke exchanged a look of mutual contempt, openly displaying their obvious hatred for one another.

"Should Mr. Brannigan be in attendance, sir? It was my understanding that this meeting was to be held with your officers only," Clarke inquired, levelling a sneer at Nick, who in turn glared back with a scowl. The infamous captain had been surprised to discover Nick conversing so closely with the general. Their apparent friendship discomfited him.

"Mr. Brannigan is here at my personal invitation," General Brock stated firmly, with just a hint of agitation. "Let us hear no more of it." Brock eyed Clarke coldly for an instant before facing his other officers.

"Now, gentlemen, let us address the task at hand." Brock then proceeded to open a large map of the Niagara frontier, spreading it open on the table. "The Americans are readying themselves for an attack, of that I am positive. The location, I assume, will be somewhere along this stretch of the river, thus gaining entry to our soil," he stated plainly, pointing to the area of the Niagara River running from Lake Erie to Fort George. "I would like a garrison posted here, at Brown's Point and here, at Vrooman's Point," he ordered, indicating each strategic site on the map. "However, I want the largest garrison to be positioned here, at the heights in Queenston, as I feel this will be their most likely point of entry for the invasion. I also anticipate that the American troops may cross the river any day now, and are quite probably planning their battle strategy as we speak.

You see, gentlemen, my brigade-major, Thomas Evans, has just returned from across the river; an errand on which I sent him with instructions to exchange prisoners. The enemy simply replied that since the captives had been sent to Albany and could not be returned for a couple of days, nothing could be done at the moment. They suggested that we wait two more days before we collect our men. Suffice it to say gentlemen, that this information, plus other evidence gained on that day, has convinced me of the enemy's immediate plans to attack, hoping to acquire yet more prisoners in two more days."

"What would you like us to do, sir?" Nick inquired, with the rest of the men echoing his question.

"Some will remain here at the fort. The Iroquois chief John Norton is camped not far away with his followers, ready to assist when needed. Regretfully, our friend Tecumseh has disappeared; his whereabouts unknown for the time being," Brock added with concern. "Captain Clarke, you will appoint one of your men to call in the militia from the surrounding neighbourhood, post haste, and Mr. Brannigan, would you be so kind as to inform all others in the outlying district to report immediately to the fort. The rest of you are to make all necessary preparations to meet the coming assault. This very evening I want everyone at the ready to defend Upper Canada. In conclusion gentlemen, you have your instructions. Let us now make haste to receive the enemy!" The small group of officers disbanded then, slowly filing out of the general's quarters, conversing loudly with each other as they left. Nick remained behind, unaware of Walter Clarke's halted presence in the doorway. He missed the dark, threatening sneer directed at him before the captain turned abruptly and stalked angrily away.

Nick left Fort George at the conclusion of his short, private meeting with Isaac Brock, acting instantly on the general's instructions. Even though he was not a British soldier, he opted to help Brock in any way possible. As he mounted his horse, he fervently wished that he could make a quick stop at the Sullivan farm, but he knew that the general was depending on an immediate response to his orders. Time was of the essence. However, Kate would be his first priority after this damned battle was over, he promised himself. Nick rode hard into the night, reaching the various locations of the scattered militiamen, relaying the general's instructions word for word.

At the completion of his task Nick could be found riding alone in the dark once again, the moon lighting his way. He was lost in his thoughts as he headed back to Fort George, the steady clip-clopping of the horse's hooves loudly intruding on the quiet stillness of the night. He was tired and longed for the comfort of his bunk. He was also troubled now by the subtle change he noticed in Brock's manner earlier this evening. The general had showed such bravado and excitement while discussing his battle plans with his men, but his exhilaration had faded later on during their private meeting together. Nick recalled how Brock had suddenly appeared slightly melancholy and edgy, expressing a sudden desire to see his beloved Sophia, even though he knew there was no time. The general also seemed distracted, Nick thought, remembering Brocks secret confession that he was plagued by a nagging premonition. He did not make much if it at the time, but thinking back now, Nick found it to be quite unnerving, and Brock's portentous words came to mind: *I feel if this war continues, I may do something quite imprudent.*

Nick himself had an uneasy feeling that he could not shake. Was he experiencing some kind of forewarning as well? Ridiculous! It was only natural to feel this way before a battle, he thought. Oh, how he detested confrontations, but he would not shirk his duty; he would do all in his power to save Upper Canada. Nick was thankful for his horse; strong, spirited, fast and sound. It is the untiring Arabian blood running through his veins, he concluded. He thought of Brock's admirable steed Alfred, who apparently was an extension of the general himself during battle. Nick was suddenly hit with an overwhelming sense of guilt, realizing that he had not even named his own horse yet.

Captain Walter Clarke dispatched two of his men from Fort George to call in all the militia residing in and around Queenston, leaving the collection of Kevin Sullivan to himself, enabling him to see the pretty Miss Kate once more. He smiled wickedly in anticipation of the visit, hoping the girl's feelings had softened towards him. Clarke congratulated himself for his cunning impulses on this evening's mission. His satisfaction was immense, knowing that he and he alone, would be the one responsible for stealing the coveted son away from the Sullivan family, throwing him headlong into the war. The captain rode with purpose up to the modest farm house just as dusk was approaching. He smiled wickedly as he thought about Nick Brannigan and all the rest of the so-called honourable men associated with him. He would fix them all, he vowed, and his revenge would one day be sweet. He would devise a most ingenious plan of both revenge and victory, which the up and coming battle at Queenston would hopefully bring to fruition.

Kate Sullivan answered the loud, repeated knocking. Opening the front door, she froze instantly at the sight of Captain Clarke, standing boldly ogling her from head to toe. She did not smile in greeting. Instead, she instantly stepped backwards. An inexplicable unease consumed her. She felt quite certain that it was an ill wind that blew this scoundrel their way.

"Katie Brianna, who is it me girl, that has come callin' at this hour?" Thomas Sullivan's short inquiry was laced with annoyance.

"It is Sir... um ... Captain Walter Clarke," Kate answered nervously, noticing his red uniform. "If you will follow me please. My father is in the kitchen."

Captain Clarke eyed her swaying skirts with pleasure, as he followed her into the other room.

Mr. Sullivan was seated at the table, his unlit pipe now forgotten in his hand. He stared morosely at the doorway, trying to squash the feeling of dread that he too experienced at Sir Walter's untimely arrival. He nodded curtly to their guest, indicating for him to take a chair. Walter Clarke doffed his hat and fixed each of them, Hannah included, with a victorious smile as he sat in the proffered seat. With a false graciousness, he recited the reason for his visit.

"No! Please, not yet!" Kate exclaimed frantically in protest a few minutes later, hugging her brother tightly.

"It is alright now, Sis," Kevin soothed, as he pulled away smiling. "You did not take on so when I left with Nick to go to Detroit."

"I was unaware that you had left then. Father told me after you were gone. Believe me Kevin, I worried about you then too. I still have not forgiven Nick for taking you with him."

"I am quite ready and willing to go dearest, and so is Carl. This is what we have been training for all these weeks."

Thomas Sullivan sat dismally in his chair, shaking his head in resignation. "Aye, me girl , t'will be alright, just as your brother says. They are soldiers now and are needed to defend our country, eh lads?"

Kevin nodded quickly in agreement, showing a confidence that made his father proud. Carl, however, stood fidgeting nervously, unable to keep still. Kevin seemed to be the only one who noticed. He shrugged it off though, figuring that his friend was just experiencing some apprehension towards the upcoming battle.

Kate and her father now directed their full attention to Walter Clarke, both fixing him with an accusing glare. The two young soldiers had vacated the room to gather their belongings so they missed the ungracious welcome that their captain received. The insufferable man, Kate thought with disdain, he displays no apparent sign of remorse in his task here this night; in fact, he actually seems to be enjoying himself. She realized that it had to be done, but this man had the audacity to show his undue pleasure at escorting her beloved brother to war. Her father, on the other hand, felt suddenly old and defeated. He was proud of his son, but frightened for him too. Lord, he thought sadly, if one of us has to die, please let it be me.

Kate, along with her father and Hannah, bit their tongues, attempting to show some small amount of civility towards Captain Clarke during his stay, even though each passing minute threatened to expose their charade. Conversation was kept to a minimum; short sentences and quick replies. No offer of a strong drink had been made to the unwanted guest, but Hannah did grudgingly serve him a cup of tea before abruptly leaving the kitchen to check on the boys.

Captain Clarke felt the coldness in the room. It was definitely not the temperature, since there was a warm crackling fire glowing in the hearth. No, he thought, as he regarded his uncharitable hosts, it was the tight smiles and ice-cold eyes starring back at him from across the table. The unforgiving coldness that he in turn felt for them, did not register on his face. Although he was attracted to Miss Sullivan, she had slighted him on every occasion, which only angered him all the more. His only desire now was to use her violently at his will. The fact that Nick Brannigan wanted her too, made it that much sweeter. He was impatient to snatch Kate away from her condescending family, and it was all he could do to remain calm.

Captain Clarke's irritation mounted as he noticed Kate averting her eyes every time he glanced in her direction. He realized then that he had erred considerably in his thinking regarding the hope that Kate's feelings would soften. He silently berated himself for his carelessness. He should have shown remorse in his duty this evening and hid the abundant joy that consumed him. In the next instant Clarke attempted to mend his folly. Switching his tactics, he tried in earnest to repair the damage to his character. "I can imagine how horrible this day must be for all of you," he stated with a forced regret. "I implore you to please forgive my seemingly elated mood; it is not directed at bringing your poor son to war, I assure you. I must apologize for my unforgivable callousness, but my enjoyment is solely from the fact that I now have the chance to finally extinguish the enemy and chase them back across the river in defeat."

Kate and her father exchanged knowing glances, neither one believing the captain's feeble explanation and both distrusting him more than ever. Outwardly, however, they just smiled and nodded at Captain Clarke without uttering a word.

Walter Clarke was satisfied. His was just arrogant enough to believe that his insincere apology pacified his hosts, unaware of their true feelings regarding him. What a simple, gullible people they are, he thought, hiding his vicious grin. How I will savour my revenge.

The silence was broken by Hannah issuing a string of instructions to both Kevin and Carl as they followed her into the kitchen. The boys were ready to take their leave, so Thomas, Hannah, and Kate choked out their strained goodbyes, with Kate silently vowing to be strong, not wishing to cause the boys any discomfort at their departure. Sir Walter had hoped for a few moments alone with Kate. Hiding his contempt and disappointment now, he too stood, reluctant to take his leave, but finding himself rudely excluded from the circle of well wishers. Kate smiled and hugged both Carl and her brother. She made them promise to return home soon, safe and unharmed. Kevin kissed her goodbye, uttering reassurances that he did not necessarily feel, his mind consumed with thoughts of battle and the secret hope that he would be able to keep his promise to his sister.

Kate had succeeded in keeping her emotions under control until the boys were out of sight and she was alone in her room; then the damn broke. All the fear, anxiety, and misery that she held inside all evening finally spilled free through her tears. She cried not just for Kevin and Carl, but for all the young men who were marching off to battle, and for all the grieving families, including her own. She thought of Nick then, knowing that he would be joining Isaac Brock at Queenston. How would he fare? Oh, I wish I could have seen him once more before ...? Kate shook herself dismally, realizing where her thoughts were going. She refused to think about Nick dying in battle. She lost control then. She cried and sobbed until her heart ached. This is what she had been terrified of all along.

"I hate this wretched war," she sobbed, raising her eyes to heaven. "I do not understand Lord. Is this the answer to my prayers? Hannah says that we have to trust you; the Lord knows what is best. How can the best for us be the onset of war? I cannot take this, God. Kevin could be killed! Nick too! He may never know how much I love him. Please! Keep them all safe," she begged. Kate threw herself onto her bed and sobbed hysterically. When sleep finally did come, it was not a blessing.

The night had turned dark and foreboding while the wind howled in outrage, matching the mood that presently encompassed the Niagara frontier. Kate lay tossing and turning, agitated in her slumber, reliving that horrible nightmare once again. Only this time it had changed slightly. The dream was in colour, and the dead soldier at her feet now had a face. It was Kevin! She desperately tried kneeling down to embrace her brother to offer him some comfort while assessing his wounds, but she could not! Her legs were paralyzed and her knees would not bend, no matter how hard she tried to move them. The fog at her feet cleared suddenly and when she looked down Kevin was gone. Kate became frantic, calling out to her brother in a panic, but her voice was lost, deep in the thick, relentless mist. The tears spilled rapidly down her cheeks as she screamed her brother's name over and over, hugging herself in grief, and begging the fog to please release him.

In an instant, all went quiet: deathly quiet. As Kate stood shivering uncontrollably in the stillness, she heard a dreaded low, eerie drumming sound that droned on steadily, growing louder as it inched threateningly closer. The dense, chilly mist encircled her now, wrapping its cold, black arms tightly about her in a smothering embrace. Once again she felt her heart race and her body convulse as a dark, unknown shape emerged from the fog. It was Nick! The drumbeats had intensified, reaching such a crescendo that Kate had to cover her ears to shut out the noise. She screamed in terror, watching helplessly as Nick, covered in blood, crawled steadily closer, his hands grasping the dirt for leverage. Kate felt her knees buckle and her body go limp, and sliding slowly to the ground, she called out his name before the darkness claimed her.

Chapter Ten

———

Nick lay wide awake in his bunk, already perturbed with the war. It was the wee hours of the morning and he was feeling restless and unnerved. Something had awakened him and he could not fall back to sleep. The longer he stayed awake, the more frustrated he became. I need to be well rested and have my wits about me for the battle that is sure to come, he thought. As he lay quietly in the darkness now, his thoughts turned to Kate.

"Damn the late hour of my return! If not for that, I could have stopped in to see Katie on my way back here. My God, that I should love her so," he whispered. Nick had always prided himself for his resourcefulness at avoiding that particular emotion in the past. Frowning in confusion, he was amazed at his giving into love so readily now; especially with one so young and innocent as Kate.

Nick's thoughts grew tender as he remembered Kate at the ball: her soft honeyed voice, her tickling laughter, and her gracefulness when she danced. He chuckled softly as he thought of her at the Powell's; playing games with the children and climbing down the tree in her gown and bare feet. He had never known a woman like her; she intrigued him as no other had in the past. Nick was also reminded of her beautiful auburn hair that he had the pleasure of running his fingers through as he kissed her. That kiss was something else too, he mused. He knew Kate to be naive, but she seemed to respond instinctively to his advances. He remembered gentle arms encircling his neck; soft, tender lips pressed firmly against his; and a young, innocent body curving eagerly into his embrace. Nick trembled slightly. Thinking this way will not help me sleep, he thought.

"Lord," he whispered. "Why should this woman haunt me now?" Nick had no time to consider the matter. The quiet stillness of the fort was suddenly shattered by the sound of booming cannons exploding in the distance.

In the predawn drizzly October morning Fort George came to life in an instant. Some soldiers sprang immediately into action, putting on uniforms and snatching up weapons, while others, still groggy from sleep, stumbled around their bunks in confusion, trying to locate various parts of clothing. Nick Brannigan jumped quickly from his bed, pulling on his boots and throwing his coat over his shoulder, before grabbing his musket and racing from the blockhouse in search of General Brock. Once outside, he collided with Kevin Sullivan searching for Carl Phillips, and Nick hollered above the bedlam that now encompassed the fort.

"Never mind Carl! Report to your first in command. There is no time to lose!" Nick spied General Brock running for his horse Alfred, and veering off suddenly, he bolted to try and catch him.

"I will not wait, Nick," Brock screamed in earnest a few moments later. "Join with John Norton and his warriors and follow me directly," he added, before turning Alfred hastily towards the gates. Nick then watched in helpless frustration as Major-General Brock, administrator and commander of all forces in Upper Canada, galloped away alone in the heavy sleet, splashing wildly through the mud as he urged his mount on in the direction of Queenston Heights.

Heavy cannon fire could be heard for miles surrounding the heights. Queenston was closest to the battle and the thundering noise was earth-shattering, not only to the inhabitants there, but in the outlying areas as well. Some were so afraid that they sat quietly in terror, praying for God's intervention. Others chose to keep busy, nervously bustling about in the early morning hours, trying desperately to keep their minds occupied with something else. Laura Secord was wide awake. She had tucked her children into bed hours ago after James left for the fort, and sought the comfort of her old rocking chair in the parlour where she now sat, her mind on James and the horrible battle. The pounding and booming woke the children. Frightened now, they hurriedly joined their mother by the fire. The three youngest, Charlotte, Charles and Apollonia, cried out hysterically with every roar of the distant guns. Mary and her younger sister Harriet tried to comfort their siblings, but they would not be soothed.

The rain had stopped, but Laura's uneasiness grew with each passing minute. If the enemy gained the heights, then she and her family could be in peril. She felt isolated and alone, longing for the companionship of others and terribly afraid for her children. A thought suddenly struck her and she ceased her rocking. They had to leave! They could no longer remain here all alone and unprotected. She told Mary to dress the children in warm clothing, and to please hurry as there was no time to delay. So it was that when the mantel clock chimed again, the Secord's fled their home, heading in the direction of the Sullivan farm.

The constant booming reverberated in Kate's nightmare, jolting her upright in bed and driving her from the room. She located Hannah and her father in the kitchen, sitting stiffly at the table, looking tired and strained. She joined them, too frightened to speak but comforted by their presence. For the longest while, they all sat motionless, listening to the pounding sounds of the war. A sudden persistent knocking startled them, and each one in turn stared blankly at the back door, uncertain if they should open it. Finally, Kate rose with uncertainty and slowly approached the door, opening it just a crack and peering cautiously out into the early morning hours.

"Good heavens," she exclaimed in surprised relief, her tension relaxing now on finding Laura and her family huddled in the doorway, looking cold and wet. "Do come in, please, and warm yourselves by the fire." Kate ushered her friends into the kitchen and with Hannah's assistance, the little group were soon dry and comfortable.

"I will make you something hot," Hannah said. "Let me see now. A pot of tea and some hot cocoa should do nicely," she reasoned. "Are you hungry too? I can heat up some stew if you wish?" Laura Secord declined the food, thanking Hannah for her most generous offer, but graciously accepting the hot drinks. While the heat from the fire warmed them, Laura explained why they had fled their home in the middle of the night.

"Now, dearie, ya' need not worry. You and yours are welcome to stay for as long as ya's need," Thomas Sullivan stated reassuringly.

Sometime later, when the room had grown quiet once more, the small group at the table, Laura and Mary included, listened with unquestionable fear to the ceaseless noise outside in the distance. The four young Secord children however, lay undisturbed by the cozy fire, sleeping soundly.

Dawn was just beginning to break, shedding only minimal light over the vast escarpment at Queenston Heights. Nick arrived just below the top of the crest at the redan, where the main cannon, an eighteen-pounder, with eight gunners, was situated, firing repeatedly at the advancing American boats. He had sent John Norton and the rest of the Natives to the other side of the line in an attempt to prevent the enemy's ascent up the cliff. He watched now as Brock stood motionless at the edge of the escarpment overseeing the battle now underway.

Nick quickly approached the general to inform him of the Indians arrival. Isaac Brock surveyed the scene below with satisfaction, as the thundering cannon successfully slowed the flow of the American reinforcements now desperately trying to cross the river. He had just ordered the light infantry company that occupied the crest above them down to the river bank to help the small force there keeping the enemy from coming ashore. Both Nick and Brock nodded a quick greeting to one another. Nick assured the general that his reinforcements were on the way, but had no time to speak further. At that precise moment a small American party who had silently scaled the cliff, gave a whooping cheer from above and immediately charged down upon them, muskets at the ready. Without hesitation, Brock ran to the cannon. He managed to hammer a ramrod into the touchhole and break it off, effectively spiking the weapon, rendering it useless for the time being.

Weapons were brandished on both sides, but musket balls showered down on the British from the crest higher up. The ground was becoming slippery from the steady drizzle, making it hard for Brock's men to hold their position as the American soldiers literally fell down on them during the attack. Nick's musket was suddenly knocked from his grasp. As he scrambled to find it, an American soldier took aim and fired. He immediately dived into the nearby bush cover, barely dodging the flying musket ball as it hit a branch overhead, splattering torn leaves everywhere. Nick realized that the odds had now changed in favour of the Americans. He watched in disbelief as General Brock grabbed Alfred's reins and followed his men in retreat down the steep escarpment to the village of Queenston below. The British had lost their stronghold of the heights with the capture of the cannon, Nick realized. Feeling defeated now, he plucked his musket from the mud and he too beat a hasty retreat. He descended the daunting cliff, following the same path that Brock had just taken.

Nick found General Brock at the far end of the village gathered with his men in a garden, preparing for a counter attack.

"Gentlemen," the general stated tersely. "Whoever controls the heights, controls Upper Canada. If the enemy takes the heights, they will dominate the Niagara River all the way to Fort Erie. Their possession of the heights along with this village will prove detrimental to our cause. Not only would it be difficult to remove the enemy from this vantage point, but they would also gain warm quarters for the winter, allowing them to build up and strengthen their army. In short gentlemen, if we lose the heights then all is lost." Nick decided to join Brock, some two hundred men from the 49th Regiment, and a scattering of militiamen, to retake the cannon on the redan. Some of his men were ordered to veer off in a flank position to attack the enemy on the left, but Nick remained with Brock.

"Push on boys! Push on!" the general cried out loudly to his company as he turned Alfred back towards the foot of the crest. He quickly dismounted, seeking cover behind a stone fence. "Muster your courage boys; I fear you shall need it," he stated. With adrenaline flowing, and spirits high and ready for battle, the men awarded the general a hearty cheer. Nick then followed Brock as he vaulted over the fence and with the general leading Alfred by the bridle, they quickly advanced up the escarpment once again. The rest of the company followed clumsily behind, slipping and stumbling on the wet, uneven ground, trying desperately to catch up to their esteemed leader. I will never forget this day, Nick thought, marvelling at the general, his sword raised high in the air, as he rallied his men for the final charge.

Isaac Brock's determination to regain the heights was apparent to all. In his exuberance, he rushed forward, undaunted even when a musket ball hit him in the hand. Above them, Nick noticed that their left flank had clashed with the Americans, drawing them immediately into a fight. The American captain ordered a charge, and the British were swarmed by the enemy, driven back once more, while shots from both musket and cannon were being volleyed down the side of the cliff in a steady assault. Nick felt his coat sleeve tear as a bullet ripped past him, scarcely missing his arm. A young soldier running alongside of him suddenly crumpled to the ground in a heap. Nick knelt down to determine the extent of the unfortunate soldier's injuries, dodging the cascading musket fire that surrounded him.

A musket ball whizzed noisily overhead, just inches from Nick's scalp. When he turned to see where it came from, he noticed an American soldier stepping out from behind the bushes, not thirty feet from General Brock. It was quite obvious that the enemy recognized Brock's scarlet tunic and large plumed hat, noting the general's rank. Before Nick could scream out a warning, the mysterious assailant drew a bead with his long border rifle and buried a bullet deep within Brock's chest. Nick watched in horror, realizing in an instant that the general was dead. He started crawling toward Brock's lifeless body, but in the next instant he faced another horrific and unbelievable sight. A cannonball had ripped through another unsuspecting British soldier, slicing him in two and his newly severed body slumped over, falling on top of General Brock. The British, at a loss now with the untimely death of their leader, retreated, dodging musket and cannon fire while gathering some of their wounded. They scrambled down the steep hill once again, this time carrying the lifeless body of their beloved general.

Nick did not retreat with the others, but veered off in a different direction, hoping to find the Native warriors. Brock's death was a blow to the British and their allies. All of his men were numb with grief and mourned his passing. Nick was devastated; he too mourned the loss of his friend, but he also thought they should pull together and win this battle for their general; Brock would have wanted them to. They just could not lose the heights! He made his way carefully up the side of the cliff, thinking that Norton and his Indians would be congregating behind the large clump of trees at the top. When Nick finally reached the crest of the escarpment unscathed, he pulled himself up, breathing a small sigh of relief. After spying the small woods just a few yards away to the right, he crept closer, trying to remain inconspicuous as he sought a better look.

The trees were clustered close together providing an excellent cover and Nick chose the largest one to hide behind. There was a small open clearing in the middle of the woods and he overheard angry voices coming from within, but there was no sign of the Indian allies. However, Nick was startled to discover Kevin Sullivan standing his ground in the centre of the glade, arguing with two American soldiers, and one of them was Carl Phillips! From his secret vantage point behind the tree, Nick watched the scene play out before him, experiencing feelings of both shock and disbelief.

"Carl, you are despicable! You fooled us all!" Kevin's face was now distorted in disgust.

"Kevin, please! Try and understand. This was not an easy decision for me, but it was really the only one I could make. Edward is my brother and I cannot possibly fight against him."

"You know, Carl, I was just thinking about a discussion that took place not long ago in our parlour, when you accused my father and I of questioning your loyalty. Do you remember that?" Kevin didn't allow Carl a response, his anger so intense now. He fixed Carl's brother, Edward, with a murderous glare before turning back to Carl. "With all we have been through together and after all my family has done for you! How can you even think of fighting against us? If this man is your brother, where was he for the past few years while you were living with us? Should you not feel any allegiance to me and my family?" Kevin hollered out in a rage.

"Enough!" Edward Phillips had heard enough. Unleashing his anger on Kevin, he ground out through clenched teeth. "Look Sullivan, he is my brother, not yours; blood being thicker and all that. He just borrowed your family for awhile, that is all. Besides," he added smugly, "I have always been able to talk my little brother here into doing whatever I wanted, and this is no different. True families must stand together," he chided with a sneer.

"It is all clear to me now," Kevin replied despondently. "That night when Captain Clarke came to collect us, you were acting strange and now I understand why! You had this planned even then. You sicken me Carl, and I am ashamed of you!"

"He is my brother; my family. I will stand with him!" Carl shouted.

"Was your life with us and our friendship just a lie?" Kevin completely lost his temper then, screaming obscenities and lashing out in hurt and anger, smashing Carl in the face with his fist. Carl, his dander up now too, retaliated by grabbing Kevin and throwing him hard to the ground, where they proceeded to wrestle much like they had done in the past, only this time it was not in fun.

Nick stared in disbelief. If he had not just lost a friend in the midst of battle, he might have found the situation amusing. He had never seen Kevin act like this before. He was just deciding whether to offer his assistance, when another of Kevin's punches deposited Carl in the mud, knocking him out cold.

Edward Phillips had watched with hate-filled eyes as the two young men attacked one another, scrambling around in the dirt, each getting licks in while showing no mercy. When his brother lay unconscious however, Edward came to Carl's immediate defence. His retaliation was swift. He turned angrily towards an unsuspecting Kevin and, using the butt end of his musket, delivered a hard blow just under his ribs. Kevin fell to the ground, the wind knocked out of him, gasping for air.

Edward then raised his loaded musket and aimed it at Kevin's head. Nick, who up to this point had been quietly observing the ruckus, sprang instantly from behind the trees, colliding savagely with a surprised Edward as he pushed the gun aside. The force of the impact toppled them both to the ground, where Nick proceeded to pound the

American in the face with both fists, rendering Edward unconscious. Kevin was lying defenceless at the edge of the clearing trying desperately to catch his breath, when Nick approached him. After ushering Kevin to his feet, he began enticing him to breathe normally, unaware of Captain Clarke, who quietly hovered only a few yards behind them.

Walter Clarke was leading his men away from the heights and feeling secretly elated at the death of General Brock when he noticed Nick Brannigan scaling the side of the escarpment, and decided to follow. He lost his footing on several occasions during his climb, but raw determination prodded him on and he was greatly relieved to reach the top. He too became aware of the angry voices and quickly headed for the nearby clump of trees. Clarke saw Nick leap to rescue the Sullivan boy. He also noticed the two American soldiers that lay unconscious in the dirt, and was astonished to discover that one of them was Carl Phillips; the Sullivan's handyman.

He smiled wickedly as a plan began to form in his mind. He had been waiting for an opportunity such as this. This is perfect, he thought, especially now that that tiresome Brock is dead. Oh, yes, my plan will come to fruition this day! Captain Clarke raised his musket and approached Carl Phillips with murderous intent. When Carl's eyes finally opened, he looked up in dumbfounded terror, seeing Clarke standing above him with his musket raised high. Realizing in an instant what was about to happen, he let out a spine-chilling scream.

Both Nick and Kevin were alerted then. They turned instantly towards the piercing cry and were traumatised as they watched Clarke bash poor Carl repeatedly in the head with his musket, silencing the young man forever. Kevin dropped to his knees, overcome with nausea, agonizing for the friend that Carl had once been. Nick turned away, shocked and disgusted by the unsavory British captain. Edward awoke. After witnessing Clarke's brutality to his brother, he gained his footing and darted towards the bushes, desperate to escape. In the next instant, however, Nick found that he was once again appalled by the loathsome Clarke, as he watched the captain quickly raise his weapon, this time firing a lead ball into Edward Phillip's retreating back; dropping him instantly. Nick hesitated a second, staring at the disturbing scene in front of him before rushing over to check on Kevin; neither of them noticing that Captain Walter Clarke was reloading his musket.

When Nick was satisfied that Kevin was fine, he helped him to his feet once more.

"He is going to kill us!" Kevin screamed at the top of his lungs.

Nick swung around, horrified at finding Walter Clarke's musket pointed directly at them. In a blind rush, he grabbed Kevin by the shoulders, and for the second time that day, he dived into the bushes to escape a musket ball. Kevin screamed out in pain as the bullet ripped into his leg, hitting him in the knee. Once again Nick's attention was momentarily drawn away from Clarke, who, seeing his opportunity, rushed over to him brandishing his raised weapon with the blade exposed. Walter Clarke, a knight of the realm, then thrust his bayonet sadistically into Nick's leg, backing off to run at him again, this time aiming for his chest. Nick bellowed in rage, yelling out in agony, willing himself to remain conscious. His mind was in torment as he desperately tried to think of what to do next. He did not want to die, not like this, not at this bastard's hands. He had always been unsure of his feelings regarding God and faith, but in that instant he found himself mumbling Kate's name and calling out for some divine intervention.

Walter Clarke stopped within inches of Nick. His menacing glare locked with Nick's hate-filled eyes. His mood changed instantly then, and his face relaxed. "No! I will not kill you. You see, Mr. Brannigan," he stated almost pleasantly, "I have a much better punishment in mind for you. Killing you now would be the easy way out, and we must not have that. No no. We must not have that. You see," he added, running his swollen tongue over his lips while rubbing the tip of his bayonet across Nick's heaving chest. "I want you to suffer, and believe me, suffer you will; I promise." The deranged captain then threw back his head and laughed triumphantly towards the sky.

Nick glanced around for any sign of Kevin, but after calling out to him, he heard nothing above Clarke's evil laughter ringing in his ears. "I will see you in hell, you bastard!" he rasped, feeling helpless and alone. Nick watched in a dream-like state as two young soldiers loomed above him. He felt himself being lifted and his body craved an escape from the intense pain. His leg had been ripped wide open, his bone exposed now amidst a pool of blood. He closed his eyes and drifted down into the cradling arms of an advancing darkness. Captain Clarke ordered his men to carry Nick's unconscious body back to Fort George.

Kevin Sullivan, who now lay silent, was forgotten in the bushes at Queenston Heights.

Chapter Eleven

In the late afternoon of October 13th 1812, the battle of Queenston Heights was over. The British had taken over nine hundred prisoners and their casualties were light; fourteen killed and seventy-seven wounded. General Sir Roger Hale Sheaffe, who had taken command after the fall of Brock, initiated a final charge that, although not as gallant as Brock's, was successful. The British had regained the heights. Not wishing to attempt another frontal attack, Sheaffe decided to approach the Americans through the cover of trees. Using the Indians as a screen, he and his men waited for the anticipated reinforcements that Brock had summoned earlier, and then proceeded to batter the enemy. The Americans surrendered to the British after losing approximately two hundred and fifty soldiers, but in retrospect, the British deemed their losses greater with the unfortunate death of Major-General Isaac Brock.

When the guns had finally fallen silent, the Niagara frontier breathed a small sigh of relief as it slowly came to life again. Most of the women stared longingly towards the heights, watching for their sons, brothers and husbands to appear. Squeals of delight mixed with anguished cries as the battered men returned to their homes. Laura gathered her family together, thanking her friends for their hospitality, but she longed to be back at her own farm to meet her returning husband. Before she left however, a passing soldier in the Lincoln Militia informed her that James had been mortally wounded during the battle, and Laura quickly decided to go in search of him without a moment's delay. Could she come back for the children later?

Thomas gave his hurried consent regarding the children, but he immediately balked at the idea of her heading out to parts unknown by herself, declaring it to be unsafe. If she was so determined to do this crazy thing, then he would have no other recourse but to accompany her.

Hannah, however, would not hear of it and had put her foot down in a blatant refusal. "You are too sick," she lamented with concern. "You will surely perish in the damp night air."

Thomas continued to argue, but Laura too voiced her objections and politely declined his offer, saying that she would never forgive herself if he were to collapse while helping her. Laura Secord was a pretty woman, with a fair complexion, dark hair and a kind face. People were quite often misled by her slender frame and delicate appearance, thinking her frail and timid, not realizing that she possessed great strength and determination.

Kate was also at a loss, unsure now of what she should do regarding Nick and Kevin. No one knew what had become of them. She was just as determined as Laura to search the heights at Queenston and bring them home too. Her ill-timed announcement however, only proved to rile her father's already ignited temper.

"I will not have ya' doin' such a foolhardy thing, me girl! I forbid it!" Thomas Sullivan stated, hearing her intentions. "I want me boy home just as much as you do, but I will not be havin' ya' traipsin' all over that blasted battleground and maybe gettin' yourself hurt or even killed in the bargain! This one, I have no say in," he blurted out pointing to Laura. "But I sure will have me say regardin' me own daughter."

"Your father is right, Kate. Surely you can see that? It would be ludicrous for you to attempt such a thing," Hannah added anxiously. Kate regarded them for an instant, praying for their understanding, but her mind was set, and no amount of pleading could sway her decision.

"I realize that this may indeed be foolish, but please Father, Hannah, I must go," Kate pleaded. "I need to find out what has happened to Nick and Kevin. Laura is going in search of James and you do not want her out there all alone, do you? I am sorry to disappoint you, Father, but I am quite determined in this matter." When she noticed the anger and fear mirrored on their faces, Kate sighed in defeat. Shaking her head sadly, she embraced them both. After wiping away her tears and quickly grabbing her cloak, she rushed out into the late afternoon to accompany Laura to Queenston Heights.

The two women stood at the crest of the escarpment transfixed for a moment, as their eyes wandered aimlessly over the disturbing sights before them on the battlefield; bodies were strewn everywhere they looked. Kate heard Laura calling out to James as she began her search for him among the dead soldiers. Since there appeared to be more American uniforms than British, Laura hoped her task would be that much easier. Upon first arriving, Kate and Laura had formed a plan that would allow them to cover the most ground in the shortest amount of time. Splitting the area in two, they would each search one side, eventually meeting in the middle of the field.

Kate immediately began scanning the area for any sign of the men folk. Some of the unfortunate soldiers that she came across were wounded beyond recognition, with dried, dirty blood covering their now still bodies. Others lay prostrate in the dirt as if in sleep, their wounds unseen. As she hastily searched the faces, Kate recognized the limp body of Johnny Thornston, once so vigorously alive, now laying silently at her feet, and she cried out at the loss of a friend. He had tried to steal a kiss from her not so long ago, she recalled, and she had refused. She now regretted that missed kiss; for his sake.

Once again she thought of the recurring nightmare, and violently shaking her head, she pushed it instantly to the back of her mind. Kate did not want to imagine the worst as she trekked solemnly through the sea of dead bodies, sickened by the sight. Such a waste, she thought, as she continued across the littered field.

"Oh, I wish I was strong and brave like Laura. Please God, let them be safe; all of them." Kate hoped she could exhibit the same determination that Laura displayed in abundance, as she diligently searched for Nick and Kevin.

A few minutes later Kate swung around abruptly, hearing Laura's cry of alarm from the far side of the field. As she drew closer, she witnessed her friend throwing herself over James, who lay wounded on the ground. In the next instant Kate experienced raw panic. After a sharp intake of breath, she watched in horror for what seemed like an eternity, as two American soldiers, muskets aimed and ready to fire, stood threateningly over James and Laura Secord. Kate stood motionless, paralyzed to to the spot, as she watched Laura stubbornly shielding her injured husband, refusing to move out of harm's way, even at his shaky plea.

Queenston Heights appeared to be abandoned by the British now, and Laura stared openly into the eyes of the two enemy soldiers, defying them to shoot and wondering at the same time if she would die here this day with her husband. Then an order was suddenly issued from behind the two soldiers and they lowered their weapons.

Kate hadn't realized that she was holding her breath until she expelled it in one long whoosh, and then she immediately crossed the short distance to join her friends.

Captain Wool, the same officer who had lead his men up the escarpment earlier that day to capture the British cannon, introduced himself as he looked speculatively at Laura and Kate, apologizing for the actions of his two men.

"We do not make war on women. I assure you ladies that these two will be dealt with appropriately," the captain stated, eyeing each of the young soldiers with disdain.

Laura, now regarding James with concern, bravely sprang into action."Captain Wool, my husband has a musket ball in his shoulder and another has shattered his knee. I will require assistance in getting him home," she declared in a no nonsense tone.

"Of course. You two, bring a horse and help the sergeant onto it," Captain Wool barked. When an unusual amount of time had elapsed and the young men had not yet returned, the captain cursed under his breath, excusing himself to search them out. A short time later Kate and Laura heard two shots fired, and Captain Wool had come back alone with a horse in tow, offering no explanation.

"Thank you for your kindness, sir," Laura stated, after James was secured safely onto the horse's back.

"Travel with caution ladies; the ride could prove detrimental to your husband's welfare. Take it easy, else the jolting may cause him to bleed to death."

"May God see you safely home," Laura replied.

Captain Wool then bowed politely to both women and walking briskly he left them, heading in the direction of the Niagara River.

"Please Kate! I cannot possibly leave you here all alone," Laura cried a few minutes later upon hearing Kate's intent to remain to continue her search.

"I have to find Kevin and Nick, Laura, or at least try. Do not fret over me. You need to get James home now; you cannot wait for me. Go Laura, I will be fine," Kate insisted, demonstrating a braveness that she didn't feel. Wrapping herself in her cloak and, after taking a water pouch from Laura, she returned to the edge of the heights to resume her search for the three missing men.

"I will send someone after you," Laura promised fretfully, as she had no other choice but to lead the horse homewards.

As Kate began to descend the escarpment, she was once again plagued by more disturbing sights. Among the lifeless bodies that littered the side of the cliff, she recognized a few friends and neighbours, now just bloody heaps lying in the dirt. She swallowed the lump of fear that rose in her throat, and as she shouted Nick and Kevin's name, her mind screamed at her to hurry. The journey was treacherous however, and as she travelled down the steep hill, acutely aware of how dark it would be soon, her foot slid in the loose dirt. She tumbled downward for a short distance, landing close to the spot where Brock himself had fallen earlier. She picked herself up and continued on, only to trip over a limp body a few minutes later. She cried out in alarm when she recognized Private Matthew Dunsford lying unmoving in the mud. She gazed down at him with compassion, thinking of Molly Hogan. Shamefully, Kate recalled the sarcastic and unfeeling words she had expressed to her friend not long ago: how Molly would meet and fall in love with a soldier at the ball only to have him die in the war. I have to try and comfort him, she thought, for Molly's sake.

"I will try to find something to cover you with if I can," she cooed tenderly.

"Help me," the lethargic young soldier rasped, raising a shaky hand to Kate.

"Matthew? Matthew, where are you hurt?" she exclaimed, her face flooded with relief. After all the dead bodies that lay at her feet this day, she was happy to finally find someone alive. She gave him some water from her pouch and quickly examined him, puzzled at finding no evidence of any blood or injury. She gently inquired again. "Please, tell me, sir, where are you hurt?"

"My back," he whispered. Private Dunsford was too weak to continue and lost consciousness.

Kate immediately checked his breathing. After placing her rolled up cloak under his head for comfort, she set off again to resume her search. Although he could not hear her, she promised to return. She stood up stiffly, her aching muscles already starting to burn. She quickly surveyed the area trying to decide where to look next. As her gaze wandered to the top of the heights she squinted for a moment as her eyes caught a flicker of movement at the top of the cliff, near the crest of the escarpment. Kate began to scramble up the steep hill again, her climb proving just as inglorious as the soldiers' descent had been earlier in the day. When she finally reached the top however, she was disappointed. No one was there! She then noticed a small wooded area just a short distance away and devoid now of any rational thought, she headed straight for it.

Kate Sullivan pushed her way through the clump of trees. Finding herself in the middle of a clearing, she stopped short in alarm. There, lying still and quiet in the dirt, were two slain American soldiers. She approached them cautiously, swallowing the nausea that engulfed her throat, all the while fighting a strong desire to turn away from the revolting sight. Kate shuddered deeply, immediately aware of the one lying on his back with his head bashed to a bloody pulp. She had no way of knowing that the faceless soldier was Carl Phillips. The other American was slumped over him with a trail of blood running behind, as though he crawled there before dying. Kate also noticed the musket wound in his back and this time she did turn away.

The gruesome sight was the last straw. "I hate this war!" Glaring at the two silent bodies, she screamed out in anguish. "This is your fault! You Americans wanted this war, so you only have yourselves to blame!" Kate sank to her knees then crying, sobbing and praying all at the same time. "Please, God, do not let me find Nick and Kevin like this, I beg you! Nick!" Her shriek pierced the air, and she continued loudly. "Kevin! Carl! Where are you? Answer me, please!" Kate lay face down on the cold, hard ground now, sobbing until her throat was hoarse, her hands balled into fists as she savagely struck the earth. So much death! So much horror and degradation! "Oh, God! This is just the beginning of the hostility. What is to become of us? When was it all going to end?"

Rising to her knees, she lifted her tear-filled eyes towards heaven, pleading to the unknown entity beyond the clouds. "Please, help me to be strong, Lord. I am so terrified of the weakness that now consumes me, body and soul, and fear I am in great danger of losing my mind. The temperature suddenly turned colder and Kate noticed that it was almost dark. A dampness clung in the air now and she watched with trepidation as a heavy mist rolled silently up the escarpment towards her. She shivered uncontrollably, her short jacket no longer offering any protection. I have to get out of here, she thought, hastily rising to her feet.

"I will not leave this field alone," she vowed, carefully climbing back down the steep ridge to retrieve Private Dunsford. Kate stopped suddenly, watching in alarm as the fog surrounded her. She stood paralyzed for a moment, seized in its clammy, vaporous grasp. "Just like my dream," she moaned. "Nick! Kevin! Carl, Matthew! Where are you? Oh, God, please do not let my nightmare come true." She looked down then, just like she did in her dream, expecting to see the dead body of her brother lying at her feet, and waited for that all too familiar loud drumming sound that would bring Nick crawling out of the fog. All was quiet though, and nothing lay at her feet or moved in or out of the mist. Kate gave in to her tears once more as she stood in the desolate surroundings, lamenting at her failure to find the men. A strained, pleading voice reached out to her through the thickening cloud, and she paused a moment to listen, recognizing Private Dunsford's muffled cries. "I am coming, sir. I will see that you get back to the fort," she hollered, wiping the wetness from her cheek. Having something to occupy her mind now, she pressed on, not only through the fog, but through her fear as well.

Kate had just knelt down to offer some comfort to Matthew, when a low, persistent drumming sound advanced towards them from the mist, growing louder as it approached. She sat frozen to the spot, her fear returning. She squeezed her eyes shut, not wanting to see the evil that was about to swoop down on them. The drumming stopped. Kate kept her eyes clenched and her body tense, holding her breath for the duration.

"Are you quite all right miss?" the friendly voice inquired.

Kate's eyes flew open in a flash and she laughed uncontrollably, almost hysterically, at the sight of a young British drummer boy who gazed innocently down at her with a bewildered expression on his young face. When she didn't reply right away, he questioned her again.

"May I help you miss?"

Kate found her voice then and felt relief flooding through her. Someone else was with her; she was not alone. Even though the boy was younger, probably no more than fourteen, he was an extremely welcome sight.

"Thank you, Lord," she whispered, smiling to herself. "Please, he has injured his back and I need to get him to Fort George," Kate pleaded in desperation.

With a quick nod, the young drummer disappeared in the mist, returning sometime later with a large piece of board, a lantern and some blankets. Depositing them all on the ground near Private Dunsford, he then turned to Kate.

"The wagon I found was of no use to us miss, but I am sure we can use this piece of it to drag the soldier home."

Between the two of them, they covered the rough-hewn board with one of the dirty blankets and carefully laid the private on top before covering him with the other. The young boy then stripped the rope from his drum and secured Matthew to the plank, assuring himself that, in this instance, the army would not mind him desecrating their property.

"Please, what is your name?" Kate asked. "Mine is Kate Sullivan."

"David Crawford at your service, miss," he replied, bowing slightly.

Kate could not help but chuckle softly at the boy's courteous display of manners. Even during such desolate times as these, the British were all politeness, she thought.

"Well, Master Crawford, I do thank you for your assistance in this matter," she said, grabbing her soiled cloak from the ground and wrapping it snugly around her cold body. "I simply do not know what I would have done had you not come by when you did."

David blushed slightly. Turning abruptly, he went to the makeshift stretcher with the pretence of checking the tightness of the already secured knots in the rope. "It is too dark now, miss. I will light the lantern and then I think we should be on our way. It is quite a trek up this hill and a long walk to the fort."

"David, one thing still puzzles me. Why were you beating your drum so persistently when you found me?"

"I was searching for my brother among the wounded. You see, Miss Sullivan, we had an arrangement before the battle that if he were lying injured somewhere, he was to listen for the sound of my drum."

"What if you had been killed?" Kate inquired, slightly bemused.

"Then miss, my brother would have known by my silence."

"You did not find him then?"

"No miss, I did not find him," David muttered, lowering his head and shaking it sadly. Sniffing loudly, he raised the top end of the stretcher and pulled it forward.

"I did not find my brother either," she replied with a dismal sigh, walking slowly beside the boy and helping him as he dragged the injured private back up the steep escarpment.

Nick Brannigan opened his eyes to dimly lit surroundings. Everything was blurry, and he frowned deeply as the room reeled about him. He heard faint voices, but they seemed far off. Weak and exhausted, he strained to sit up, but collapsed back onto the bunk, feeling drained and shaken. He was thirsty, the dryness of his mouth made it difficult for him to speak. He was hot! The heat was so unbearable that he felt as though he was being consumed by fire. A long, black, never ending tunnel appeared before him and he clung to the bed as he felt himself slipping slowly into it, and the dim light of the room vanished.

As Nick lay in a delirium on his bunk, he felt a gentle, cool touch on his brow. Opening his eyes, he smiled at the woman sitting by his bed. It was his mother! She had found him. He had cried out to her as she stroked him gently, cooing softly to him while coaxing him to drink.

"*Come Nicholas; finish this broth like a good little boy.*" A warm liquid trickled down his throat then and he winced, pushing the cup away.

"I cannot Mother. It hurts too much to swallow." His mother smiled down at him before she floated away in a fog, replaced suddenly by another vision, that of a drunken man with cold eyes and a mirthless sneer. "Where is my mother? What have you done with her? I remember, they dragged her away! Why did she not come home?"

"*Your dear mother refused to follow the rules boy; she wanted to become one of them. I could not let that happen. You understand?*"

"Mother!! How could you do that to her? I hate you, you bastard!! I never want to see you again! You are dead to me! You hear me old man!!" Nick screamed in torment, thrashing from side to side on his bed, the fever causing him to slip in and out of delirium.

"Please Nick, you must drink this. It is just a little broth I made for you. The doctor says you need the nourishment to get well." Kate managed to get another small amount of the liquid down his throat before he commenced his thrashing again, as the man with the cold eyes returned.

"*Think of where your loyalties lay, boy. You are my son, remember?*"

"How dare you send that man to entice me back, Father. How can you think I would have anything to do with you after what you did to my mother?"

"*Then if you will not come back with me, maybe your sister will.*"

"You leave Ellen alone or I will kill you!" Nick cried out in panic as the vision silently faded away again. Even in his semi-conscious state, he was aware of the intense heat burning his body and he rolled and tossed on the bunk, trying to escape it. A moment later he moaned in delight as something cool slid over him, gently dousing the burning fire.

"Swallow this Nick. Please?" The honeyed voice of an angel penetrated through his delirium and when he opened his eyes he saw his Katie, holding a cup to his dry lips and coaxing him to drink. "Just take a little Nick, then I can cool you off again with the wet cloth."

"Is he any better Miss Sullivan?" Kate turned abruptly at the grating sound of Captain Clarke's voice, noticing with disdain that his face was devoid of any concern.

Nick had heard him too, and in his crazed state, the sound drove him wild on his bunk. After Kate calmed him, Nick thought of Kevin. I have to let her know about her brother. "Kevin," he called weakly. He had to say more but all the thrashing and yelling had proved too exhausting and once more the fight left him. "Katie, I am sorry about Kevin," he whimpered, reaching out for her before falling down into the black hole once again.

"Captain Clarke, what did he mean? Do you know what has become of my brother Kevin?"

"In good time my dear, all in good time. I am attending a meeting with General Sheaffe tomorrow to which you will most certainly be invited. All will be disclosed then, I assure you. I am confident that you will find it a very informative assemblage. In the meantime however, your duty is to make this traitor well enough to stand trial."

Walter Clarke turned to leave then and Kate stared open-mouthed at his retreating form, wondering at his pompous accusation regarding Nick, and missing the look of glorious victory that had lit up his ugly features.

Sometime later Nick regained consciousness. Opening his eyes, he lay unmoving for a moment. He was stiff and sore, but his head was clear now. His fever had broken, but he was unsure of where he was. I do not even know what day it is, he thought. How long had he been here? Where was Kate? Nick was still experiencing some difficulty deciphering what was real from what he had imagined in his feverish state. Had Kate really been here? He looked quickly around trying to ascertain where he was and discovered that he was lying on his bunk in the blockhouse, which for the time being seemed to be filled with injured and dying men. It must be a makeshift hospital, he concluded, surveying his dim surroundings.

The old stove that stood in the centre of the room was stoked now, and heated pots and steaming kettles sat on top. Nick also noticed the wooden hanging racks that stood in the far corner, where sterilized bandages hung to dry. All around him he could hear the ramblings of other soldiers, some quite noticeably out of their heads, while others were dictating letters to other soldiers' wives, acting as nurses, with the hopes that their messages would reach their loved ones. Some wounds were fatal, with soldiers crying out in agony, while others just whimpered quietly in their pain.

He remembered then the wound that he had sustained at the hands of Walter Clarke, and he tried to move his right leg, only to cry out at the stabbing pain that travelled from just above his knee to his groin. Nick gently rubbed the bandaged area, cursing violently as he recalled the horror that took place on the heights. He thought of their glorious charge up the hill, only to be followed by their inglorious defeat, ending with Brock's death. He shook his head sadly, thinking of the loss not only of his commander, but his friend. Nick could not understand why, in the great scheme of things, a great man like Isaac Brock, who was a much valued officer and a hell of a man, should die, while a detestable, evil blackguard like Walter Clarke, good for nothing at all and serving no purpose, should be permitted to live.

His fear of Clarke was just as strong as his hatred for him. Nick had always known the man was evil, but now, in his weakened condition, he felt helpless against him. He suddenly thought of Kevin, and wondered if he also had been brought here by Clarke. I need to get word to Thomas, he thought. But how? Another disturbing thought struck Nick and he cursed once more. If Kate really had been here, then she was sure to be at the mercy of Walter Clarke too. Damn my blasted luck. Oh, Katie. Where are you? I need you here with me now. I need to know that you are safe."

Major-General Isaac Brock was buried on October 16th 1812. After the battle of Queenston Heights had concluded, the general's lifeless body was taken to the Government House in Newark and made ready for burial, a bereaved Sophia Shaw at his side. On the day of the funeral the procession left the Government House, following a route to Fort George, where he would be laid to rest. Captain John Glegg, who had served with Brock for many years, had requested the bastion at the front left corner of the fort to be Brock's grave site. Captain Glegg explained that this area was the most strategic artillery battery in the fort, and therefore, the most appropriate final resting place for their beloved general and friend.

Kate accompanied Sophia and the Powell family to the funeral, offering her comfort without uttering a word. There is nothing that I can say to my dear Sophia at this time to make her feel better, so it is best to remain silent, she decided. Many people attended the ceremony, too many to count, and all seemed greatly distressed, some lamenting loudly while others just shook their heads in sadness and disbelief. Kate realized then how these people, herself included, had come to rely on this man to send the Americans home, and to put this terrible war behind them. She understood now how everyone here felt, most grieving for a man that they had never even met, and some had never even seen. They were mourning the loss of more than just a great man; they grieved for the loss that his death would certainly bring to Upper Canada.

Kate had sent a message to her father informing him of all that had happened since she had last seen him, and wondered if he and Hannah had come. Was Laura here too? Kate quickly searched the throng of people that gathered near her, surmising that it would be impossible to find anyone in such a crowd unless they were standing close by.

The procession slowly made its way to the fort with the remainder of the British army, the Militia and various Indian tribes lining each side of the travel route. Brock's trusted horse Alfred, dressed out in a full military attire of his own, and led by four grooms, preceded his master's coffin as the procession marched on. When they arrived at Fort George, Isaac Brock was buried in his appointed grave while the British fired a twenty-one gun salute in a gesture of respect. Across the river at Fort Niagara, the American garrison respectfully fired a similar salute. This war had already claimed the lives of so many men, but this death seemed more disastrous and unforgiveable. Kate lost control and finally gave into the sudden tidal wave of emotions that washed through her and she and Sophia clung to each other, both crying bitterly. Through her tears, Kate thought of Kevin and Carl, still missing, and of Nick, who lay wounded and close to death in the blockhouse nearby. There were other families too who had already lost so much. Kate ached for them all.

A melancholy mood prevailed at Fort George and throughout the Niagara region. Captain John Glegg had later informed Sophia Shaw that over five thousand people had attended General Brock's funeral.

Chapter Twelve

The following morning was cold and blustery, the wind playing havoc with everything that was not tied down, leaving the undefended fort at its mercy. Kate Sullivan shivered uncontrollably as she entered the private headquarters of General Sheaffe, accompanied by Captain Glegg, who at the moment was still mourning the loss of Isaac Brock, his mood somber. She had remained at Fort George at the present general's request, as her assistance was still required in caring for the injured. It was also her hope that Kevin might return to the fort. She knew that Nick was in a very bad way, causing her much alarm, but as yet, she did not understand the full extent of the trouble he was in. Captain Clarke had seemed rather evasive in regards to Kevin when he informed her of this meeting. This piqued her curiosity as well as her fear.

"Please, come in my dear and take a seat." General Sheaffe bowed to her as she entered the room, indicating a chair on the opposite side of his desk, which Captain Glegg graciously held out for her. When seated, Kate glanced around the small group. Her eyes fell on Captain Clarke, who stood arrogantly in the corner. She stared openly at each man in turn, looking bewildered and uncertain, and she shivered slightly as that old feeling of dread crept through her once again. The general offered Kate a cup of tea, which she politely declined, and the meeting commenced.

"Now then, it has been brought to my attention, Miss Sullivan, that you have been inquiring after your brother who seems to be missing;

one Private Kevin Sullivan. Have I been informed correctly?" General Sheaffe raised a questioning eyebrow to Kate. At her brisk affirmation, he continued. "Miss Sullivan, Captain Glegg has provided me with the information that you are seeking and I am now able to enlighten you, however alarming it may be."

Kate swallowed hard, trying to squash the fear that was quickly rising in her throat, as she squirmed uncomfortably in her chair. "Please sir, what has become of Kevin?" she whispered, her tear-filled eyes fixed intently on the general.

"I am sorry my dear, but your brother was murdered during the battle at Queenston Heights. I say murdered, because he was deliberately killed by a traitor."

"No!!" Kate buried her head in her hands shaking and crying in anguish, as though her heart would break. "Kevin! Oh, Kevin! You promised you would come home safe! You promised!"

General Sheaffe was growing impatient now; he had more pressing matters to attend to and he wanted this business to be concluded immediately. He had no time for the silly emotions of females when he should be rallying his men together. He knew all too well that it would not be easy to replace the deceased Brock, but he was determined to win their loyalty. He had to admit that he was uncomfortable with the way they all still seemed to idolize their dead commander. He was just a man, for heaven sake! In his hurry to have this whole tiresome matter behind him, the general's speech was clipped and to the point. His annoyance with her grief plainly showed. General Sheaffe missed the darting glance of disapproval from Captain Glegg and continued on with his gruesome report.

"Miss Sullivan, unfortunately there is more to tell, and at its conclusion, an escort will see you home where this dreadful news may be divulged to your family. But for now," he added in a slightly demanding tone, "you must pull yourself together and accept this distressing situation with bravery. Terrible things happen in war miss, and yours is not the only loss, I assure you."

Kate blew her nose and dried her eyes, trying desperately to concentrate on what the general was saying over the loud drumming in her head and the deep aching in her chest. I cannot bear this, she thought wildly. How can he be so cold and callous? Kate did bear it however, but not well.

A little while later Kate sat quietly in a wagon as a kindly old soldier clucked to the horses, coaxing them slowly through the gates of Fort George. She was on her way home, a place of refuge when she was tired, despondent or frightened. Tonight there would be no peace and comfort awaiting her. After everything that has happened to me in the past few days, she thought dismally, I feel drained and exhausted. There was just no way to soften the blow to her loved ones. Even though she had been gone for awhile, she was not looking forward to facing her father and Hannah this night. "Lord," she prayed quietly. "Please let me find the strength to deliver this horrible news."

The hour was quite late and Kate lay motionless in her bed gazing quietly at the bright moon that was peeking through the open curtains of her bedroom window. The night was calm now. The terrible rain storm that had accompanied her home had finally ceased. The dismal weather matched the mood of both her and her family perfectly, and they had all cried so much that they had no more tears left to shed. It was with swollen eyes and a dry throat that she now felt the storm brewing within her heart. Her jumbled emotions were raw and painful. Her dear, sweet, loveable Kevin! How could they go on without him? Earlier this evening, when she had broken the dire news to Hannah and her father, they had both crumpled pathetically together, clinging to each other while they cried. She had hated to hurt them further, but she had no choice. They deserved to know the truth and she held nothing back.

Repeating General Sheaffe's words, she told them of how Nick was a traitor, and that the British captain who had brought him back to the fort did not kill him when he had the chance, because he wanted Nick to pay for what he had done. Kate told her father and Hannah how Nick had fooled them all; even poor General Brock had trusted him. Kate had also repeated the general's words:

'A man's entire personality and behaviour could suddenly and drastically change during battle, sometimes leaving a stranger in his place. You would be surprised, Miss Sullivan, what a man is liable to do when he succumbs to his fear. I have men awaiting execution at this moment for that very thing. They ran from battle you understand.'

When her father and Hannah had both sadly questioned her about the validity of the horrible, yet unbelievable story, she stated plainly that, since it was the general himself who had delivered the news, how could it be doubted? And even if she were to have doubts, she argued, the very fact that she had overheard Nick uttering Kevin's name and then deliriously apologizing for some wrong done to him, should more than prove the case.

"No," she had admitted to her father. "It must be true."

Lying alone in her bed now, she ached for her father. He had lost his son. She recalled his mumblings when she had first told him this evening. He kept repeating that it was not right for a child to die before his da'. We will never recover from this, she thought and at that moment she felt her heart harden. She finally drifted off to sleep, hating the war and hating Nick Brannigan.

The next morning the sun shone brightly overhead in complete contrast to the dark, sour mood that encompassed the Sullivan household. During breakfast, Thomas kept shaking his head and mumbling repeatedly to himself that something was wrong. He did not understand why Nick would want to harm Kevin. It just didn't make any sense. Hannah had asked Kate if there was any news regarding Carl. She sadly replied that there was not, feeling guilty for her easy dismissal of him during her search for Kevin and Nick. Poor Carl! She promised to make some inquiries when she returned to the fort.

Kate welcomed the chance to leave, feeling ashamed of her thoughts. If she were to stay here, she would only succumb to the tragedy that haunted them all. She feared that her mind would truly be lost. She desperately needed something to do! Kate was confident that Hannah would take care of her bereaving father, so the next morning she bid them a tearful farewell. She left with a heaviness in her heart and an uneasiness in her mind, saying that she hoped to see them soon, and promising to make a quick stop at the Secord farm.

Mary Secord answered Kate's impatient knocking and immediately led her upstairs where Laura was nursing an immobile, but slightly improved James. They too were devastated by the terrible news regarding Kevin, Mary especially, who cried torrents of tears in Kate's arms. When it came to the telling of Nick's treason and his hand in Kevin's demise however, James shook his head in blatant denial, saying that although he had only known Mr. Brannigan for a short time, he refused to believe him capable of such a vile and traitorous thing. Kate thought that it was easy for Mr. Secord to believe in Nick's innocence, as it was not his brother that was killed.

When Kate was leaving Laura followed her out, seeking a chance for a private conversation. "I must tell you Kate dear, I am so relieved, as we all are, that you have returned safely from the heights. I sent the young Collin's boy after you, but you had already gone. We were deeply concerned," Laura added, hugging her close. "Listen to your heart my girl, and hear what Nick has to say. Please, do not let your overwhelming remorse over the loss of your brother cloud your already confused judgement. Remember, if you ever need us, we will be right here." Laura's smile was tinged with sadness. She watched her young friend's departure, feeling helpless. She has been through so much, Laura decided; I will not burden her with anymore unpleasantness.

What Laura refrained from telling Kate was that when she returned home from Queenston Heights with James, her lovely home had been ransacked by a vengeful group of American soldiers. Laura had been so thankful that the house was empty during the assault. Luckily, the children were still at the Sullivan's farm, so no one was hurt. The band of miscreants had broken some furniture and stolen some food, despoiling their home and leaving it in shambles. Shaking her head sadly then, she turned to enter the house, and without knowing why, Laura suddenly felt the misery of all Upper Canada descending heavily upon her small shoulders.

When Kate arrived at the blockhouse, the first person she checked on was Private Dunsford, avoiding Nick for now, although she was very aware of his presence.

"I see you are being well taken care of," she said, observing Molly Hogan dabbing a cool cloth over the private's hot forehead. Just as I did for Nick only a few short days ago, she thought miserably.

"Oh, Kate, thank you so much for bringing him back to me," Molly cried, turning with a smile when she heard her friend's voice. Rising from her chair she gave Kate a hug. "Matthew thanks you too," she added.

"It warms my heart to discover you considerably much improved, private. I was so relieved to finally find someone still alive on that field. I am glad it was you." Suddenly Kate's thoughts were jumbled. She silently berated herself. Tell the truth, she chided, you know you would much rather have found Kevin. I could have saved them both, she thought adamantly. A woman beckoned to Kate then, appealing for her assistance at the far corner of the large room. "Take care," she whispered softly to the bedridden private, lightly touching his shoulder and offering a parting nod to both him and Molly. "I will come back later if I can." Uttering a small sigh, Kate walked steadily in the direction of the summons, realizing that she was nearing Nick's bunk. Deciding to ignore him, she kept her face void of any feeling when she passed by.

Molly Hogan watched her friend's departure with grave concern, noticing how despondent her friend had become, and how Kate seemed to have aged since the night of the ball.

Nick lay in pain. Staring up at the ceiling and deep in thought, he wondered what had become of Dr. Ramsey. There had been no one to tend to his needs recently, and he was quite concerned. Where was Kate? He calculated in his mind that it must be about five days since he had last seen her. The pain in his leg was throbbing intensely now, so he called out impatiently for the doctor with the hope of getting something to ease his discomfort. He could see the doctor, but the man seemed to take no notice of him. Nick had the distinct feeling that he was being ignored. Come to think of it, he thought, no one has spoken to me for three days. Twisting himself painfully around and rising up on one elbow, Nick hollered as loud as he could in his weakened state.

"What is going on here? Can you hear me, Doctor?" After his sarcastic outbreak, Nick dropped back down heavily onto his soiled mattress feeling spent and forsaken. Receiving no immediate answer, he searched the room once again. This time he noticed the doctor approaching him, a daunting scowl marring his usually pleasant face.

"You just lay there and keep quiet, you traitor; you are disturbing the other men. No one wants to listen to you. I will come to you when I see fit. Do not, I repeat, do not call for me again! My orders are to keep you alive for your hanging; that is all!" Doctor Ramsey spat out each word in contempt, eyeing Nick as if he were the scum of the earth. "Thank the Lord that you will not be in my company much longer, but while you are, I will tell you once and for all, stop your belligerent hollering! No one here will waste their time seeing to your comforts!" The doctor stomped off in a huff, leaving Nick to stare after him in bewilderment.

He recalled how cordial and genuinely concerned Doc Ramsey seemed, and everyone else for that matter, just after he was brought here. His wounds were dressed quite frequently and he was given laudanum for the severe pain. Nick was lost in a state of confusion with this drastic turn of events. What happened? Where is Kate? He needed her now more than ever. Did the doctor call me a traitor? He turned his head from side to side on his pillow, perspiring heavily, sickened by his own odour as he gently rubbed the stained bandage that was now sticking to the nasty gash in his leg.

Sometime later Nick became aware of Kate's presence when she entered the building. He silently watched her through bleary, unwavering eyes as she stopped at Private Dunsford's bunk. Why is she not coming to see me? he wondered. Nick followed her every move and he was gravely concerned with what he saw. Kate seems different, he thought. He noted how tired and broken she appeared and his anger and frustration dissipated. He was suddenly reminded of a horse he had rescued once when he was a young boy. The owner had worked the poor animal from sunup to sundown, feeding it only enough to keep it alive, and beating it severely when it could no longer work. Dear God! Something terrible has happened to her.

Nick heard a woman's voice from somewhere behind him, beckoning for Kate. She responded immediately, passing him by without a glance. He reached out to her, but she ignored him. The light has gone from her eyes; there is a heavy sadness in them now, he thought disquietly. What is the matter Katie? Has Walter Clarke gotten to you? He thought of Kevin again. The memory of what happened at the heights haunted him still and he needed to speak to Kate about her brother; but would she listen? For the remainder of the day, Nick noticed that Kate busied herself with the other patients, continuing to keep her distance from him. His thoughts remained in a turmoil. He had wanted desperately to call out to her, but his pride and the stone look on her face stopped him. Finally, he had lost consciousness, once more gaining a temporary relief from the pain. When he awoke it was late, and his Katie had gone.

The following morning four soldiers, two of them armed, entered the blockhouse and directly approached Nick's bunk. He watched with uncertainty as they spread a canvas stretcher on the floor beside his bed. His agony was relentless as they lowered him roughly onto it, causing Nick to scream out in sudden anguish at the unsympathetic ears all around him.

"Where am I going?" he rasped out through clenched teeth.

"Just a slight change of quarters," one of the soldiers replied gruffly.

They left then as quickly as they had come, a man at each end while the armed soldiers marched along beside, no one saying a word. Nick was jostled carelessly across the green, where once again the 41st Regiment practised their drills. He recalled an earlier day before the war when he had visited here with Kate, and how much they had enjoyed the day. He could almost see her shy smile and hear her soft giggle. Oh, how he longed to see that side of Katie again! Nick was suddenly jolted back to reality as another searing pain travelled sharply up and down his leg. If something is not done soon, he thought in frustrated anger, I am certain to lose it.

"Where the hell are you taking me?" The soldiers chose to ignore Nick but his answer came a few moments later, and his stomach tightened into knots. He cursed loudly when the guardhouse came into view. Again Nick recalled his previous visit to the fort, remembering how sorry he felt at the time for any poor soul forced to stay in that hell hole.

The dankness of the room was apparent as the soldiers lifted Nick from the canvas stretcher and deposited him roughly onto the cold, hard floor of the cell. "What the hell is happening? Tell me! What crime have I committed?" Once again Nick was ignored and the soldiers locked the cell door and left him without saying a word. As he lay there in the dark, shivering from the cold, he tried desperately to sort out this terrible madness. Nick was unaware of the jail's other occupants; two British soldiers who ran from the heights during the battle were now awaiting execution.

He knew from listening to the other wounded men in the block-house that the British had regained the heights and after the battle had taken many prisoners. He silently wondered what had become of those unfortunate men. What is to become of me? he thought. Brock's promise rang in his ears now and he scoffed at its recollection: 'Remember, my friend, whatever happens, I am on your side. I stand by my men.' Nick's head pounded and he felt sick. "If Brock had lived, I would not be in this mess now," he muttered aloud. "I would rather die than lose my leg." He suddenly felt nauseated at the thought of them torturing him first, by removing his leg before hanging him.

Captain Walter Clarke opened the wooden door to the small cell, a look of self- satisfaction smeared on his miserable face, as he gazed down at the sorry-looking inmate. "I knew that one day, if I were patient, I would be sure to have my revenge, Nick Brannigan, and let me assure you, it is indeed sweet." He laughed wickedly as the prisoner stared up at him with contempt, not making a sound. "Oh, but there is more sweetness to come, sir," he continued. "You see, with a little black-mail, the fair Miss Sullivan will be mine, in every way of course." His laughter reached a terrifying pitch as he watched Nick's struggle to rise, hate filling his whole demeanor. Walter Clarke was well aware of the prisoner's weakened condition, so he continued on boldly without fear, bending even closer to Nick's face. "Let me enlighten you dear boy, for I am sure you are at a loss as to what has transpired since that dreadful day at Queenston Heights.

Let me see now, where to begin? Oh yes. You see, when I first learned of Brock's demise, I was of course elated. I knew that at last there would be nothing or no one to stop my revenge. General Sheaffe would be eager to have Brock's men align with him, so naturally he would hasten to act on their behalf, would he not? I was undecided as to whom I should first approach regarding this matter, but I quickly settled on Captain Glegg. You see, Mr. Brannigan," Clarke added with a smirk, "he was a dear close friend of the dead general's and mourns him still, so why would he not believe me? I am after all a captain in the British army and a knight of the king, am I not?"

"What the hell have you done, you bastard?" Nick ground out weakly through gritted teeth. He was more terrified than angry now, and he wanted to close his mind to the raw evil of this man.

Walter Clarke's jovial mood vanished in an instant and leaning in even closer to Nick, he snarled out his next words. "I, along with my two witnesses, told Captain Glegg, who in turn informed General Sheaffe, who then held a short meeting with Miss Sullivan, that we happened upon you and your American friends just as you killed Private Sullivan. And while we were disposing of your two allies, you hurriedly pitched the dead body of Kevin Sullivan over the cliff into a burning wagon. You then tried to escape, so of course we had no choice but to stop you, only leaving you alive so we could return you to the fort and make you suffer the consequences."

Nick snarled, wishing at the moment that he had the strength to beat Clarke senseless.

Undaunted, Captain Clarke continued on. "Oh yes, and I intend to inform the lovely Miss Sullivan of the identity of one of your American friends. You see, she will have to succumb to me now, or I will accuse her, and the rest of her family, of being not only traitors to the crown, but to all the people of Upper Canada. I assure you, Mr. Brannigan, I will be believed! After all, Mr. Phillips was in their employ, was he not? And you, a known traitor, were seen quite often in their company. Also, just to make sure that you are tried for treason, I will convince our new commander and his officers, especially Captain Glegg, that you had fooled their beloved general, and that the man that shot Brock was indeed a friend of yours. Tsk-tsk. I sincerely hope that you did not arrange that death too?"

Nick growled like a rabid dog, low at first and then growing louder as his body filled with an agonizing and insatiable hatred. He used his last surge of strength to kick Clarke hard with his good leg, knocking him backwards onto the floor, before collapsing against the wall of the wooden cell.

Captain Clarke pulled himself up slowly, and retaliated by delivering a resounding whack across the side of Nick's head with the stock of his musket, rendering him unconscious yet again. The deranged captain then bounded from the cell, slamming the door and hastily snapping the lock back into place, unaware of the young prisoner who watched his departure with great interest.

Chapter Thirteen

A small Georgian style cottage had been built inside Fort George; its sole purpose was to house any important people that might be visiting. Nestled privately behind blockhouse one, it was there that Kate resided during her stay at the fort. The location proved beneficial for both her and the British, as she was close to the wounded and could offer assistance at any time during the day or night. It was early evening now and Kate was bent over the fire stirring a large pot of stew. The wounded men had been fed already and she was now reheating the contents to serve the prisoners their meal. As she filled the pewter bowls with the steaming mixture, her mind wandered to Nick. He was gone when she had returned to the hospital and the doctor had told her that they had finally taken the murderous traitor to the guardhouse. Laura's parting words suddenly came to mind and she wondered if maybe she should talk to Nick after all.

The guardhouse was just as bleak, dark, and damp as Kate remembered; only it was worse now since there were prisoners inside. The sentry unlocked each cell that held the two young British soldiers, and while they were given their bread and stew, she could not help but feel sorry for them. They do not look any older than Kevin, she thought sadly: my poor Kevin! Her features suddenly hardened at the thought of her dead brother and she followed the sentry to Nick's cell, ready to give him a tongue lashing along with his dinner.

When the door was opened Kate gasped in alarm, her hatred forgotten for the moment, and after quickly shoving the food tray at the surprised young sentry, she entered the small chamber for a closer look at Nick. His clothes were torn and covered in blood and filth, and there was an ugly gash on the side of his head that was bleeding profusely. The bandage covering his leg was dirty and bloody, and the stench of him was so overpowering that Kate felt like retching. Her supposed hatred for Nick turned instantly to despair as she gazed down at the pathetic prisoner. No one has taken care of him in days, she thought.

Kate swung around, unleashing her temper on the unsuspecting sentry, shouting out orders for him to bring a basin of hot water, bandages, wood for the stove, and some salve for Nick's wounds. After witnessing her angry outburst, the soldier complied immediately. When he returned, he lit a fire in the stove and set up a small portable bathtub near the heat. After depositing the items she requested, plus a few extras, onto a wooden shelf in the corner, he left, colliding with Captain Glegg on his way out.

Captain Glegg's curiosity had been aroused when he first noticed the guard doing Kate's bidding and he followed the young soldier back to the jail. Upon entering the dark building, he stood quietly in the doorway for a moment, regarding Kate with interest. "Miss Sullivan, what is the meaning of this?" the captain inquired softly.

"Captain, this prisoner's condition is deplorable," Kate stated. "No man deserves to be treated in this fashion. I am just as guilty as everyone else; I too have neglected his care. I feel thoroughly ashamed of myself as we all should, especially Doctor Ramsey. I am now taking steps to rectify this situation, and I assure you, sir, I will not be stopped." Captain Glegg frowned at her obvious determination, but secretly he found himself admiring her compassion. He himself had some qualms regarding Nick's guilt, knowing how much Brock had liked and respected the man, but it was not his brother that Brannigan was supposed to have killed. "Miss Sullivan. You would help him after all he has done?"

"He is only charged with the offenses sir, not proven guilty of them." Kate could not believe her ears. Was she actually defending Nick?

Captain Glegg observed her for a moment longer, his thoughts turning to Brock and how this man may or may not have deceived the general. "We shall see," he mused softly. "In the meantime, you may clean him up; we do want him alive and well turned-out for his hanging." Glancing directly at the bathtub, he grinned openly. "I will send someone to assist you with the more delicate parts miss. Maybe one of his own militiamen will volunteer." The captain noticed Kate nervously averting her eyes from the tub and his smile broadened. Showing his amusement with the situation and bowing politely, he took his leave.

Kate frowned deeply when she watched him go. Muttering angrily at his laughter, she proceeded to rifle through the items on the shelf while she waited for the promised help to arrive. The sentry had been more generous than she had first hoped, bringing soap, towels, blankets, bandages, laudanum and even a small straw mattress to cover the cell floor.

Collin Wentworth carried two pots of boiling water into the guardhouse, setting one on top of the stove to keep warm while he emptied the other into the small tub. The private was a large pleasant fellow who had served under Nick in the militia, and was quite willing to offer the young lady any assistance that she may require. The private's ample size allowed him to gently lower Nick into the bathtub, mindful of his injuries and drawing only a slight whimper from him, as the prisoner was too tired and weak to object.

A short while later, with the private's help, Kate had Nick laying comfortably on the mattress; bathed, shaved, clean clothes and both wounds washed and dressed. Miraculously, neither injury appeared infected at the moment, but Nick had lost a lot of blood. She had just finished feeding him some broth when he took her hand, gently rubbing his thumb across her palm.

"Katie," he croaked. "Katie, listen to me, please. I have to tell you about Kevin." Kate's mind screamed at her to let him talk, but she knew that he was too weak. Even in her confused state, she was determined to save him.

"Sh-Sh-Sh." Kate whispered softly. "No talking now. You need your rest."

"No, I need to te...ell...y...ou...ev...er...y...th..." Nick faded quickly with the laudanum and he drifted off to sleep, his hand still holding hers.

I will not soften towards him, she promised herself, jerking her hand away.

"He should sleep for a while now," Collin stated reassuringly. "Miss Sullivan, I have to say, I do not believe he did what they are accusing him of. I have known Nick Brannigan for some time now and he just would not do such vile things. He deserves a chance."

After Collin Wentworth had left, Kate found herself wondering if he might be right. There were some who believed in Nick, so why could she not? Burying her head into her hands, she exclaimed out loud. "What chance did my poor Kevin have?"

Ellen Brannigan had just returned to the little rooming house in Newark where she had been staying since first coming to Upper Canada six months ago. She had hastily left her aunt's home in Baltimore, successfully fleeing her father's possessive grasp, intending to join her brother in the great country that he so often raved about in his letters. Ellen had been happy and content with her new life, but her rapture suddenly turned to anguish on receiving Kate's dreadful news about Nick's recent incarceration. She now threw a few toiletries and clothing into a cloth bag in preparation for her visit to Fort George. Miss Sullivan had assured her that Nick was fine and that she personally was seeing to his welfare. She also warned Ellen to stay clear of the British military post. Nick was being held for treason, Kate had warned, and surely would not want his sister to become involved. Ellen Brannigan was gravely disturbed by the news to say the least, and she certainly had no intention of staying away. Her brother needed her now. Right or wrong, she was determined to go to him, hoping to see Nick by nightfall.

Kate sat quietly in a rocking chair in front of the blazing fireplace inside her cozy cabin at Fort George. The steady rhythm of the to and fro movement lulled her into a false sense of tranquility, and her thoughts drifted back to a more peaceful time before the war. She thought of the problems that were so concerning then, realizing now just how trivial they all were. If this war had not come, there would have been many more dances to attend, and such fun to be had, she thought bitterly. Kate recalled her time spent with Matthew Dunsford when they had both laughed so gaily in the drawing room at the Newark ball. I should have devoted the entire evening to him and left Nick Brannigan alone. Maybe we all would have been better off if I had. Hannah is right. She is always telling me that: 'You never really know what you have until it is gone.' Kate sighed wistfully. Oh, how tired she was, she thought, wishing that this horrible war would just end. She groaned loudly in frustration as Nick secretly crept back into her thoughts and she began mulling over the events of the past few days, trying to make sense of all that had happened.

Kate had taken care of Nick with such love and compassion the other night, although she had displayed a slight shyness when bathing him. It needed to be done, so she had rolled up her sleeves and with the kind private's assistance, the task was accomplished. Nick should rest easy again tonight, she thought with satisfaction. But will I? She had purposely stayed away from Nick since that evening, so she could try and make sense of the situation. She turned it over in her mind so many times without any definite conclusions.

Kate was still plagued by the accusations that were directed at Nick, contemplating everything she had heard. Major-General Sheaffe was an intelligent military man, was he not? she argued. Surely he would be confident of Nick's guilt before arresting him on such horrendous charges as treason and murder? He must have had positive evidence. It must be true! How could she have been so wrong about Nick? How could her father? Kevin had been suspicious of him from the first and had said as much to the family, but father always defended him.

" I just do not know what to think." Kate shook her head in confusion. "I love my family, but God help me," she admitted wearily, "I still have feelings for Nick." She ceased her rocking then, and closing her eyes, she issued a silent prayer that Nick was innocent of any wrong doing toward Kevin and Upper Canada.

A continual aggressive knocking pulled Kate from her thoughts. Opening the cabin door, she was surprised to find an angry, dishevelled Ellen Brannigan standing there, her cheeks damp with tears. Her face was flushed and her eyes were dark, and following her curt greeting, she pushed past Kate and entered the room.

"How dare he treat me so!" she spat out indignantly.

"Miss Brannigan, whatever has happened? Who has upset you?"

"That despicable man who met me at the gates." Oh, the first young soldier was a gentleman right enough, but then this Captain Clarke came along and dismissed him, saying that he would take care of me personally. He proceeded to forcefully shove me into the sentry box and tried to take liberties with me. I have never been so humiliated in all my life. I would have still been at the mercy of that disgusting man if the dismissed sentry had not returned." Ellen gave way to her tears and Kate ushered her immediately to a chair by the fire.

"Please, Miss Brannigan, do sit down and I will make us some tea." Ellen dried her eyes and thankfully took the proffered chair, momentarily basking in the warmth before removing her cloak. When the kettle had finally boiled, Kate filled the awaiting teapot and set out two china cups. "These were loaned to me from the officer's kitchen," she commented, taking a seat beside Ellen. "Now, Miss Brannigan, General Sheaffe will hear about this, I assure you. Mr. Clarke is a crude, lecherous man who should not be above disciplinary action."

"I cannot believe that a kind, loving and decent man like my dear brother is locked away, while that man is allowed to roam free." Ellen Brannigan stared at Kate for a moment and then slowly shook her head. "No, please, I beg you, we shall say nothing of this dire incident. It will only make matters worse. I must see my brother, Miss Sullivan."

Kate offered no reply. Instead, she lifted the pot and began to pour the tea.

"I know that you advised me not to come," Ellen admitted. "But I simply had no choice. He is the only family I have left and I cannot lose him."

"Miss Brannigan ... may I call you Ellen?" At Ellen's immediate nod Kate continued. "Surely you can understand the seriousness of this situation. I am quite certain that I declared as much in my recent note to you."

"You did. But please understand Miss Sullivan ... may I call you Kate?" At Kate's affirmation, Ellen continued. "I need to help him if I can. My brother loves this country, he told me so. He is not a traitor."

"I am not sure what to believe, I am so confused. General Sheaffe has conclusive evidence. Listen Ellen, these soldiers hate Nick and it has become much worse since we buried General Brock. It is as if the army is blaming him for what has happened and are directing all their revenge on him. Do you not see the danger you are in?"

"I simply do not care," Ellen replied. "Nick would never leave me in the face of danger. My brother has spoken of you often, Kate. He cares for you and your family. Surely you must feel some kindness towards him?" Ellen inquired softly.

"You have admitted your love for your brother to me Ellen, but are you also aware that he stands accused of killing mine? I assure you that the love you have for Nick is just as great as the love I have for Kevin. Believe me when I say that I understand what you are feeling, but at least you know the whereabouts of your brother, while I remain uncertain of where mine is, or if he is even alive."

"That is precisely why I need to see Nick! Kate please, if it were Kevin lying in that horrible cell, would you not feel as I do?" Ellen rose abruptly from her chair, wringing her hands together in frustration. She approached Kate. "Please, can you help me?"

Kate stared at the agony on Ellen Brannigan's face. "I shall try," she replied, sighing in defeat. "Nick is not going to like this, of that I am certain."

Ellen smiled then, thanking Kate with a quick hug. "You just leave him to me," she said. Since the hour was growing late, Kate suggested that they wait until morning before visiting Nick, to which Ellen reluctantly agreed.

The autumn moon shone down on the cabin, casting a bluish glow around the room. The two ladies had retired for the night and now lay in the dark, talking in hushed tones. The small cabin had only one double bed. It was not what either lady was used to, being constructed solely of rough wood and a weaved rope bottom, but Ellen had been too tired to care. Relieved to finally have a place to lay her head, she declared that if it was good enough for Kate, then it certainly would be sufficient for her.

"Ellen?"

"Yes Kate?"

"I am still unsure of my feelings for Nick. I thought I loved him once, but now after all that has happened, I am confused. I promise you though; I will take care of him." Ellen and Kate closed their eyes, feeling somewhat comforted by each other's presence. As they lay quietly in the blue darkness of the room, they listened to the night sounds before drifting silently into slumber.

The morning sun invaded the cabin with an unusual brightness, but the air in the room was still crisp and damp, as the fire in the hearth had all but died. Kate slowly opened her eyes, rubbing them lightly as she stretched. She spread her arms wide, pulling them back instantly the moment she remembered Ellen sleeping beside her. However, when Kate rolled over, she was surprised to discover that Ellen's spot was empty now and she was all alone. She called out, but there was no reply. Ellen had gone.

Nick too was just waking up. His eyes fluttered slowly open, trying desperately to adjust to the dimly lit cell. No mirror was available to him, so he did not see the paleness of his skin or the darkness beneath his eyes. Nevertheless, he was aware of the debilitating weakness that still invaded his body, knowing that he was lucky to be alive, but still yearning for his strength to return. His heart seemed lighter this morning though, and he felt refreshed, recalling how affectionate Kate had seemed when attending to him the other night. Where was she? he wondered. He smiled leisurely then, remembering the soft touch of her fingers on his raw, wounded body as she bathed him. How shy she was, he thought, especially when she tried to avoid that secret part of him that was hidden under the water. Nick was relieved that the dirty, sickening smell of his body had gone, and when he moved his leg now, he noticed that the intense stabbing pain had dulled slightly, becoming more tolerable. He was wide awake and aware of the noisy rumblings in his stomach, wondering if Kate would be bringing him his breakfast today. He had not seen her or anyone for a couple of days, other than the sentry who brought him his meals, and Private Wentworth, who cleaned his wounds. When the door to his cell slowly opened a few minutes later, Nick flashed a warm smile, hoping to welcome his Katie along with the food tray she may be carrying. His friendly greeting changed instantly to disgust as he stared into the cold eyes of Walter Clarke, who now stood complacent in the doorway.

"Get out of here and leave me alone, you soldier from hell." Nick's warm, comfortable mood had vanished, and in its place he felt only cold hate and fear. "I still cannot believe that you were able to convince everyone that I am a traitor and a murderer. As God is my judge, and yours, you will be found out; I promise you." Walter Clarke doubled over with laughter and Nick's anger was ignited. "What the devil do you want of me now?" he lashed out in contempt, wishing he could throw something hard at the captain's offensive head. "I am glad that you find this situation so amusing."

"I am here simply to offer my condolences, Mr. Brannigan. You see it is rather amusing when you think about it really."

Nick scowled and turned his face away, trying his best to ignore the obnoxious man.

"Here you are waiting to be hung for the murder of Miss Sullivan's dear brother and your traitorous actions against the country, and all the while you are longing for the beautiful Kate's affections; the woman you admire and owe your very life to." When Nick continued to ignore him, Walter Clarke proceeded undaunted. "I find it rather hard to believe that the dear woman cares anything for you, not after what she has done."

Captain Clarke had the prisoner's full attention now, but Nick still continued to look away. That old feeling of dread that seemed to always accompany Clarke's visits crept slowly through his body once again and he waited for the bastard to lower the boom.

"It seems Miss Sullivan has taken an eye for an eye so to speak," Walter Clarke alleged, approaching Nick then, and kneeling in close. "You see, she is convinced that you killed her brother, so last night she took her revenge by sending your dear, sweet sister Ellen to her demise," he added maliciously.

Nick roared out his rage with tears filling his eyes and hate filling his heart. He was like a caged animal gone wild, and Walter Clarke, momentarily fearing for his own safety, jumped away.

"You are a lying bastard," he ground out venomously. "Kate would do no such thing." Following his sudden outburst, Nick felt the little strength that he did possess ebb slowly from his wounded body.

"Well, console yourself if you must, but Miss Brannigan is gone. Miss Sullivan sent her a note informing her of your predicament here and asked her to come to see you. I did feel obligated to meet her at the gates, and of course she is so lovely I could not help but have my way with her in the sentry box, not an easy task to be sure, but quite rewarding."

Nick remained quiet and still, his head pounded and his eyes burned. His brain was in turmoil and he experienced some difficulty sorting out his thoughts. He felt that he would explode at any moment but Clarke insisted on plunging the knife in deeper.

"It was all a ploy dear boy, do you not see? Miss Sullivan delivered your beloved sister into the waiting hands of your father. You see, my good man, it seems your father was still vexed with you for not returning home with him and he became quite adamant that your sister would. When she blatantly refused however, I am afraid that his temper got the better of him. Unfortunately, there was a terrible struggle and alas, dear Ellen was lost. Miss Sullivan did not kill your sister, you understand, your father took care of that, but she was responsible for summoning her here, knowing full well what the outcome would be." Walter Clarke stole another uncertain glance at Nick, and was surprised to find him still silent. "Your father left in haste of course, for fear of capture."

Nick's breathing grew heavy as he listened in disbelief, overwrought by the news that Ellen was gone. His strength had deserted him and he had no will left to fight back. His sister was dead and Kate had betrayed them both.

"Oh, come now Mr. Brannigan, you could not possibly imagine that Miss Sullivan was taking care of you because she loved you?" Walter Clarke added, "you could not be more wrong. You see, I was present when General Sheaffe informed the lady of your vile deed to her brother, and she vowed her revenge. She told the general that she would nurse you back to health so we could hang you. Oh yes, she did make a suggestion to General Sheaffe that you visit the punishment triangle to endure a much deserved lashing."

Walter Clarke left the guardhouse feeling somewhat disappointed by Nick's reaction. He had felt vindicated at first with the prisoner's sudden transformation into a wild, crazed beast, but then he weakened suddenly and the cell turned silent. The captain was satisfied, however, confident that the damage was done. Miss Sullivan would soon be his, and even if Brannigan were lucky enough to escape the noose, he would no longer lift a finger to help her.

Private Grant Cameron was huddled quietly in his small cubicle across from Nick and had been privy to Captain Clarke's unsolicited visit for a second time. He knew the officer was lying and he tried to inform Nick of that fact, but his numerous hails were ignored, as no answer came from Nick's cell. The private was also aware that the general had been absent for the past two days and could not have possibly ordered the whipping. The young condemned private also recalled how readily Mr. Brannigan had come to his defense during the battle at Queenston, and was determined now to find a way to speak with General Sheaffe when he returned. He might not be able to save himself, but hopefully there would be time to help Mr. Brannigan, before they were both hung.

In the early afternoon Nick was awakened once again by two British soldiers armed with muskets and swords. There was also a drummer boy, David Crawford, pounding out an aggravating rhythm. With the aid of the soldiers, the prisoner was led to the punishment triangle. Nick's glare was filled with icy shards as he silently locked eyes with the soldiers that now shackled him tightly to the whipping post. A quick look around showed that he was surrounded by British officers on three sides, while the other militia men and low ranking soldiers stood a short distance away to observe the corporal punishment. Nick noticed a few familiar faces in the group, most looking away when their eyes met. He also discovered that Captain Glegg appeared extremely uncomfortable with his task, his hand trembling slightly as he held the cat-o-nine-tails.

The captain had flogged men before, but he detested the duty today. The prisoner's condition was deplorable and his guilt was uncertain. He only agreed to this whipping upon receipt of a signed document from General Sheaffe, indicating his desire for this corporal punishment to take place. Captain Glegg felt no pride or satisfaction in performing this task, and secretly questioned the general's motives for this particular punishment. The drumbeats altered suddenly, signaling to the captain that it was time to begin. Nick's shirt was removed and he braced himself for the impact.

Kate had searched all morning for Ellen, but no one had seen her. She asked the sentry at the front gate if he had noticed her leaving, but he politely replied that he had not seen the lady since her arrival. Kate decided not to inform Nick of Ellen's visit or disappearance; there was no sense worrying him. He could do nothing anyway, she thought gravely. Kate's features brightened suddenly as a new thought came to mind. "For goodness sake, Ellen must have gone to see Nick without me," she exclaimed. "I do hope he was not too angry with her."

Making her way quickly along the path towards the jail, Kate noticed that the green space where the soldiers usually practiced their drills each day was deserted, and she wondered where they had gone. It was then that she heard a continuous loud cracking sound coming from the other side of the guardhouse, and she realized in horror that some unfortunate man was being flogged. She hurried to Nick's cell then, alarmed at finding it empty.

"No," she whispered in dismay, "It cannot be. They would not do this to him. Not in his condition."

Kate ran outside, rudely pushing her way between the soldiers that were gathered by the dreaded whipping post. She stopped short, momentarily shocked at the sight before her. Nick was straddled at the post, scarcely able to remain on his feet, looking pale and weak. There was a spattering of blood running freely from the torn flesh covering his back. After all her painstaking efforts to care for him! How dare they do this! She screamed at the crowd that surrounded Nick, venting her outrage and disbelief. Catching Captain Glegg off guard, she forced him aside, grabbing the disgusting whip and throwing it to the ground in a violent fit of temper. She did not take the time to think about what she was doing or how she was interfering in a military punishment. She did not care! That was Nick they were abusing and she would stop it any way she could. Kate chastised the men then, her chest heaving as she eyed each soldier in turn. Not even Captain Glegg escaped her unrelenting fury.

"Have you all gone mad?" The soldiers didn't know what to do. They just stood silently inspecting the ground beneath their feet while Kate rested her accusing gaze on Captain Glegg once again. "Cut him down. Has he not been through enough at the hands of this army?" She went to Nick then, agonizing at the sight of his ripped flesh. "This man has not even had a trial yet; how can you punish him so?" Kate cried out in anguish.

Captain John Glegg was overcome by a sudden feeling of compassion as he witnessed Kate's grief stricken accusations. "I am sorry you had to witness this Miss Sullivan, but it is being done by order of General Sheaffe."

"I issued no such order, Captain. Cut that prisoner down!" All heads turned immediately upon hearing the booming voice of their approaching commander.

Captain John Glegg cleared his throat loudly, gaining the attention of the other men before turning to the general. "Sir, I have your written order here for the flogging," Glegg stated firmly. He then handed the letter to the awaiting officer, while Nick was cut loose.

The general briefly examined the paper before thrusting it back at the bemused captain. "I repeat Captain Glegg; I did not issue this order. Who delivered this message?"

"Captain Walter Clarke received it at the front gate, sir. He said that it was delivered by your messenger. I examined the document myself and recognized your penmanship. I assure you general, I had no reason to suspect deception." Captain Glegg was now flooded with feelings of sorrow, uncertainty, anger and regret.

"Where is Captain Clarke?" the general inquired.

Glegg quickly scanned the crowd of officers but there was no sign of Walter Clarke. "I do not know, sir. I expected him to be here with the other men."

General Sheaffe strongly requested that the missing officer be located and that they should all meet in his quarters posthaste. He then instructed two soldiers to escort the prisoner to the blockhouse where he could have his wounds attended to. After regarding Kate with a surprising look of sympathy, he turned and abruptly left.

Captain Glegg too departed hastily from the scene. He had always felt pride in the past when carrying out his regimental duties; but not today. He was determined to find Clarke and get to the bottom of this.

Kate was so preoccupied with Nick for the time being that she completely forgot all about Ellen.

Nick was lying on his stomach, his back burning intensely. Kate began to clean the bloody slashes that had unmercifully ripped through his skin, using a strong soap and warm water, and finishing with a cool, healing salve. He was awake but made no sound during her gentle ministrations, his gaze fixed on some focal point across the room. His mind was once again in torment, agonizing over Ellen's death, the whipping, and Kate's possible involvement in both. With each stroke of the cloth, he grasped tightly to the bed sheet, wincing at her touch.

Kate spoke softly in a soothing tone, whispering his name repeatedly, but still there was no response from her patient. When she'd finished, she gazed warmly down at him in his sore, vulnerable state, and her heart filled with love. She knew then that he could not possibly have done the things he was accused of and she also knew that she had to help him somehow. Kate cooed softly to Nick. When he slowly turned towards her however, she gasped in shock. His eyes, now open, glared back at her with contempt. It shook her to her soul! She reached out to him in earnest, only to have her heart shattered when he recoiled from her touch.

"What have you done to my sister?" Nick ground out furiously.

Chapter Fourteen

Ellen Brannigan woke slowly, moaning in discomfort as she opened her eyes. She tried rubbing her throbbing temples, only to find that both her hands and feet were bound securely with a rough piece of rope. She immediately became frantic and tried to call for help, only to discover that her mouth had been covered tightly with a smelly old rag. I have been unconscious, she quietly surmised. What happened to me? Ellen was confused; struggling with her muddled brain she tried to clear her head. She sat quiet and alone, rocking back and forth as the unforgiving darkness pressed in against her. She wanted to scream! She wanted to cry! Tears immediately filled her frightened eyes and overflowed down her cheeks and her body began to shake uncontrollably. Ellen felt her heart race; the tormented organ threatening to explode within her chest as a scream rippled in her throat.

Ellen turned her head in every direction, trying desperately to focus on her surroundings. She suddenly felt something small scurrying over her legs, causing her to thrash wildly about where she sat. She was terrified now. As her muffled screams penetrated the eerie darkness, a door opened above her and she watched with trepidation as a large, older man descended the stairway in an obvious drunken state. He almost lost control of the lantern he was carrying and it swayed precariously in his grasp, causing the light to flicker haphazardly around the room. Stumbling over some invisible obstacle at the bottom, he cursed loudly before turning his attention back to her. Weaving excessively with each step; he approached.

Ellen shrank back against the wall in horror when the grossly intoxicated figure held the light to his face, and she recognized the pathetic drunken smirk that was plastered there. Squeezing her eyes shut, the memory of what had transpired over the past few hours came flooding back, hitting her so hard that it caused an escalation of the unbearable throbbing in her temples. Ellen rubbed them vigorously, thinking of her brief visit with Kate Sullivan and how it had ended so abruptly. Something had awakened her in the middle of the night, she recalled, and she left the warmth and comfort of the bed to investigate. Yes, she remembered, she had been looking intently out the window of the cabin, marvelling at the quiet stillness of the fort, when she was suddenly grabbed from behind.

Ellen recalled too, how someone had roughly covered her nose and mouth with a vile smelling cloth; and then there was nothing but a pit of darkness. Kate was going to take me to Nick, she thought. My poor Nick. In an instant her eyes flew open and she began a screaming tirade through her gagged mouth, shaking her head as she stared up in disbelief at the once handsome man. This dishevelled, drunken lout was her father!

Mr. Nicholas Brannigan Sr. laughed mirthlessly. Leaning down towards his daughter, he reached out, yanking hard on the cloth covering her mouth and pulling it roughly down over her chin.

"I warned your damned brother that this would happen if he refused to return home and fight on our side," he slurred, his foul whiskey drenched breath making her nauseous. "Now you have to pay the price for his stubbornness my dear."

Ellen stared at the polluted man, realizing that her father was strange to her. He had never been an over-affectionate man, and she did expect him to be quite over-bearing at times, but she could not understand his actions now. Nick had sheltered her from most of the debasing things their father had done, she realized, and she was just discovering how far this man was willing to go, and it frightened her. Just the idea that her own father would resort to kidnapping was unthinkable. When Ellen tried to respond to him, she found it difficult. Her mouth was dry and sore. "I do not know what you are talking about Father. Why am I here?" she rasped. "Please, may I have a drink? I am so thirsty."

"You are just like your mother my dear and don't think you can soften my heart on that score. You are just as expendable as she was." Raising his voice a notch and swaying on his heels, he continued with his slurred admonishment, jabbing his index finger at his daughter to make his point. "Your brother refused to join me. That is why you are here now! You see, my girl," he added with a sneer, you are bearing the brunt for him deserting me and our country. Damn his treasonous hide!"

"Nick is incarcerated; he could not come even if he wanted to," Ellen replied with certainty, her fear dissolving with each spoken word. In the next instant, however, she watched in pity as her once proud and handsome father slumped shamefully to the cellar floor, finally succumbing to his inebriated state.

"We are well aware of your brother's unfortunate predicament, my dear, make no mistake."

Ellen gasped, her bravado fading rapidly upon hearing that voice and the evil laugh that accompanied it. Slowly tilting her face upwards she shook her head in denial, her eyes wide, magnetically locked on what appeared to be Satan himself. "W-why are you doing this to me? I have done nothing to you," Ellen complained weakly.

Captain Walter Clarke leaned down menacingly, inches from Ellen's frightened face, rudely letting his spittle fly with each enunciated word. "Your wretched brother has been a thorn in my side for too long and I will end it now; I have been fooled for the last time." Captain Clarke stood then and began to pace the floor in front of her, hands clasped tightly behind his back. He continued in a matter-of-fact tone. "There is no doubt that the younger Mr. Brannigan is well aware of your disappearance by now. You see, he has been informed recently that not only was Miss Sullivan privy to your abduction, but she also displayed a great eagerness to assist us." The unrelenting captain beamed then, treating her with a satisfied smile.

Ellen could not believe that Kate would do this. She had trusted and liked her, so sure of Miss Sullivan's true concern for Nick.

Clarke laughed cheerfully at the apparent shock and desolation that tainted Ellen's lovely features before turning to regard his drunken assistant, kicking him roughly with his boot. "Get up you lazy, disgusting creature." The elder Mr. Brannigan groaned loudly, swearing violently in his drunken stupor.

Indignant now with the way both of these men had treated her, Ellen's anger was aroused, momentarily defusing her fear, and she lashed out at Walter Clarke. "You are a cad sir, a jackanapes of the worst kind and I can understand why everyone abhors you. Your title as a knight is laughable. If not for your financial wealth, you would be nothing. I am also quite convinced that your money is the result of ill-gotten gains. You are a defiler of women and hold yourself as more prominent than you deserve. How can you rationalize allowing an innocent man to hang? You, captain, are nothing but a coward and a fool, and I despise you!" Ellen Brannigan was breathless. Her chest heaved rapidly as she finished her condescending attack. Her bravado ebbed once more.

. Walter Clarke stared blankly ahead as if in a trance, looking straight through her at nothing in particular, with no reply on his lips. His unresponsiveness unnerved Ellen to the point where she almost wished he would yell at her. However, the only sound she heard was the groaning of her father, now trying to rise, using the wall behind him for support. Clarke turned his attention back to the elder Mr. Brannigan for a moment, cautioning Ellen at the same time. "A word of warning my dear. Never underestimate what I am capable of. A defiler of women you say? I treat them as they deserve. I will see your brother hang for his abominable treatment of me. He deserves no less. When he is dead, I will have Miss Sullivan. Of that you may be sure, as she in turn deserves me." Captain Clarke issued this disturbing speech while assisting the elder Mr. Brannigan to his feet.

"I find it hard to believe that even a man like you could resort to such dire measures. Are you not afraid of God and his wrath? Should I fear for my own safety as well?" Ellen inquired desperately, trying to disguise the tremendous fear that flowed throughout her body.

"God does not scare me, and I pay no heed to his wrath. I do suggest however, that you fear for this man's safety at the moment." As Walter

Clarke pinned Ellen's father to the wall with one hand, he pulled out a British dueling pistol from underneath his coat with the other, and aiming it inches from Nicholas Brannigan's skull, he fired.

Clarke then tucked the weapon back into its hiding place as the corpse slumped to the floor in a crumpled heap, blood streaking the wall behind him. Walter then turned his gaze to Ellen once again, issuing an ultimatum as he leered dangerously down at her.

"If you promise to be quiet and not make a fuss, I will leave the cloth off your mouth and give you a drink of water. If, however, you become a nuisance to me, I will not only cover your mouth again, but I will leave you down here for the rats to play with. Now, do I have your promise?"

Ellen couldn't speak. She couldn't scream and she did not cry out. Her fear had intensified. She was struck dumb by the horror of what she had just witnessed. She knew that her father had become a vile, despicable man, but it was still horrible to watch him die like that. She now understood in full measure what this monster standing above her was capable of. He was insane! Just as mad as the war-ravaged world around her, and she feared not only for her life, but for her sanity as well. Ellen's manner suddenly became more compliant. With frightened eyes frozen to his, she nodded her head meekly, and surrendered.

The temporary hospital was noticeably empty now and the hustle and bustle that followed the battle at Queenston had ceased. Dr. Ramsey was absent, no longer barking orders at his nurses, and all was quiet. Most of the injured soldiers had vacated the building; some died or were sent home, while others returned to active duty. The empty beds were beginning to fill once more with healthy men who had taken their original places back in the blockhouse, as the War of 1812 continued.

Nick Brannigan was stretched out on his bunk sleeping soundly, propped on his side with pillows, lying on clean linen and covered with a warm blanket. A young woman who was busy folding laundry in the back corner accidentally dropped a metal bucket.

The loud crash broke the silence as it reverberated throughout the room. Nick jerked impulsively in his sleep, startled by the thunderous noise, and his eyes flew open. The sudden movement caused his features to distort dramatically. Wincing in pain, he gently rubbed his throbbing head and massaged his wounded leg. He needed to sit up, he thought, but his body objected fiercely when the feat was first attempted. Straining to rise again, Nick now sat in confusion on the side of his bed surveying his surroundings.

He was relieved to discover that his stay in the dreaded guardhouse had ended. He became acutely aware of a burning pain in his back, the excruciating fingers of flame licking mercilessly at his shoulder blades before traveling lower, causing every muscle to tighten.

Nick recalled the brutal whipping he had sustained. When was that? Feeling sore and miserable, he eased himself slowly back down onto his side, aimlessly wondering how long he had been here, as thoughts of both Kate and Ellen stormed his brain. Clarke! He suddenly remembered Walter Clarke's previous visit to the guardhouse and his mirthful declaration that Ellen was dead, implying that Kate had somehow been involved. Nick's pain was forgotten for the moment, replaced instead by a gripping coldness as intense hatred consumed him, and he rose up on his bunk once more. I will kill him! Feeling a sudden rush of adrenaline coursing through his veins, he wrapped himself in a sheet and went in search of his clothes.

Chapter Fifteen

Kate had no idea where to begin her search for Ellen, but had decided to return home and request help from her father. She had left Fort George in a state of misery and frustration following Nick's horrible whipping incident and his hostility towards her afterwards. He thought she was involved somehow in Ellen's untimely disappearance and she wondered how he'd even known that his sister had been at the fort. She was consumed with melancholy thoughts as she travelled slowly in the direction of home. *How could he think that of me?* Kate had forgotten for the moment that it was only a few short days ago when she'd had the very same opinion of him in regards to her own brother.

She recalled Nick's recent rage. It was so intense; it chilled her to the very bone. How ironic, she mused sadly, that now, just as her feelings were softening towards Nick, his for her had become hate-filled. *I will never forget that angry, accusing look in his eyes,* she thought dismally. To make matters worse, Kate had no idea of Ellen's whereabouts. Where could she have gone? Desperation engulfed her now. There was a strong desire in her heart to prove her innocence and gain Nick's forgiveness, but she also feared for Ellen's safety. Where could she be? Kate liked Ellen and was determined to find her, desperately hoping that Nick would be alive to be reunited with his beloved sister.

The inclement weather had turned bitterly cold all of a sudden as Kate slowly made her way home. She clumsily followed along the deserted road with her head down as the wind pelted icy shards of snow against her unprotected face. She was uncertain of the date, guessing that it must be sometime in late November. How grand it would be to sit in front of a cozy fire enjoying the comfort and being fussed over by Hannah and her father. Oh, how she longed to be home! Kate had tried to push all thoughts of Kevin to the back of her mind, but not one day went by that she didn't think of him, and it tore at her heart. I hope that father has not plunged himself into a deep pit of despair over the loss of his son, she thought sullenly, longing to find both him and Hannah well. Kate felt a recurring sense of guilt wash over her for the way she had abandoned her family so soon after relaying the horrible news about Kevin. Keeping our minds occupied with finding Ellen will be a good thing for all of us, she reasoned.

Kate had been through so much of late that she no longer concerned herself with being alone during this uncertain time of war. Was it not just last spring that she journeyed home from Laura's on this very same dark and deserted road in an agitated, frightened and most indecisive state? At present there was still some daylight left, but the sun had already begun its descent. The cold, wet, driving snow persisted in making Kate's trek slow, but she diligently pushed on, comforted in the knowledge that she was nearing the Secord farm and could stop there for a rest. Oh, Nick, she thought sadly, I will find her; I promise. Kate quickened her pace as the welcoming sight of Laura's home came into view, and she gazed wistfully at the tendrils of smoke that were now swirling slowly upwards from both chimneys.

"My goodness, Kate dear, but you are worn to a frazzle and soaked right through to your skin," Laura Secord declared, opening the door and finding her young neighbour perched there, wet and shivering. Once inside, she immediately relieved Kate of her drenched coat and boots before escorting her into the parlour, where she proceeded to remove the remainder of her saturated clothing. After Kate was dry, she was wrapped snugly in a blanket and coaxed into a wing-back chair, where she sat contentedly in front of the warm fire. After hearing all of the commotion downstairs, Mary Secord decided to investigate. When she entered the room, she was shocked to discover her friend in such a miserable state. Mary had not seen much of Kate since the beginning of the war and she now stared at her friend with concern. Laura, noticing her daughter's entrance, requested Mary to please bring some tea. When Mary returned a few minutes later with the tray, Laura was vigorously rubbing Kate's half-frozen hands.

"Thank you so much for everything," Kate whispered a short time later, as she sipped the steaming brew and offered both Laura and Mary a small exhausted grin. "I do not know what I would have done had you not been here to help me."

"Please Kate, tell us what has happened to upset you so," Laura inquired gently. "Is this sadness you feel in regards to Kevin?"

Kate had been guarding her frantic emotions for weeks but she suddenly lacked the strength to keep them buried behind the invisible wall built up inside her. Now that she found herself being gently coddled by her friends, she finally allowed the dam to break. In the midst of her anguished cries and floods of tears, she related every drastic event that took place following the battle of Queenston Heights, even lamenting once again for her lost brother. Laura listened to her friend's outburst with compassion, hugging her closely and cooing softly in a well-meant, but futile attempt to soothe her. Laura cast a quick glance at her daughter then, realizing that she too was upset.

"Come, Mary, we had best leave her be now to cry it all out and maybe she will fall asleep," Laura whispered, pulling her own grief stricken daughter from the room.

Kate was so immersed in misery that she was not even aware that her friends had left. "I am so terribly exhausted," she whimpered, finding herself alone. Her crying had ceased now and only the occasional sob escaped through her much calmer resolve. Squeezing her eyelids shut, she allowed the few remaining tears to fall silently over her flushed cheeks. "Dear God," she prayed aloud. "Thank you for watching over me during this mess and keeping me safe, and I thank you for such loving, and caring friends. Oh, and God, please let Nick's heart soften towards me, and let me find Ellen alive and unharmed." She knew that she was asking a lot, but she confessed to the Lord that she was ready to do whatever was necessary to achieve that end. Kate's prayers ended then and she quietly drifted off to sleep in the large winged chair in front of the blazing fireplace.

The next morning dawned cool and crisp with only a light dusting of snow covering the ground. There was a peacefulness surrounding the farm, belying any evidence that a war even existed. The wind had softened to a slight wintery moan, barely moving the weather vane at the tip of the barn roof, and the outside temperature had risen slightly. The livestock had been tended to by Mary and ate their morning feed quietly; too cold to make any sounds. Inside the house bustling noises from the kitchen drifted into the parlour awakening Kate, who yawned and stretched noisily, reluctantly dragging herself up out of the chair where she had spent the night.

"I am sorry that we left you there Kate, but you were sleeping so soundly and we did not have the heart to wake you," Mary explained softly as she slowly entered the room. "Mother said you needed rest and it did not matter much where you found it. I do hope you slept well in that old chair."

"Good morning, Mary," Kate replied. "Please, do not apologize. I did sleep well indeed." Kate felt more refreshed and most anxious to be on her way. "Is your mother occupied in the kitchen?"

"She was a moment ago, but now she is upstairs with Father. He is still quite immobile, you see, and his injuries still plague him dreadfully, keeping him a prisoner in his room. Mother spends much of her day seeing to him, only coming downstairs to help me prepare the meals and do the cleaning up. Since the beginning of this bothersome war we have lost the one helper that we had left, after you were gone, so I now help wherever needed; mainly with the house and barn chores and seeing to the children."

Kate studied her young friend, noticing the dark puffiness around her eyes, the drawn appearance of her lovely face, and the slowness of her step. Mary is exhausted, she thought shamefully, and mourning Kevin. "Oh, goodness Mary," she gasped, taking Mary's hand and leading her to the chair. "Do sit down. How could I have been so selfish? I let you dote over me when you yourself are tired and grieved? I would hate to think that you are becoming ill. Your poor mother has been busy too;

I should imagine that she is fatigued as well." Neither Kate nor Mary noticed that Laura had silently entered the room.

"Whatever is the matter child?" Laura questioned with concern, rushing to her daughter's side and feeling her forehead for any sign of a fever. Mary was fussed over then, with Laura echoing Kate's unease. The eldest Secord child was instructed to retire immediately upstairs to rest for the remainder of the day.

"It was my intention to venture home today Laura now that I am quite well, but considering the most recent events with Mary, I will stay and help you until she recovers. It is the least I can do," Kate offered, trying to quell the disappointment in her voice. She had so wanted to begin her search for Ellen today, but knew that her loyalties to this family must be met.

"Thank you, my dear, but there is no need. Mary is only tired, not ill, I assure you. After a good day's rest she will be restored, just as you were. She still suffers with Kevin's death, but that too will lessen in time, for the both of you. Now, come to the kitchen for a bite to eat. Kate's indecisiveness lingered. "Do not concern yourself with us," Laura added. "Truly my dear, Mary will rest today and I can manage as I have always done. I know you are anxious to be home; you confessed as much last evening, remember?" Laura placed her hand under Kate's chin, lifting it slightly. "Go home Kate, you may be needed there and your family will be overjoyed at seeing you again." After Kate had finished a light breakfast, she visited James Secord and his daughter Mary once more before setting out for home, expressing a heart-felt wish that they both enjoy good health in the future.

Kate quickly closed the distance to the Sullivan farm, her strength returning with the mounting excitement. As she approached, she noticed how quiet and deserted the place appeared. There was smoke rising from the chimney however, and upon further speculation Kate heard their cow Sadie lowing in the barn, and a strange, gruff voice hollering for her to move over and stop trying to upset the milk bucket. Frowning, she assumed that her father had acquired a new hand, and by the sounds of it, he was definitely not used to milking cows.

Upon hearing the front door open and slam shut, Kate's attention was drawn immediately to the house. Watching in horror, she saw an all too familiar figure step out onto the porch. Kate gasped, quickly ducking behind the nearest tree.

"Clarke!" she whispered in alarm. Her mind was swimming and reeling at the unexpected sight. Why was he here? She watched hesitantly as he marched away from the house in the direction of the barn. Kate was uncertain of what to do next. She trembled inwardly, her whole body quaking in panic, knowing instinctively that this man's presence did not bode well for either her father or Hannah. Her heart raced. She was determined to investigate the matter further. Kate swallowed hard and smothered her fear. After double-checking that Clarke was out of sight, she stalked quietly towards the house; Ellen's rescue forgotten now.

Kate did not consider herself to be a brave woman; in fact the opposite was often the case, but at the moment her worry and anxiety for her family overpowered her fear. She was desperate to find out what was happening in her home so she crouched low. After a darting glance in all directions, she stealthily made her way to the front door, quietly sneaking inside. Kate quickly searched each room, upstairs and down, but found no trace of her father or Hannah. She could not call out to them for fear of being apprehended by Clarke, so she was at a loss as to what to do. Where are they? She was frantic. What has happened to them?

When Kate entered the kitchen, she quietly approached the back stairway leading to the cellar and heard muffled voices drifting up to her. After cautiously opening the door, she gasped, recognizing Clarke's evil declaration and Ellen Brannigan's fearful plea. Kate was confused. I was so sure he was in the barn, she thought. He must have returned while I was searching upstairs. How did I not hear him? How did he not hear me? What is Ellen doing here? Once again, Kate was uncertain of what to do. She was so pre-occupied with her troubled thoughts that she didn't hear the back door open, nor the footfalls that silently approached. Suddenly, she was pushed hard from behind. Screaming loudly, she tumbled down the rickety stairs, landing in an unconscious heap at the bottom.

"You imbecile!" Clarke bellowed, realizing that it was his beautiful Kate that lay sprawled and unmoving at his feet. "Max," he ground out viciously, grabbing his unsuspecting assistant threateningly by the throat. "You had better pray that she is still alive or I promise you, you will indeed suffer an extremely painful death." Clarke shook the unfortunate man off, his face darkening to an almost purple colour. He kneeled down to Kate, relieved at finding her alive, and then turned back to his assistant. "Carry her upstairs to one of the bedrooms, and be careful about it," he barked. Clarke snatched the lantern from the floor and raced up the stairs behind them.

Ellen Brannigan hollered out in protest, sadly realizing that Clarke's thunderous reaction could only mean one thing; the injured woman must be Kate Sullivan. Kicking her unbound feet in frustration, she cried until she was exhausted.

General Roger Hale Sheaffe was alone in his quarters, sitting uncomfortably at his desk, the very one that had once been occupied by the late General Brock. He held a quill pen tightly in his hand and tried to give all his attention to the documents that were set out in front of him, only to find himself distracted by his own thoughts. His mind was on Brock, and how he was still being plagued by the late general. Sheaffe threw the writing implement down onto the desk and rubbed both hands over his face in exasperation. That blasted man's memory was a thorn in his side at times and he was well aware that his men would never think of him as they did their favoured general; but he was determined to adapt. He did his best to make these quarters his own, but occasionally there were still subtle reminders of Brock, such as certain letters he came across and the few toiletries he found. Sheaffe respected the general too, but the man was gone, and like it or not, life needed to go on. "I will prevail," he said aloud, before returning his attention to the forgotten paperwork.

General Sheaffe was just completing a letter of his own when he was interrupted by a knock on the door. He remained seated but bid the visitor to enter, looking up with interest as Captain John Glegg approached. The aspiring general made a special effort with this captain, as he had been a friend and confidant of General Brock, and he now desired this gentleman's absolute approval. If he could gain the respect of this man, then the others would surely follow.

"Please excuse the intrusion, sir," Glegg offered. "I have a matter of great importance to discuss with you."

"Certainly, my good man. Please, take a seat." The general indicated the chair in front of his desk and held out a cigar box to the captain. He also held up a whiskey bottle, and offered him a drink.

"Thank you, sir," Glegg replied with a nod, reaching for the tumbler and taking the proffered seat.

"Now, captain, to the business at hand. What is this important matter you wish to discuss? Have you located Captain Clarke as yet?"

"No, sir, unfortunately we have not. But in fact, my report does indeed pertain to Mr. Clarke, and to that of Mr. Nick Brannigan as well. You see, general, I am afraid a lot has been revealed since the battle at Queenston and we, the British army, have made a ghastly error."

General Sheaffe jumped to his feet and pulled the cigar abruptly from his mouth. While he paced nervously back and forth behind his desk, he felt a great uneasiness wash over him as he momentarily ceased his gait. "What mistake could we have possibly been guilty of Captain Glegg?"

"We, all of us here at Fort George, have treated Mr. Brannigan abominably ill, sir," the captain admitted regretfully. "I see no recourse but to offer some explanation to the gentleman, post haste, and pray that following our most humble apologies, he may be amiable enough to forgive us."

"Please captain; tell me all that has transpired." The general resumed his pacing as he listened intently.

"Well, sir, it seems that Captain Clarke visited our prisoner and proceeded to proudly confess to Mr. Brannigan of a certain ruse that he had just accomplished. You see, sir, it was in fact the infamous Captain Clarke himself who performed all the offenses that Mr. Brannigan is now being charged with, including the murder of Private Kevin Sullivan. But, as much as I would like to believe otherwise, sir, there is no conclusive evidence that Clarke played any part in General Brock's demise. It seems that Clarke took advantage of the sentry's temporary absence from the jail and entered, unaware of the two other prisoners occupying the guardhouse: Private Grant Cameron, and Private Joseph Styles. These are the two soldiers that were incarcerated for desertion at Queenston and are scheduled to be hanged as we speak. Private Cameron overheard the conversations between Clarke and Brannigan and gladly recounted the information to me. Joseph Styles on the other hand, claims to have heard nothing."

"What are our assurances Captain Glegg that this particular prisoner is telling the truth? Why is it that one claims to have heard everything while the other appears to have heard nothing at all?"

"Sir, let me just say that Private Cameron is just as guilty as Private Styles. However, I feel that he does posses some scruples and knows that he did wrong. Since he is now fully prepared to face the consequence of his actions, he does not want to see an innocent man punished for something that he did not do. He also informed me that this is his chance to return a favour to Brannigan who apparently came to his aid during the battle at the heights. Then there is Styles. That man is so consumed by his own grief and so terrified of the gallows, that he just sits in his cell muttering to himself, unaware of what is going on around him. He has not even eaten any of the food offered to him since his incarceration. I feel certain, sir, that the first man, Cameron, will walk bravely to the gibbet while the latter, Styles, will be dragged there, shamefully kicking and screaming. I wish to also add, that Private Cameron was quite adamant that I bring this information to you." Captain Glegg then produced a sworn statement containing all the facts that the young private overheard from Nick's cell and handed it to his commander.

The general read it thoroughly, shaking his head at its conclusion. This letter, coupled with Clarke's actions of late: the flogging incident as well as his sudden disappearance, led him to believe that Mr. Brannigan just might be an innocent victim in all this chaos, while Captain Clarke was not only a ruthless, evil man, but a disgrace to the British army. General Sheaffe felt uncomfortable with this outlandish injustice and hoped he could make amends for his army's wrongful accusations. He did not want to admit that he also erred in his judgement of Mr. Brannigan.

What about this nuisance of the two women disappearing? he thought. He had not even known that Brannigan had a sister, let alone that she had been here at the fort.

What of Miss Sullivan? Was she involved in all this confusion too? Maybe it is just a coincidence that she had also suddenly vanished. The general wrestled with his troubled thoughts, all too aware of what Captain Glegg's feelings were at the moment regarding this obtrusive situation. He was desperate to satisfy him yet again. Oh! What is to be done? the bemused general lamented to himself. What a terrible state of affairs!

Captain Glegg, who had been eyeing the general expectantly, now offered a suggestion of his own. "I wish to visit Mr. Brannigan at the blockhouse, sir, to offer our apologies and inform him of the unfortunate circumstance regarding his sister and Miss Sullivan's disappearance."

"Indeed, Captain, rightly so. I intend to accompany you," replied the general.

"There is one more subject that I wish to broach," the captain added reluctantly. "Although Private Cameron did run from battle, he has now displayed an inordinate amount of integrity in his defense of Mr. Brannigan. Can he not therefore be spared the hangman's noose, sir? He is only a young lad after all."

Once again General Sheaffe felt the silent pressure in attaining this captain's approval, but he was determined not to ignore British military law entirely. He was confident that he had appeased Captain Glegg enough by condemning Walter Clarke and freeing Mr. Brannigan, so he decided to hold fast to his original decision regarding the two deserters. He cleared his throat before answering.

"I appreciate your sentiment captain, I truly do. I too would like nothing more than to save this young private, but alas, our British law is steadfast and must be obeyed at all costs. We must not be remiss in our duties and appear negligent in front of the men. No, Captain Glegg, I am sorry, but I feel we must 'deter by terror of example.' Therefore the sentence will be carried out. The men must realize that they will indeed be punished for their crimes."

"I understand, sir," Captain Glegg replied with a satisfactory nod. "And may I say general, that the prisoner was not promised freedom for divulging this information."

"Come now, captain, you have still gained something this day. Let us go and inform Mr. Brannigan of his imminent release. I shall ask for his forgiveness and hope that we can put this sordid matter behind us. General Sheaffe was certain that he had pacified his captain satisfactorily and he promised that Walter Clarke would be punished for his actions the moment he was apprehended. Captain Glegg and General Sheaffe entered the blockhouse a few minutes later in a more jovial mood, only to have their hopes dashed when they could not deliver their good news in person. Nick Brannigan was gone!

Chapter Sixteen

———

Kate heard someone calling to her from far away. She seemed to be floating through a long winding tunnel of darkness as she followed the persistent voice upwards, towards the light. Her eyes blinked a few times and finally she was able to keep them open, squinting slightly as the brightness of the room invaded her vision. She instantly became aware of a heavy, relentless pounding in her head. Kate moaned out in distress and tried to speak, but was shushed by a soothing, familiar voice.

"Hush now, Kate. Do not try to rise. You are hurt from your terrible fall of last evening," Ellen Brannigan coaxed as she set a cold cloth on Kate's head, covering the large bandage that was already in place there. "Captain Clarke had you brought up here to rest and recuperate, and thankfully, I was allowed to accompany you and see to your care."

Kate slowly surveyed her surroundings. When she discovered where she was, it shocked her. Was it not just yesterday that she was anxious to be home? At any other time she would have enjoyed waking up in her own bed, but under the present circumstances, she only felt frightened and appalled. "Ellen, do you know what has happened to Hannah and my father?" Kate moaned, searching the other woman's face.

"Oh, Kate, I am so sorry, but I do not. You see, I was unconscious when they first brought me here, so I am just as much in the dark as you are. I did not even know until last night that this was your home. I must say my dear, my present lodgings are much more desirable than that smelly, mouse-infested cellar of yours."

"This is my room," Kate stated, sounding confused, as she gently rubbed her throbbing temples before trying to sit up. She was indeed perplexed. "And to think that I was coming here to find comfort and to ask for my father's assistance in locating you. Well, I now know where you are, Ellen, but where is father and Hannah? I need them. They must have gotten away before Captain Clarke arrived. At least I pray they did."

"Please Kate, you must lie still," Ellen replied as she lowered Kate gently down onto the bed.

"Ellen, I was so puzzled that morning when you disappeared. When I awoke and discovered you were gone, I thought you had visited Nick without me, so I went to the guardhouse to find you. Oh, my poor Nick!" Kate cried out in dismay, covering her face with her hands.

"What has become of my brother, Kate? Please, I must know," Ellen begged in alarm.

"Oh, Ellen," Kate sputtered. "When I went to the guardhouse, Nick was not there. I heard a terrible cracking sound coming from outside the building. When I followed the noise, I discovered Nick, tied to that dreadful whipping post, being flogged repeatedly with a cat-o-nine-tails. It was horrible!"

"Nick." Ellen whispered her brother's name through her own tears, shaking her head in sadness.

"I am afraid that is not the worst of it Ellen. The British army not only blames him for Kevin's death, but they also accused him of taking part in General Brock's murder." Kate was sobbing loudly now as Ellen looked on, stricken with shock and disbelief. "I am so ashamed to confess that I too thought that Nick had murdered my dear brother, but in my defence, the news was delivered to me by General Sheaffe himself, who assured me that he obtained all the pertinent facts. I was convinced that he would not have disclosed such horrendous information otherwise."

Ellen had given in to her own remorse, sadly repeating her brother's name while continuing to listen to her friend's emotional recounting of the incident.

"The general then went on to tell of his recent discovery that Nick was born in America, so he could not have possibly fought for our cause at the battle of Queenston Heights. They intend to hang him for treason, Ellen!" Kate cried.

Ellen Brannigan was bewildered. "This cannot be possible Kate; Nick loves this country and has strongly declared it so in every letter he has ever written to me. You must know that to be true," she pleaded. "He is innocent of all they accuse him of."

Kate's head continued to throb from the exertion that her outburst had caused, and she pressed her hands to her temples in an attempt to stop the persistent hammering in her skull. "Ellen, all I knew at the time was that my beloved brother was gone, swept away from me and my family in an instant. I had thought then of when we were children and how he protected me and doted on me, and how I loved him. Brock was dead too, and my mind was in utter chaos. I was so confused then and suffering from such a tragic loss that I could not make sense of anything at all. I know Nick to be innocent now, Ellen," Kate woefully confessed.

Ellen blew her nose and dried her eyes, pushing her own grief aside for the moment, and made an honest attempt to console a very despondent Kate. "You are in love with my brother, are you not?" Ellen inquired when Kate had calmed.

"Yes, Ellen, I love him," Kate whispered softly, slowly rising once again to a sitting position. "Unfortunately, I do not think that the feeling is mutual; in fact I believe the opposite to be true. He hates me now." At her friend's perplexed expression, Kate added, "You did not see the loathing on his face and hear the growl in his voice when he accused me of being involved with your disappearance. I will never forget the hardness I saw in him then. Sadly enough Ellen, I knew I truly loved him at that moment, fully realizing at the same time that he despised me so." Kate's shoulder's shook with every heaving sob, and Ellen tried once more to comfort her while controlling her own misery.

"I am afraid that this catastrophe is all Captain Clarke's doing," Ellen said. "You see, he confessed to me that he told Nick that you had a hand in not only my disappearance, but in my murder as well." Kate sobbed all the louder upon hearing this latest information, and Ellen quickly continued with her heartfelt explanation. "I believed him at first, but when I witnessed him shooting my father in cold blood, I realized then what a detestable creature he really is and that he lied about everything." Ellen trembled at the dreadful recollection. "There was such an evil calmness about him, Kate; I was frightened beyond belief." Ellen noticed that her friend was near exhaustion and searching for relief, so she gently laid her down on the pillow for a second time.

"I am so tired, Ellen, and so terribly sorry."

"Hush, Kate, try and rest now. You have done nothing wrong my dear, and Nick will come to realize that by and by. You just wait and see," Ellen soothed. "You just leave him to me."

"Oh, Nick," Kate mumbled sleepily as she closed her eyes and drifted quietly off to sleep. Kate found herself lost in the thickening mist once more, racing hysterically away from the ever-encroaching fog as it relentlessly chased her through the darkness in the same horrible dream. The misty fingers were reaching threateningly towards her and no matter how fast she ran, it was always just behind her, waiting to strike. Suddenly, her legs became paralyzed and she could no longer run. Some invisible evil lurched towards her from the blackness and she let out a blood-curdling scream. In reality though, she had only cried out in a feverish pitch, but it succeeded in waking her, thus bringing an end to the frightening nightmare, and alerting Ellen to her distress. On waking, Kate related all she could remember of the dream to Ellen, confessing that she had experienced this same frightening vision several times in the past. At the conclusion she closed her eyes for a moment, listening hypnotically to her friend's warm, relaxing voice as it gently soothed her.

Kate calmed, but the recurring dream was still very prevalent in her mind. Was it a warning of things to come? She felt restless, even in her feverish state, and most anxious to be away from Walter Clarke. They needed to be back at Fort George convincing the general of Nick's innocence, but how were they to accomplish that? Think Kate, think, she berated herself, trying desperately to collect her incoherent thoughts. After a few moments her eyes opened and she brightened a little as an idea finally came to her.

"I find myself confined to my bed Ellen, but you are in no such predicament; you are well and unhindered," she stated in a matter-of-fact tone.

"Yes, Kate, but what of it?" Ellen's confusion showed plainly on her face.

"Do you not see? I am afraid that you will have to leave here and seek help."

Ellen was instantly taken aback at the ludicrous suggestion. "And just how am I supposed to accomplish that, my dear girl? Have you forgotten that I too am a prisoner here? That little fall you took has definitely affected your thinking."

"Listen to me, Ellen," Kate persevered weakly, feeling her strength beginning to ebb. "I am dizzy and my head pounds so hard whenever I move. There is such an excruciating pain in my side, and my left ankle is so sore that I am sure I could not even bear to stand up. It is not my intent to complain, you understand, but you must see that I am rendered useless for the time being, so the duty of escape must fall on your shoulders. Ellen, you do see the importance of our getting away, do you not? Listen, if you were quiet, I am confident that you could easily make it as far as the Secord's farm; they live only a short distance down the road."

Ellen shook her head vehemently. "I am sorry, Kate, but I simply refuse to even attempt such an expedition. I will not leave you here."

"We need to have help, Ellen," Kate persisted, a hysterical edge to her voice now. "Have you forgotten that Nick is to be executed at Fort George any day? And have you also forgotten Walter Clarke's involvement in this mess? That madman has to be stopped Ellen, and we will need help to accomplish the task. I only pray that we are able to clear Nick in time, and that we are not already too late," she added wistfully.

"Believe me, Kate; I too am aware of the importance of my brother's release and the shortage of time involved, but I do not think you know how deep the insanity runs in our captor, and what he is capable of? No one realizes the depth of evil lurking within Captain Clarke's soul more than I." Ellen's reserve floundered slightly as she related to Kate all the horrific events that took place in the cellar, and she elaborated on the cold-blooded killing of her own father at Captain Clarke's hand. When she had finished, Ellen stared intently at her friend with tears flowing silently down her face.

Kate tried to comfort her while absorbing the horror of what she had just heard.

Ellen stood up directly, sniffing loudly and wiping her face, gaining control of her emotions once again. "Kate, you know I want to help my brother more than anything, but what you are asking of me is impossible. How am I to leave here unnoticed? That evil man and his accomplice hide in every shadowy corner of this house, always watching. Even if I could escape this room undetected, I could never leave this farm."

"Ellen, we have a privy behind the house that has two loose boards on the back wall, held in place by only one nail at the top of each one, and a wooden wedge at the bottom." At Ellen's apparent look of confusion, Kate explained further. "You see, when we were children I locked Kevin inside the privy and refused to let him out. He retaliated by screaming at me as he kicked a hole in the back wall to make his escape. As I recall, it was a terrible prank to play on him though, as he was extremely claustrophobic. Anyway, I remember how furious our father was at the time and he made us both repair it. So, you see Ellen, if you express an urgent need to be escorted there, you can make your escape by separating the boards and squeezing through. Once you are out, you could run to the tree cover directly behind the privy, and then on to Laura's."

Ellen sighed loudly, shaking her head in resignation. "I will do this thing Kate, for you and for Nick, but I do not mind telling you how terrified I am." Footsteps were heard outside the bedroom door. When it opened, both women gazed fearfully at Walter Clarke's sneer laden face, the conversation they had just shared still fresh in their minds.

Nick Brannigan's injuries were proving to be a major hindrance to his escape from Fort George. His progress was slow at best and he was tiring easily as he stumbled awkwardly over the rough terrain. Unfortunately, he had to avoid the main road, which would have made his journey much easier, for fear of being discovered by the soldiers that were surely pursuing him. Often, since leaving the fort, he found himself thinking about his unraveling life and wishing it were a bad dream. How could his circumstances have changed this drastically in so short a time? He loved this country; his life was here now. He still found it hard to believe that the British, Brock's British, were intent on hanging him for treason. That damned Clarke. Someday he will pay for all his evil and deceitful ways; Kate's God will surely see to that. Unless I find him first, he vowed. Thinking of Kate then, his worry for both her and his sister grew stronger.

"Kate! Ellen! Where are you?" he shrieked. The area was deserted, and only the forceful wind answered back. Nick felt lost and alone, much like he did all those years ago when his mother was taken from him. He remembered the heated argument that he had had with his father before this blasted war began, and how he declared emphatically that this was his country now and he no longer wanted to live south of the border. How ironic, he thought mirthlessly. If he was guilty of treason, it should be to America; it was the place of his birth after all. His jumbled thoughts settled on Isaac Brock and how much he missed the general. They had shared an unspoken trust and had been through a lot together in such a short time. Even now in his painful and confused state, Nick felt the immense loss of his friend. He also wondered what had become of Tecumseh. How could the British army believe that I would have anything to do with Brock's death? What were their accusations based on? The vile, lying testimony of a scoundrel like Clarke!

"Damn," he swore loudly. All the pain and bitterness of his life was centered on two men: his father, and Walter Clarke. As Nick continued his painful journey, certain events of his past came suddenly to mind. First, the horror of watching his mother being taken and then later killed, and the outrage he lavished on his father for what he had done. He also remembered the fear he had felt for his tiny sister, how concerned he was then of what would become of her. It was too much for a young boy to experience, and here he was again at the mercy of another madman!

Nick never really cared for anyone since his mother, with the exception of Ellen of course; until now. Katie! He tormented himself with thoughts of not only his beloved sister but of Kate as well. He swore out loud. He was angry at himself, regretting his unforgivable treatment of Kate: the cold looks and hate filled accusations, especially after she single-handedly rescued him from the whipping post. He prayed that she would forgive him. His thoughts turned to Walter Clarke once more. If that devil has brought harm to either of the women that I love ... ? He couldn't let his thoughts progress any further, refusing to think the worst and determined to find them both very much alive. He would consider no other outcome.

Nick ambled along with difficulty, dodging between the brittle, entwining branches of the dense forest that skirted the roadside, slipping in the mud and wet snow with each misplaced step. His wounds troubled him, but raw determination drove him on. He intended to reach the Sullivan farm before nightfall; where he hoped to find Kate. What day is this? he thought pensively. He had lost track of the time since the battle at the heights and his incarceration that followed, and was uncertain of the date. It must surely be close to the end of November, he surmised. He was cold, tired and hungry, and his mind teased him as he thought of a hot bowl of stew and a comfortable warm bed. Nick shook his head sadly, too deep in thought to notice his immediate surroundings. When he mounted the top of a steep embankment, he lost his footing and slipped unexpectedly in a small quagmire of mud. He immediately cascaded roughly down the side of the ridge, grunting and yelling in pain as he fell head over heels, landing in a painful heap at the bottom.

Walter Clarke's visit to the bedroom did not cause any undue stress and both women were surprised to find him almost cordial. He inquired with concern if Kate was well and praised Ellen for her excellent care. Just as the captain turned to take his leave however, Ellen bade him wait, confessing her dire need to visit the outhouse as soon as possible. He nodded his consent, stating that Max would escort her and that he would remain in the room with Kate to await her return.

Ellen was momentarily elated to be finally outside, briefly forgetting Max, who lumbered lazily along beside her, and the dire reason for which she was enjoying this short reprieve. The cold wind, along with Max's surly growl, brought her abruptly back to reality. Her escort was a tall, miserable looking man, and Ellen remembered that he was the malicious brute that viciously pushed Kate down the cellar stairs. She cast a sly glance at him before wrapping her shawl snugly around herself and quickening her step to the privy.

Moments later, Ellen could barely control the quaking in her limbs as she quietly squeezed through the hole in the wall of the outhouse, with Max being none the wiser. She was thankful that the wind moaned loudly enough to cover any noise she might have made during her escape. She was out! It had been easier to accomplish than she had first imagined, she thought. Without a moment to lose, Ellen ran immediately towards the woods and the Secord farm.

Kate had heard the commotion outside in the same instant as Walter Clarke, and the latter quickly left the bedroom to investigate. Kate lay still, concern for Ellen uppermost in her mind. Quaking with apprehension, she awaited the vile man's imminent return. Only a few minutes had passed before Clarke burst into her room, slamming the door when he entered, his face livid. She lay defenceless on the bed, her eyes never leaving the captain as he loomed above her, the colour slowly draining from his face as he spoke.

"How very clever you must feel, my dear."

Kate felt uneasy with his quiet tone, suspecting that at any moment he would cast his merciless retribution upon her. She closed her eyes, praying that Ellen's escape had been successful.

"Look at me!" Clarke whispered dangerously, as he bent over her so closely that his hideous face was only inches from her own.

Kate opened her eyes just as she felt her assailant's claw-like hands clutching her neck. She stared as if in a trance, noticing the ugly glare in his eyes and the beads of smelly sweat that covered his face. He is going to kill me, she thought, and could not move. She was paralyzed again and she felt his fingers begin to tighten; this time she was not dreaming. Her whole body was wracked with pain and now this devil was squeezing the life out of her. Kate instinctively grabbed his hands, trying to pry them from her swollen throat. She realized that in her weakened state she was no match for this crazed man, so she reached up and viciously clawed at his face.

Clarke screamed in pain, instantly withdrawing his hands. In the next moment he shrank back from her, crying out passionately like the madman she had always believed him to be. "That bastard's sister has escaped!!" he exploded, as anguished tears fell rapidly down his face, mixing with the bloody scratches on his cheeks. "How could you do this to me?" He approached Kate then with his arms extended out and his palms facing up, pleading with her, whimpering at times like a small child, as he implored her to love him. "Please, my love, do not reject me. I could not stand it if you did. I beg you, my dear, do not make me hurt you."

Kate was bewildered and frightened. After mentally measuring the extent of his insanity, she quickly determined that he needed to be handled with great care; her very life depended on it. "Please, my dearest Captain, do not distress yourself so. Whatever has happened to upset you?" Kate's tongue stumbled over her false benevolence, and just as it happens with an unstable mind, Walter Clarke's mood changed instantly to that of an enraged aggressor.

"Do not waste your simpering tones on me, my dear; I know you despise the very sight of me." He was becoming infuriated again and Kate softened her voice even more, trying to lure him into a false sense of security.

"But I have done nothing, my love. Why do you berate me so strongly?"

"You helped that bitch escape!!" he bellowed.

Kate swallowed hard, realizing with dread that he did not seem to believe her, and tried desperately to gain control of the horrible situation. "In truth I did not, sir. Why would I? Was it not her traitorous brother who murdered Kevin? I have not as yet had the opportunity to relay that particular information to my family, sir, but believe me, I shall," she lied. Kate's chest heaved as her heart pounded and she could feel the intense pain from her wounds circulating throughout her entire body. She was more frightened now than she had ever been in her life as she watched Walter Clarke pacing back and forth at the foot of her bed. Suddenly, he seemed calmer, and that terrified her. She knew that he was unbalanced, but she was not prepared for his next horrific revelation.

"Your family?" he chuckled then in wry amusement. "Your family will never know my dear, for I have taken the liberty of disposing of them. Yes, you may rest assured, I made them extremely sorry for their obvious contempt and degradation towards me. Suffice it to say that they will certainly not bother us in the future. No, my love," he stated, leering in close to her face. "We are quite alone now. Come, my dear, do not look so stricken. I did it for us. They were trying to keep you away from me." Walter Clarke leaned in even closer to Kate then and kissed her quite ardently, brushing his wet, disgusting lips over hers.

She gagged in repulsion. With her mind screaming and her ears ringing, she pulled herself up slowly. Leaning over the side of the bed, she vomited, overcome by the horror of it all; her mind in agony. She stared at him in wild-eyed dismay. This man had killed her entire family and soon Nick would follow. Her chest heaved and her head pounded. The ringing in her ears grew steadily louder as her initial numbness dissolved. Kate finally let herself react, as a low, guttural moan crept up from her throat evolving into a piercing, blood-curdling scream.

"I hate you! I have nothing but contempt for you! Who could ever love such a vile, despicable, repulsive animal like you? You sicken me!!" Kate was hysterical now and out of control. "If I were able to and had a weapon, I would kill you myself!"

Walter Clarke pulled back at once, stunned at the onset of her hysteria and crazed confession, but after her hate-filled tirade, his anger too was inflamed. He approached her slowly, pulling the hunting knife from his belt and rubbing it threateningly over her face, neck and chest.

"Be careful, my love," he replied wickedly. "You should guard what you say, for surely you know me to be a man of conviction." He sneered menacingly then. "I will have to kill you eventually, knowing what your true feelings for me are, but I promise you before that happens, I will show you how a man and woman act in the bed chamber. I will have you, my love, and your precious Nick Brannigan will never have that particular pleasure."

Kate felt her insides heaving once more. Without thinking, she blurted out a reply. "Ha, sir; the joke is on you. Mr. Brannigan has already taught me the ways of men and women, and believe me when I say this to you, captain, I am quite certain that anyone else would pale in comparison." Kate had no time to be shocked at her own words.

Walter Clarke turned instantly into the very devil himself and plunging his knife down onto the bed, he just missed Kate's ear as he stabbed it violently into the soft pillow, close to her head.

"You will both pay for this atrocity and all the others that you have lain at my feet!" Clarke shrieked in outrage before continuing in a much quieter tone. "I cannot accept this. I will not accept this. You were mine to enjoy! Well, my dear," he added, a disturbing calmness returning once more to his voice. "That bastard will not have you again. He is already paying the price for incurring my wrath, is he not my love? I would imagine that he has already been executed for the crimes of treason and murder," he continued, his tone smug now. "Just the very thought of him swinging at the gallows is a great comfort to me." Walter Clarke laughed insanely then and pulled himself away from a devastated Kate.

"Know this, Miss Sullivan; your friend may have escaped, but you I fear, will not be as fortunate. People have to pay when they displease me; Max learned that lesson all too well. He should never have let Miss Brannigan trick him. Even if the bitch is able to bring help, it will not be in time. You see, my dear; you are home now and will never leave. No," he added with conviction, pulling the dagger from beside her head. "I will not take you now, as you were to be my treasure. The very thought of that bastard's hands on you sickens me. I was to be your first! Walter Clarke's volatile temper cooled and his tone was quiet once more. No! Our love has been tainted and I will not have that bastard's leavings. Alas, my dear, I cannot allow anyone else to have you either. Rest assured, you will not die by this knife. I have something more appropriate in mind for you, my love."

Kate felt her body shake uncontrollably at the realization that she was indeed going to die. When her jailor exited the room, she sat up in a panic, listening to his shrill laughter resounding through the house. A few moments later the front door slammed with a reverberating bang, and all was quiet. Kate lay immobile for a second, before suddenly giving in to her tears. "Have I truly lost everyone?" she lamented loudly, overcome with misery and fear. She could not bear it. First Kevin, and now Father and Hannah. Nick! Kate screamed out for the man she loved before collapsing on the bed feeling frightened, lost and alone.

Chapter Seventeen

———

Laura Secord stood at the kitchen window looking pensively out at the deserted road, pausing in her work to briefly luxuriate in the peace of the moment. It had been a tiring day so far and it was not even noon yet. James had awakened this morning with such a burning pain in his knee that she had been unsure if he would ever settle down. Mary, who seemed to have recovered sufficiently from her debilitating grief and fatigue of the previous day, occupied the other four children with a quick game of blind man's bluff, before taking them outside with her to finish the chores in the barn.

As the dark clouds gathered threateningly overhead, Laura sighed heavily. If only this dreadful war had not come. She knew of no one who claimed any benefit from it. When asked, the general consensus seemed to be that it was just a dreadful bother, a nuisance in everyone's life. Life had been hard enough for those who inhabited the Niagara peninsula before this calamity reared its ugly head, with most families working diligently from dawn to dusk, but now it promised to be ten times worse. We are only slightly better placed than our neighbours at the moment, she thought, the Sullivan's included, and we too are exhausted by the end of each day. She was thankful, however, that the war only remotely touched their lives at present, with the exception of James' injuries of course, and for the most part they merely heard the sounds of random gunfire far off in the distance.

Laura was suddenly overcome with such a tremendous feeling of anxiety. She experienced a discomfort that could not be ignored. She knew in her heart that before long, and through no choice of their own, they would all be thrown head-first into this ghastly war. The wind moaned eerily on the other side of the window as small shards of ice began to pelt against the glass in a constant ticking rhythm.

"A storm is brewing," Laura muttered out loud. "And I do not mean just the weather." Shaking her head she returned to her bread dough, angrily punching it in frustration while kneading it smooth. Laura had just put the bread in the oven when Mary and the other children came bursting into the kitchen, immediately followed by a gust of wind.

"Mother, there is a stranger staggering down our laneway," Mary exclaimed.

Laura rushed to the window and peered out; noticing at once that the man looked as worn out as his clothes and as frozen as the shards of ice that continuously pelted him in the blustery weather. As the unfortunate creature drew closer, she could see the loose, bloodied bandage that now lay askew on top of his head. One long strip had come unbound and hung down limply over his chest; it too was flapping in the wind. The woolen scarf that was wound tightly under his chin and around his head seemed to be the only thing holding the rest of the bedraggled binding in place. His gait was clumsy and he stumbled along purposefully, his eyes never wavering from the front door. Laura regarded him intently until recognition finally dawned. She gasped in shock and hurried to the door, grabbing her coat from its hook and quickly throwing it on as she headed out to the injured man, leaving her five children staring after her in wonder.

"Oh, Nick," she cried, taking hold of his arm. "Come this way into the kitchen." Laura led him around the house to the side door and, once inside, she and Mary helped him out of his wet coat. Since they could not manoeuvre him up the stairs, they brought the mattress from the trundle bed down to the parlour and placed it by the fire for Nick's comfort. Unlike Kate, he needed more than just rest and food; his wounds had to be attended to.

Mary brought him a bucket of warm water and lye soap, placing them on the table beside the clean wash rag and towel. "Mother said to give you this," she stated shyly, nervously handing him one of her father's nightshirts. "Are-are you able to wash up and dress yourself?" At Nick's affirmation, she continued. "I will return later to collect your wet things then." She turned to leave, pausing at the doorway, debating whether she should inform him of Kate's whereabouts. Mary decided she had best heed her mother's wishes that they wait until morning to speak to him about Kate, and silently closing the door, she left the room.

The hour was late and the house grew quiet as Nick lay on his bed, feeling both sated and exhausted. He was clean, his belly was full, his wounds had been dressed and two women occupied his mind: Kate and Ellen. He had informed Laura and Mary earlier of his earnest intent on locating them, but neither mentioned seeing Kate or his sister. As he drifted off to sleep, he wondered what had become of them.

The harsh weather had calmed considerably throughout the night, and the morning dawned with sunshine and a slightly warmer temperature. Laura enlisted the help of Mary to ensure that all was quiet on the main floor of the house and that no one bothered Nick, sound asleep in the parlour. A few events in the war had taken place following the victory at Queenston Heights, but most people were unaware of them, including Nick, whose incarceration left him bereft of all pertinent information regarding this war of 1812. Three of His Majesty's ships - The Frolic, The Poictiers and The Macedonian - were all defeated by the Americans. Then there was President Madison's re-election last fall. The British, however, had set up a blockade in both South Carolina and Georgia, and the Americans decided to retreat from eastern Canada. The war seemed so far away from the Niagara region and the Secord farm; for the time being all was quiet on the peninsula.

Nick finally woke when Laura entered the parlour with his breakfast. He voiced his disapproval at first, kindly declaring that they need not wait on him. He could just as easily eat in the kitchen. It was only after Laura's gentle insistence and his inability to rise that he accepted the proffered meal. While he ate, Laura seated herself in a chair near him and they began to converse quietly, exchanging personal views on the war and the crumbling world around them. When Laura inquired about Fort George though, Nick conveniently omitted any information regarding his escape. He in turn inquired if the war was having any effect on her family at present and further commented on how mysterious Kate and Ellen's disappearance was. He informed her then of Clarke's declaration that his sister had been murdered, but that he did not believe it. He also reiterated to Laura that he would not give up his search until both women were found.

"I cannot imagine how you managed to travel this far, considering your injured condition, not to mention the rough terrain you crossed and the inclement weather."

"It was not easy, Laura, I assure you. I am ashamed to say that there were a few occasions along the road when I was tempted to just lie down and give up. I slipped and fell over an embankment a short distance from here. I found myself lying prostrate in the mud; the pain was such that every part of me whispered just to lie there and die." At Laura's inquiry as to what drove him on, he continued. "In my half conscious state, I saw both Ellen and Kate coming through the brush towards me. I heard General Brock's enthusiastic order *to Push on, boys,* and somehow I was rejuvenated enough to drag myself back up that hill."

"You impress me, Mr. Brannigan. You possess a strength and determination that I am envious of, and your courage defies anyone from hindering your mission. I am sure that you will indeed find your sister."

"I thank you for your praise," Nick said in a matter-of-fact tone. However, I would like to point out that you yourself are an angel of mercy. I know of no other woman who scoured the battlefield at Queenston looking for her husband."

Laura was taken aback for a moment, and then remembered she was not alone in her search. "What of Kate? She was with me on the heights that day looking for both you and Kevin."

"I am corrected then, madam, and somewhat astonished, I might add," Nick replied, smiling slightly and harbouring a whole new respect for Kate.

After Nick had finished his meal, Laura grabbed the tray and was collecting the dirty dishes, feeling that now was the time to tell him of Kate's whereabouts, when Harriet, her second oldest, entered the room.

"Papa's leg is burning again mama and he needs you upstairs," the young girl stated, eyeing Nick with youthful suspicion as she slowly approached her mother.

Laura cradled her daughter lovingly while presenting her to Nick with a proper introduction. "Mr. Brannigan, this is Harriet. My dear, this is our friend, Mr. Nick Brannigan."

"Hello, sir," Harriet replied with a smile and a quick curtsy.

"Hello, Miss Harriet," Nick said, returning a friendly smile of his own. "And how old might you be, young lady?"

"I am nine years old," she replied. After studying Nick for a moment, she approached him shyly. "Are you looking for our Kate?" she innocently inquired.

The dishes suddenly rattled on the tray and when Laura turned quickly towards Nick, her eyes locked with his startled expression. "You may tell your father that I will be up directly," Laura said, nervously clearing her throat as she gently ushered her daughter from the room. Returning to Nick, she smiled sheepishly before explaining. "I was just going to tell you of Kate's brief visit here Nick, before my daughter's untimely interruption," she confessed.

"Kate was here?" At Laura's slight nod, he hastily threw back the covers and attempted to stand up. "Why did you not inform me of this last night? You knew how anxious I was to find her," Nick complained, his voice rising.

"Please, Nick. Lay still. You are not well." Laura gently pushed him back down onto the mattress and covered him once more before offering her explanation. "We decided not to speak about this last evening because you were badly in need of rest. You were sick, exhausted and wounded. Knowing where Kate was would have served no purpose to you then." Laura stood, her frustration just as apparent as Nick's. "I have to see to James for the moment, but I will return as soon as I am able. Do not move from this spot!" she ordered. She left him alone then to stew over the matter, quickly making her way to her husband's bedside.

Later, Laura related the whole story of Kate's visit, informing Nick of her cold and exhausted condition and how sad she was about not only Ellen's disappearance, but also for Nick's unfair anger. Laura regarded Nick with an accusing expression then, and his response surprised her.

"I am such a fool. Kate did not deserve that," he admitted, shaking his head and casting an apologetic glance at Laura.

"There will be no argument from me on that score, sir." Laura also spoke of Kate's anguish over his upcoming hanging, and of her plan to find Ellen with the high hopes of returning her to him safe and sound. "She was determined to enlist the help of her father to find your sister, Nick, so she left here two days ago, her health much improved. She said that when Ellen was found, they would all return to Fort George and somehow convince the general of your innocence." Laura laughed then, lightening the mood, and shrugging her shoulders at Nick, she elaborated. "I do not know how she planned to accomplish that feat, but suffice it to say that if persistence and determination held any importance in the matter, and with the good Lord's assistance, she would succeed. Now it appears that she need not concern herself with your whereabouts; only your sisters."

"I see that you were indeed very wise to keep this from me Laura," Nick stated, ignoring the speculative glance that Laura gave him. "But of course you realize that I do intend to follow her. Would you be so kind as to bring me my clothes." Nick was thankful that Laura had made no further reference to his escaping the hangman's noose.

"I am so sorry, Nick, but they are wet. I laundered them this morning and they are still drying by the fire in the kitchen." Nick scowled, impatience clearly distorting his handsome features. "It will serve no purpose to be cross with me, Mr. Brannigan. You cannot go anywhere before this afternoon, and that is that," Laura scolded sternly. In the next instant however, her voice softened. "I promise, sir. Mary will bring them to you just as soon as they are dry. In the meantime, I will clean your wounds again and then you can rest while you wait."

Nick hid his annoyance and smiled lamely up at her in defeat. "I am sorry for my thoughtless behavior madam. It is inexcusable. I cannot thank you and Mary enough, and am in your debt for the care that you have not only given to me; but to Kate as well. Truly, Laura, I did not mean to be rude; I apologize. I am just so worried about my sister and am anxious to see Katie."

Sometime later Nick woke, but this time it was to a quiet household. No one puttered in the kitchen and there were no noises of children scampering through the rooms. It is getting late, he thought as he sat up. Looking around the parlour, he noticed his clothes now laying neatly folded on a chair. He rose from the mattress, carefully at first, but after feeling some of his strength returning, he grasped tightly to a table and pulled himself up. Experiencing some difficulty, he slowly put on his clothes before entering the kitchen in search of his overcoat and boots.

Nick found Laura and Mary outside, pulling dry laundry from the line in the late afternoon sun. He lumbered unsteadily towards them, relieved to find that he could still walk, dodging the children who were playing close by.

"G-Good afternoon, Mr. Brannigan. I-I am happy to see that you seem much improved, sir." Mary spoke first, smiling in embarrassment at the conclusion of her greeting, thinking to herself how lucky Kate was for holding this handsome man's interest.

"Thank you, Mary," Nick replied, treating her to one of his most charming smiles before turning his attention to Laura.

"I wish to borrow a horse Mrs. Secord, as I am extremely anxious to see Kate. I intend to join with her to find my sister."

"Of course. There are two in the barn, sir, and you are welcome to either one. I must confess though, I am concerned for you riding at the moment, even if it is only as far as the Sullivan farm. Are you quite sure you feel up to such a strenuous journey?"

Nick attempted to soothe Laura's fears, but was interrupted by Mary's excited cries and frantic gesturing. When following the direction of her avid pointing, they were all surprised to discover a woman running towards them, screaming and flailing her arms madly about. Nick recognized Ellen at once and immediately set off to meet her, cursing his damned limiting wounds all the way. Ellen flew into her brother's awaiting arms, giving in to both her happiness and distress as she sobbed out his name. Nick could not believe his eyes as he held his coveted sister in a tight embrace, listening attentively as she continued her outburst; laughing and crying with relief. He silently thanked God for Ellen's safe return before subjecting her body to a hurried inspection, inquiring concernedly about her welfare.

"Are you all right? Are you hurt?" Nick didn't give Ellen a chance to reply before charging on with his questions. "Why did you leave the fort? You must have known how worried I would be. You should not have come in the first place." Nick embraced her once more and Ellen too, blubbered out questions of her own, fussing over him in distress after noticing his wounds.

"Oh, Nick! We were so afraid that you had been hung. Captain Clarke led us to believe that it was inevitable."

"Clarke! Where is he, Ellen?" Nick gently pulled away from his sister, holding her loosely by the shoulders as he made his inquiries.

"He... he is with Kate," she stammered between sobs. "He was holding us both hostage upstairs in her bedroom until Kate convinced me to escape."

"Why did she not escape with you?" Nick asked apprehensively.

Ellen stumbled over her words as she replied. Her worry for Kate was apparent.

"She was unable to, Nick. You see, she is injured and bedridden. Captain Clarke is with her. Oh Nick! I am terrified of what he will do to her when he discovers our treachery," Ellen wailed. She clutched her brother tightly, fretfully disclosing everything that had taken place while she had been held captive. She told him of their father's involvement with Captain Clarke and how he was killed. Ellen informed him too of Kate's treacherous tumble and the injuries she sustained. She also informed him of the calculating, leering looks that Clarke bestowed on Kate. She left nothing out of her story.

The more she spoke, the more devastated he felt. At the conclusion, Nick experienced a coldness that crept steadily inside him, bringing with it a fear such as he had never known before. That crazed monster had his Katie! There was no telling what he would do. Clarke's mind was unstable, he was certain of that, and Nick knew he had to find her. There was no time to lose! He gently handed Ellen over to Laura's care with a soothing promise that she need not worry, that everything would be all right.

As darkness descended, Ellen Brannigan watched with trepidation as her brother galloped away from the barn and sped off in the direction of the Sullivan farm, his wounds all but forgotten now.

Nick was close to his destination and just rounding a corner, when he was almost forced off the road by another rider. The lunatic was travelling at a ghastly speed and almost succeeded in knocking him off his mount. Nick was forced to pull up suddenly, turning an angry, accusing glare at the retreating horseman. He felt the panic surge through his body, as he recognized the evil, high-pitched laughter and cursing accusations of Walter Clarke.

"You are too late! You cannot save her! Tell that bastard that since I was denied her, no one else will have her either!!"

Nick heard Clarke scream out his insanity with the night wind. In that moment he was convinced that the madman only saw a rider on a horse, and had no idea who he was. It was in that instant too, that Nick smelled the smoke. He kicked his horse in the flanks and galloped off towards the blaze.

Nick arrived at the Sullivan farm unaware of the blood now oozing from his head and leg. He dismounted and set off immediately, hampered by a limping gait, towards the burning house. Peering up at the second floor windows he frantically called out Kate's name, but all he heard was the loud roar of the wind as it made the flames dance. Nick then watched in horror and disbelief as the thick smoke swirled relentlessly out of the windows and the hungry flames licked the walls and curled about the roof. Weakened by his pain and loss of blood, he fell to the ground before reaching the porch. Clarke had been right! He was too late! The whole house was engulfed in flames and he could not enter. Nick pulled himself up to a sitting position and, tilting his head back, screamed his torment to the night sky, his face grimaced and wet with tears, overcome now by the smoke and heat that erupted from the blaze.

So many times since this war had started, Nick had felt anguish and torment, frustration and pain, but nothing had prepared him for this. His mind reeled at her memory and his body ached for her. He needed her and he loved her, but had never let her know how much. And now she was gone! He screamed Kate's name over and over, his voice overpowered now by the thundering clamour of the inferno. Nick felt the sanity slowly draining from his mind. He shot a wild, hateful glare towards the road where his nemesis had just escaped, lamenting loudly through his tears. He cursed Walter Clarke for what he had done, vowing to avenge Kate's death.

"You are a dead man, Clarke! I will hunt you down and kill you if it takes the rest of my life; I promise you that!" Nick's voice reached such a pitch that he too sounded like a madman. Shaking his head helplessly, he covered his face with his hands, whimpering Kate's name, and cursing the war and Walter Clarke for bringing such devastation to his life. He was overcome with bitterness, feeling heartsick and alone. He could not believe that she was gone.

Kate's relentless sobbing, ceased abruptly when she smelled the smoke. She pulled herself carefully out of bed, intensely aware of the shards of pain that shot through her broken body. Kate stooped over slightly, hanging on to the furniture for support as she warily made her way to the bedroom door, the pain attacking her unmercifully from head to toe with each step. She reached out to turn the handle, but pulled back directly, wincing at the pain from the burning metal. Feeling her strength beginning to ebb, Kate slid slowly to the floor. Leaning against the wall, she sat dazed for a second. A choking cough brought her immediately out of her stupor. She watched in horror as the menacing smoke slithered up towards her through the large gap under the door, just like the ominous serpent from the bible story, she thought, as it wafted dangerously throughout the room.

"Dear, God, he has set fire to the house!" Kate began to cry, trembling with the knowledge that she was trapped. "This wood frame house will light up like a tinderbox," she wailed. "Oh, God! What am I to do?" Her mind was flying wildly in every direction at once, desperately trying to think of any possible escape. The smoke grew thicker, causing Kate to cover her nose and mouth with her nightgown, and her choking cough intensified. The room was heating quickly. She felt that she was on fire.

Her eyes stung through her tears. She felt an unbearable burning in her throat and nostrils. It was difficult to breathe now and as she sank lower to the floor in defeat, she pleaded once more for God's mercy.

'Get up, Katie Brianna. No time to sleep now, me girl. Come Daughter, there is work to be done this day.' Kate quietly moaned her father's name as she heard his voice coming from far away. She opened her eyes then and turned to face the window, hearing her father beckoning to her once again from the other side of the glass.

"Help me, Father," she choked out deliriously, as her tears fell to the floor.

"I cannot darlin'. You got yourself up that blasted tree, so now you can just get yourself down. If you lose your footing me girl, I will not let you fall. I promise."

"No! Father, I am in my room. I am burning, Father. Please find me. I am not in a tree. Oh, please help me," she pleaded. From somewhere deep within the farthest recesses of her muddled brain came an immediate dawning. "My tree! I almost forgot about my tree. Do not fret Father," Kate called out, "I am coming." She struggled to crawl to the bedroom window; her body screamed in protest while her mind willed her to continue. She somehow managed to climb through onto an awaiting branch, knowing that she only had a short amount of time before the hungry flames devoured the house. Her head pounded. She felt sharp stabs of intense pain throughout her body. With gritted teeth and short raspy breaths, she managed to keep moving. Each branch she held onto was a trial, and she prayed that she could descend safely.

There was no time to test each limb before stepping onto it, but she persevered, knowing she had no other choice. Kate was not far from the ground when she heard an angry crashing sound above her. Pausing, she looked up. She watched helplessly as the explosive flames engulfed her bedroom, sending live sparks spewing out the open window and onto the tree, filling her with fear as it began to burn. Kate climbed steadily down to escape the ravenous fire, pain continuously torturing her body. She finally dropped to the ground, crying out in agony as she crumpled in a broken heap at the base of the tree. She willed herself to remain conscious. Concerned now for her safety, she slowly and piteously crawled as far away from the burning house and the now blazing tree beside it.

Kate's body was wracked with severe pain and there was also an over-powering hurt that presently invaded her mind. She thought back to when she heard her father's voice. Oh, how overjoyed she had been to discover that Clarke had lied to her, relieved that her father was alive and had come to save her. The moment she realized that her mind had played a cruel trick on her, the devastation was too much to bear and she completely fell apart. Kate cried out in anguish above the din of the blazing inferno, releasing all her pent-up suffering and horror through her anger and tears.

Nick slowly and painfully pulled himself to his feet, the soreness in his body matching that of the ache in his heart. He did not want to move, but he knew that he could not remain here. He would return to the Secord's for now to see Ellen, but as soon as he was strong enough, he would hunt Clarke down and deliver his retribution.

"I will make him pay for this, Katie," he vowed. "He will rue the day that he took you from me" He looked behind him at the raging fire for an instant. Shaking his head sadly, he turned on his heels and slowly limped back to the borrowed horse. Nick was climbing carefully onto the mare's back when he stopped abruptly, straining to listen as a feeble cry floated towards him on the wind. In a state of confusion, he noted that the sound, now growing louder, had come from the far side of the house, and he carefully set out to discover its cause. As he rounded the corner of the burning building, he found that a tree there was ablaze right alongside the house, and a few yards away from it was ..."

Katie!!" Nick screamed out his rapture and reaching Kate, he gathered her gently in his arms, hugging her close while moaning her name repeatedly. He pulled away, noticing her pale face, stricken with grief and pain. Ravaged by the suffering in his own body, Nick managed to carry her a short distance to an old wooden garden bench, where he proceeded to examine her injuries. They were both in a bad way, he surmised, but he deemed her wounds to be more severe. He suddenly remembered the large blanket laying under the saddle on his horse, and left to retrieve it. Moments later, they were both wrapped within its warmth and sitting together, each so thankful at finding the other alive, that no words were spoken.

Nick experienced some fleeting emotions: the agony of thinking Kate was dead, to the sudden elation at finding her alive, and then the distress over her unbearable condition. He was overjoyed at having her safely back in his arms once again; his own misery forgotten. But, no matter how happy and relieved he felt, Nick was still concerned for not only the apparent injuries that afflicted Kate's body, but also for the hidden ones that troubled her heart. She has lost her home and sanctuary, he thought sadly, and I pray that she is able to recover from the devastation of it all.

Kate too tried to take control of her over-powering emotions. She was overjoyed at finding Nick alive, but her ecstasy was overshadowed by the great loss of her family. Just like the flames that were swallowing up her home, she was overcome by an intense state of melancholy that threatened to engulf her completely. She looked at Nick then, gazing absentmindedly into his deep blue eyes, and when he stared back at her, she could see her love mirrored in them. He leaned into her then and placed a soft, tender kiss on her mouth. When he released her, they both sat silent for a time, watching the farmhouse burn to the ground; both feeling an unbearable sadness as they stared at what was now a smoldering heap. Kate suddenly started to cry, collapsing against Nick's chest. He embraced her lovingly as she sobbed out her misery.

"Kevin's gone. Hannah and father are gone. You were almost hanged. The terrible man that pushed me down the stairs is dead. Your father is dead too. Walter Clarke killed them all!!" she wailed, looking up at Nick with a crazed, fearful expression. "He is such a hateful man! I cannot take this anymore, Nick," she whispered forlornly and shaking her head. "There are just too many disastrous things happening to me now. I hate all the conflict and devastation that Clarke and this terrible war has caused. The cost is too high! I...I just want it all to stop!" She screamed out now as the tormenting sobs wracked through her slender, pain-ridden body.

"Come now, Katie love. Do not take on so. You are not yourself at the moment. I am just so thankful that you are alive. When I saw the burning house, knowing that you were being held upstairs, I had thought you were dead. I came too late and could not get in." Nick rocked her gently back and forth in his arms, placing soothing kisses on her face and forehead. Your pain and loss will heal in time," he cooed reassuringly. "We know Clarke to be a liar my love, so there may be a chance that Thomas and Hannah are still alive. If however, we discover the worse to be true," he whispered, "then we will never forget them."

Kate tried to take some comfort in his words, but she had buried herself too deeply in despair. She reached a shaky hand up to his face, noticing his wounds. "Oh, Nick," she moaned. "Look at you. You are bleeding."

"I am alright," he shrugged, "but I must get you to Laura. You are hurt my dear, and in need of rest."

"I wish that we could have been together after the ball and have life continue on normally, with dances, and laughter and ... everything wonderful," she sighed in remorse. "At least we can be thankful that Ellen is alive."

"I love you, Katie," he confessed.

Chapter Eighteen

Nick and Kate were returning to the Secord farm, mounted uncomfortably together on the borrowed mare. Kate was seated in front of Nick, wrapped in his embrace, with the old blanket covering her tightly, even around her feet. Her head pounded so incessantly that she leaned against him and closed her eyes, trying to ignore the rest of her injured body which screamed out in protest against the slow, painful journey. Oh, how she longed for the comfort of her bed, she thought. She agonized over her recent loss and knew that her whole existence had been sorely affected now. No more would she flounce down the stairs in the morning to see her father sitting at the kitchen table, or hear the sounds of Hannah singing while she prepared their breakfast. Her family was gone, and her home along with them. Kate was heartsick, knowing instinctively that they would always remain in her thoughts. She thanked God that she still had Nick, although, in the next instant, she openly blamed the Divine Being for bringing these horrible tragedies to her life. So now, she thought dejectedly, not only had she lost her family, but her faith in the Lord was vanishing as well.

Kate had a very pessimistic view of the future. Even though Nick held her close and the Secord's were anxiously awaiting their return, she still felt lost and alone. She was oblivious to the biting wind that now mercilessly ravaged them both. It whipped their clothes and loose bandages haphazardly about, the frigid air piercing through the cloth; chilling them to the bone. Their horse also protested to the severe weather, snorting and flinging its head with every step. Kate's mind was filled with tumultuous thoughts regarding the war and Walter Clarke, focussing intently on how they were both viciously ripping her life apart. A complete hopelessness consumed her soul. Welcoming the numbness that gradually seeped through her now, she allowed herself to be drawn down into such a deep pit of despair that the pain in her heart seemed to fold up inside somehow, leaving her very spirit broken.

Nick was more optimistic than Kate regarding the future, although he too found the ride difficult. However, he could not deny his enjoyment at having Kate snuggled into him so closely, even if only for her warmth and comfort. His mood turned dismal though as he tried to block out the freezing weather, finding himself surprisingly disturbed by the death of his father. Nick hated the man that his father had become, but the way he had died was indeed shameful; just one more murder to lay at Clarke's door. *I wonder if that bastard thought he was getting even with me by killing him,* he mused dryly. There had been bad blood between him and his father for years, but Nick still experienced a feeling of remorse for the loving parent of his youth; before drinking, betrayal and a divided country separated them.

Yes, he thought dismally, *Katie and I have been through hell these past few months, Ellen too,* and no doubt there were still a vast number of other people in Upper Canada who suffered from their own misfortunes as well. Nick gave Kate a gentle squeeze feeling an abundant relief at having her back with him once more. His thoughts turned to Thomas Sullivan then and he made a silent vow to his absent friend. *I will see Kate through this terrible war, sir, and continue to take care of her afterwards; have no fear. She will want for nothing, I promise you.* There was no doubt in his mind that he would survive this war; he had to; they both did.

Throughout the following weeks Nick and Kate eventually recovered from their physical injuries, although Kate still struggled with depression. She was miserable. The hopelessness and despair were relentless, clinging so strongly to her mind, body and soul, that no matter how hard she tried, she just could not shake free. It affected her whole demeanor and she continuously scolded herself for her weakness.

Christmas was fast approaching, but try as they might for the children's sake, there was very little joy at the Secord's this year. Many families throughout Upper Canada were suffering. Some were short of money while others had little hope of lasting out the winter. Still others had lost husbands, fathers and brothers, leaving almost everyone in low spirits for the upcoming season. With Nick's improved health came an over-powering restlessness that he could not ignore. He needed to confront the British regarding their charges against him and to free the ongoing turmoil that now aggravated him, even in his sleep. Maybe, he thought, without Clarke's interference, I just might be able to accomplish that end. He was tired of his disturbing dreams of incessant torture and punishment that always seemed to leave him feeling drained and bitter.

The night before Christmas Eve, Nick was visiting with the convalescing James in the upstairs bedroom, accompanied by Kate, Mary, Ellen and Laura. He confidently informed all present that he would be returning to Fort George early the following morning.

"I intend to plead my innocence to General Sheaffe," he declared. "I will inform him of all the terrible things that Clarke has done." Secretly, Nick hoped that the spirit of the Christmas season would soften the general's heart, granting him the leniency he craved.

For the first time since her rescue, Kate protested loudly against the idea, pleading desperately with Nick to at least stay until after Christmas, as things were desolate enough. She asked him to wait before making such a rash decision, hoping that he would change his mind. Nick gently refused however, stating that he was determined to proceed; Christmas or no Christmas. There was no need to drag this out any further. He explained too, that since he had no desire to fight with the Americans, he could not find refuge in the States, and there was nowhere else he could hide from the British in Canada. He also added that he was sure it would go much better for him if he were to approach them first, rather than having the army forcefully descend upon Laura's home, possibly opting for his immediate execution instead of captivity.

That would only make an already gloomy situation worse, would it not? If they caught him here and decided to hang him, they would not care if it was Christmas, he had remonstrated.

"The only reason I left in the first place was to find the two of you," he insisted, looking fondly at both Ellen and Kate. "And as I do not intend to hide from the British army for the rest of my days, I find that I have no other choice. No more excuses now. I must face this!" Nick felt torn when he noticed Kate's quiet, alarming look, not wishing to add to her current suffering, but he remained steadfast in his decision. Sighing heavily, he continued, his attention on her now. "I have done nothing wrong Katie. I have to trust in that God of yours that General Sheaffe will be merciful. It is not my intention to give you false hope though, as the British are known to be an unrelenting lot when it comes to rules and law, especially in the military. I need to plead my case and not back down like a coward or I would be no different than that bast... uh ... Walter Clarke. I need to at least try and clear my name. Tell me you understand."

Kate nodded her head but proceeded to make a declaration of her own. "I am going with you." At Nick's immediate refusal, she quietly informed him that if he did not let her accompany him, she would only follow along behind.

Nick knew that he was defeated. He groaned in frustration, but pronounced with a wagging finger that if she was not ready first thing in the morning, he would leave without her.

The following day, after arriving early to the fort, both Nick and Kate were pleasantly surprised, while somewhat baffled, by the sentry's welcome. He freely admitted them through the gates, not insisting on any application of restraints to Nick. The sentry then proceeded to escort them to General Sheaffe's quarters. Joined by Captain John Glegg, Sheaffe greeted them amicably and invited them to please sit down. They were not long into their conversation when Nick learned of the circumstances that had turned in his favour. Had he heard correctly? Had all the charges been dismissed? Both Nick and Kate were ecstatic; rising from their chairs in unison, darting glances at each other and at the two officers.

"Please, do not misunderstand me, sir," he stated to Captain Glegg. "I am exceedingly grateful but find that I am confused at the same time. I came here in utmost trepidation, thinking the worst of endings would prevail. How could this fortunate circumstance have come about so neatly?" Nick learned of his pronounced innocence, thanks to the testimony of his neighbour in the next cell. "I did not realize that there were others imprisoned in the guardhouse. Where is he?" Nick inquired of Captain Glegg as they stood alone now. "I wish to thank him personally."

Since the general was preoccupied for the moment in a silent discussion with Kate, Captain Glegg seized the opportunity, informing Nick of his sorrow at having tried most urgently to gain a reprieve from the general for the unfortunate and well meaning young soldier, but alas, he had failed. Private Cameron's punishment was set in stone and British army law had to be appeased. Captain Glegg further explained to Nick how he and the general went to the blockhouse intending to relate the happy news of his imminent release, only to discover that he had vanished.

"One more day's wait, sir, and you would have known all," the captain added, stressing that had urgent war matters not detained him, he would have sought Nick out. "On the other hand, Mr. Brannigan, had you not been proven innocent, I would most assuredly have tracked you down and you would have been forced to face your allotted retribution. I admire your courage in returning here however, especially since you were unaware of the favourable turn of events. May I also add, sir, that I did indeed have misgivings about your incarceration, especially when seeing how dearly Miss Sullivan cared for you. I also regret my part in the detestable flogging that you were subjected to. Please understand, Mr. Brannigan, that at the time, I was convinced I was acting under the general's orders. I do apologize and hope that you can forgive me. If I had thought for one moment that it was strictly Captain Clarke's order for the whipping, suffice it to say, sir, it most definitely would never have been carried out."

Nick was saddened by the hanging of his cellmate, but elated at his newly found freedom. He clasped hands with the captain in a friendly shake, and in that moment he understood the trust that General Brock had once set on this man. Nick marvelled at the captain's ability to hide his apparent frustration with Brock's replacement, knowing that, try as he might, Sheaffe would never be the bold, decisive leader that Brock had proven himself to be. I almost feel sorry for the general, Nick thought.

"Yes, Mr. Brannigan, you are free to go," General Sheaffe's voice loudly declared as he and Kate returned to the conversation. Nick laughed blissfully, not fully believing his luck. Suddenly taking hold of Kate, he picked her up in his arms and she squealed excitedly as he whirled her ceremoniously around the room in an airborne dance. Captain Glegg grinned as he watched, but the general cleared his throat loudly, revealing his impatience to continue with the urgent matter at hand. Nick sobered then, lowering Kate gently to the floor before turning his attention back to both men.

"I wish to inquire if we can still rely on you to fight alongside us once more, Mr. Brannigan?" General Sheaffe questioned in a serious tone. "We do still suffer from a vast shortage of men at present and it is our hope that you will forgive and forget, as they say, and join with us once again." General Sheaffe then extended his hand out to Nick in an offering of friendship, and Nick, reluctant at first, grasped it in acceptance, amazed by the audacity of the man.

Later, when they had left the fort behind them, Nick confessed to Kate that he did indeed have doubts. He would forgive Sheaffe, and the rest of the British army for the time being, but it would be a long time before he could forget, if ever, what they had done to him.

"I hope this war ends soon," he told her. "I find that I am reluctant to fight with them now and I cannot seem to fully trust them as I once did; excluding Captain Glegg of course. Brock trusted him, so I know I can trust him. It is too bad however, that the captain is not in charge at Fort George. I now have an inkling of how Tecumseh and our Native friends feel towards some of the British." His mention of the Shawnee Chief's name brought Tecumseh instantly to mind. He too was a great leader who demanded obedience from his followers. He too had the respect of General Brock.

Nick's mood saddened for a moment. "Katie, I am positive that if Brock were alive today, this war would be handled with skill and expertise, instead of the bungling, disorganization persisting now. Our only saving grace is that the Americans seem to be just as inadequate as we are." As they rode towards the Secord farm, Nick realized where his thoughts were taking him and he suppressed the uncertainty that threatened to squash the excitement of the day. Even so, he could not completely deter his uneasiness, wondering at the part he would play in the war over the next few months.

Kate sighed quietly, nestled beside Nick on the wagon seat, lost in thoughts more comforting than Nick's at the moment. She did not offer any reply to his statement, but silently rejoiced in their sudden turn of events. She felt the tiny seed of relief slowly growing within her as she luxuriated in their good fortune. This terrible war had finally taken pity on her. So apparently had God she thought, smiling happily for the first time in weeks. She snuggled more closely into the handsome man at her side as she felt her trust and faith in the Lord returning. He had given Nick back to her, and for now she would be content with that.

Christmas day was celebrated more joyfully than anyone had first anticipated. The children were delighted with the few handmade gifts they had received and filled their bellies during the simple feast that followed. Even though the gifts and meal were not as elaborate as the previous year, no one seemed to mind. Kate had knitted a scarf for Nick, who wrapped it lovingly around his neck. When he handed her the beautiful coloured bracelet that he'd traded Tecumseh for, she squealed in delight and slid it on her wrist. Kate, like Nick, respected the prominent Native and she held the treasured gift in the same high regard as she did the Indian chief.

The New Year dawned, bringing with it hope for the future. Would 1813 bring an end to the war? Some inhabitants of the Niagara frontier looked to the next few months in anticipation, longing for a change; most hoping that the Americans would go home. Unfortunately, the war did persist, but the year began on a victorious note for the British with the battle of Frenchtown in the Michigan territory. Although the British and First Nations were repelled during their first bungled attempt at surprising the Americans, due to the inadequacy of their commander Lieutenant-Colonel Procter, victory was theirs after the second assault. That bold attack succeeded in catching the enemy off guard, bombarding them with artillery fire and capturing their commander, Brigadier General James Winchester. Unfortunately, Tecumseh wasn't there to keep the natives in line, and following the battle some of the American prisoners were brutally killed by a few drunken Native soldiers, marring this British victory. In the months that followed there were a few small skirmishes that were fought on both water and land, lasting hours, days or longer; the Americans winning some while the British army and their allies, were victorious with others. Ships were captured and destroyed, and towns and forts taken.

In the latter part of April, Kate was presented with the news that the town of York had been captured by the enemy and she immediately became anxious for her friends: Betsy, Lillian, and their mother Charlotte, She had not seen Sophia since Brock's funeral and wondered if her friend had left the Powell's home to rejoin her other sister in York. Nick too had recently departed for places unknown, so she also had the worry of where he was and how he was faring. She was abundantly thankful at the moment for the large workload at the homestead, and Kate immersed herself blindly into her chores. She attempted to push all thoughts of Nick, her home that now lay in a burnt rubble, and her family that disappeared, back into the furthest recesses of her mind. One evening before retiring Kate peered out the window, and after watching a falling star cascading across the sky, she closed her eyes for a moment to make a wish. She wished whole heartedly that both armies would do whatever was needed to bring about the end of this terrible war; briefly forgetting that: one should always be careful of what they wish for.

Chapter Nineteen

The large calibre cannons resounded their thunderous booms, followed immediately by the continuous lesser wails of a few nine-pounder guns. The threatening weapons continued to blacken the bastion with a sooty fog as they fired back repeatedly in retaliation against the invading American army. The previous attack on York earlier in the spring had left the British with no doubt of their vulnerability when the enemy plundered that defenceless town: pillaging, looting, and burning, before they turned their attention to the capture of Fort York itself.

Major General Roger Hale Sheaffe happened to be visiting York when the Americans assaulted the town. He immediately gathered the eight hundred soldiers with him, plus the local militia and a few Native allies, and together they rallied to face the enemy. They had not been fighting long when Sheaffe realized just how outnumbered they really were. The outcome was sure to be certain death for not only himself, but for his men too, so he made the decision to pull back in retreat, all the way to Kingston; two hundred miles away. That previous decision now left Fort George, the principle garrison of the whole Niagara frontier, at the mercy of the invading Americans.

Brigadier General John Vincent was presently in command at Fort George in Sheaffe's absence, and he was now loudly barking out orders to his men as the Americans infiltrated the British stronghold in a steady stream. He was anxiously watching over a smoke covered wall, instructing some of the soldiers to move in a flank position and attack the enemy, while others were sent scattering in every direction to defend their post in any way possible. The Americans were relentless. Once again the British army and their militia were all too aware of how outnumbered they were. They watched in horror as the enemy emerged from the thickening fog in an unceasing barrage, descending upon the battered military post at a steady pace. General Vincent continued to scream out orders while cannons roared overhead, rallying his men with exuberant cheers of charge! His army was somewhat discomfited though, for the enemy troops seemed endless. As soon as the British and their allies cut down an advancing American line, there always seemed to be another one waiting in the wings, ready to pounce.

The British and the local militia were fighting a losing battle. General Vincent looked on in dismay as, in many sections along the perimeter of the fort, the enemy had succeeded in breaking through their main lines of defence. They were surrounded on all sides now and in great danger of being cut off. The order was given to fall back, and the men fought fiercely as they made good their escape, leaving their dejected fort far behind them. Ironically, this was the mighty structure that was primarily put into place to ensure the safety of all the Niagara frontier. General Vincent shook his head in disgust before bounding over the nearest damaged wall to accompany his retreating men.

Nick Brannigan was in command of a small group of local militia-men who were not quite ready to relinquish their post yet, choosing to remain until most of the ammunition had been spent. During the incessant fighting, he and his men had tried their best to extinguish many of the buildings set fire by the enemy's red-hot cannon balls, but alas, some had been rendered useless in the flames. Nick paused momentarily to reload his musket and quickly surveyed the scene that stretched out unbelievably before him. The Americans were everywhere, methodically striking down any British, Canadian or Native soldier that they came upon. It was at that moment when he sadly realized that all was lost. Since defeat and surrender were inevitable, he ordered his own men to disband, sending them scattering in retreat, over the ruined walls of their beloved fort, heading straight into the surrounding battlefield; every man for himself.

Nick followed behind, dodging cannon fire and musket balls. He felt a sharp, searing pain rip through his left arm just under the shoulder. The impact dropped him instantly to his knees and, grunting out loudly, he stared in alarm at the lead ball that was deeply imbedded in his now throbbing limb, his shirt sleeve slashed to shreds and sticky with blood. He was lightheaded and nauseous. With the fear of losing his arm prevalent in his mind now, he quickly tore the remainder of his tattered sleeve and, using his teeth and right hand, he did his best to securely bind the wound. He seemed to be momentarily ensconced in the middle of hell, as all around him there was an onslaught of yelling and screaming. Men, both British and American, fell from musket fire and bayonet piercings. Nick sat dazed for a moment as he witnessed the bedlam that surrounded him, listening to the wailing and whimpering of the wounded before death claimed them. A musket blast exploded close by, dragging him back to his present predicament.

Nick decided to crawl towards the nearest palisade at the back of the fort, feeling the gritty scraping of the imbedded lead ball as he dragged himself roughly forward using his good arm, his entire body now soaked in sweat. He reached a deserted bastion, cannons silent now, the wall partially blown away, exposing the large battlefield that lay before him on the other side. There, a smaller war ensued, equipped with more screams, sharp orders, musket fog and bodies haphazardly littering the wet grass. The intense throbbing in his left arm seemed to seal his fate. An immense feeling of defeat washed over him. I am going to lose my arm, he thought, and there was no humour in the mirthless laugh that followed. He leaned tiredly against a damaged wall, catching his breath and collecting his thoughts. He had been lucky enough to keep his leg when it was wounded. Maybe his luck would hold for his arm too, he thought optimistically. If only I could stay here and rest, he groaned as exhaustion threatened to overtake him. After shutting out the noise of the battle, Nick closed his eyes for a moment, wondering if he would ever see Kate again and waited for the expected unconsciousness.

Somewhere at the back of Nick's mind there was a tiny nagging voice that continuously implored him to keep moving, and he slowly responded. He had to try, for himself and for the life he wanted, no needed, with Kate. Cautiously he scaled the desecrated wall of the bastion then, holding his wounded limb carefully bent at the elbow. Lowering himself gingerly to the ground on the other side, he crouched down. After scouring the immediate area, Nick quickly devised a plan. Lifting himself up on unsteady legs and gaining his balance as he slumped over slightly at the waist, he ducked unnoticed into the nearby tree cover. He would find a safer place to rest before continuing his escape, but running away did not sit well with him. I feel like a coward, he thought shamefully. Once again, for the umpteenth time during this godforsaken war, he thought of Isaac Brock and his enthusiastic cheer of 'Push on boys!' Push on! Nick shook his head scornfully. Looking up towards heaven, he muttered quietly to his deceased friend, attempting to justify his decision to retreat.

"Yes, Brock, I will push on. I can do nothing more here. I am tired and wounded. I am going to regroup and come back stronger. This I vow." Nick raised his right fist skyward to seal the bargain. "No, sir, this damnable thing is not over yet; I promise you that. This new country of ours will not be lost," he continued loudly, his voice now mixing with the din of the war.

An angel of mercy was skirting the hectic open field beyond Fort George, drifting among the tired and injured soldiers as the deadly battle raged, risking her own life to bring them food and hot drinks, also offering comfort to the wounded or dying soldiers. Nick was leaning against a fallen tree. Weak from the loss of blood, he watched her with great interest as she approached him. The lady seemed to be advancing as if in a dream, he thought, a ghostly vision floating calmly towards him. He wondered if maybe he was feverish and slightly out of his head. She stood quietly gazing down at him and he uttered a small sigh of relief, realizing that his head had cleared and the lady was now offering him some refreshment.

"Please, allow me to tend to your wound, sir," the woman said softy, after noticing Nick's arm. She untied the hastily applied bandage to quickly examine the extent of the injury, and he winced, feeling every muscle in his body contract with the pain, as she pulled the sticky, soiled cloth from his arm.

"Please, my lady, I must know your name," he whispered.

"Mrs. Mary Henry, sir," she replied with a warm smile. Nick liked the sound of her voice; it was soft and soothing. "My husband Dominic is the lighthouse keeper Mr... ?"

"Brannigan... My name is Nick Brannigan," he replied, treating her with a grimacing smile.

"Well, Mr. Brannigan, I am going to have to take you home and treat this wound properly. I simply cannot do what is needed here. Promise me, sir, that you will sit and rest until I return with help."

Nick had no intention of moving. After all, he could use some sleep and maybe with this lovely lady's assistance, the good Lord would let him keep his arm. "I assure you, Mrs. Henry, I will not move one inch." Nick felt pride for this remarkably brave yet unknown woman. He watched her silently weaving her way through the trees until she disappeared. While awaiting his rescue, he reflected on the dismal capture of their fort and he was suddenly overcome by a great feeling of loss. I know exactly what Kate would say, he thought tenderly. She would scold me and tell me that I should be thankful that I managed to survive the battle in the first place. But, even Kate would be saddened by the fact that Fort George now lay in the hands of the American army, who without a doubt, will be commandeering all of Newark soon.

Nick finished the last crumb of bread and cheese. Draining his now cold coffee, he closed his eyes once more and drifted gently off to sleep. When Mary Henry returned, she was accompanied by Captain John DeCew, who had two more injured soldiers in tow. Travelling northward, the small and inconspicuous group headed for the lighthouse that stood proudly erect overlooking Lake Ontario, not far from the Niagara River.

The British, Canadian, and Native forces had indeed completely abandoned their stronghold in Newark to the enemy, some retreating as far away as Burlington Heights. The small town of Newark, along with the many farms and homesteads that scattered in all directions as far away as Queenston and beyond, were now left defenceless and at the mercy of the enemy. The Americans were free to enforce their selves and their rules on the inhabitants. Some people were forced to billet officers for short periods in their homes. The American soldiers would simply approach a house and instruct the occupants that they required food and lodging, and it had to be done. Many of the local retreating men headed home in secret to see to the welfare of their own families. If any were caught, they could be shot or taken prisoner, eventually to be removed to parts unknown across the border.

Captain John DeCew was one such man. He had left the lighthouse, confident the men were in capable hands, to venture forth in the direction of his own home. He wanted to make sure that Katherine and the children were safe, and to reassure them that he was unscathed by the ordeal. Captain DeCew kept to the bushes that skirted the roadside for most of his journey, and under cover of darkness he was able to pass through Queenston undetected. His good luck held until just a few miles from home. Thinking that he heard a noise behind him, he paused for a second to listen. Suddenly, enemy soldiers burst through the trees, surrounding him in an instant, their bayonets drawn and ready. Cursing loudly and realizing that there was nowhere to run, he plopped himself callously down onto the ground in complete and utter defeat, berating himself for his carelessness.

Laura Secord was upstairs in her bedroom seeing to her husband, who'd been unusually cantankerous all day as he had listened to the cannons exploding in the distance. Although his wounds still plagued him, there were signs of improvement and she told him so.

"You are very fortunate, James. Kate said that some of the men recuperating at the fort had died when their injuries became infected, some with even lesser wounds than yours." She then placed a light kiss on his lips. "Try to sleep my dear. The guns have stopped for now and whatever has happened we can do nothing about it at present." She pulled up the covers and passed him something to help ease his pain, before quietly leaving the room to check on her children across the hall. Satisfied that they were all sound asleep, Laura then went to join Kate, Ellen, and Mary in the kitchen. They too seemed nervous today, listening to the disturbing gunfire coming from the direction of Newark.

Kate awoke the next morning to the sounds of spring. She lay quietly on the little trundle bed that she shared with Ellen, unconsciously listening to her friends rhythmic breathing as she slept. The birds were waking up along with the sun that was making its daily ascent above the treetops. Bessie and Mildred's incessant lowing could be heard coming from the barn, and the unceasing cackling and clucking of the hens drifted noisily up to her from their coop. Such reassuring sounds, Kate thought. She closed her eyes for a moment, imagining that it was just an ordinary day in May on the farm and that she was safe in her own bed. She could pretend that the sounds she heard from the kitchen below were just Hannah making breakfast for her father and Kevin, and there was no war.

She smiled broadly at her happy imaginings but, all-to-soon her joyful dream was shattered by her own traitorous thoughts, making her feel miserable. Was it not just last May when she first heard the news of war? She shook her head in disbelief, realizing that an entire year had passed by. They had suffered so much during that time, she thought dismally, thinking again of her family's disappearance. As Kate lay there, it suddenly dawned on her that quite some time had passed without the recurrence of her awful nightmare, and her mood brightened a little. At least that was one thing she could be thankful for.

They had just finished breakfast. Kate was helping Ellen with the cleaning while Laura went upstairs to James. Mary, accompanied by her younger siblings, was outside in the barn, seeing to their few livestock. Laura noticed the three American officers first, as they rode silently up to the house. Without a word to James, she left the room, meeting up with Kate and Ellen who were also on their way to greet the visitors. All three women stood bravely in the drive, hiding their uneasiness as the officers approached.

"Ladies, I am Lieutenant-Colonel Charles Boerstler of the 14th US Infantry," the officer in charge stated, politely introducing himself. The women eyed the men with apprehension as he presented the other two soldiers by his side. "This is Captain Harold Bennett," he said, indicating the first soldier. "And the tall one there beside him is Captain Bryce Tanner." The officer in question stepped forward and each man smiled warmly at the women during the introductions, conveying their pleasure at meeting them, and the ladies too gave their names. Captain Tanner's bold smile suggested a special interest in Kate, and he slyly conveyed just how pleased he was to make her acquaintance, when he allowed his eyes to roam freely over her body in apparent appreciation. She turned away in haste to hide the heated colour of her cheeks, missing the captain's devilish grin.

The colonel now looked directly at Laura and continued. "I assure you Mrs. Secord, we are not here to cause you or your family any harm." He went on to elaborate in great detail their overwhelming victory of the previous day, and how they had been out all night and now needed rest. He also stated that although he and his men required immediate food and lodgings, they intended to return to their newly captured fort early the next morning. Laura took the news calmly, thankful that their stay was a temporary one. However, Ellen and Kate struggled to hold back their tears of distress at this most recent information, worry for Nick uppermost in their minds. Was it not just last week that they received news of him being back at Fort George?

The following morning Colonel Boerstler and his captains left the Secord's, thanking Laura for the delicious meals and confessing wholeheartedly that no fort anywhere could produce such fine food. He also informed her that there might be other occasions in the future when he, or other soldiers, would need to impose upon her hospitality again, as the men frequently found themselves away from the fort. Captain Tanner had made a nuisance of himself during his short stay, much to Kate's chagrin, and she was greatly relieved at his departure. He unnerved her with his bold humiliating stares and lecherous smiles. Kate thought of Nick then, with his laughing eyes and rakish grin. Quite often when in his company, she found that his bold stares made her blush profusely too, but somehow she never felt uncomfortable or insulted by them. I must admit though, she thought, Captain Tanner is a handsome man, but he still could learn a lot from Nick.

After the soldiers left, Laura and Ellen returned to the house, but Kate wandered alone to the end of the laneway. Peering expectantly down the road that lead to Newark, her thoughts became preoccupied with Nick once more.

"He will come home to me," she stated optimistically, her eyes scanning the deserted road. "He has to. I love him and I need him; so does Ellen."

Chapter Twenty

———

Nick slowly opened his eyes, forgetting for a moment where he was and what had happened. When realization finally dawned, he felt for his arm, heaving a huge sigh of relief at finding it still attached.

"God bless Mrs. Henry," he muttered with a laugh, as he gazed around the small room. The bed he was lying on was comfortable. He felt well rested, now that the pain had subsided slightly. The bedroom had darkened in the advancing twilight, with only a single candle on the table beside him, its flame burning steadily in the still evening air. All was quiet, and he wondered why no sounds drifted to him from other parts of the house or from the other injured men. He had no time for further speculation though. Just then the door opened and Mary Henry entered the room carrying a tray.

"I am pleased to see that you have awakened Mr. Brannigan, as I have brought you some nourishment."

Once again Nick regarded this lady that had literally scooped him from the pit of hell and had saved his life, at the risk of her own. He owed her so much, he thought, conscious now of his empty stomach. She even resembled an angel with her bright caring eyes, tiny rosebud mouth and porcelain skin. Yes indeed, he concluded, Mr. Dominic Henry was an extremely fortunate man.

"Thank you, Mrs. Henry. I am ravenous," he stated, as he sat up and leaned against the headboard, eagerly awaiting the food. "Could you please tell me about my wound? You see, I remember nothing after you brought me here. I am grateful however, to find that I am still in possession of my limb." To demonstrate his point, he reached across with his good arm and gently massaged the wounded one just below the bandage. Then he fervently attacked his meal.

"Well, sir, in answer to your question, as you know, Captain DeCew assisted me in delivering you to my home, along with the two other injured soldiers, after which all wounds were cleaned and dressed. He also helped me to free your arm of that terrible musket ball. We were both very concerned that you might lose the limb, and you still may if it becomes infected. The ball was not too deep Mr. Brannigan, but it did not come out as easily as we had hoped. We shall keep an eye on it however, and I am determined that you will remain here until you are much improved." She eyed Nick tentatively, searching for any signs of protest, but all she noticed was a confused expression marking his brow.

"I seem to recall, dear lady, that when I first sustained this wound, the ball was imbedded deeply within my arm." Noticing Mrs. Henry's uncertain glance, he chuckled with amusement. "Please, make no mistake, I am greatly relieved at the favourable outcome, only confused with how it came about."

Mrs. Henry smiled at him then, shrugging her shoulders. "Indeed, sir. Evidently good fortune was with you as the ball must have worked itself loose during your ordeal."

"Well, whatever the reason, my arm feels much better now, thank you. The throbbing seems to have subsided for the moment."

"I suspect, sir, that that is largely due to the tincture of laudanum which I gave to you when you first arrived. Also, it is most likely the reason you were able to sleep so soundly over the past twenty-four hours. I also applied a homemade poultice under the bandage that is now in dire need of changing I expect, and I am sorry to say that the procedure will probably be quite painful. The last time it was changed you were lucky enough to be unconscious." When Nick had finally finished his meal, Mrs. Henry removed the empty tray from his lap. After placing it on a nearby bureau, she picked up another one containing soap, hot water, a milky bread mixture, a cloth and some clean bandages.

Nick swallowed nervously as she approached. He tried to ignore the tension that suddenly assaulted his body. He hated pain, but it seemed to be his lot in life now, and he was determined not to let it show. He began to chatter nervously, trying to keep his mind occupied while she worked.

"How long did Captain DeCew remain here Mrs. Henry, and are the other two still recuperating?" Nick winced as he asked, biting down hard on his lip when she removed the soiled bandage.

"The captain has left, sir. He was intent on returning home to see if he could arrange to have his family taken to safety, and I for one cannot blame him. As for the other two men, their injuries were not as severe as yours, and only required a good cleaning and bandaging; while yours needed stitching. They too left yesterday with the captain, to search out their family and friends.

"Mrs. Henry, you seemed so determined to reach as many soldiers as possible that day. Did you venture out to the field again?" Nick squeezed his eyes tight, his arm now wracked with pain as she cleaned, dressed and bandaged the raw area. Holding his breath, he waited for her reply.

"I did indeed, Mr. Brannigan. I re-stocked my provisions and returned to offer assistance to as many as I could." She looked at him then, her eyes misted in sadness. "There were just too many. It distresses me that I could not help them all. Thankfully the fighting has stopped for the time being, and I expect that the hoards of wounded will stop for now as well."

Nick gently clasped her small, delicate hand, surveying her tenderly. "May I say, Mrs. Henry, that you are one of the bravest women I know, and I am sure your husband is very proud of you. Is he here? Perhaps I could meet him," he suggested in an afterthought, before letting go of her hand.

"My husband should return shortly, sir. I shall introduce him when he arrives."

"I look forward to it, if I am still here. You see, I too have concerns for my family and am most eager to know how they are faring. They may even be anxious about what has become of me," he added jokingly, returning his now-throbbing arm to its sling. "I too must leave soon. I feel well rested now and hopefully the pain will become more tolerable. I thank you again Mrs. Henry for all you have done for me and I promise that if I can ever be of any assistance to you in future, all you need do is ask."

A few days later Kate was helping Ellen in Laura's small vegetable garden, clearing the weeds and planting seeds. Her thoughts drifted to Captain Tanner as she worked, reminded of his several annoying visits over the past two weeks. She had been oblivious however, to the warm gazes that Ellen had bestowed on the American, dwelling only on how much he bothered her and how edgy she became whenever she saw him. At the conclusion of his last visit, his ongoing advances had made her more angry than flustered. Oh, I wish he would just leave me alone, she thought. Rising to her feet, she arched her back, tilting her face up to the hot sun. The weather had been mild this spring. She usually found it quite relaxing to work in the garden, but not today. She was restless and impatient to discover what had become of Nick.

"I wish he was here too Kate," Ellen said, not even looking up but guessing what was on her friend's mind.

Nick was crouched in the bushes at the back of the house observing the two women he loved, relieved at finding them both unharmed. He made his way home from Newark and had been hiding in the bushes nearby for the past few days, staying out of sight while he decided where he would go. He had kept a close eye on the enemy troops as they patrolled the area, noticing one officer in particular who seemed a frequent visitor to the Secord homestead, and who also appeared to be a great nuisance to Kate, which annoyed him immensely. Nick glanced around cautiously, noting that all seemed well at the moment. He realized with regret that he could not stay for long; the enemy was too close. At least there is no sign of that fancy captain yet, he thought arrogantly, knowing all the while that it was only a matter of time before the buffoon returned. Nick's blood boiled at the mere thought of the captain's freedom to openly pursue his Katie when he could not, and he envied the time that the man spent with her. He was determined however, that he was not going to leave here today without saying good-bye to both Kate and Ellen.

"We should be ready for more seeds soon," Ellen noted. "I can finish here Kate, if you want to get them."

Kate nodded. She stretched her aching muscles before turning in the direction of the garden shed.

Nick saw his chance and acted immediately, cautiously following Kate and making his way behind the building. In his urgency to reach her he didn't hear the horse cantering down the laneway or see the rider dismount and talk briefly to his sister. Nick was just about to turn the corner and follow Kate into the large outbuilding when he was alerted by a noise. Nick ducked out of sight, watching irritably as the self-same American officer slowly approached, pausing for a long moment in the doorway before entering the shed.

"Damn," he muttered quietly through clenched teeth. How many times since meeting Kate has someone or something stood between us? First there was Walter Clarke, he thought, then there was the war and his imprisonment, and now this! Nick silently cursed the man, wanting nothing more at the moment than to throttle him.

Kate had just opened the seed box and was examining its contents when she felt the small hairs at the back of neck stiffen. Turning quickly, she gazed apprehensively at Captain Bryce Tanner, who stood in the doorway blatantly admiring her once again.

"Oh, for goodness sake Captain, you startled me!" Kate admonished as she slammed the lid shut on the box. "Have you not heard, sir, that it is impolite to stare?"

"Please, dear lady, do forgive me, but I could not help it. I was immobilized by your loveliness," he replied.

Kate was embarrassed as he continued to ogle her. Ignoring the instant blush that rose to her cheeks, she offered an indignant reply. "You should not say such things, sir; they are not gentlemanlike. We have been all through this before. Please, believe me when I say that I desire no such admiration from you. Are you not the enemy captain? I beg you, sir, leave me be!"

"Come, Kate. It is not my intention to discomfit you, only to convey how ardently I admire you." He approached her then, taking the box from her hands and thrusting it onto a nearby shelf, before continuing with his explanation. "Whether I am the enemy or not my dear, I am first a man who appreciates beauty such as yours. Surely you do not find my attentions so intolerable and unwelcome?"

Kate gazed back at the officer for a moment, reluctantly concluding that he was indeed a very attractive man. Maybe it was the uniform, or the blonde, wavy hair, or the dark hazel eyes. Whatever it was, Kate was flustered and confused, cursing her naiveté once again, as she wondered how to handle the situation. My goodness, the man is as handsome as Nick, she thought, but that is where the similarities ended. She turned to face him now, confident in her growing love for Nick, and tried once more to deter him.

"As I have already stated, captain, you are the enemy, so therefore no good could possibly come from your unwelcome attentions. So, if you will please excuse me, Ellen is waiting for me in the vegetable garden." Grabbing the seed box off the shelf again, she turned to leave.

"Not even if I know the present whereabouts of one Kevin Sullivan?" he inquired steadily, with one eyebrow raised in her direction.

Kate halted abruptly. Turning now, she stared in wide-eyed astonishment at the captain, unconsciously dropping the forgotten container to the floor. "Y-You truly know where my brother is, sir?" Kate whispered. "Is he alive?" At Captain Tanner's positive nod, Kate cried out in pure rapture, tears falling loosely down her cheeks while laughing and crying at the same time. "Please, captain, I beg you, tell me where he is."

Captain Tanner closed the short distance between them. Placing his hands gently on her shoulders, he confessed apologetically, sadly shaking his head. "I am sorry, dear lady, but I cannot. I am not at liberty to disclose that information; not even to you. You do understand? He is a prisoner of war at present, but I assure you my dear, that he is most definitely alive."

"You swear this to be true? You would not play such a cruel joke on me, sir?"

Captain Tanner gazed into her pleading eyes, declaring on all that was holy that the information was indeed true. "You can well imagine how surprised I was to find that Captain Bennett was present when your brother was captured," he admitted freely. "I overheard your discussion with Mary Secord when we first arrived, regarding the concerns you had for Private Sullivan, and I decided to look into the matter. When questioned, Captain Bennett confessed that he did indeed know of your brother, and proceeded to inform me then of the news that I have just now related to you."

Kate squealed out in elation and twirling around in delight, she hugged herself happily. "Imagine, sir, all these months I had questions in my mind regarding Kevin's plight, and now here you are giving me the exact answers that I have craved. I am truly overwhelmed by this news, sir, and I thank you." In her apparent delirium, Kate threw her arms around the surprised captain's neck, laughing excitedly and displaying her gratitude to him with a hug.

Captain Tanner too was caught up in the moment. Laughing with her, he slipped his arms around her waist, and tilting her head back slightly, he pressed his lips softly to hers. Before she could pull away, the captain's arms tightened and the kiss grew deeper.

Kate tore her mouth away from his and twisted from his grasp managing to free herself, her chest heaving in shock and disbelief for what he had just done. She smacked him hard on the cheek, fixing him with an icy glare. "How dare you! Is that why you told me of Kevin?" Kate gave in to her indignant tears then. Feeling the humiliation flowing through her, she responded harshly. "You, sir, have the manners of a boar!"

Captain Tanner tried desperately to reason with Kate, apologizing for his mistake and professing that everything he stated was true. He admitted that he was lost in the moment, but that it was not his intention to insult her. His only desire was to make her happy. He shook his head in frustration. He watched Kate stomp angrily out of the building, her gardening all but forgotten. He may have felt somewhat vindicated however, had he known that she was just as displeased with herself as she was with him. When he turned to leave, his foot bumped her discarded seed box. Picking it up, he carefully set it back on the shelf. After scolding himself for being all kinds of a fool, he left the shed.

Nick Brannigan peered hesitantly around the corner of the shed, watching in concern as the American entered the building. He found a window around the back and he stood quietly beside it now, secretly peeking in at the unsuspecting occupants. His angry mood vanished and he found himself smiling with amusement when Kate sternly reprimanded the man's behaviour. He recalled briefly the time when she berated him for thinking she was a boy.

"I almost feel sorry for the lout." Nick chuckled quietly. He was distracted by a busy squirrel that bustled noisily about in a nearby tree chattering loudly, and his attention was momentarily drawn away from the window and the occupants inside. When he turned back to them however, his temper flared. Once again his face darkened with an angry scowl that instantly wiped away all traces of his previous good humour. He stared in raw disbelief at the sight before him. Kate was hugging and kissing the American officer! Nick's jaw tightened immediately and his fists clenched as his temper rose. He wanted to barge in and rip them apart, pummeling the man profusely in the process. It took all of his willpower to remain still; he would not risk capture. He only watched for a second before turning away hurt and disgusted. With his temper ready to explode, he returned to the safety of the bush.

The ugly green monster sleeping inside him came fully awake now, and his jealousy surfaced. Nick's thoughts turned unreasonable and his ability to rationalize faltered. He had had enough, lashing out at the unfairness of it all. How could she allow that man to kiss her like that? To make matters worse, his wounded arm was throbbing incessantly, aggravating his already foul temper. What a fool he was. He could see now just how worried she was over him. One thing is for sure, he thought, I am not going to waste any more time worrying about her.

"Well, Miss Kate," he stated with conviction. "I fully intend to say goodbye to you." Nick waited impatiently for the American captain to leave. He swore under his breath once more when, a short time later, he noticed the man conversing pleasantly with Ellen, before mounting his horse and galloping off in the direction of Fort George.

"Oh, Kate! What news! Can we truly believe the captain?" Mary was excited when Kate related to her what the officer had recently divulged regarding Kevin. They were in the summer kitchen; Kate was stoking the fire for the evening meal and Mary was sweeping the floor. Having uninvited house guests periodically, increased their workload, adding extra chores to an already tiring day. Most times it was the same soldiers who came, but at other times they found themselves having to house more strangers.

"All I can tell you Mary, is that he gave me his word that it was true," Kate replied, neglecting to enlighten her friend about the unwanted attentions that she had encountered in the garden shed. "But I am indeed very hopeful," she added with assurance.

"Then so am I," Mary replied firmly, hugging herself and then Kate. "I am finished here," she said. "I am impatient to share such welcome news as this with Mother and Father, especially considering what we are all going through at the moment." Mary hugged Kate again and displaying more enthusiasm than she had in months, burst happily from the room.

Kate had finished her work and was sitting on a stool in the summer kitchen drinking tea and quietly thinking of Captain Tanner. She had come to the conclusion that aside from the unpleasantness earlier today, he had proved to be quite amiable. Yes, she reflected, he should not have kissed her, but she had to admit that she was more embarrassed than hurt. She reprimanded herself for her part in the matter, feeling foolish and silly. Why did she let herself get so carried away in her excitement? She should not have hugged him. For goodness sake, the man has been vying for my attention ever since we met. I should not have let that happen; I know better, she thought regretfully. It would have been different if I were in love with him, she reasoned. Nick suddenly invaded her thoughts and her desire to see him was unbearable. He was the one she wanted. She only hoped that he was safe. For the second time that day Kate felt as though she were being watched. She turned inquisitively towards the door. After uttering a loud squeal of delight when she saw who was standing there, she jumped instantly to her feet and rushed over to embrace the welcome sight.

"Well, hello there Miss Sullivan, surprised to see me?" Nick inquired sarcastically, while treating her with an insolent grin.

"Nick!" Kate hugged him to her ecstatically, overwhelmed at seeing him again. She pulled away slightly. Noticing that his arm was in a sling, she cried out in dismay. "Your arm! Are you hurt badly, Nick?"

"Just a little musket wound," he replied tersely. Kate's happiness had blinded her to the fact that Nick was anything but cordial, so she missed the scowl on his face and the sarcasm in his voice.

"Oh, Nick! I am so glad to see you," she cried, embracing him once more before pulling away to search his face. "You need to be careful, my love," she warned, eyeing him tenderly and leaving him for a moment to close the door. "There are American soldiers all around this place. Have you seen Ellen? She will be so thrilled that you are home. She was desperately worried for you, we all were. Oh, how long can you stay?" Kate realized that she was blubbering but couldn't help it. All these weeks of not knowing if Nick were dead or alive weighed heavily on her emotions. Seeing him standing safe before her now, her excitement was instantly unleashed.

Nick could not believe the nerve of this young woman who had once been so shy and naive. Well there was certainly no evidence of any naiveté earlier with the American captain, he thought maliciously. He listened to Kate in rude astonishment as she chattered on, seemingly unconcerned at his foul mood, while her voice dripped with what he saw as false sincerity. Where was her shame? What of the guilt she should be feeling now? He shook his head in anger and turned away from her, unable to believe what he was hearing. She was telling him of how the Americans just stayed whenever they pleased, and what an imposition it was having them here. They took control of the house, she had said, and everyone in it. Still thinking of the American captain, Nick swung around, an angry sneer plastering his face.

"I am aware of that," he growled. "In fact Miss Sullivan, I am aware of a lot of things. You do not appear to be too put upon, my dear," he added disdainfully, grabbing her roughly into his embrace then, and covering her mouth in a vengeful, tortured kiss. He wanted to hurt her the way she had hurt him. In the back of his mind he heard a little voice screaming at him about how wrong he was and how ungentlemanly he was acting, but he did not care. He had been through so much lately and now this young woman whom he loved, had deceived him.

Kate squirmed in his arms and Nick's body reacted. His mouth softened, allowing him to enjoy the kiss for a moment. Then he heard that warning voice again, urging him to stop. He listened to it this time and pushed her away in disgust. He was angry at her for bewitching him and angry at his own body for its betrayal. Nick glowered at her, powerless to stop himself even when she stared back at him hurt and confused.

Kate could not understand his anger, once again feeling helpless and humiliated, accosted by his dark, accusing glare. Her hand trembled uncontrollably as she slowly lifted it to her bruised lips. Her eyes filled with tears. "Nick," she whispered. "What is the matter? What has happened to you?" She reached for him again.

Nick grabbed her hands in his. Holding them tightly together in his right hand, he leaned in close to her face and ground out cruelly. "I will tell you what happened, my sneaky little darling. I trusted you. Imagine my surprise when I discovered you in the garden shed today, kissing an American officer!"

Kate shook her head wildly in shock and disbelief. He was there? Oh God. The full force of her previous actions came brutally to mind, and she regretted them now, more than ever. When she attempted to explain, he would not listen. Instead, he cut her off, dropping her hands as he immediately continued to berate her in a hurtful, sarcastic vein.

"Really, my dear Miss Sullivan, did you enjoy kissing him?" That little voice inside his head was trying desperately to reason with him again, telling him he was being too overzealous and there was no need to be so cruel, but again, he refused to listen.

Kate could only stand dumbfounded, sadly shaking her head.

"Do not even try to deny it. I saw you!" he asserted, fixing Kate with a steady, contemptuous glare.

"Nick, you have to listen to me," Kate pleaded, reaching for him yet again.

He shook his head with impatience. As he gazed miserably down at her, he rebuked himself for letting her make a fool of him. "No more," he said out loud. "I truly thought you were special, Kate. Let us just blame this entire misunderstanding on the war, shall we? I was under the impression that we had an understanding," he said, hurt now replacing his anger. "I guess I was wrong."

Kate cringed at his mocking tone, her heart shattering once more at his angry accusations. "Nick, please, let me explain. You do not ... "

Nick grabbed her roughly by the shoulder with his good arm, wondering for a second how he could possibly hate someone that he loved so much. He had to get as far away from here as he could.

"I do not have time for this; I need to say goodbye to my sister before your American friend returns."

"Nick, please." Kate's pleading fell on deaf ears as Nick continued harshly.

"You will please tell me where Ellen is."

Kate backed away from the cold unfairness that had infected this man she loved. He was a stranger to her now. Holding back her tears, she choked out her reply. "You will find Ellen in the barn."

Nick turned to leave, but looked back at her decisively.

"When this war is over, I will be back for Ellen." Nick then pushed passed her and without even a backward glance, he left.

Chapter Twenty-One

A few changes had taken place since the British victory at Stoney Creek at the beginning of June. The American invaders had been forced to retreat back to Fort George, engaging in numerous skirmishes along the way, losing even more of their soldiers to capture, injury and death. The enemy had also been forced to abandon Fort Erie along with a handful of their other captured posts along the Niagara River, only managing to hold on to Fort George and the town of Newark, along with the village of Queenston. The British now began to slowly recover from the initial American invasion and were slowly regaining the Niagara peninsula, but the situation was still a stalemate and far from peaceful. The British army and local militia were not strong enough to drive their American adversaries out of Fort George and for the time being, the enemy lacked the power to take any offensive action against the British. There were many residents in both Newark and Queenston whose homes and farms had been ransacked, some even destroyed by American raiding parties, while a large number of able-bodied men were taken prisoner on both sides.

Lieutenant James Fitzgibbon of the 49th Regiment of Foot received permission to try and rid the area of these marauding raiders. He immediately handpicked a group of men who had been trained in guerrilla warfare. His impressive corps were dressed in grey-green uniforms and given the nickname: the *Green Tigers* by some and *Bloody Boys* by others. Fitzgibbon was considered to be a very popular leader, a skill that he had learned from Isaac Brock, one of his first commanding officers. The prominent lieutenant and his *Bloody Boys* were proving to be quite a nuisance to the American army; so much so, that the enemy was just as determined to stop their interference.

The insidious war dragged on with no relief in sight and the days that followed Nick's brusque departure left Kate and Ellen each basking in their own private misery. Ellen had remarked to Kate one night not long after her brother had gone that she was puzzled by his tense manner and his impatience to leave.

"I worry for him Kate, just as you do; he seemed very unhappy when we said goodbye. I know Nick so well. Something was bothering him."

Kate felt a twinge of guilt for causing her friend such worry, but she could not let Ellen know the truth about what had occurred between her and Nick on that regrettable day. Kate was embarrassed by her recent episode with the handsome American captain and she was uncertain if Ellen would understand her behaviour. She may even blame me for forcing Nick to leave so abruptly, she thought. Kate was afraid of Ellen's condemnation and her heart still ached from Nick's.

They trudged on daily with the abundant workload at the homestead, each day the same as the last, with very little news of the war. There were rumours circulating however, that it was all over. Since the enemy was still occupying the area, many believed that the Americans had won. Most of the locals did not seem too concerned with who had won or who had lost, just as long as life could return to normal again. Kate too, was hopeful that there might be some truth to the talk, except for the part that pertained to the Americans winning of course. They were all so tired of this war.

One evening, during the second week of June, Kate was sitting alone in the parlour sewing as she listened intently to the loud discussion that was taking place in the next room. They had more American visitors this evening who, after gorging themselves at the kitchen table, decided to enjoy some drinks and cigars while conversing on some most pressing matters. Kate rolled her eyes, realizing that the officers were a little heavy in their cups as she heard their voices slurring every word and rising with every sentence. She was exhausted. Her back ached and her neck was sore. She sighed softly. After replacing the unfinished sewing to its basket, she yawned and stretched as she stood, deciding to leave the men to their pompous discussion and seek the comfort of the trundle bed upstairs.

As she quietly entered the foyer, she paused momentarily unseen at the kitchen doorway. Peeking into the smoked-filled room, her earlier thoughts were confirmed. She witnessed both men standing across from each other at the table, gyrating unsteadily on their feet and using pronounced, exaggerated gesturing to make their points known. Rolling her eyes once more, Kate shook her head at their idiocy as she started to climb the stairs. In the next instant though, she stopped abruptly, listening with new-found interest as the officers discussed all the mistakes made by both sides during the recent battles.

Kate bristled when she overheard the Americans boldly regaling their great victory at Sackets Harbour. She cringed when they laughed in heightened amusement at the British general's inadequacy and sudden withdrawal from the fight. In the next moment however, her spirits soared when hearing that the officers mourned the loss of their ship - *The Chesapeake* - that had recently been captured by the British. The men spoke of how the damned British had the gall to take their stolen vessel into service with the intention of using it in the Royal Navy. Kate desperately tried to stifle her giggling as the two men went on to discuss how inept their own American commander had been when he allowed two of his senior officers to be captured at Stoney Creek, before succumbing to British threats and persuasive demands of surrender.

"We all know by now that we outnumber the damn British," one of the officers slurred indignantly, hiccupping loudly as he continued. "They are not now or ever will be any stronger in force than we are; less so, I would imagine," he boasted drunkenly.

Kate welcomed the news. Thinking it quite amusing, she laughed quietly, muffling the noise with her hands so as not to be discovered. Then the other officer was saying that unfortunately, the battle at Stoney Creek would most likely prove to be a turning point for the control of the Niagara frontier. Good Heavens, she thought, why do they not just give up and go home and leave us in peace? Kate impatiently mounted the stairs, anxious to share this information with the others, if they had not already overheard.

It was late afternoon of June 21st, 1813 and the unseasonably high temperature caused an intense, uncomfortable heat to permeate the whole Niagara region. Many of its inhabitants were left feeling hot and lazy, so much work to do, but they had no energy to complete their chores. Some just gave up and lounged leisurely in the sweltering afternoon sun, praying that evening would soon bring the coolness that they all desired. Others laboured tiredly while sponging the sweat from their bodies and swiping angrily at bothersome insects. Even the livestock on the small farms that dotted the landscape, suffered in the heat. They too became lethargic, lounging in the shade while constantly swishing their tails in aggravation at the pestering swarms of flies hovering around them.

The situation was much the same at the Secord homestead. Kate and Ellen had left for the Powell's house in Newark early that morning, upon finally receiving word from Sophia Shaw. She had written to Kate stating that she had now returned from York after visiting her sister Charlotte and the two little girls, declaring how devastated they all were with the American invasion of their city. Sophia had also announced her intention to remain with Isabella in Newark until John came home, and how she longed for her dear friend to visit her. Kate wanted so much to introduce Ellen to them and was anxious to see Sophia again, knowing that her dear friend still suffered the loss of the man she loved. Ellen informed Kate though, that she already had the pleasure of being introduced to both Sophia and Isaac Brock at the Newark ball the previous year, but would love to accompany her on the trip just the same. Kate felt torn at the thought of going. Sophia needed her, but so did Laura. She felt guilty for leaving, especially with the burden of extra work at the homestead. But when she voiced her concerns to Laura, they were pushed idly aside.

"Do not concern yourselves," Laura had stated. "Mary is an excellent help and Harriet is old enough now to take care of the younger children. I am sure that we can manage quite well in your absence."

The sun, gradually dipping below the horizon, cast dark shadows over the Secord homestead while candles flickered softly inside. The household was quiet. The children had gone to bed, all except Mary, who remained with her mother in the kitchen, helping her to tidy the room following the evening meal. A noise outside distracted them and they recognized the sounds of horses pawing and snorting in the lane. Laura instantly ordered Mary upstairs, well aware that any company at this time of night could only mean one thing: hungry American soldiers. She quickly dried her hands, discarding the towel onto the table before heading outside, a wan smile of greeting adorning her face. Two of the soldiers had already dismounted by the time she arrived. The other one, she noticed with chagrin, was injured and slumped over in his saddle. Laura nodded curtly in answer to their gruff greeting, taking an instant dislike to these men who left her feeling tense and uneasy. There were no apologies for the late hour of their arrival, only blatant expectation that they were to be fed and lodged for the night, and the injured soldier's wounds attended to.

For the second time that evening Laura brought disarray to her kitchen, only this time she was extremely disturbed. While she prepared a meal for the two unwelcome officers, she slammed dishes and banged pots in her frustration, all the while grumbling quietly to herself. Her family had billeted a number of enemy soldiers in the past, but these particular men were different. They appeared to be ill-mannered and ill-tempered with their barking orders and ungrateful attitudes. They insisted on lingering over their meal, taxing Laura's temper all the more. She felt tired and miserable, her body craving the comfort of bed, while the two officers in the parlour leisurely sipped their wine and discussed the war, seemingly unconcerned for their wounded companion in the kitchen.

It was while she was attending to the injuries of the unconscious soldier that Laura suddenly became aware of the muffled discussion that drifted towards her from the other room. She realized that their talk had now turned to more serious matters. With a puzzled expression, she quickly crossed the hall and listened silently through the partially closed door.

The two Americans were discussing Lieutenant James Fitzgibbon, who was presently in command at the British outpost at the recently vacated DeCew home. They were confidently planning a surprise attack on the British stationed there and Laura listened in horror as she overheard their conversation.

"If you arm your men against Fitzgibbon... the whole of Upper Canada will fall," the first voice stated.

"How many soldiers can we assemble?" the other inquired.

"We could probably gather approximately five hundred infantry and a large succession of weaponry. Our messengers tell us that Fitzgibbon has no more than fifty men at his disposal, plus a small band of Natives. A surrender is anticipated, sir," the first man declared.

"Proceed with the attack in two days time," the other voice ordered.

Laura was frozen to the spot; mortified at what she had just overheard. They were planning to surprise the unsuspecting British by launching an attack near Beaver Dams, she thought. A sudden movement on the opposite side of the door startled her, so she withdraw immediately back to the kitchen and the wounded soldier. As soon as she was able however, she rushed upstairs to tell James of the dire situation that they now faced, unaware of just how soon she would help to change the events of the war.

"Do you not see, my love? I have to go. There really is no one else," Laura whispered. "Fitzgibbon has to be warned, or the whole frontier will be lost to the Americans." Laura stood pleading her case to her convalescing husband. He was sitting up in bed now feeling frustrated and annoyed with their present dilemma, helpless in the knowledge that there was nothing he could do to rectify it.

"I am well aware of our predicament my dear, but I do not like the idea of you traipsing out in the wilderness all alone. What if you are stopped by enemy patrols? You do realize my love, that John DeCew's house is about twenty miles from here? You will require courage to do this thing?" James Secord had always considered himself to be a strong, resourceful man who would never shirk his duty, but now he could only silently curse the debilitating wounds that held him imprisoned in his own bed. He wracked his brain, but there was simply no one else that he could appeal to for help at this moment, and he realized that a warning message had to be delivered to the lieutenant almost immediately. Oh, why did those damned soldiers have to stay in their house this evening?

"I understand your worry, James, but I promise to be careful, and I shall not be alone," she added with conviction. "My brother Charles is sick, so I will stop there on my way to check on his recovery and also appeal for Elizabeth to accompany me on my journey. If an American patrol should question me, I will offer that excuse as my sole reason for venturing out." Laura leaned carefully towards her husband and, after dropping a soft kiss on his lips, continued on with her urgent assessment. "We will make it my dear, if God so decrees. My courage will come from my surrender to His will and purpose in my life. I trust in the Lord, James, and so must you."

James Secord sighed in defeat, acutely aware that there was no other choice; he had to send his beloved Laura on this most pressing mission. "I must confess, my love, that I would be greatly relieved if someone else delivered that blasted message." James Secord groaned in frustration. "Very well, my dear, I will give in to you, as I seem to be bereft of any other choice at the moment, but I must insist on doing what I can from this abominable perch," he declared, slamming both fists down on his bed in annoyance. Laura then pulled a chair up and sat close to her husband's bedside, listening intently to his instructions.

The next morning, just after dawn, Laura was ready to begin her tedious and dangerous journey, her anxiety mounting as she waited for the obnoxious American soldiers to leave. When the enemy finally vacated her home, she said good-bye to her family, promising to return the next day, and after grabbing a satchel of water, she departed quietly. Her nerves were on edge as she left Queenston behind, heading steadily towards her brother's home in St. David's. Although she was worried about him, the uncertainty of her mission was uppermost in her mind. I am sure that Kate would have come with me today if I asked, or Mary, Laura thought, not looking forward to travelling with her niece. Elizabeth was younger and less experienced; she also frightened easily. She would have been much happier with Kate's company. Laura regretted her promise to James, certain that Lizzy would most likely prove to be a hindrance instead of a help.

Later, when Laura arrived at her brother's house she didn't stop long. She offered them a quick explanation of her enterprise, and after appeasing herself of her brother's improved condition, she collected a hesitant Elizabeth and headed out once more. There had been an absence of American patrols thus far on her journey and Laura prayed that her luck would hold. The sun was climbing higher in the sky, casting its heated rays onto the travellers, and a slight stickiness engulfed the air. They were in for an unusually hot day, Laura surmised with regret, as it was still early yet and the temperature had already started to escalate. As they neared the small village of Homer, Laura and Elizabeth came upon a large mosquito infested swamp and decided to rest a moment. Elizabeth, who had already started to complain, rebelled at the idea of sloshing through the murky water.

"Rest assured, my dear Lizzy," Laura commented dryly. "Your Uncle James warned me to avoid this swamp. He told me to follow the First Nations Trail and cross the bridge over Ten Mile Creek near Homer. We are not far from there now." Later, when they found the trail and were heading towards the village, Laura tried to lighten the mood and calm Elizabeth's fretting. "You know, Lizzy," she said thoughtfully. "When I first came here, the village of Homer was called Upper Ten Mile Creek."

"Why did they change it?" Elizabeth inquired.

"Of that I am not certain," Laura shrugged. "Maybe the villagers just decided that the name was too long."

After they crossed the bridge, they skirted around Homer and headed for Shipman's Corners, avoiding the main roads whenever possible. Laura's frustration increased and so did her impatience when she noticed Elizabeth's lagging pace. I have such a long way to go yet, she thought fretfully. I must reach Fitzgibbon in time! The temperature had continued to climb all morning and the heat was becoming unbearable. Laura felt like a wilted flower as she mopped the perspiration from her face and neck, feeling sorry for her niece now whose step had slowed to an almost-limp. They stopped yet again to rest and share a cup of water while Laura attempted to settle her nerves, but she was still anxious to put the next town behind them. When they finally reached Shipman's Corners however, Elizabeth collapsed from exhaustion, stubbornly declaring that she could go no further.

"I will have to leave you then," Laura announced. "You understand that I cannot stop now? This is my task. I have to see this through." Laura soothed her niece, trying to quell her own mounting reservations about continuing on alone. Although Lizzy had proved to be a hindrance some of the time, she was company on the trip. I must do this, she thought, I have no other choice. Elizabeth was soon lodged with the village minister and his family for the night and Laura set out once more, promising to collect her the next day.

Laura crossed the bridge at Twelve Mile Creek, and followed the small waterway, swatting madly at the marauding insects, as she was once again forced to avoid main thoroughfares. She passed by the village of Power Glen and the Tourney house, wishing that she could go inside for a nice long visit and escape the scorching heat. James and Laura had been friends of the Tourney family for quite some time. The desire to enter their home now was overpowering, but Laura pressed on, more determined than ever to reach the British outpost at the DeCew home. She had travelled so far already, uncertain of the way, trudging through woods thick with brush and wildlife and tramping recklessly through fields filled with tall grass and a variety of snakes.

Laura Secord peered aimlessly up to the sun, trying to determine the amount of daylight that remained, as she continued to follow in the general direction of Twelve Mile Creek. It was late afternoon when she finally crossed the creek, and there, in front of her, stood the magnificent, yet imposing, *Niagara Escarpment*. Laura gazed up in awe for a moment, wondering how she would ever reach the top. This section of the cliff was even more daunting than the steep ridge at Queenston Heights, she mused, searching for an easier climb. Laura was fortunate when a few minutes later she spied an area of the incline where the slope was a little more gradual. The climb still promised to be an extremely difficult one however, but at least there were a few small trees and bushes in place that would prove an advantage during her risky ascent. As she fought her way slowly to the top, she continuously slipped on the loose rock and dirt, threatening to hurl her down to the bottom at any moment.

When Laura finally reached the peak, daylight was fading rapidly. She collapsed in exhaustion. She closed her eyes for a minute, trying to catch her breath before moving on. In the next instant however, her eyes flew open, alerted suddenly to a movement above her. As she lay motionless on the ground, her heart racing, Laura stared up into the puzzled faces of a small band of Natives. She was momentarily frightened at the unexpected sight, but after realizing that she was in the DeCew's field and that these Indians were probably camped here, she guessed that they were friendly. Anyway, I have come too far to give up now, she thought, extending her arms up to the curious Natives.

"Please. Take me to Fitzgibbon," Laura rasped. She was tired, sore, dirty and hungry, but she allowed the Caughnawaga Natives to help her stand. Laura Secord was then peacefully escorted to Lieutenant James Fitzgibbon, where she delivered her all important message.

The following morning dawned clear and bright, finding Laura all alone on the road home. Fitzgibbon had bid her to 'go with God,' and although he was very impressed with her determination, he still felt uncomfortable with her refusal for an escort. Laura had declared that with a good night's rest, she would be well able to travel, and since she had arrived unattended, she could surely return the same way, without putting any escort at risk of capture or even death. The stoic lieutenant finally relented, his attention now drawn to other pressing matters.

Laura had left John DeCew's home with the hope of rejoining her own family by early evening, the cooler temperature proving a welcome relief for the day's travel. She stopped quickly at Shipman's Corners as promised, to collect her niece before continuing stealthily on her way. After depositing Elizabeth safe and sound, and checking on her brother once again, she set out alone for her homestead, impatient to see her own family. Laura was only a few miles from home when she spied two enemy soldiers riding directly towards her in the distance. Her heart raced and her pace quickened, apprehension mounting with each step. Her anxiety eased however, when she recognized one of the American soldiers as Captain Bryce Tanner.

"Mrs. Secord, what a pleasure it is to see you again," the officer stated, touching the brim of his hat in greeting before introducing the young private at his side. "What a beautiful day for a leisurely walk." The captain eyed Laura suspiciously, but she just smiled at him and calmly offered her rehearsed excuse.

"I wish it were a leisurely stroll, sir, but you see, I have just come from my brother Charles' home where he suffers still from illness. His wife assures me that he is improved however, so I must return to my own convalescing husband."

"Well, dear lady, let us offer you an escort," Captain Tanner insisted lightly, accepting her seemingly sound explanation. The captain assisted Laura onto the younger soldier's horse. After handing the reins to the private for the purpose of leading her, he mounted his own horse and rode along beside, making light conversation.

They finally reached her laneway and Laura suspected that the captain was intending to stay and visit.

"The lady is not here, sir," she kindly stated, noticing his interest in the excited group that now came running towards them from the house. "You see, both Ellen and Kate are in Newark at the moment, and are not expected to return until the end of the week."

Captain Tanner appeared disappointed, but smiled a greeting to Laura's approaching family. "You must inform the lady on her return that I will stop by in a week's time with the hopes of visiting her then," he said.

The two American soldiers rode away unaware of the courageous trek that Laura had just completed. They left her to the welcoming arms of her family and she was then bombarded with kisses, hugs and squeals of delight.

The following day, a large band of American troops travelled quietly along Mountain Road near Beaver Dams, to attack the British post. They had just reached the crossroads however, when their siege was forestalled. A small group of Natives that had been encamped near St. David's earlier in the day spotted the six hundred American soldiers marching in an extended column towards the DeCew house. Fitzgibbon was ready. Following Laura's warning, reinforcements had been called in.

A large band of Mohawk and Caughnawaga Natives were hiding in the woods all along the road, waiting to ambush the unsuspecting American soldiers. As the enemy drew near, they sprang into action and the battle raged on. The Americans, led by one Lieutenant-Colonel Boerstler, knew they were losing, so they withdrew to regroup. The enemy planned to make another charge against the British before returning to Fort George, but were stopped by Fitzgibbon. The British Lieutenant arrived and requested a surrender; it would be a way out for the defeated soldiers, but the Americans refused. When the British reinforcements came however, the enemy had no choice but to abandon their position. The battle of Beaver Dams proved a very sound victory for Upper Canada.

Chapter Twenty-Two

———

People all over the Niagara frontier were feeling the full effects of the war. There was a dominant food shortage now. The American raiding parties from the previous year had escaped with some of the local residents' smoked meats, garden vegetables and winter preserves, so families had to ration their stores, many retiring to their beds at night hungry. The soldiers on both the land and water, British and American alike, also found themselves tightening their belts. The blockades in place on the surrounding waterways hindered the arrival of provisions to both sides of the war.

The American soldiers occupying Fort George had become disillusioned. The mass excitement that followed their initial capture of the prized fortress, had all but disappeared. Sickness was spreading rampantly amongst the enemy soldiers garrisoned there. Many had succumbed to their illness as their bodies were too weak to recover. The British were relentless in their efforts to try and regain all that had been lost to them, which now put more pressure on the American patrols to constantly guard their captured villages and military posts. A large number of the discontented American soldiers found themselves entertaining thoughts of desertion and some of those that were able silently left the fort by cover of darkness, anxious to be home. The enemy's stronghold was now finally beginning to crack against the growing strength of the British army and their Canadian and Native allies.

Kate and Ellen had returned from Newark at the end of June, accompanied by Captain Bryce Tanner and his small patrol. The meeting was supposedly quite unexpected as the captain and his party, which also included Captain Bennett, had come across the ladies earlier that morning just as they were leaving the Powell residence. Samuel Forbes had just clucked at the horses to *get on there*, when all eyes turned apprehensively in the direction of the approaching Americans. The patrol was cordial however, much to everyone's relief. Kate turned her head away in shame as Captain Tanner rode leisurely towards them, but Ellen smiled warmly as she gazed into his handsome face. The captain returned Ellen's smile, greeting each of the ladies in turn, chuckling softly to himself at Kate's self-conscious reaction.

He glanced quickly at Mr. Forbes ready to relieve the man's apparent alarm, but Captain Bennett interjected, assuring the old gentleman that he had nothing to fear from them. Captain Tanner nodded in agreement, proclaiming that although they did not make war on women and old men there may be others who might, so therefore it would be safer for all if they accompanied the ladies home. Mr. Forbes reluctantly vacated his wagon and the two American captains left with Kate and Ellen, escorting them back to the Secord farm. Poor Mr. Forbes. He was left staring after them in concern, knowing he had no choice in the matter. Despite their friendly manner, he was still uncomfortable leaving the women in the hands of the enemy.

The heat of June had given way to an even hotter July, while the inconceivable war battled on sporadically, with no immediate end in sight. A notorious man by the name of Joseph Willcocks was presently making quite a name for himself throughout the peninsula, causing every able-bodied man and boy in the vicinity to be on their guard. Mr. Willcocks was considered to be no better than the American's Benedict Arnold with his traitorous ways. He had originally worked with General Brock in his pursuit to convince the Native people to join them against the Americans, but eventually the two men had developed a mutual dislike for one another. Brock did not trust Willcocks, finding him to be overly ambitious and extremely cagey. Willcocks proved immensely jealous of the general's fame and adornment, all the while growing disillusioned with the British cause. Joseph Willcocks then offered his services to the Americans, who in turn used him, but also did not trust him. The notorious Willcocks then gathered volunteers amongst some of the disloyal Upper Canadians. Together they roamed the Niagara frontier maliciously searching for, and capturing, any man who refused to join them. If taken prisoner, the men were soon deposited somewhere in the States, their location unknown.

Kate and Ellen were both fearful for Nick. Where was he? It had been so long since either had heard from him. They were now both anxious for his safety. So much has happened to him already, Kate thought desolately. She ached from not knowing what had become of him. Even if he did not care for her any longer, she knew that if it were at all possible, he would surely contact his beloved sister. The not knowing was proving extremely troublesome for Kate; not just her worry over Nick but in her unsettled thoughts regarding her own family. Captain Tanner's words regarding Kevin had been spoken when he was attempting to woo her. Walter Clarke had made his dreadful confession about her father and Hannah in the midst of an insane tirade. After all, Nick had been right about Captain Clarke being a liar. She was uncertain if either man spoke the truth. She often thought that it was quite possible that the house had already been abandoned when Clarke arrived. Maybe her father and Hannah had been alerted to his coming and escaped. If that were so, then where were they? Kate was greatly troubled over the matter. She decided to return to her deserted home to see if they had went back there. The worst thing that could happen will be that I find the place empty, she thought. Besides, it will do me a world of good to go and remember all the wonderful things that happened there.

The next day dawned brightly, the sun was already sending its warmth to the solemn world below. Thankfully, all was quiet. The unrelenting guns were silent for the moment and both the British and American commanders had not called any of their troops to arms as yet. No, there seemed nothing in the early morning stillness to disturb the present tranquillity. Yet Kate felt an uneasiness rising slowly within her as she, along with Ellen, approached her desolated farm. They both stared gloomily at the scene before them. They'd made their journey on foot, travelling the same route from the Secord's that had become so familiar to Kate, but only this time there was no comforting farm house to greet them. All that remained were the few outbuildings, looking out of place now amid the vacant, charred ground. This is such a terrible waste, she thought, as a huge wave of melancholy washed over her. Kate was thankful for one thing, however, their few livestock had been taken to Laura's after that horrible night.

Ellen had desperately prevailed upon Kate to leave well enough alone and forego her visit home, convinced that she would only stir up all the tragic events that had taken place there not long ago. After witnessing Kate's obvious determination however, Ellen had reluctantly agreed to accompany her for support.

"Oh, Ellen, I just cannot fathom all that has happened here," Kate confessed. They were standing amongst the long grass near the spot where the house had once stood. This was my home," she whispered quietly, feeling the desolation creeping inside again. Both women stared blankly at the bleak pile of blackened rubble that littered the ground. Kate couldn't hold back her tears as they flowed slowly down her cheeks. "My home, my place of refuge where loving arms always waited to comfort me, and laughter rang happily through its walls. I remember it all, Ellen! I want that life that was stolen from me. It was mine, and I miss it so much!" Kate stood rigidly beside her friend, overcome with a mixture of grief, frustration and anger. It is all gone now, she thought miserably, and dear Ellen had been right. She was beginning to relive the horrendous incidents that had happened, stirring up all the dreadful circumstances leading to the fire, and blocking out all the good memories that she had come back here to seek. Kate shuddered suddenly as the sour memory of Clarke penetrated her thoughts.

Ellen, sensing Kate's distress, reached out then, gently encircling her one arm around Kate's shoulder in an attempt to console her. "Come, dear, let us walk about the property and you may share all your happy memories with me," Ellen murmured, leading Kate away.

"I know the Christian thing to do now would be to forgive Captain Clarke for what he has done here," Kate lamented a moment later as she dried her eyes. "Oh, but Ellen, it is so hard."

Ellen fixed Kate with a speculative glance before speaking. "You need to forgive him Kate; for yourself. Remember what the Bible says? Forgiveness, no matter how hard, will help you begin to heal."

"Well, I may forgive that man someday, but I will never forget what he has done." Kate gave in to her tears once again.

Ellen too, was drawn back, thinking her own private thoughts concerning the terrible ordeal, recalling what they had both been through, and the narrow escape that had followed.

Kate shook her head decisively and wiping her eyes and nose, she faced Ellen, determined to lighten the mood of the visit. "I think we should check the outbuildings for any sign of father and Hannah," Kate suggested. As they walked on, she proceeded to entertain Ellen with her many cherished stories of the life she enjoyed here, laughing once more with the retelling of how she locked Kevin in the privy. They were both still chuckling over the matter as they approached the barn. Kate's face turned to stone and she stopped abruptly. "Ellen! Look there." Gaining her friend's attention, she pointed to the alarming site. "Oh, God, no! Crosses Ellen, three of them!" Kate wailed, running hysterically towards the wooden symbols.

Ellen followed quickly behind, only catching up to Kate after she had thrown herself violently to the ground, sprawling over two of the graves, clutching handfuls of dirt as she cried. Ellen pulled her grief stricken friend into an embrace, tenderly rocking her back and forth while staring in horror at the names that had been neatly scratched in two of the crosses. Thomas and Hannah! "Dear God, my poor, poor Kate." Ellen continued her efforts to soothe her friend. "Oh indeed, how awful," she wailed.

Thomas Sullivan had been such a jolly man. Ellen's thoughts transported back to when she was a little girl and the first time she had met him. It had been raining that day, she recalled, and their carriage had broken down in front of her house. Her mother had taken pity on the Sullivans and invited them inside. Her father had not been home at the time, so Nick went for help. Ellen remembered Kate's father as being a slightly loud gentleman, who seemed to be always laughing, and she had taken to him instantly. Mrs. Sullivan however, seemed rather shy in contrast. Nick had also found a certain kinship with the jolly man, spending much of his time with Mr. Sullivan while they waited for the wheel to be repaired. In fact, she recalled sadly, Nick seemed closer to Thomas during that short visit than he had ever been with their own father. Such a pity the way some things turn out, she thought, gazing once more at the bedraggled graves. Ellen noticed that the crosses were made from partially burned wood. They were obviously taken from the remains of the farm house, she surmised. She was just wondering who had buried them when she noticed Kate, who had now stopped crying, looking at her so dejectedly.

"Well, I wanted to find some answers did I not?" Kate choked out through her sobs. "I must confess, however, that I was hoping for a much happier ending. I am not even sure what I thought I would gain by coming back here. Oh, God in Heaven, this is all too horrible, Ellen. You did try to warn me; I should have listened. I carried this silent hope inside of me that Walter Clarke only said he killed them, to get even with me. There was a small part of me that believed they were still alive. Oh Father; Hannah, I love you both so much. How am I ever to go on? Ellen, you and the Secords are all I have left and I am afraid that I may even lose you, now that Nick no longer cares for me." Kate collapsed into her friend's comforting embrace once more.

"Hush now, Kate. I believe that I was wrong. You needed to come here. How else would you have known for sure about dear Thomas and Hannah? And what is this nonsense about my brother not caring for you? Nick loves you, I know he does, and so do I. You could never lose either one of us."

Calming slightly for a moment, Kate lifted her head to gaze broken-heartedly at the crosses. "I wonder who buried them. That man Max must be in the other grave," she mused raggedly. "Oh, Ellen!" Kate succumbed once more to her uncontrollable grief as a searing pain ricocheted unmercifully through her tortured mind and soul.

Nick Brannigan had been hiding out on the Sullivan farm for well over a month, sleeping in the barn at night, and keeping an eye to the road during the daylight. He had been lucky so far in avoiding the few

American patrols that infrequently scanned the area, still, he found that he often awoke feeling uneasy, listening intently to every little noise. He had obtained some medical supplies from Ellen before he left, and he spent most of his time during the first few weeks recuperating from his wounds. He cleaned and dressed his arm with diligence, resting whenever possible. He spent most of that convalescing time thinking of the past. Many memories flooded his mind, and one recollection in particular repeatedly invaded his thoughts; the night of the horrible fire when he thought Kate was lost to him forever. He remembered too how dead he felt inside. What a cruel joke life had played on him, he reflected gloomily, when after finding her alive, he was now at risk of losing her to an American officer.

Nick had also rehashed his feelings about Kate during those quiet moments in the barn, and his anger dissipated. He recalled the hurt expression on her face and the sadness in her eyes, and he berated himself for the way he had treated her.

"I always seem to turn on Katie," he growled loudly, startling a few sparrows that were roosting in the rafters. "I am forever depriving her of the chance to explain and for the life of me, I cannot fathom why? She did try to reason with me, but I would not listen! Blast my damnable stubborn pride! Have I learned nothing from past experience? Things and situations are not always what they seem. I have to see her again," he said, looking up at the roosting birds. A scowl darkened his features then, just for an instant. "But I will do all in my power to dissuade her from that American Captain!"

If he wanted, Nick Brannigan could probably have almost any woman he desired. His handsome looks, tall frame and muscular build, usually left most women observing him with interest. He no longer craved meaningless and trivial dalliances though, this war had changed that. His heart now yearned for something more; something true. He needed someone who would love him unconditionally and stand by him through any circumstance. He had convinced himself, that woman was Kate.

Nick had only been on the Sullivan property for a couple of weeks when his food stores started to diminish. Since his arm seemed much better and the enemy was scarce, he decided to hunt up some rabbit. He needed to eat, he reasoned, promising himself to cook the hare over a low fire. Nick had wandered out into the bush to set his traps, but what he found instead, devastated him. He had come across three bodies and one grave; he didn't recognize the first corpse, but the other two were Thomas Sullivan and his housekeeper Hannah. To his complete and utter horror, he discovered that they had both been bludgeoned to death and left for the wolves, causing him to retch violently at the odious sight. He had buried them, his injury balking at every shovelful of dirt, later digging another shallow grave for the third person. He wept for his friend Thomas.

He cursed the war and Walter Clarke who he knew was responsible yet again for another atrocity. The one lonely grave that he had come across later was quite a distance from where he had found Thomas and Hannah. Remembering Ellen's confession that their father had been in league with Clarke, Nick believed that his disreputable sire lay beneath the unidentified mound of dirt, and he stared at the unexpected sight, devoid of any emotion whatsoever.

"Katie." He had often called out to her in his sleep, agonizing over the unimaginable circumstance that now awaited her at her beloved home. He wished with all his heart that he could spare her the inconceivable hurt that was sure to come. She had been through so much of late and now this. He had decided to tell Kate about her father and Hannah and he needed to do it soon. It would not be easy, he surmised, especially in light of the way they had parted.

Nick was walking out of the thick bush surrounding the farm one morning carrying a cracked pewter bowl filled with berries, when he heard the low mumblings of people talking. He immediately raced back to the barn for cover, thinking that it must be an American patrol. However, when he peered cautiously out towards the laneway, he was surprised to discover that it was his sister and Kate who were approaching the barn. After emitting a loud sigh of relief he suppressed his overpowering desire to join them and quickly ducked back into the barn unseen. He wasn't certain if they were being watched. That annoying captain could have followed them here. Nick gazed at the two ladies he loved most in the world with a growing interest, wondering what had brought them here. He loved his sister dearly, it was true, but at his first glimpse of Kate, he knew that he would not give her up to the American captain without a fight.

Nick was still reflecting on this sentiment, his attention drawn away from the ladies for a moment, when he was jarred back to reality by a sudden horrendous, earth shattering scream. He knew instinctively what Kate had found. He cursed himself for not returning to the Secord's sooner to inform her of the deaths, saving her from this torment. Nick watched helplessly as she poured out her anguish over the dejected graves and he immediately bolted from his hiding place, quickly closing the distance between himself and Kate. Ellen squealed at the unexpected sight of her brother's concerned, but welcome face, happy at finding him here of all places, looking very much alive and well. Nick leaned down and kissed the top of his sister's head before gathering Kate into his arms. Cradling her gently, he carried her away from the excruciating sight, back in the direction from which he had just come, with Ellen following behind.

It was early afternoon and the sun was beginning to play hide-and-seek behind the many heavy clouds that riddled the sky, leaving a slight, premature darkness over the land. A warm, restless wind tossed itself haphazardly about the ragged farm, whispering a warning to all of the summer storm that was now brewing. The three solemn occupants inside the barn spoke quietly together while they finished their noon meal. Kate and Ellen had brought a picnic with them, and they had generously shared their small feast with Nick. Kate remained quiet for a time, staring off into space, lost once again behind a thick wall of gloom. Ellen sensed her brother's desire to be alone with Kate so she rose suddenly and left, declaring her need for some fresh air, in spite of the threatening weather outside.

Nick slowly approached Kate, clutching her in his embrace as he sat down beside her on the wooden bench. "I am sorry for the way I treated you when we last spoke. My only excuse is that I was in such pain and consumed with jealousy. You see, I love you, and I intend to fight for you." Nick turned then and gazed down at Kate, seeing the shock and devastation on her tear-stained face, realizing that she needed his comfort now, more than anything. "Katie? Listen to me, please. I know how you feel, but you need to find the strength to go on. You have been through so much since the start of this godforsaken war, but you will overcome this."

"Y-You were the one who buried them," she stated flatly. Seeing his quick nod, she continued. "P-please Nick, where did you f-find them?"

"They were lying together just inside the tree cover at the back of this barn."

She looked into his eyes, then turned away. "Oh, why did I not return to look for them after the house burned? I should have come back! I should not have left them there. Kate shook her head in dismay continuing to berate herself for not discovering Hannah and her father sooner. "I cannot bear to think of them lying there alone and unattended for all that time. Oh, God, why did I not try to find them?"

As the thunder roared outside, Nick pulled Kate close again in a comforting embrace, gently stroking her hair and cooing softly in her ear. He too grieved for yet more losses due to this war that nobody seemed to want. It is bad enough that she has found their graves, he thought regretfully, but it will serve no purpose for her to know the terrible circumstances surrounding their death.

"Katie, calm yourself." he choked out. "There was nothing that anyone could have done for your father or Hannah. Yes, my dear, I did bury them and I was honoured to do so. I even spoke a prayer over their graves. I found them a month ago after arriving here from Laura's, so you see, they did not lie here long, I assure you."

"D-do you know how they died?"

"I am sorry, Katie. I can only assume that they met their end at the hands of Walter Clarke. I have to think that what he confessed to you that day was indeed true." Kate collapsed in his arms once more, sobbing quietly now as he gently stroked her hair, his own eyes filling with tears. "I have known your father ever since I was a young boy," he stated thickly. "Sadly enough, he meant more to me than my own father did, even though we had lost touch for a few years. When I was finally old enough and able to escape my father's house, I packed up Ellen and headed for Upper Canada. I left her with a maiden aunt before I reached the border and went in search of your father. I was not acquainted long with Hannah, but I supposed her to be an extraordinarily loving woman. I had met your brother Kevin when he was little, but oddly enough, I had never met you." Kate, who was listening quietly to Nick's soft words, had no time to comment.

The sudden noise of a snapping branch drew their attention to the doorway of the barn. Nick, uttering a low guttural snarl, pulled away from Kate with fists clenched and gravely approached the visitor, who had his arm looped around Ellen's waist as they stood hesitantly inside the building to escape the rain.

"First, I witness you trying to lure Kate into your arms, and now it seems you have enticed my sister? Really Captain Tanner, can you not make up your mind? I do not intend, sir, to give either of them into your care." Nick scowled darkly at the American captain, their faces only inches apart now.

"Nick, no!" Ellen screamed, pushing her brother back, while positioning herself in front of Bryce Tanner.

"I assure you, Mr. Brannigan, that it is indeed your sister's heart I crave. I do confess, however, that I did pursue the lovely Miss Sullivan in the beginning, but she would have none of me." Captain Tanner levelled a kind smile at Kate, who had now risen from the bench and approached the two men. "It is true that I became a constant visitor at the Secord's home during these past two months with the intention of wooing her, but it was during those meetings and Kate's refusals that led me to notice your lovely sister. Put very simply Mr. Brannigan, since Kate's affections were obviously directed at another and her love undaunted, I found myself spending more time with Ellen, drawn instinctively to her beauty, her elegance, and her ease of manner. It did not take long for me to realize that she had become very dear to me."

Captain Tanner squeezed Ellen lovingly as he continued, noticing the perplexed expression on Nick's face. "I love Ellen, Mr. Brannigan, and she loves me. I also know that if I had indeed loved Miss Sullivan this deeply, her many refusals would not have deterred me. Make no mistake, sir, I do still care for the lady," he stated, bowing to Kate. "I am well aware of what she has been through and greatly admire her courage, her steadfastness, her love of family and," he added with a chuckle, "her faithfulness to you."

Nick turned then to regard Kate, relief now flooding his mind. He ran his hand quickly through his hair, scratching his head in confusion before turning his attention back to his sister and Bryce Tanner. He believed the captain, for he could not mistake the look of love that the man directed at Ellen. Had he himself not looked at Kate in the exact same way?

"Nick," Ellen whispered, taking hold of her brother's arm. "Bryce has recently confessed to me what transpired between himself and Kate that day, declaring that his intentions were completely honourable, insisting that Kate was merely excited and overjoyed at the glorious news of Kevin being alive. She simply lost her head for a moment, as did he. Yes, he kissed her, but you missed her rebuttal. She pulled away and struck him hard in the face."

All eyes turned towards Kate as she quietly approached Nick. With her eyes locked on his, she choked out a confession of her own. "I have never loved anyone else, Nick. You captured my heart from the very first moment at the Newark ball." Looking regretfully at the American captain now, she continued. "If my heart had not already been given to Nick, I may have accepted you; I do not know. But in truth, I was relieved when your attentions turned to dear Ellen. I have observed the two of you together on many occasions and you seem to be so happy and content with each other. I do not even mind so much that you are considered our enemy. You see," she stated miserably, letting her tearful gaze slide freely over each of her companions as she spoke. "All the odious things that have happened to me since the start of this terrible war are the fault of one man, Sir Walter Clarke, and he is British!" Nick shamefully gathered Kate in a hug, while casting an apologetic glance at Bryce Tanner.

"I will never doubt you again," he promised.

All eyes had been centred intently on Kate and all ears engrossed in what she and Nick had been saying, so they were oblivious to the two men that now stood smirking silently just inside the doorway of the barn. When the first soldier spoke however, the startled occupants turned quickly towards the noise and stared in shock at the intruders. While both Bryce Tanner and Nick Brannigan swore heatedly under their breath, an intense feeling of dread spread swiftly among the surprised group.

"Well, captain, it appears that you have taken a prisoner; am I correct?" Captain Tanner was momentarily at a loss as to what to do next, unsure of how much his comrades had overheard. He quickly found his tongue though and snapped into action.

"Yes, sir, Major Willcocks," he replied. Captain Tanner recognized the infamous Joseph Willcocks at once. He cursed quietly again, familiar with the major's reputation and knowing all too well what the outcome of this unfortunate meeting would be. Bryce Tanner also knew that it would prove to be in the best interest of all concerned if he went along with the major for the time being. His emotions were indeed jumbled. He did not trust Willcocks, he never would, but he also realized that he had no other choice at present but to take Ellen's brother prisoner, feeling sorry for the injured man. He had begun to like this Brannigan. This damn war, he thought, as he watched his beloved Ellen tear away from him to cling to her brother, all the while screaming at the two men in the doorway. I will not lose her because of this, he reasoned, turning abruptly and presenting his back to Willcocks. After quickly pulling Ellen from Nick's side Bryce Tanner looked her brother in the eye and whispered that he would do all he could to help him.

Nick had no choice at the moment but to trust the inscrutable captain. For both Ellen and Kate's sake, he allowed himself to be led away, offering no resistance.

Kate, who had sat in a daze since the arrival of the American major, came to life in an instant. "No-o-o!!" She screamed in outrage, choking and crying while flinging accusations and threats at Captain Tanner and the other two American soldiers. Her chest was heaving and her eyes were as wild as the summer storm that rumbled outside and she called to Nick who twisted forcefully around at the sound of her pleading.

"Katie! I love you! Ellen take care of each other until my return!" Nick was silenced by Joseph Willcocks, who yanked him roughly round by his injured arm, causing an anguished cry to escape his angry lips.

The two women who loved him watched despondently as Nick, already soaked to the skin and chained to the back of the wagon, was being led dishonourably away in the direction of Fort George. Kate called out his name once more and started out after him but Captain Tanner held her back. Nick's arrest, coupled with finding the graves of her father and Hannah, pushed Kate over the edge. She swung violently at the surprised captain, pounding him madly in the chest with her fists while hot daggers shot from her eyes. Ellen watched, horrified for a moment, before gaining her senses and rushing to Kate.

"Kate! Kate! Miss Sullivan, please! You must control yourself," Captain Tanner implored, holding her arms in a tight grip while gently pushing her away. But she wouldn't comply. "I am not going to let anything happen to Nick!" he shouted. Kate ceased her struggling then and the bewildered captain stared pleadingly at both women, now silent. "Ladies, I have to catch up to them. I promise you that I will do everything in my power to free him." Captain Tanner then pulled a bewildered Ellen into a quick embrace, before running out to find his mount. He galloped after the retreating wagon in the driving wind and rain, leaving Kate and Ellen alone in the barn, each staring after him in despair.

"We can trust him Kate," Ellen stated quietly, as she tenderly observed her darling captain's departure.

"Dear God," Kate uttered out loud. "I cannot believe that you would let us find each other again, only to have us so viciously torn apart. Please bring him back to me; I love him so." Kate and Ellen stood together at the barn door, each one thinking of the man she loved, and watching while the violent storm ravaged the Niagara frontier.

Chapter Twenty-Three

The month of August seemed to come and go very quickly. The warm summer weather gradually cooled throughout the Niagara peninsula while the tempers of its people grew increasingly hotter. The British army and their navy seemed to lose at every turn during those terrible thirty-one days, the biggest disappointment being Fort Stephenson. They had decided to attack the American fort, but failed miserably in their attempt and were forced to retreat, causing anger and desolation to spread throughout Newark and the surrounding communities.

Although the enemy emerged victorious from Stephenson, there was a horrible incident that took place at Fort Mims far to the south. The Americans had been involved in an Indian war of their own down in Alabama with the *Creek Nation*. After the conclusion of that particular battle, the consequences were grave indeed. Fort Mims was a stockade that housed a company of militiamen, some settlers, slaves and even a few Creek natives whose loyalties lay with the Americans. On August 30, 1813, the Creek warriors attacked the enclosure, forcing their way inside, and after both parties struggled violently for hours, the battle was over. In its wake, most of the inhabitants were killed or captured and the fort was engulfed in flames.

The fall of 1813 rolled in with the Americans adding insult to injury by defeating their enemy yet again. On the tenth of September the Americans engaged in another conflict with the British, this time on the water. A raging battle broke out on Lake Erie off the shores of Ohio. The

British suffered another terrible defeat, with the Americans capturing six of His Majesty's ships. The British commander, Robert Barclay, and his small flotilla were outgunned and under-manned, with most of his men lacking the experience needed to succeed in battle. All ships were lost, causing the subsequent surrender to the American Commander, Oliver Perry. The British too realized the full effects of their loss at that battle when the American's strategic victory allowed them the complete control over that very important lake.

Nick Brannigan sat quietly in the dark, confined in a small room with the other captives, preoccupied for the moment with his previous incarceration by the British. The torturous memories grew in his mind, fouling his mood even more, and he cursed angrily at the unwelcome recollections. Am I to experience misery at the hands of the armies on both sides of this war? He shook his head in disgust as another thought struck him. He recalled the words he uttered after he escaped his ominous confinement at Fort George almost one year ago, marvelling at the obvious irony of it all. He had said then that since he was born south of the border, it would have made more sense if he were imprisoned by the Americans for treason; not the British. Nick realized with regret that those words were now coming back to haunt him. He uttered a short, dispirited laugh as he tugged lamely on the tight leg irons that bound his feet together. There was still a persistent ache that resonated in his injured arm and he gently rubbed the area as his gloomy thoughts continued.

Ten men were captured on that fateful day, but Nick was the only one who nursed an old wound, and Joseph Willcocks took a sadistic pleasure in jabbing and pulling on his sling, inflicting additional pain to his already injured arm. The journey had been a long and tiring one, with Nick occasionally having to run just to keep up to the military entourage. He had been chained behind the wagon for a good part of the way and they had even come close to dragging him at times. Nick was tired and hungry, his current train of thought only ripening his already foul temper. Why the hell am I being ostracized more than the other prisoners? Why were they allowed to sit more comfortably in the back of the wagon? Nick was indeed puzzled. What he did not know, was that as soon as his identity was made known to Joseph Willcocks, it had invoked the condemnation of the traitorous major.

Nick was unaware of the fact that General Brock had sung his praises to Tecumseh within Willcocks' hearing. The major had also overheard Nick's small company of men voicing their respect for Mr. Brannigan, which angered him all the more. Willcocks' resentment towards Nick was almost equal to his loathing for Brock. Nick shook his head once more. He slowly dragged his good arm across his forehead, scowling bitterly, as he dried the perspiration that had accumulated there.

"That bastard has a lot of gall imprisoning me," Nick snarled out savagely. "He is the traitor, not I." He was thankful for one thing, however, the soldier that locked him in the cell had taken pity on him and unchained his hands, assuming that his injured arm would hinder any escape attempt. Like his imprisonment at Fort George, his present lodging was also small and dank, and here too, he felt the unbearable loneliness. His mind wandered and his thoughts turned to Kate as he leaned back in the darkness, resting his head against the wall of the cell. What a woman she has become, he thought proudly. With everything that this war has done to her, she refuses to give up. Instead, she seems to gain strength and resilience with each hardship. Nick thought of how much his Katie had grown since their first meeting and he felt reassured with her admission of love just moments before his capture. Those words would pull him through. Even in these dire surroundings, Nick felt somewhat blessed. He had the love of a good woman and was fortunate enough to meet three of the bravest females that he had ever known: Laura Secord, Mary Henry and of course, Kate Sullivan.

"Hey Brannigan, you awake?" a raspy voice called out in the dark, interrupting Nick's silent reverie.

"Yes," was his weary reply.

"What day is this?"

Nick frowned then, mentally counting the days since they left the Sullivan farm and their time spent here. "Tomorrow should be the first of August," he replied.

"Where are we?" the confused voice inquired.

"I believe we are in Ohio U.S.A." Nick stated laconically. "At a place called Fort Stephenson."

Nick awoke the following day to the sounds of an early morning rain that left him feeling just as desolate as the weather outside. He was overcome by an annoying restlessness, much like that of caged animal, wishing he could break the bonds that held him captive and run back to Kate and his freedom. There was an eerie stillness hanging in the air as the prisoners finished their meagre breakfast in the obtrusive guard house. Aggravating insects and rodents rustled around in the dark; there were no windows to let in the light even if the sun were to shine. Somehow, he had to get out of here, he thought impatiently, before he succumbed to madness. He had not forgotten Captain Tanner's promise to help him, but sitting here now with his head aching, his belly hungry and his wound throbbing, he did not hold out much hope.

He recalled his adamant declaration to his father not so long ago, of how he was no longer an American and chose to continue to support the King of England.

"Upper Canada is my home now," he stated out loud. "I will not allow the enemy to bury me in a prison where I could quite possibly die before this war ends." Nick felt a growing sense of pride in his new country and a strong determination for his future freedom, knowing full well that he intended to escape. Oh, how he longed for this war to be over. He was anxious to begin his life with Kate. He thought tenderly now of the time when he would be able to spend his days languishing in this heartfelt dream.

The prisoners' stay at Fort Stephenson was to be a short one. Upon arriving at the American military post, Willcocks was informed that the stockade was too small, and it could not possibly house any additional people. He was instructed to transport the prisoners to a much larger facility. Joseph Willcocks did not even attempt to hide his frustration. He loudly voiced his outrage to Major Croghan, who was presently in command at Fort Stephenson, declaring that he did not appreciate the inconvenient change of his plans and that there would be no more wild goose chases at his expense; he would see to that! Nick had overheard two sentries talking about 'the captives' and that they were going to be moved to Albany New York early the following day. The mood among the prisoners was dispirited to say the least, and they now wondered what other hell hole awaited them further down the line. Nick knew that they were destined to be led further away from the Niagara River and home; detained in an American prison for the duration of the war.

The following morning Nick and his cellmates were roughly escorted outside and loaded once again into the wagon that was to deliver them to perdition. Joseph Willcocks was nowhere to be seen, a fact from which Nick had derived great pleasure as he sat in the back of the wagon with the others. The two armed guards travelling with them said nothing as they headed east towards Albany. Not long after the prison cart left the fort however, dwindling spirits lifted suddenly as the inmates heard the booming sounds of cannon fire in the distance behind them. Fort Stephenson was being attacked! The driver of the military conveyance stopped, undecided for a moment whether to turn back to the fort. After recalling their commander's stern words: *Make haste and travel forthwith to Albany without delay, allowing nothing to impede your progress,'* he clucked to the horses and continued on.

All eyes were cast backwards now, prisoners and Americans alike, as the wagon jostled away. The unfortunate men who were squeezed together in the back of it silently cheered for a British victory as the guns continued to roar relentlessly.

The British under the command of General Proctor, opened fire on Fort Stephenson from their gunboats in a continuous bombardment. Alas, their endeavour proved frustrating. Their shots had a very minimal effect on the stalwart walls of the American fort. Late in the afternoon of the following day though, the British changed their tactics. After deciding to give it another try, the general ordered his infantry waiting impatiently on land, to commence their attack. Since this assault was a spontaneous one from the onset, it too failed. The infantry was not equipped with scaling ladders or the proper weapons to blow holes in the side of the palisade. The British found themselves, much to their dismay, unable to forcefully enter the fort to wreak their havoc inside. General Proctor had no other choice but to call off the attack, causing not just disappointment to the British soldiers, but some embarrassment as well. Sadly, Nick and his fellow prisoners could not have known the outcome of the unsuccessful siege. They were unaware that their initial escalating hopes when first hearing the guns would soon be dashed. Each man now searched the direction from which they had just travelled, anticipating a rescue that would never come.

Kate Sullivan clung savagely to a constant hope that Nick would return to her safe and unharmed. She had heard much of the gossip that now circulated throughout the region, knowing full well that other families suffered as much or even more than they did. Her heart cried out to God anyway stating that Nick had endured enough, and so had she. Kate realized how selfish she sounded. She had nothing but contempt for her own feelings but she was helpless in her effort to change them. Nick Brannigan was her future. She just could not imagine the rest of her life without him. Hope was all anyone could cling to these days, and Kate was proud of the inner strength that she witnessed in others. "We will survive this atrocity," she vowed, feeling determination rising within her.

It was late in the month of September and the air was growing cooler. The days were more comfortable and the bothersome insects had all but disappeared. The people of the vast Niagara region had harvested their skimpy fields and vegetable gardens, some sharing with others who were not so fortunate. The Secords, who were considered a most prominent family before the war, now struggled right along with their neighbours in their efforts to survive. James Secord, in spite of everything, seemed to recover daily. Laura spent less time upstairs as her husband was now able to navigate to the main floor with her assistance. He seemed content to sit in his favourite wing chair in the parlour, or at the kitchen table for meals, taking his place among the family once again.

September had come and gone and October was just beginning. The night was still and serene as a lone rider galloped steadily towards the Secord homestead, now highlighted by the brightness of the moon. Once again Laura and her family welcomed an American officer into their home. Captain Bryce Tanner dismounted quickly. After tying his horse to a nearby bush, he approached the front door.

"Mr. Brannigan has been sent to a prison barracks across the border," he later stated, sitting comfortably in the parlour with Laura, James, Kate and Ellen. Looking encouragingly at the latter now, he pledged, "I will do all I can to help him gain his release Ellen. You may rely on that," he added affectionately.

Ellen's gaze touched everyone in the room, lingering slightly longer on Kate, desperately willing them all to forget for the moment that he was an American and to wish them both well. She rose from her chair. Going to the man she loved, Ellen allowed herself to be held in the handsome captain's embrace, so very grateful for his love and for his determination to save her brother.

Kate however, was not quite as pacified as the others. She liked Bryce Tanner and urgently wanted to trust him. She held no ill-regard towards him when his interest had suddenly switched to Ellen. She had not loved him, so she was genuinely happy for her friend. Kate surmised however, that since her own feelings were not clouded with passion towards the captain, she could not help but worry for the man she did love. Observing the two of them now and hearing the captain's arduous promise to return Ellen's brother to her, she wondered about the validity of his long-ago vow to her regarding Kevin's release.

"What news of my dear brother, captain?" Kate inquired rashly. "I am sorry, but you did make a similar promise to me and I have yet to see Kevin."

Ellen was taken aback, noting the apparent look of distrust that now marred her friend's pretty face. Of all present in this room, she was sure that Kate had understood her love for this man and the high regard and immense trust she had in him.

"Kate," Ellen scolded, pulling away from Captain Tanner to approach her friend. "How could you?"

"It is quite alright, my dear," Bryce interjected, squeezing Ellen lovingly and searching the other faces in the room before turning a kind eye toward Kate Sullivan. "You are indeed right to be concerned dear lady, as I have been remiss in my duty to enlighten you. Please, forgive my neglect for your feelings and allow me to finally shed some light on this most obtrusive situation."

Captain Tanner stood before Kate, appraising her quickly before continuing with his explanation. "Now Miss Sullivan. Kate. I did in fact locate your brother and arranged for his release. However, not long after that course of action, I learned that he was severely injured, and ascertained that it would be dangerous to move him. Please, forgive me dear lady, but I purposely refrained from informing you of these events until such a time when Private Sullivan's health had greatly improved. I am positive that as soon as he is fit to travel, your brother will most definitely be returned to you, along with Nick Brannigan of course." Staring intently at Kate now, Bryce Tanner longed for her trust. Enemy or not, he would move heaven and earth if he could, to save both of the men she loved. He loved Ellen. She was the right woman for him he was sure of that. However, there was still a small part of his heart that held a softness for Kate Sullivan.

Kate now felt ashamed for her clipped words. Biting the corner of her mouth nervously, she glanced apologetically at both Ellen and Bryce. "I am sorry for distrusting you, sir, but please understand that I have already lost my family and desire to at least have my brother restored to me," she replied with regret.

"Apology accepted Miss Sullivan, and I do understand. Now, ladies, Mr. Secord, I must be off," he declared with a sigh, bowing to Kate, Ellen and Laura, while grasping James' hand in a firm handshake. "I know that we are technically enemies, but praise God, I hope that at the conclusion of this tired war, we can all be friends." The American captain held out his arm to Ellen.

Kate watched with a slight tinge of jealousy as they left, following them out as far as the front porch. She stared longingly after them, noticing their tender kiss of farewell before he mounted his horse and rode away. She recalled a similar shared embrace with Nick, which left her feeling momentarily disheartened.

"Nick," she whispered softly to the night air, pulling her shawl tightly around her shoulders and glancing skyward. "Come home to me."

The infamous American general, William Henry Harrison, had arrived in Upper Canada at the end of September in full force and just in time to accept the reinstatement of Fort Detroit to the Americans.

Ironically, it was just the year before that General Hull had surrendered the same fort to Isaac Brock and his ally, Tecumseh. In doing so, he had portrayed his obvious cowardice in the matter. Now, the British general was of the same mind. General Proctor demonstrated his own cowardly behaviour with his order to evacuate the captured American fort, retreating with no apparent thought given to the allying Natives that accompanied him; the very ones whom Brock had so ingeniously procured to fight alongside the British at the onset of the war.

Tecumseh, who had marvelled at General Brock's steadfast courage and stamina during battle, now felt only contempt and embarrassment at this new redcoat leader's actions, becoming furious and disillusioned with his lack of courage and his indecisiveness. The Shawnee had become all too aware of the loss of control that General Proctor now displayed with his men, instantly appalled at his spending most of the time with his family while delegating his command to a lieutenant. After this cowardly withdrawal, Tecumseh had pleaded with Proctor to stop and face the enemy, who presently pursued their retreat. Tecumseh had accused him of being a coward when he refused to stand and fight. The Native warriors had no choice but to follow desolately behind the redcoat general. After stopping to demolish a bridge at McGregor's Creek in an ill-made attempt to slow the American troops, they decided to hide in the woods and wait for the enemy soldiers to make their way across the water.

Chapter Twenty-Four

―――――

Nick Brannigan could not believe that he had been a prisoner of war for over two months, during which time he was incarcerated inside one of the few old army barracks in Albany, New York. All of the buildings were filthy and in dire need of repair, but Nick and his cellmates deemed themselves the lucky ones, as sickness and disease seemed more prevalent in the other broken down buildings that surrounded them. While Nick had noticed the small mice and insects that shared their unpleasant quarters, he knew full well that others were not so fortunate, with their dismal space being overrun with larger vermin. The prisoners housed in those dire conditions were dying, some from hunger, while others succumbed to sickness and food poisoning. Still others fell prey to infection as medical treatment was nonexistent. All of this made the carrying out of deceased captives almost a daily occurrence. Nick thanked God every day for his apparently strong constitution. Although weakened somewhat by the ordeal of his untimely confinement, he still remained reasonably healthy.

Nick was incarcerated, along with his nine other companions, in a small square room behind four wood-rotted walls which sported two locked doors and a small barred window. There were also a set of rickety stairs leading to a second floor where the door at the top was kept locked. Each prisoner had his own wooden cot covered with a filthy, mangled mattress and a tattered Indian blanket. They were given skimpy rations each day, but thankfully, were only chained when they went outdoors. All things considered, Nick was happier with his incarceration here than he had been with his confinement at Fort George.

Not long after they arrived, Nick and his cellmates overheard their jailors speaking of the *special prisoner* on the second floor. He also found out that the man had been up there for quite some time and was still recovering from a near fatal wound. No one knew anything else about him, except that the secret captive was hidden away, sequestered in solitude upstairs. On a few rare occasions, all eyes would stare at the floor above whenever any unexpected noises would filter down to them, increasing their curiosity all the more. Nick could not help but wonder why the unknown soldier was treated differently, and what had made him so special?

Now, as night settled in on the prison and the roughly housed inmates grew quiet, sleep eluded Nick for the time being. He shook his head scornfully, reminded suddenly of Captain Tanner's parting words. I am sure he only spoke them to pacify Ellen, he surmised dismally. Nick thought of his sister and her obvious love for the American captain. In a different time and place he would have been overjoyed with Ellen's choice. The man seemed to possess some admirable principles, but in these desolate days of war, what was he to think? Brock had stated once, he recalled, that: *'One should never turn their back on an enemy but keep him up front in plain view, then you will always know what he is about.'*

Nick's musket wound had healed to a point now where he could tolerate moving his arm without a great deal of pain. He no longer needed the sling, but was determined to keep the injury clean, using whatever he had left in his dwindling rations. His leg still bothered him on occasion, and he had sadly realized that both injuries would probably always plague him. With his thoughts still focused on his sister however, he clenched both fists, vowing that if Captain Tanner should prove false and hurt his Ellen, he would surely avenge her. He also secretly hoped it would not come to that. Realistically, he knew that Bryce Tanner would be a very worthy opponent. Nick yawned, lying back on his unstable cot. He wondered once more what had become of Tanner's promise? He finally drifted off to sleep, unaware of just how soon he would receive his answer.

A few days later when the men were chained to benches outside their barracks soaking up the sun in the crisp morning air, two unfamiliar soldiers approached them, sporting wide, toothy grins. It was the end of October now and the wind, although chilly, proved refreshing to the shut-ins as they watched the advancing Americans with scorned interest.

"Well, what do you think, boys? Another victory for us and oh, dear, such a terrible loss for you." Each prisoner eyed their intruders coldly but spoke not a word. The two American privates were not put off by any means however, and continued on with their malicious badgering. "It is old news you understand, but still worth the telling, I think. You see, a month ago there was another battle gents, and your British army ran away. We have been listening to your seedy accusations against our generals ever since this damned war started. Now it is your turn. Tell me, how does it feel to know that one of your own is a bloody, stinking coward? Even the Indians who tagged along after your precious General Proctor despised him in the end."

The two enemy soldiers had the full attention of the captives now, as they continued to relay the shocking events that had occurred at Moravian town, making sure to elaborate on the recent devastation that the British had suffered. All of the prisoners, Nick included, stared up at them in stunned disbelief, having no way of knowing if what they were saying was true. They boasted to the now dismal prisoners how the conquering American troops came across Tecumseh and his painted warriors in a swamp and an outrageous battle commenced. Many of Proctor's Indian allies died, they said, and were left floating face down in the murky water, with the Shawnee Chief screaming angrily at Proctor to stay and fight.

"But, you see gentlemen, your British soldiers could not help them," one private had joked. "It has been said that they had only one cannon and no ammunition. Besides," he added laughing while the other private joined in, "General Proctor was too busy running away to offer any assistance to the great Tecumseh. He left them redskins to us! When the mighty Shawnee Chief was finally killed, the rest of his warriors that could run hightailed it into the bush. We looked for Tecumseh's body, but unfortunately, it was nowhere to be found."

"Now that is a shame," the other private interjected. "I would have liked to scalp that red skinned savage." The two American soldiers confessed that they had it under great authority that the warriors carried Tecumseh's body with them when they fled, burying him somewhere by the swamp.

The mood in the barracks that night was grim. Could these accounts be true? If they were, then we could very well be doomed, Nick concluded. First Brock and now Tecumseh, he thought angrily. Nick recalled his first meeting with the Shawnee Chief, and what a prominent figure he was. Again his thoughts turned to Brock. If he had lived, the British soldiers would not be running from the Americans now, and Tecumseh would soon realize his dream of acquiring land to house his whole Indian nation; of that I am certain!

"Where is Moravian town exactly," one of the prisoners inquired, breaking the dreary silence of the room.

"I think it is quite a ways west of here, on the other side of Lake Erie near the Thames River," another answered.

"General Proctor is nothing like General Brock, is he?" one of the other prisoners stated. "He has no boldness or determination. In Proctor's defence though," he added, "the American soldiers did say that our general and his men had lost their resolve. Maybe they were all tired. You know what it is like in battle," he said, as he surveyed each man in the room. "It is quite possible that morale was indeed, very low."

For the second time that day Nick was dumbstruck. Do not defend the coward, he thought bitterly, glaring intently at the unsuspecting prisoner who had just finished giving his opinion. With his mind reeling at the distasteful news his anger flared, and Nick found his voice at last.

"Brock accomplished so much in such a short time," he declared. "And had he lived gentlemen, he would have effected so much more. Do you realize that? He was my friend and so, for a short time, was Tecumseh. Now they are both gone! Can any of you even grasp the magnitude of all we in Upper Canada have lost?" The other prisoners just stared at him, openly displaying their astonishment and confusion. Nick pulled violently at the chains on his ankles, recklessly berating the men as he continued.

"Now this bungling fool of a general, with all his cowardice and military ineptness, has managed to undo all the good that Isaac Brock has done." Nick slumped down onto his cot, feeling tired and miserable, frustrated with the men around him. They are fools, he thought, and in good company with Proctor himself. During Nick's loud outburst, no one heard the low, pleading voice that called out from the unknown cell above, before it grew silent again. A short time later the prison too was quiet, all except for the occasional snoring that erupted from a few of the sleeping captives.

The following evening when the sentry brought the food trays in to the prisoners, Nick received more than just his usual meal. He was surprised to find a note secretly lying on his tray, underneath the gouged wooden bowl that was filled with a watery gruel. He turned his back on the other men then and quickly read the words:

'The time has come, sir, for your imminent release. With the commencing of the nightly fifes and drums, ready yourself, for I shall ensure that the door to your barracks is opened temporarily, just long enough for you to make good your escape. Do not delay, as this will be your only chance. I warn you, sir, do not try to release the others or you will be caught! You will find no hindrance at the front gate. When you are free head for the tree cover, which should allow you a safe journey home. Drop this note as soon as you leave the barracks .I will of course deny anything if you are caught, and you will undoubtedly be executed. Please, sir, I beg you, follow my instructions to the letter and all should be well. I do this for the woman who loves you and who wishes you back in her arms, and for the woman I love, who wishes you home again too.'

Nick regarded the welcome note without suspicion. Tanner had come through. He had no choice at the moment but to trust the American captain and he was quite willing to risk it all to be back with Kate and Ellen. Nick felt a small stab of guilt at leaving the others behind but was determined to heed Captain Tanner's warning. He waited for what seemed like an eternity for the music to start. When the fifes and drums were finally heard, he made sure that all his cellmates were asleep. Nick silently approached the door. He experienced an overwhelming sense of relief upon finding it unlocked. Stealing out, he hastened to the front gate. Once he had gained his freedom, Nick raced unseen to the nearby tree cover, unaware of the smiling eyes that followed him, or the satisfied grin that was plastered on Captain Tanner's face, as he stooped to retrieve the incriminating note.

Nick's journey proved uneventful for the most part, with only a few close calls along the way. When he set out, he surmised that it would take him over a month to get home. Now, creeping silently through enemy territory, he remained alert, exercising a great deal of caution while attempting to elude American sympathizers. He was thankful for one thing however, besides that of his newly acquired freedom of course, and that was that he had not been incarcerated in a far off Kentucky prison as some British soldiers were known to be; his trip home would have proven an even greater challenge if he had. He also knew that the closer he neared to Queenston and the Niagara River, the more enemy soldiers he was liable to come across.

Nick was tired and hungry, but luck had remained with him thus far. He secretly scrounged food when needed, and stole some warm clothes from a abandoned farmhouse he passed. It was evening now and the temperature had dipped considerably. Nick was relieved at finding a small cave in the woods and from inside its seclusion he watched the snowflakes, mesmerized by the sight of them floating and dancing in the crisp night air. Wrapping himself snugly in the old Indian blanket brought from the prison, he wondered what he should do next. I am going to need a weapon, he thought, but how am I to acquire one? After mulling it over briefly, he decided that a knife or sword would be best; nothing noisy like a musket would do. He needed to remain as inconspicuous as possible; his success depended on it. Nick's whole body trembled in anxiety as he longed for home.

Darkness was just descending as Nick drew closer to the Niagara River and his long-awaited crossing to Queenston. He spied the object of his attentions straight ahead and patted the long knife that was secured safely to his belt, relieved at its presence should any trouble befall him. Nick had recently come across a dead American soldier. Since the man appeared to have no further use for his blade, he was only happy to relieve him of it. He also absconded with the man's shoulder pack, extremely useful now for storing his blanket and other stolen articles.

The moon was out in full force and the snow was falling quite heavily as Nick travelled just inside the thick bush that skirted the roadway. He thought he heard a noise and stopped for a moment to listen. Hearing nothing, he pulled the collar of the stolen coat up around his neck and continued on. In the next instant however, Nick hollered out in surprise as a few unknown assailants suddenly broke through the bushes behind him. He had no time to react before being yanked abruptly off his feet and thrown roughly to the ground.

"What the hell?" Nick sputtered loudly, glaring up at a small group of scruffy young men who, in turn, were regarding him with frightened interest.

"Sh-sh," the fearsome creatures all echoed in unison, all eyes focused on Nick. "We will have to kill you, sir, if you persist in making another sound."

Nick observed the bedraggled crew that surrounded him, also noticing their unmistakeable red coats, caked now with dried mud, and the obvious fear that was so evident on their faces. He prayed that he was correct in his assumption that they were British sympathizers.

"I have escaped from an American prison," Nick whispered, holding both hands up in surrender to the group whose weapons were now levelled at him.

"You are one of us then, sir?" At Nick's acute affirmation, all muskets were lowered and he expelled a breath of relief as he was guided to his feet. Nick frowned at his soaked clothes, but his anger subsided as he stared once again at the unfortunate young group before him. They are barely men, he thought, feeling a sudden disdain towards the British army and wondering what chain of events had led the poor fellows here. After conversing with them at length Nick discovered that they were not really soldiers yet, but had only volunteered to fight alongside the British, much like himself. He wondered, but did not inquire, about the red coats that they wore. Nick was also annoyed to discover that not only were these young men captured by Joseph Willcocks too, but that the inglorious blackguard was now wreaking havoc all across the Niagara frontier.

"He wasted no time at all, sir, him and his cagey volunteers, making those of us who are loyal to the crown pay dearly for our choice," one of the young men declared in a tone that was just above a whisper. "Women and children included. He is even arresting any of the prominent men that he and his gang happen upon. No, sir, not one person on the whole Niagara peninsula is safe from his clutches."

Nick shook his head in disgust, not wishing to believe it, but at the same time, knowing it to be true. Nick advised the group of young men of his own recent dealings with the infamous Mr. Willcocks, stating that he would like nothing better than to seek revenge for all the harm that the man had inflicted on the population of Upper Canada. The young British sympathizers agreed wholeheartedly, but stated that Joseph Willcocks was presently of the same mind.

"We were on our way to meet with Captain Merritt, sir, when we were taken by Mr. Willcocks. Our Captain is afraid that the odious man is bent on revenge. There are rumours circulating that he is planning a rampage of the most foul sort. They say that he intends to pay back anyone who scorned and ridiculed him for his defection to the American side."

Nick was also told that Captain Merritt instructed his men, which included this young troop before him, to try and catch the traitor before he could inflict his retribution on the innocent people of Newark. He also wished to make a public example of the despicable traitor, as a warning to any others who maybe harbouring thoughts of defection. The young men then went on to say that in order to escape they had no choice but to kill the unsuspecting guards escorting them to the American prison.

After listening to the startling tale, Nick informed the dishevelled bunch that although sympathetic to their present plight, he was on his way back home to Queenston, and was quite anxious to be off, but wished them good luck all the same. Although the inexperienced young men were uneasy with his decision to leave, they were on a mission of their own. However, they were pleasantly surprised a short time later when Nick, frustrated beyond belief, found that his path across the river was blocked by a heavy American patrol.

"Damn! I was afraid of this. It is impossible for me to cross here." While he squashed his mounting disappointment, his young recruits silently rejoiced. He would travel with them now, and they would cross the river together, before leaving to go their separate ways. "Well, gentlemen, I travel with you as far as Newark," Nick announced in defeat. So it was, that with the moon casting just enough light to guide them on their way, the small group, that now numbered one more, stalked quietly through the night in the direction of Newark.

Chapter Twenty-Five

Kate found herself in Newark once again. She was alone this time, visiting her friend Sophia, who still suffered over Isaac Brock's death. Kate had no hope for her friend ever recovering from the loss of her fiancé as the two ladies now sat by the fireplace in the Powell's parlour. Kate was trying diligently to encourage Sophia out of her doldrums, only managing to frustrate herself when her efforts seemed to fall on deaf ears.

"I am so sorry, Kate," Sophia lamented. "I fear I shall never forget my dear Isaac."

"I do not think anyone expects you to forget him Sophia, and quite frankly, I cannot imagine how any of us could ever forget him for that matter. Your General Brock will remain in the hearts and minds of a great many people for a great period of time, I should think. Unfortunately, that may make it all the more difficult for you to recover from his loss." Sophia Shaw buried her head in her hands once again, pouring out her despair while Kate gently stroked her friend's arm in a comforting gesture. "You are a young woman still, Sophia, with your whole life ahead of you. You need to live it in the way God intended my dear; you cannot give up. Do you honestly think that the general would have wanted that?"

Sophia Shaw shook her head slowly, sniffing before drying her eyes. "Please, do not concern yourself with me, my dear Kate. Thankfully these dismal moods of mine pass quickly enough and come less frequently now. My Isaac was knighted, were you aware of that?" Sophia added in an afterthought. Kate shook her head in reply but was not surprised. General Brock was the epitome of a real knight and deserved to be called 'sir', unlike Walter Clarke who was an insult to the title. Words of congratulations formed on Kate's lips but she didn't have a chance to respond. At that precise moment they were interrupted by Sophia's sister Isabella, who came charging into the room short of breath, chattering enthusiastically.

"Ladies! I have some most gratifying news," she chirped. "It seems our British troops have scattered the American soldiers from Twenty Mile Creek, sending them all the way back to Fort George." Both Kate and Sophia jumped to their feet in complete and utter astonishment. "Oh, but there is more," Isabella continued excitedly as she approached. "Now this General McClure, the American commander who is now in charge of our fort, has found himself in quite a pickle it seems. I have heard that the enemy feels trapped, knowing that our army is on the way, and their general has ordered a withdrawal from our fort. They will soon be retreating across the river to their own Fort Niagara. Is this not exciting?"

"The Americans are leaving?" Kate inquired with disbelief.

"Yes, my dear, we shall be rid of them."

Since arriving one week earlier Kate was becoming increasingly infuriated with the boldness of not only Joseph Willcocks and his raiding party, but also with the American soldiers that infiltrated their town. They were all striking fear into the hearts of most of the population of Newark, some forcing their rude behaviour and military power over everyone, causing strained nerves and stretched tempers. Yes, Kate thought, we will all be overjoyed at their leaving. After Isabella's startling announcement, the women moved abruptly to the window and peered expectantly out at the town, Kate and Isabella secretly rejoicing at the sudden turn of events. Each of the women were lost in thoughts of their own, with Isabella wishing for her John to be home, and Kate longing for Nick's return. Poor Sophia, who tried desperately to feel elated, was just relieved to have the enemy gone, silently rebuking them for taking her beloved Isaac from her. Each of the women surveyed the comings and goings outside the window with new- found interest, sadly unaware that in just a few short hours, the whole town of Newark, and all its inhabitants, were to be plunged into a devastating pit of hell.

The next morning the sun rose high, suspended brightly in a blue, cloudless sky. It was still winter though, so the air was cool and crisp. When the ladies had finished their tea and toasted biscuits and tidied the kitchen, Kate invited Sophia out for a refreshing walk

"It is such a glorious day," she said happily. "I suspect the fresh air will be most beneficial, besides, I am returning home today if you will recall, and I would love one last look at the town before I leave." Sophia had balked at the idea at first, saying that the temperature was not to her liking, but after Kate's persuasive reasoning, she finally relented.

By the early afternoon Kate's cheerful mood had vanished. The sunshine had disappeared and a heavy snow had taken its place. The weather had suddenly turned cold and blustery, whipping the snow into high drifts, causing quite a disturbance throughout the town.

"I know how disappointed you must be, my dear," Isabella stated. "But your leaving for home today is simply out of the question now."

"You are right, of course, Mrs. Powell. I will be home soon enough I should imagine. I am already tired of this dreadful snow though, and there is still so much more winter to come. I do hope this day does not worsen," Kate remarked blandly.

Joseph Willcocks was furious with General McClure's decision to abandon Fort George, loudly voicing his contempt, wanting revenge on all those who mocked him. "I will burn them out before I leave!" he declared wickedly. The American general decided to appease the major's raving temper by giving Willcocks the freedom to burn the town of Newark, justifying that with this action, the advancing British troops would find no shelter or solace when they arrived. Willcocks was elated!

"The first homes to go will belong to those who slighted me after my unavoidable defection, and then I will make all of these people suffer," he vowed menacingly, holding a fire brand high in the air. "Nor will my old friends and neighbours be spared." Some of Willcock's volunteers' were not as cold hearted as their leader however, and they scattered throughout Newark ahead of him, banging on doors and shouting to the occupants to get out quickly and take what they could, before their homes were burned. Joseph Willcocks, and a few of his men, proceeded to thrust themselves boldly into most of the households of Newark, setting them to flames and leaving devastation in their wake.

The sun was just beginning to descend and the Powell home was peacefully luxuriating in the stillness of the evening. The women had retired to the parlour after their slight dinner of watered-down stew, and were presently sitting quietly in front of the fire mending some torn garments. Kate was alerted suddenly to the sound of fifes far off in the distance. For the second time that day, she rushed to the window. What she saw was mortifying! American soldiers were advancing towards the town from as far away as her eyes could see. She moaned loudly, drawing the attention of Sophia and Isabella, who also ventured to the glass covered opening. They were stunned. An insurmountable foreboding coursed swiftly through Kate as she stared at the unbelievable sight advancing towards them in the distance. What could this mean? Many of their neighbours also alert to the enemy's approach, began gathering in the streets, while others stayed indoors to hide from the intruders.

"They are going the wrong way, Kate," Isabella whispered in confusion. "Those troops are supposed to be heading away from Newark, to the river, back to their own fort."

"Oh, why can they not just leave us alone?" Sophia's frustration mounted along with her fear. She left the window, throwing herself down onto the settee.

"We are unprotected," Kate whispered in alarm, her eyes laced with panic. "Our own troops have not yet arrived." After darting a hurried glance at Sophia, she decided to change her tone. Engaging herself in a more confident manner, Kate emitted a bravado that she did not feel. "Come, ladies, it is too early to fret. Whatever happens we will meet it head on. We will not give in to the Americans."

A short time later however, all three ladies looked out in horror and remorse, as ferocious flames devouring Newark lit the sky. The continuous musket fire and loud exuberant cheers from the enemy, drowned out the noise of the townspeople who now fled hysterically from their burning homes.

"Those hateful Americans are celebrating just like it was their Independence Day all over again," Kate remarked with disgust.

Nick's escape from the Albany prison baffled all concerned. Since it was considered to be a lightly manned and derelict facility however, no suspicion was attached to the incident. The American army had more pressing matters to attend to at the moment and Captain Bryce Tanner was relieved.

Nick could see the flames long before he entered the town, but scrambling down the main street, he was inundated with the raw desolation of his surroundings. The abominable scene that greeted him was bleak to be sure, and his whole insides quaked at the sight. He came upon women and children who only fixed him with a fearful stare, as they stood huddled together in the foul weather as he approached them. The desecrated town was filled with refugees, people who had lost almost everything they owned. Nick was sickened by what now lay before him.

Most of the population were forced out of their warm homes and left exposed to the severe elements. He even noticed that quite a number of them were close to nakedness. Some people were scattering to and fro in a state of hysteria, rummaging through the rubble to find blankets, coats and boots. Although night had fallen, the blazing fires lit the streets. Thankfully, the blowing snow and forceful winds had dissipated for the time being. This atrocity is beyond belief! I cannot leave these poor creatures like this, Nick thought. With a sudden surge of determination, he scrounged some wood from a still smouldering building close by, one piece still burning in his hand. He piled the wood in a heap beside a snow bank and when he added the flaming board, the small fire was ablaze. He pulled one dazed woman and her children to the heat, and the group around her followed in a zombie-like state.

Nick left them basking in the warmth, and continued his appraisal of the town. He witnessed other dire incidents as he made his way slowly amongst the ruins, his feelings torn. He was anxious to be home, but he also thought that he should try and help some of the residents of this sadly destroyed town. He did not need to decide. Not far ahead he spied

Mrs. Henry bringing aid to some unfortunate souls and he knew what he had to do; so he quickly approached.

Mary Henry smiled broadly when she observed Nick coming towards her at a steady pace.

"Mr. Brannigan, thank goodness!" she exclaimed with relief.

"How can I be of service madam?" Nick inquired, returning a wan smile.

"These barbarians have thankfully left my home and the lighthouse intact," she stated flatly. "They very kindly informed us that since they still required my husband's services for navigating safely on the lake, the lighthouse would be spared. Was that not very hospitable of them Mr. Brannigan?" Mrs. Henry added sarcastically. Mary Henry had been busy wrapping blankets around a large group of cold and destitute people when Nick had first arrived. After shaking his head sardonically at the audacity of the harassing Americans, he instantly repeated his offer of assistance.

Dominique Henry had returned with warm clothing for the half frozen individuals. After Mary issued a hurried introduction, the two newly acquainted men aided her in transporting the unfortunates back to her home, each also carrying a small child on their shoulders. Sometime later, after he helped all he could, Nick left the Henry's, finding himself free of duty once more, and anxious to reach home. As he hastened steadily through town, he was determined to let nothing else impede his journey.

Kate ventured outside as the burning flames began to rapidly consume the small village, and she too offered her assistance. Since the Powell house had thus far escaped the torch, for reasons unknown, she set out to gather as many of the refugees as she could, directing them to Isabella and Sophia who waited expectantly to offer them food and warmth. They too were short of provisions, but were quite willing to share what they had. Kate kept up her vigil of searching through the rubble, overwhelmed by the number of destitute people.

"There are too many to save," she wailed. The temperature was frigid and still plummeting. Kate felt desolate and defeated with every frozen corpse she came across. She cried bitterly at the many bodies now coloured blue and lying stiff in the snow. Isabella had finally implored her to please stop searching, as they were now short of room. Kate was saddened, not only for the anguished people, but also for her desolate surroundings. The beautiful, quaint little town, the one she had so joyously showed Betsy and Lillian that day, had disappeared; and she mourned its loss. '*Our whole way of life will change; property will be destroyed.*' Recalling her frightened prophecy of a year ago, she cried bitterly. Moments later, Kate was jolted from her sad reverie. Hearing a series of screams emanating from a dilapidated old barn nearby, she raced madly towards the sound. Flinging the door wide she gasped in horror, as once again she found herself staring into the heinous face of Walter Clarke.

Captain Clarke was just as astonished to see Kate, but he instantly noticed her stunned expression, silently rejoicing at her delayed escape. She had paused just long enough for him to throw the young girl that he was debasing towards her, causing enough of a distraction that Kate was left off guard. He leaped forward instantly, grabbing Kate roughly by the arm and twisting the limb painfully behind her back. She screamed out in pain, and her anger intensified at finding herself trapped once more by this despicable monster. The poor frightened young girl fled the scene, screeching at the top of her lungs, as Clarke leaned in close to Kate, his foul, acrid breath causing her stomach to heave.

"My dear, this is indeed a pleasure," Clarke purred wickedly. "I am overjoyed at finding you alive. I am not sure how you escaped the fire, but know that I have long since regretted my rash decision to kill you. Really, my darling, now that Nick Brannigan is dead, I see no reason why we should not continue where we left off."

"You are a vile, despicable, loathsome creature, and I hate you," Kate growled out through her tears as her throat twisted into a tight knot, restricting her speech for the moment. She fixed him with an agonizing stare, wishing that she could wipe the smugness from his face and tell him that Nick was not dead, only imprisoned somewhere, but she could not form the words. Instead, she spit at him, the dire insult of what she had just done evident on her assailant's face which now darkened with rage. Clarke pulled back his one arm and swinging it hard, he brutally connected with Kate's jaw, knocking her backward against the wall of the barn.

He fell on her then, like a man gone mad, driving a hard punch into her stomach and another to the side of her head. A tormented, anguished scream, ripped from her throat as Clarke dragged Kate to her feet and pulled her roughly against his chest. He devoured her for a second with his wild, evil eyes. Kate stared up into the malicious, domineering face of Satan for a split second, quaking deeply before he swung her around, her back now leaning against him. Walter Clarke then yanked down hard on her now dishevelled hair and pulled her face up to his. He lifted her chin while savagely drawing out a large, sharp knife, and tracing it threateningly across her vulnerable throat.

Nick was tired and his wounded arm plagued him as he continued his trek through the war-torn town of Newark. He felt a deep sorrow for these people, pushed out so cruelly into the night, with their homes burning all around them. The weather worked against them now as the wind picked up and snowflakes cascaded from the sky. He knew that his plight, however gloomy it may be, could never be compared to the severity of theirs. He had almost reached the edge of town, grateful to be leaving, when a young girl ran frantically past him shrieking madly in the blowing snow, her clothes torn and hanging in shreds. Nick stopped short. Releasing a low, frustrated grumble, he turned to follow her, and as another earth shattering scream rippled through the air, he immediately raced in the direction of an old run-down barn at the top of the hill.

Nick charged through the open door of the small structure, only to stop abruptly in the doorway, shocked at the scene before him. That bastard Clarke had his Katie by the hair, and a blade to her throat! Nick lost all sense and reason then. Like a wild animal he leaped forward in a blind rage, emitting a low rabid growl while throwing himself hard against an astonished Clarke, scattering the knife and sending them both crashing through the wall and out into the snow. Nick was stunned by the impact and rubbed his injured arm as he tried to rise. Walter Clarke however, had gained his footing and now raced back into the barn to recover his dagger. Nick reached for his own knife and he too entered the decrepit structure.

Kate screamed once more as Clarke lunged forward, surprising Nick and knocking the knife from his hands. With a sadistic cry of victory, he brandished his own weapon, stabbing out repeatedly at Nick's face and body. Clarke's attack was thwarted however, when his arm was suddenly grabbed and his knife pushed away. The two men toppled in a heap to the floor. Kate stood motionless, riveted to the spot, her worry for Nick so intense that she momentarily forgot about her own pain. She knew by the fierceness of the fight that this was a battle to the death. She watched fearfully as the two savage beasts rolled over each other, both grunting loudly in anger and pain, and she earnestly prayed that Nick would be spared.

Nick's injury was proving to be a great hindrance. I may lose this fight, he thought with alarm. He had managed up to now to restrain Clarke's arm, staying the blade for a time, but his wounded limb was throbbing intensely. Nick kept his attention levelled on the knife, but his hold on Clarke was weakening. He knew something had to be done soon; saving himself and Kate was uppermost in his mind. Grimacing furiously, he tightened his grip on Clarke once more, recalling all the many atrocities that this monster had inflicted on them. His wrath intensified. Nick felt a sudden rush of adrenaline coursing through his veins and a momentary strength seemed to engulf him. In the split second before his strength was sapped, he quickly lifted his knees and braced them steadily against Clarke's stomach, knowing that this was his last chance to save himself and Kate. With a sudden surge of energy he pushed up violently, sending Clarke sprawling backwards. He landed hard against a nearby post and slumped to the floor. Nick gained his footing. He noticed that the heavy wooden support beam was teetering precariously overhead, ready to fall. Clarke lay unconscious beneath. Nick's body screamed out for revenge but at the same time his mind shouted that only a coward would kill an unconscious man.

Kate whimpered softly and Nick turned to face her for the first time since entering the barn. What he saw devastated him.

"Katie," he moaned, as he slowly approached her. Dear, God! Her face was bruised and her head was bleeding. She appeared hunched over slightly at the waist, as if favouring an injury there. Nick's anger knew no bounds then as he glared ferociously back at Clarke, now coming to. Kate cried out in anguish and Nick's eyes blazed with fire as he watched his nemesis struggle to rise. He had no weapon and neither did Clarke, but he was all too aware that if attacked again, he would surely lose. Nick heard Kate's broken whimper and he quickly turned, meeting her eyes and locking them in an impassioned gaze, as their mutual love shone through. In the next instant the spell was broken and Nick's scowl returned. He told her to stand back out of the way before turning his attention back to Clarke.

"You vile, despicable bastard!" Nick screamed, racing towards the pole that Walter Clarke was now leaning against in a daze. With the last scrap of his remaining strength, Nick purposely threw his weight full force into the already unstable wooden rod. He sent it sprawling over in a cloud of dust and debris, falling with it to the floor, as a large section of the decaying roof came crashing down. Kate darted back to safety, and Clarke screamed out in terror, throwing up his arms to cover his head as the heavy pile of rubble cascaded down on top of him, crushing him to death. No sound came from the pile of wood that covered Nick.

Kate rushed over to the place where Nick was buried, hysterically calling out to him while coughing uncontrollably. She waved her hands back and forth in front of her face in a feeble attempt to dispel the choking dust that now encircled the air around the fallen rubble. She began to lift the boards off Nick, mumbling through her tears, willing him to be alive. The boards were heavy and she stopped for a moment to catch her breath, her own injuries forgotten once more. Darting a quick glance over her shoulder, she was relieved to notice that most of the shattered roof had fallen on Walter Clarke. When Kate resumed her digging, she had only lifted a few more pieces of wood before finding the rickety post, and she cried out thankfully upon hearing Nick's scratchy voice. Kate saw him lying seemingly unscathed beneath the heavy post. There did not appear to be any sign of blood seeping through the dust that covered his body, so she thanked God, realizing in that second how close her beloved Nick had come to being crushed.

"Katie?" he rasped.

"I am here, my love," she replied happily, her tears falling freely now.

"I should be dead," he muttered in confusion. "Crushed by this heavy wood. Katie, how is it that I am still alive?"

"By the grace of God, my love." Kate found a large, heavy board. Securing it under the fallen crosspiece, she used it for leverage to slowly pry the beam off Nick. Luckily, she was able to raise it high enough for him to crawl out, before she herself collapsed in a heap of pain and exhaustion. Nick gradually pulled himself to his feet and reached for Kate, gathering her into a tender embrace. They both felt very relieved and thankful to have one another again, but Kate was overcome with emotion as her rapturous tears poured over her bruised cheeks. She was overjoyed to be in his arms once more and her heart was full of love. The war is not over yet and more terrible things may happen to us, she reasoned, but for now we are content. We have each other.

Nick pulled away from Kate and gazed with concern at her wounds, anxiously listening to her assurances that they were not too serious. He looked despondently at the pile of debris that he had just crawled out of and frowned slightly at a private recollection. "What exactly did you mean Kate, when you said that I survived by the grace of God?"

"It is truly amazing, Nick, perhaps even a miracle," she said, her voice now laced with excitement. "It appears that when the post fell, you were thrown underneath, but the one end was jammed by other fallen debris, halting its plunge to the floor. It stopped just inches from crushing you!" Kate hugged Nick tightly to her then, quietly thanking God again for saving him. "I am afraid my love, that Walter Clarke was not so fortunate," she declared, drawing Nick's attention to the pile of rubble that covered the man. As they drew closer, they noticed a bloody hand sticking out through the wreckage, looking as stiff as the boards that buried it, but they could feel no pity.

"We need to take each other home," Nick declared softly.

The burning fires in Newark turned gradually to smouldering embers as the new day dawned. Nick and Kate stayed at the Powell's taking care of each other, waiting impatiently for the time when they could begin their journey to the Secord farm. That day came with the arrival of the British troops two days later, and they rode together in an army wagon, leaving the horrors of the past few days behind them. However, they did not go alone.

Chapter Twenty-Six

The devastated survivors of Newark were immensely relieved at the sight of the returning British army. The troops had arrived at Fort George first, surprising the American rear-guard that still remained there, killing some of them and taking the rest as prisoners. When the army finally reached the town however, they too were mortified by what they saw. It was gone! Almost all the buildings were reduced to smouldering piles of rubble, with only a few left standing. The soldiers gaped in disbelief at the crowds of half frozen people. Some had taken shelter in ramshackle huts they had just thrown together from the debris. The British soldiers who had taken part in many a gruesome battle, were sickened now by the sight of dead bodies strewn everywhere, laying stiff in the snow, with some even sequestered amongst the broken furniture that now littered the streets. Many of the men wiped their eyes, their piteous emotions suddenly turning to rage, as their anguished gaze penetrated the settlement.

Captain Merritt stared in bewilderment at the few small fires that were scattered throughout the town, and at the surviving townspeople gathered around them, and he wondered why the others did not seek warmth too before they froze to death? Many people were heard wailing for their deceased loved ones while others, men and women alike, were seen walking around in a hypnotic daze, their eyes vacant and their minds gone. Some of the inhabitants, when seeing the arrival of the British soldiers, began to make their way to Fort George. The army was shocked by these atrocities brought about by the Americans, especially when told of a sick, elderly woman who had been carried out of her home by the enemy, bed and all, and after being deposited roughly in a snow bank, she had no choice but to watch her house burn. Captain Merritt had also been informed that some of the devastated people were leaving town, trudging through the deep snow, probably chilling themselves to the bone, all in the hope of finding some comfort at the neighbouring farms. When he heard this news, he agreed with the reasoning behind it and dispatched a wagon, along with a handful of soldiers, to assist the refugees on their journey.

The Secord home was filled to the rafters with the families that had accompanied Nick and Kate home from Newark. They even had some of the survivors housed in the summer kitchen. Anyone who brought belongings, stored them in the barn. There was plenty of work to be done, and an abundance of help to do it. Most of the families that occupied Laura's home were fatherless, as many of the men in Newark were taken prisoner by Joseph Willcocks. Rations were low but the women managed to serve scantily prepared meals anyway, with Laura commenting that thankfully women and children did not eat as much as men. Kate and Ellen kept themselves busy by helping the mothers with their small children. Ellen tried in earnest to keep her mind from dwelling on Bryce Tanner. She had no idea of where he was or when he would return, if ever, and she prayed that he was not involved in the devastation that plagued Newark. Her spirits were lifted however, with Nick's confession that Captain Tanner did honour his promise by helping him escape. Sadly though, for Kate, there was still no news of Kevin.

Just over a week later a soldier rode up to the Secord's door. This time it was a British officer. Captain Merritt was not alone however, and the small group of misfits accompanying him were looking for Nick Brannigan. Nick met the captain cordially. He laughed heartily in surprise upon recognizing his young friends, greeting them with an exuberant handshake before welcoming them all inside. Once the proper introductions had been completed, the visitors were assembled comfortably in the Secord kitchen, drinking a hot grog and enjoying the warmth of the fire. Nick noticed that the boys still wore their bedraggled red coats, but at least now they were clean. He chuckled along with the others as they listened with amusement to the young soldiers' version of how they had first met Mr. Brannigan.

It wasn't long before the conversation turned to more serious matters. Captain Merritt had stated that he was visiting the local farms to see how the refugees of Newark were faring, and to let them know that they would soon be home.

"Buildings are being erected as we speak," he had declared. He was also trying to get an idea of how many families had survived, before dismally confessing that they were still unsure of how many had perished on that fateful day. "This was nothing more than an act of barbarity," he voiced angrily. "I still find it hard to believe that the Americans would do such an abominable thing."

One evening just before Christmas, Nick found Kate sitting quietly on her bed, huddled in a blanket and feeding a tiny baby. He watched her quietly at first, thinking to himself what a tranquil sight they made. It reminded him of a drawing that he had seen in a church once when he was a young boy. Of course he was not comparing Kate and the tiny child in her arms to the holy mother Mary and her son Jesus, but the thought did strike him of how spiritual the moment seemed. Nick smiled, gazing warmly at the peaceful scene before him, feeling strangely comforted by what he saw. Kate, sensing his presence, lifted her head slowly and stared back at him, smiling sweetly with love emanating from her eyes. He approached and sitting down beside her, he stared down into the angelic face of the infant.

"Would you like one of these someday?" Nick leaned in closer, placing a soft kiss on her cheek.

"I am sure I would like a few of these someday," Kate replied, turning to smile up at him. In the next instant Nick found himself overpowered by an urgent sensation, a feeling that he was not even aware of until that exact moment. It certainly was not his intention when he came upstairs to find her, but seeing her now with this tiny baby and the look of adoration in her eyes, he could not help himself.

"Marry me, Katie." He gazed at her adoringly, his steady look penetrating right through her, while he waited for her to speak.

"Yes," she whispered softly without a moment's hesitation, happily searching his face through her tears. "Oh, Yes." Kate leaned into Nick and kissed him tenderly. The kiss intensified almost as soon as their lips met and Nick pulled her even closer, but they were too close for the baby's comfort. The infant protested loudly when the make- shift bottle was knocked from his mouth. They pulled apart giggling, voicing to one another how silly they must look. Nick gently wiped the dampness from her eyes. After they had eagerly professed their love for one another, Kate smiled up at him apologetically, and returned her attention to pacifying the agitated infant.

"There will be another time Katie," Nick promised in a slightly more serious tone. He left her then, happy with the knowledge that he would soon be her husband.

The days passed quickly since the burning of Newark, all things considered, and some of its residents were restless to be home.

"Christmas was coming," they had declared in frustration. "We wish to be home for Christmas." They did express their gratitude for all that had been done for them, but couldn't help the mounting homesickness that seemed to infect them daily now. Laura sympathized with their misery, stating that she herself would not like to be away from her home either, especially at Christmas. She promised them that her family would do everything possible to have some kind of celebration for the children.

The men brought in an evergreen tree and it was trimmed with odds and ends that were found in both the house and the barn. Small gifts too were secretly made from scraps of wood, straw, and some old rags. Kate had thought briefly of the previous Christmas, and how it was considerably less abundant than the year before, knowing that this one would be even more so. Laura watched with great interest and sly amusement, helping whenever possible, as the holiday preparations were being made. She joyfully realized that just maybe her family and friends would make Christmas happen after all.

Kate was outside in the barn early one morning, the sleeves of her coat rolled up slightly as she sat on a small, wobbly stool to milk the cow. The weather had turned crisp, but the sky was clear and there was no wind. The snow lay deep in some sections of the farm where it had drifted the night before, but she was able to navigate from the house to the barn quite easily as the men had graciously cleared a path. There was another such footpath made, stretching from the house all the way to the road, making that trek considerably easier too, for any approaching visitors.

Kate had just left the barn with a pail full of milk, some of it sloshing over the sides as she struggled with the weight. Not wanting to lose her footing in the snow, she was happy when Nick came to her rescue. They had met at the halfway point on the path, and Kate immediately let him take the bucket, thankful to be finally relieved of the heavy load. He moved steadily along the path while Kate lagged behind, laughing merrily as she pelted his back with snowballs. Nick had just set the pail down onto the porch and turned abruptly, ready to punish his bothersome attacker, when their attention was suddenly drawn to the drive. Both Nick and Kate stared with great interest at the lone figure who, with cane in hand, was slowly limping towards them; Nick felt slightly annoyed with yet another mouth to feed.

"Where did this one come from I wonder? I would have thought all the homeless people in Newark had been attended to by now," he said. "I should go and inform Laura."

When Kate did not answer, he cast a questioning glance in her direction, instantly noticing the look of unbelieving shock that was pasted on her lovely face. He took hold of her arm, but she stood frozen to the spot, pulling away from him instantly when he tried to lead her into the house. He reached for her once more, and again she pulled away. This time she uttered a strangled cry and Nick watched helplessly as her face contorted, and the tears streamed over her cheeks. He was shocked however, when in the next instant she raced down the laneway laughing and crying, stopping only when she reached the welcoming arms of the stranger. Everyone within earshot heard the ruckus and soon a crowd of people gathered at the front of the house.

"Dear God in Heaven," Mary exclaimed happily, her eyes on the stranger. "Kevin has come home at last!" All eyes were focused on the couple in the driveway now, as an exhilarated Nick ran towards them.

Kate was in her glory. Her brother was home! He would not be returning to the war; his leg injury would not permit it. Although Kevin's once proud stride was now reduced to an extremely pronounced limp, he seemed resigned to his limited mobility and was indeed, over-joyed to be home. Kevin had informed them all that Captain Tanner was responsible for his freedom, involving him in a prisoner exchange. He went on to state that no sooner was the trade completed, when the British attacked Fort Niagara, capturing it the following day.

"Thankfully by that time we were all on our way home," he stated. "I was in no condition to do battle." Kevin then relayed all that Captain Tanner had told him. He knew about the farm and that his father and Hannah were gone. He knew about the devastation in Newark, relating how he and the others had overheard the British troops crying for ven-geance. He had also been told about the deaths of both General Isaac Brock and Chief Tecumseh. What Kevin did not know however, was that his little sister was going to marry Nick Brannigan. He could not have been happier.

Later, when they were alone, Kevin also related to Nick that after the British and their allies left Queenston Heights, he was found by a couple of American privates. They had carefully carried him down the escarpment where they were met by a Captain Bennett, who then escorted him, and others, to Albany New York. At Nick's sudden intake of breath, accompanied by his complete look of surprise, Kevin laughed jovially and attempted to describe the situation he was in at the prison.

"You see, Nick," he continued. "I heard your voice and cried out to you, but thankfully I was not loud enough. Captain Tanner warned me after that incident not to let you know I was there. He said you would never leave that blasted prison without me and as he had a carefully arranged escape planned for the both of us, we were to trust him."

"I had no idea you were there," Nick stated. "The Captain was correct in keeping that little secret from me."

"I cannot tell you how relieved I was to hear the captain's words Nick; I will never forget them. He said: "I have promised your sister Private Sullivan, that I would free you from this prison. I assure you that I have a plan even now as we speak, but you must trust me as Nick did, and be patient. I greatly admire your sister and am deeply in love with Mr. Brannigan's so you need not fear. I will see you home.'

"Nick?" Kevin looked serious now, as he gazed at his future brother-in-law. "I do not desire my sister to know the identities of the two American soldiers we came upon at the heights. She loved Carl as a brother, and I am afraid she would be extremely devastated by this information."

Nick assured Kevin that he was confident Kate knew nothing of the matter. "She had made some inquiries," he said. "But she was informed that Carl's whereabouts still remained unknown."

"I still cannot understand Carl," Kevin said, shaking his head in wonder. "He was a part of our family for a long time, and to just turn on us in that way. Why would he do that?"

Nick thought for a moment, considering carefully before answering. "War and money can bring about such sudden changes in a person, Kevin. Men; and women too for that matter, have been known to adopt a whole new personality when either or both of those culprits come into play." Nick had broached the subject then of both his and Kate's dealings with Walter Clarke, adding that he did not think the war had anything to do with the wretchedness of the man in this case, but that he had been born evil.

Kevin said nothing for a moment, silently lost in his own private thoughts, his face hardened in anger. Finally, when he spoke, his voice sounded grating. "If you had not killed that monster Nick, then I most assuredly would have. The slimy, worthless, murdering bastard," he spat out through clenched teeth,

"You know Kevin, in that one instant before I knocked over that pole, I had an attack of conscience. But when I looked at what he had done to Kate, I went completely mad. In that one moment I was no better than Walter Clarke, and I did not care."

Kevin regarded Nick then with a melancholy stare, sighing deeply before he spoke. "We have all lost so much already because of this damnable war." Then brightening slightly, he added, "I am very proud of my little sister though, Nick. I barely recognized her. The frightened little girl is gone now. In her place stands this incredibly beautiful, confident, strong woman. Father and Hannah would have been so proud of her too," he stated sadly. "I am thankful that so far the war seems to have brought about an encouraging change in my sister, instead of some unfavourable one that could so easily have emerged."

"Well, although I too am proud of Kate, there are still some traits of hers that I would indeed miss if they disappeared completely." Nick chuckled then. Trying to lighten the mood, he regaled Kevin with some of Kate's humorous exploits of late, which included the tree climbing at the Powell's, omitting the romantic interlude that followed, and was heartily gratified when hearing Kevin's uproarious laughter as the pigpen incident was also recalled. The two men remained in the kitchen long into the night, enjoying the peaceful stillness at long last, conversing quietly together while the rest of the household slept.

Kate was happy and content for the time being, even though she was well aware that this War of 1812 would continue on. It was Christmas Eve, and she was standing with Nick in the parlour. She was admiring the small decorated evergreen tree, thinking how excited she actually was for the coming holiday season, when he made his unwelcome announcement.

"It appears that this war may not be through with me yet, Katie." Noticing the sudden dismal look in her eyes, he mentally chastised himself for spoiling her peaceful reverie. "Men are still needed to defend our country, my dear," he explained. "Captain Merritt has declared to me that if my wound will allow such physical exertion, then the army could indeed use my services once more. This country is not free of the invaders as yet. It never will be if men refuse to fight."

Kate reluctantly gave in to his reasoning and uttered a small sigh of defeat, knowing in her heart that he was right, no matter how much she dreaded the thought of him returning to the battlefield.

"When this dreadful war is over Nick, I want to rebuild my father's farm. I know Kevin would like nothing more."

"Will he let us live there too, my sweet?"

"Maybe he will bring his own wife to live there." Kate smiled once more, as she and Nick both observed Kevin conversing secretly with Mary Secord.

"Well, my dear," Nick stated quietly. "Maybe we can all be one happy family."

"By the grace of God, Nick; by the grace of God," Kate offered with a sly smile.

"You know something Katie? You even had me talking to that God of yours," Nick chuckled softly, tugging gently on a strand of her hair.

"Oh? I do hope you listened to each other," she expressed warmly.

"We did indeed my love, we surely did. He is the one who brought me home to you." Nick turned her to face him then, neither of them uttering a sound as he slowly and steadily lowered his mouth to hers, capturing her lips in a loving, rapturous kiss.

Epilogue

Kate Brannigan stood solemnly outside the Secord homestead, her son's arm encircling her gently around the waist. This visit had pulled at her heartstrings, leaving her mood sad and muddled. One moment she felt like crying. Then in the next instant she would recall something amusing and bubble with laughter. There had been so much good then she thought, mixed with so much bad.

"Yes, Thomas," Kate declared softly still staring into the past. "Unfortunately that war did go on. It left this beloved Niagara peninsula of mine in a state of confusion and remorse for quite some time. I have never forgotten General Brock." Kate gave a short laugh then as she spoke of the general's funeral. "The most surprising thing to me that day was that General George Prevost was one of the those who mourned Brock's loss. This is the very man who held poor Isaac back almost every time he tried to carry out his plans. Apparently, Sir George cared for General Brock more than he ever let on. Isaac would have been pleased." Kate then sighed, her mood turning sad once more. "We lost our treasured Fort George too, following the brutal American attack. When the British returned to it following the siege on Newark, they had to pitch tents, as there was only a few small buildings left standing. Yes, my son, that was indeed such a sad time."

"The British did retaliate, didn't they Mother"

"They did indeed, but not before the Americans returned to wreak more havoc on us. Battles continued to be won and lost on both sides."

She sighed once more. "It was just so bleak and dismal a time. More people were killed and even more taken prisoner. The Secords assisted many a destitute family before the invasion was over. James could no longer fight, you understand, his injuries proved too severe, but your father surely did. I was hard pressed to keep him off the battlefield, but thankfully it was late in the year of 1814 before he could fight again. Even then his damaged limbs plagued him constantly," she reflected.

"You have never told me, Mother. How long did it take for Newark to be rebuilt?"

"Thomas, it seemed like it took forever. I do not remember, Son." Kate stared off into space once more, letting many thoughts roll through her mind. "After that terrible ordeal the night Newark burned, the British waited for the right time to heave their vengeance on the enemy, and Lord when they did, it was catastrophic. They crossed over the Niagara River with the intent of lashing out their revenge on the Americans. It was terrible! They destroyed Lewiston and then they attacked Buffalo, leaving that poor town in a shambles."

Kate spoke through the remembered misery. "It was such a sad time my boy, for us and our enemies, and I blame Joseph Willcocks and his counterparts, including that dreadful General McClure, for instigating that whole horrific mess in Newark. With a strong retaliation, our army proved no different than the Americans. You see, the British went to Washington and burned down the home of the president! I do not think they should have gone south of the border, Thomas. There was no need that I could ascertain; the Americans had already left our country."

"That was a long time ago Mother. You may not recall the reasoning behind their decisions. Let's just be content that there is peace between our countries now."

"Well, I do know that both sides of that war had set their vengeance on one another and innocent people suffered because of it. It served no purpose that I could see. God forgive me, Son, but I was relieved to hear that justice had been served somewhat with the death of Mr. Willcocks during the siege at Fort Erie."

Thomas Brannigan smiled down at his mother, wrapping his other arm around her in comfort, while noticing the pain that now showed in her eyes as she retold more calamitous stories pertaining to the war of 1812. He had felt guilty when he first heard her relating these disturbing tales, some he had never even heard before, thinking that it might be best to change the subject. He knew now that this experience was acting as a balm for her. She always felt better for a while after the telling.

"Whatever happened to Captain Bryce Tanner, Mother? Why was Aunt Ellen not married to him?"

"Captain Tanner had promised to come back for her, enemy or no, Thomas. They had planned to get married and live here in Queenston. That dear man who came to mean so much to us for many reasons was killed at Lundy's Lane."

"Poor Aunt Ellen," Thomas stated, shaking his head remorsefully. "Poor Aunt Ellen."

"Yes, dear, it was indeed sad. She was devastated. Ellen mourned his passing for a long time. Then one day she met your Uncle William. He brought her back to life again, and we were all very grateful to him for that. She was happy, and although she loved your uncle, it was not with the same intensity that she had loved Bryce Tanner. It is ironic Thomas. Your Aunt Ellen and I started out with each other. We were the greatest of friends then, and here we are together again. Since both our husbands are gone we seem to rely on each other now, just as we used to before we were married."

"Mary Secord was a close friend of yours too, Mother, and of Uncle Kevin's, I thought? Why didn't they ever marry?"

Kate thought quietly for a moment, her mind drawn back to that night when Kevin came home to the farm with his bride, and it was not Mary Secord. Mary had been distraught, she recalled silently to herself, and never forgave him for not wanting her. Kate had always felt that Mary secretly blamed her too. Although nothing was ever said, they were never close again. Kate didn't confess any of this to her son, however.

"Oh, I guess their interests changed Thomas and they found different partners who suited them better," she fibbed. "On a brighter note, however, Molly Hogan did marry Private Dunsford. But, alas, I have not seen them in years either and have since lost touch. I have often wondered if they moved to England to be with his family. I know Molly had no family here. Even Sophia Shaw was lost to me, and those in her family as well, so I never knew what had become of dear Betsy and Lillian. I have often thought of them over the years though. I had written several times, but with no response, so I stopped trying." Kate shook her head then, sadly remembering her lost friends. "No dear," she said. "Ellen is all I have left of my friends. Your father was my best friend. I will never forget him. He was such a man!"

Thomas Brannigan noticed his mother's growing fatigue and slowly began to usher her toward the waiting carriage. This trip had tired her considerably, he thought, but she is a strong woman. She always has been.

"Oh my dear Mother, what you have been through," he chuckled, holding her gently by the arm now. "I seriously doubt that my Lottie could have stood as much. You mean the world to us Mother, you truly do. We all love you and we treasure all your stories."

"You may not think so after we arrive at Chippawa, dear boy," Kate warned teasingly, giving his hand an affectionate pat. "I am afraid that Laura and I may do quite a bit of reminiscing too." Kate stopped for a moment. They were in the middle of the drive and she wanted one last look at the house that had come to mean so much to her over the years. "Thomas," Kate stated, staring back and pointing to the front porch of the homestead. "That is the very place where your father lowered the boom. We had not been married too long before he glibly informed me that he was going to Chippawa to fight alongside the British once more. I was so upset with him, let me tell you, and him just standing there staring at me with that handsome, devilish grin of his. People always told me that I had your father wrapped around my little finger, but I think it was the other way round." Kate laughed then and gazed merrily up at her son.

"The way I see it, Mother dear, is that you both had each other snug around the fingers. We children basked in the security of just knowing you two loved each other so much."

"Well, your father's winning smiles and dancing eyes were all-for-not the day of the battle, and he should have left well enough alone," she giggled. "The Americans forced the British to retreat and they all had to leave Chippawa in defeat. As you can well imagine Thomas, that failure did not sit well with your father. The last battle he participated in before that was when the Americans captured Fort George, so he really wanted the British to win at Chippawa."

"He was at Lundy's Lane, wasn't he? The British won that battle," Thomas interjected.

"Yes, they certainly did Son, and what a victory. Your father was elated when he arrived home. I was elated too, but not because they won. I was so happy to have him home safe. Just like when the Americans invaded Queenston Heights, we could hear the roar of the guns all the way to Laura's house. They were faint, but we still heard them. I was petrified. I could stand anything that had happened to me during that awful war, anything except the loss of your father, that is. That man could rile me like no other, but I loved him more than life itself. I still do." Kate's eyes filled with tears at her remembrance of Nick.

"Father once told me that when the war ended he had no desire left to build a winery, so that was why the two of you decided to raise your family in the wilderness. Did you ever regret that decision Mother?"

"No, Son, not for one minute. So much had happened to us during the war that we sought peace and solitude to restore our souls. Oh, we came back briefly to visit Laura and James, and since your Aunt Ellen and Uncle William were with us, I was indeed very happy, your father too. We were living out the dream that we had promised ourselves, if we both survived the war."

They had reached the carriage now and Kate paused for a moment, dropping her son's hand and turning to tenderly search his face. He laid a hand on her cheek and listened intently as she spoke, her eyes once again mirroring the pain that she felt in her heart.

"One of the saddest circumstances regarding that awful war, Thomas, was that after the Treaty of Ghent was signed, the fighting should have ended then and there. The American's greatest victory throughout that whole terrible war was probably the battle of New Orleans. So many more injuries and deaths for both the British and Americans that could have been avoided. All those mothers and sweethearts lost their loved ones needlessly. In our eyes though, the victory was overshadowed by the fact that the War of 1812 was actually over when that great battle took place, but no one fighting it had heard the news."

Thomas Brannigan clasped his mother's hand then and gently helped her into the open carriage, pulling the door shut behind them. He motioned to the driver and the conveyance rattled noisily down the still deserted road towards Chippawa and Laura Secord. Mrs. Kate Brannigan did not look back!

Printed in Canada